DIPLOMATIC IMMUNITY

BANTAM BOOKS
NEW YORK   TORONTO   LONDON   SYDNEY   AUCKLAND

DIPLOMATIC IMMUNITY
GRANT SUTHERLAND

Sutherland

This book is a work of fiction. The story takes place primarily within the New York City headquarters of the United Nations, the physical setting and organization of which are realistically depicted. However, the names, characters, and incidents portrayed are the product of the author's imagination. Any resemblance to actual persons, living or dead, is entirely coincidental.

DIPLOMATIC IMMUNITY

A Bantam Book / May 2001

All rights reserved.
Copyright © 2001 by Grant Sutherland.

BOOK DESIGN BY GLEN EDELSTEIN.
Map Illustration by Hadel Studio.

Library of Congress Cataloging-in-Publication Data

Sutherland, Grant.
Diplomatic immunity : a novel / by Grant Sutherland.
p.   cm.
ISBN 0-553-80186-4
1. International relations—Fiction.   2. New York (N.Y.)—Fiction.
3. United Nations—Fiction.   4. Diplomats—Fiction.   I. Title.

PS3569.U824 D5 2001
813'.54—dc21   00-050807

Published simultaneously in the United States and Canada

Bantam Books are published by Bantam Books, a division of Random House, Inc. Its trademark, consisting of the words "Bantam Books" and the portrayal of a rooster, is Registered in U.S. Patent and Trademark Office and in other countries. Marca Registrada. Bantam Books, 1540 Broadway, New York, New York 10036.

PRINTED IN THE UNITED STATES OF AMERICA
BVG   10   9   8   7   6   5   4   3   2   1

*"The most dangerous of all moral dilemmas:
When we are obliged to conceal the truth in order
to help the truth be victorious."*

—*Dag Hammarskjöld, United Nations Secretary-General,
1953–1961. Died in a plane crash while on a UN mission
to the Congo. The cause of the crash was never determined.*

United Nations Headquarters

New York City

1. **Secretariat Building**
   Office of the Secretary-General, 38th floor
   Office of Sam Windrush, Legal Affairs, 29th floor
   Room Seven, 35th floor
   Surveillance Room
   Basement level

2. **General Assembly Building**
   Delegates' Lounge
   General Assembly Hall
   North Concourse entrance and exit
   Basement level: bookshop and Room B29

3. **Dag Hammarskjöld Library**

4. **Conference Building**
   Security Council chamber and sidechamber

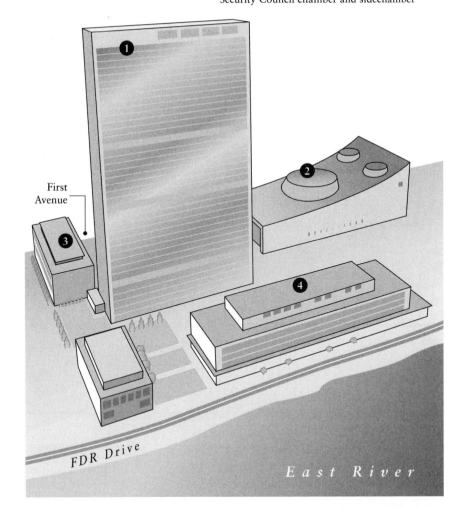

PROLOGUE

ON MANHATTAN ISLAND BY THE EAST RIVER THERE are eighteen acres that are not legally part of the United States. This fact was impressed upon me throughout the first week of my induction, but acquired the force of reality only when I was called upon to pledge allegiance to a charter that was not the U.S. Constitution and to a flag that was not my own.

After the ceremony that year, the Secretary-General invited me and my fellow inductees up to his private dining room for drinks on the thirty-eighth floor. He made a speech.

"You have come here from many lands to dedicate your working lives to the service of all nations," he proclaimed, sweeping his hand regally to embrace us, the newest and lowliest members of his team.

Twenty-two of us, as I recall. Three, like me, U.S. citizens, the others from all quarters of the globe. And all gathered to join the great United Nations enterprise, to aid the downtrodden of the earth, to build bridges of trust between nations, and to free mankind from the scourge of war.

The Secretary-General was eloquent. He painted the big picture. Duty. Responsibility. Hope. The greater good of mankind. A practiced politician, though I did not see it at the time, he offered us the words we wanted to hear. I was twenty-six, my fellow inductees mostly younger, each of us playing at being maturely levelheaded but underneath that, burning, lit with personal ambitions and universal ideals that seemed not only compatible but inseparable, as if the world's good was somehow at one with our own. We were united too, of course, by youth's universal belief—the evidence for which was all around us—that our parents' generation had screwed up badly; that we could do better; that, given a chance, we could build a finer world.

I sat by the window. The view from the thirty-eighth floor was splendid.

"Each of you has a part to play, a real part in this endeavor. To serve all nations. All nations. Not merely your home countries. Not even that greater number, those nations with which you feel some affinity, some tie of culture or language or race. But all nations. Those with whom you agree and those with whom you disagree. Those which you believe good and those which you believe bad. Once accepted by the General Assembly, once a signatory to the UN Charter, each state has a legitimate call on the services of the Secretariat." His hand swept over us again, not regally now but inclusively. "On me. And on you."

Then he put on his glasses. And he opened the UN Charter, a red morocco-bound copy, which he held in one hand.

"You have undoubtedly heard this several times these past few days. It will do you no harm to hear it again." His smile was wry, our laughter dutiful. But when he looked down and began to read, his grandiloquent and somewhat showy manner of address fell away. His tone became dry, almost professorial. And though we had as he surmised heard Article 100 of the Charter frequently during the course of our induction, we listened. Attentively.

" 'In the performance of their duties the Secretary-General and the staff shall not seek or receive instructions from any government or any other authority external to the Organization. They shall refrain from any action which might reflect on their position as international officials responsible only to the Organization.' "

He closed the morocco-bound copy. "The Secretary-General and the staff," he intoned. He removed his glasses slowly. He looked up. "Me," he said. "And you."

A weight seemed to settle over the room, a moment of pure silence. And at that moment we were not merely young, ambitious men and women embarking on careers as international civil servants; at that moment we were acolytes, novitiates of a secular order, receiving final instruction from the high priest of our faith. A final warning. We would be leaned on. Attempts would be made, through us, to subvert the UN's high ideals.

Then the Secretary-General raised a hand. And smiled somewhat equivocally.

"Good luck," he said.

ELEVEN YEARS LATER

When Toshio Hatanaka called, I was alone at my desk. I picked up the phone and said my name, then listened to the crackling coming down the line.

"Windrush," I said again, louder this time. "UN Legal Affairs."

The distant crackle continued. I was on the point of hanging up, when I heard a voice calling forlornly into the ether. "Sam?"

There are not many voices I would recognize under those conditions—just family and maybe three or four colleagues and friends—and I guess it says something about how close I'd become to Toshio over the years that I picked out his voice immediately. Smiling, I kicked back in my chair.

"I can't hear you, Toshio. Speak up."

The line broke up again, Toshio's fragmented words reaching me faintly, like some indecipherable code. I'd held more than a few of these conversations with Toshio since he was appointed UN special envoy to Afghanistan. He spent half his life in places where a portable satellite-telephone was not a luxury item but a piece of equipment as essential as a four-wheel drive or a guard with a gun.

"Sam." His voice emerged from the static. There was some more that I missed, and then, "Abatan."

I took up my pen. Abatan was one of the UN-controlled refugee camps on the Pakistan border, a place to which we had recently sent out a relief medical team. One of the relief doctors, on sabbatical from her real job in New York, was my wife. I asked Toshio what the team needed, what inevitable bureaucratic and quasi-legal hassles they were having that I, as first deputy of UN Legal Affairs, could help straighten out.

"No," he said. "Can't contact—" And then the line faded.

I told Toshio I was losing him; I asked him again to speak up. His voice suddenly crested.

"The tribesmen went to Abatan. Into the camp."

My pen froze over the notepad. The Afghan tribesmen should not have been anywhere near the camp; the Pakistani military guaranteed us full security.

"Who do you want me to speak to, Toshio? The Pakistani ambassador?"

For several seconds there was only static on the line, audio waves swelling, then receding. "Toshio?"

"I will find them," he said. "I will contact them."

"Who?" The Pakistani military? The Afghan tribesmen? I could hear the concern in his voice. Something was not right. I dropped my pen, then rose from behind my desk. "Who do you have to find? What's going on out there?"

"Medical team," he said, his voice breaking up. "Hostages."

The line faded, crackled like gunfire, and was gone.

TUESDAY

1

"WE'RE GOING TO BE LATE," PATRICK O'CONNER REMARKS unhappily. We have just emerged from a twenty-minute session in the local Starbucks, Patrick, over two light grandes, telling me his woes. Now he considers the thickening crowd on the sidewalk before veering right, wiping the last muffin crumbs from his mouth with a handkerchief as I fall into step beside him.

"You know," he says, continuing his complaint as we walk, "it's unbelievable. This thing's been on the cards how long? Years. And here we are, the whole jamboree set to start—for chrissake, they'll be voting on it in two days—and still no one knows the numbers. Tell me, Sam. Really. What kind of cockass thing is that?"

This question, in variations, is one I have been listening to every day now for at least a month. So I incline my head but offer no comment, and as we push our way through the sightseers, Patrick goes on delivering his latest thoughts on the subject, the main matter of debate at Turtle Bay, in fact, for over a year: the elevation of the Japanese to a place at the top table of international diplomacy, a permanent UN Security Council seat. What Patrick refers to in private moments, in his inimitable Australian way, as the Nip Question.

"Every tinpot bozo lining up for his say, and the Japs still walking around like a buncha zombies, like it's in the bag, as if it'll all go through on a nod from Uncle Sam." He shakes his head, disconsolate. He swears.

And then, mercifully, he lapses into a thoughtful silence. He is not a tall man, and is in his late fifties, but as he barrels forward, the crowd parts around him like water around a stone.

Patrick O'Conner, the UN's Undersecretary-General for Legal
Affairs, has been my boss for almost three years. I have become ac-
customed to his moods, but today, this morning, his disgruntlement
has gone into overdrive, reached an altogether higher order of mag-
nitude. He sweeps a hand across his forehead. He sets his bulldog
jaw tight. He does not look happy.

Patrick, as everyone in the Secretariat knows, has fallen out of favor lately with the thirty-eighth floor. Breaking with his usual practice, the Secretary-General no longer calls Patrick to his side at the
onset of any crisis. He has ceased to find Patrick's speechwriting tal-
ents indispensable. He does not invite Patrick back to his grand
Upper East Side residence, as he once did so often, to shoot the
breeze and drink whiskey till all hours of the night. And everyone
knows, too, that the reason for Patrick's fall is the vote, just two
days away now, on Japan. Following Patrick's advice, the SG has
forced the pace on the vote, driving it to the top of this year's
General Assembly agenda. Patrick, in a rare miscalculation, was certain the Japanese had the numbers. In fact, they still may. But the
whole thing is so delicately balanced now that no one can call it, and
if the worst should happen, if Japan loses the vote, then the SG, after
all his efforts, will look like a fool.

Which is why for the past several weeks Patrick has been kept at
arm's length from the thirty-eighth floor. Should the need for a
scapegoat arise, Patrick is shaping up as ideal material.

Now Patrick shoulders his way impatiently through the sightseers
and tourists who have gathered near First Avenue. It is not just me.
Patrick O'Conner is unhappy with the world.

"Speak to Hatanaka," he tells me as we bump together in the
throng.

Right, I think. Okay, now I get it. Why Patrick has asked me to
Starbucks for a quiet word, why I have just spent twenty minutes listening to his beef. He has been softening me up, priming me to com-
ply with this request. Speak to Hatanaka.

When I pretend not to have heard, Patrick touches my arm.

"I want you to speak to Hatanaka. Get him to ease off this crap
he's talking, trashing his own bloody country. Who's he think he is
anyway, running a private campaign? Is that what he's paid for?"

I concede, reluctantly, that Toshio Hatanaka has probably overstepped the mark.

"Overstepped? Christ, the way Hatanaka's playing it, there is no
bloody mark." Patrick shakes his head in disgust. "You hear the latest? He's sent out a letter to all the senior delegations telling them

how a Security Council seat's incompatible with the Japanese Constitution. Can you believe it?"

"It won't change the vote."

"Says you."

Unfortunately, he has a point. Toshio Hatanaka, committed pacifist and twenty-five-year UN veteran, has become more involved than he has any right to be in this. Now I ask Patrick exactly what it is he wants me to tell Toshio.

"Tell him he's out of line. Pull his bloody head in."

"You can't?"

"You think I haven't tried?" We turn face-to-face, edging our way through the crush toward the steps down to First Avenue. Part of the crowd down there is chanting, placards held high. "Of course I've damn well tried, he's just not listening. But you two seem to get along, yeah? You've wasted enough time on that Third Committee bullshit with him. Anyway, try to speak to him, will you? See if you can talk some sense into the man's thick head, make him see this isn't just some pissy point of procedure he's screwing around with here. This is the big game."

"And you want Toshio to butt out."

Patrick shoots me a look. "Sam, I'm asking you to speak to the man, that's all. If you don't want to, don't. But I don't wanna be hearing any more about your principles. You know he's in the wrong. Speak to the man."

We emerge from the crowd at the head of the steps and pause; even Patrick is momentarily silenced by the sight. Turtle Bay, UN headquarters, in all its General Assembly opening day glory. Sightseers line First Avenue both ways; a motorcade of black limousines slowly snakes its way into the forecourt of the Secretariat building, the thirty-nine-story office tower where Patrick and I both work. Delegates are strolling across to the garlanded entrance, the rainbow colors of the African national costumes shimmering in the long line of gray suits. Everyone shaking hands. Smiling. One hundred and eighty-five flags flapping in line. There is, undeniably, a real sense of occasion.

Just below us on this side of the street, the maroon-robed Tibetan monks—a shaven-headed cluster, they have been camped here on a hunger strike for two weeks—cease their chanting as the Chinese delegation disappears into the UN buildings. The monks lower their FREE TIBET placards and peer curiously through the line of New York cops to see what might happen next. Or maybe in this age of celebrity they're hoping for the same as the ranks of sightseers crowding behind them: a glimpse of somebody famous, a face they recognize from the style magazines or TV.

Well, I think, here we are. My fourteenth time and the thrill, though muted by the passing years, still rises. The flags fly. The limos disgorge the mighty. It is the third Tuesday in September, and here we are once again at the gathering of all the nations of the earth.

Patrick turns to me. "Speak to Hatanaka." Then he looks at his watch as he begins shouldering his way down the steps. "We're going to be late," he says.

———

We are not late, of course. The delegates and the presidents, the prime ministers and the foreign secretaries, various senior UN staff, all of us are gathered in the Delegates' Lounge, everyone busy seeing and being seen, the only two things you can do at a gala occasion like this. The moment he spots James Bruckner, the U.S. ambassador, Patrick moves in swiftly to press the flesh, leaving me alone by the wall. Most days this place has the feel of some airport lounge built and decorated in the fifties. Long rows of high windows and clean, spare lines. Today the effect is enhanced by all the suits, the different-colored faces; it looks as though half a dozen jumbos have just arrived and unloaded several hundred VIPs.

Mike Jardine, deputy head of security here at the UN, weaves toward me through the crowd. He finishes delivering some command into his walkie-talkie, then turns to stand at my side. He tugs at the collar of his jacket and straightens his tie.

"Fun day?" I venture.

He tilts back his head. "Shit fight of the year. All we need now's the frigging ticker tape."

There is not the trace of a smile on his pallid face. His hooded eyes continue to sweep left and right as he tells me that we appear to be down one delegation.

"Who?"

"The Japanese."

But the Japanese, with everything they're playing for this session, will not be staying away from the opening. When I offer him this judgment, Mike grunts.

"No-shows I can deal with. You ask me, they're just holding back for the grandstand entrance, the Streisand thing. Get here last, everyone's gonna notice." He makes a face. "Jesus. And I used to think I had problems down at the Hall."

City Hall, he means, a reference to Mike's old job of running security for New York's mayor. Mike left the NYPD five years ago to come and work here at UN headquarters, an appointment that has turned out to be one of the more inspired of the last Secretary-General's tenure. Just before Mike joined us, relations between UN Security and the NYPD had hit an all-time low. On one celebrated occasion a fistfight broke out during some ambassadorial lunch at the Park Plaza, four of NYPD's finest versus four of our guys, eight grown men slugging it out in the john over who was protecting whom. That those days are now behind us is largely due to Mike. He is respected on both sides of First Avenue.

I ask him if he's seen Toshio Hatanaka. He shakes his head.

"But I've seen your girlfriend," he says.

When I give him a look, Mike grins. I'm starting to wish I had never told him. Then someone reports a "red" over Mike's two-way. Mike groans.

"Red?" I say.

Code, he tells me. Something the security guards don't want to broadcast. "Basically, a first-class screwup," he says. Backing away into the crowd, he tells me to enjoy the big party.

This seems to be my cue to mingle, so I do, drifting through the crowd, nodding pleasantly to the half-remembered faces from some committee meeting last week or last year, talking briefly, moving on. Unlike Patrick, I have none of the politician's instinct for working a room, so no one I speak to here is a name. English, the Latin of our age, rolls around me in a hundred different accents. Other languages too; my ear tunes in to the Spanish conversations, scraps of French, but I can't see Toshio anywhere.

"Mr. Windrush," says Jennifer Dale, sidestepping a Pacific Islander, planting herself in front of me. "What brings you here?"

"The food."

"You're too early."

"The drink?"

She holds up her nearly empty plastic cup. "Too late."

Glancing over her shoulder, I tell her I seem to remember something about an agreement we had. She looks around.

"Yeah, well, some places are so public, they're private." Then she faces me, smiling now, a professional woman at ease among suits. "Relax, Sam," she says quietly, "I'm not going to jump you."

I take a moment with that. Jennifer Dale and I, as Mike knows and some others have guessed, enjoy a relationship that goes well beyond the professional. But she's probably right—there is nothing wrong with a senior bureaucrat like me from the Secretariat exchanging pleasantries with the U.S. ambassador's legal counsel at a gathering such as this. So gesturing around, I ask if she's made many new friends this morning.

"Everybody wants to be my friend, Sam. That's one of the joys of being an American."

"I'm an American."

"You're Secretariat," she reminds me, grinning. "That puts you firmly in the twilight zone." She waves to someone behind me. "You know, this isn't as bad as you said it was going to be. I think I might even be liking it."

Give it time, I tell her. Wait for the opening General Assembly speeches.

She nods and sips her drink and looks past me. There is a stir over by the door. The Japanese delegation finally arriving.

"I guess you heard we got a letter from Mr. Hatanaka."

"I heard," I say.

"We're considering a formal protest."

"Bruckner not happy?"

James Bruckner, the U.S. ambassador to the UN, Jennifer's boss. The U.S. has been lobbying for decades now to get Japan a permanent Security Council seat; Bruckner has been spearheading the campaign all this last year.

"Ballistic," Jennifer tells me.

When I reprise the assurance I gave Patrick, that it won't affect the vote, she simply raises a brow.

"Anyway, we'll know Thursday," she says, referring to the day scheduled for the vote. "And I tell you, Sam, ballistic's going to seem mild if the Japanese lose. Bruckner will be out for scalps."

Her drift is clear, but I ask anyway. "I'm meant to pass this on to Toshio?"

"We'd be much obliged."

"You think I'm going to?"

"It was worth a try."

She smiles and I smile back. If she wants the message passed, she is going to have to do it herself. Then our conversation slides into a lighter vein. We start comparing notes on the celebrity guests, mine just the usual remarks, so much smaller in the flesh than on TV. But Jennifer has a gift for verbal caricature, which she uses now, skewering several of the big names with words, imagined anecdotes, solely for my entertainment. She is dry and ironic, and really very funny, a quality I completely failed to notice when I knew her the first time around. Which was, incredibly, almost twenty years ago now.

We went through Columbia Law School together. Correction. We enrolled the same year and joined the same study group our second semester. After that our paths diverged. We'd see each other in class or around the campus, but we weren't friends, and after graduation we totally lost touch. Yet, when she appeared in the doorway of my office six months ago, I recognized her immediately. Her honey-colored hair is a shade darker—dyed, I have since learned, to disguise the first wisps of gray—and her face, lined at the corners of the eyes, is somewhat fuller, but otherwise the years have treated her well. In many ways she seems to have grown into herself, become the formidable presence she always promised to be. But formidable or not, and despite her nonchalant air, the upcoming vote on a permanent Security Council seat for the Japanese has her worried.

If the Japanese win, it will be a political coup for Bruckner. Every big hitter in his party from the president on down will be endorsing him for next year's gubernatorial in New Jersey; and if he makes governor, Jennifer Dale, naturally, will be along for the ride. If the Japanese lose, however, Bruckner's political star and Jennifer's prospects will be on the wane. And Jennifer is an ambitious lady. And determined. Which I guess is why she finally cannot resist returning to the subject of the vote.

"Anyway," she says, "what are you hearing? Good guys still in front?"

"Which team's that?"

She makes a face, then lowers her voice to tell me how Bruckner's calling the numbers: one hundred forty for the Japanese seat, twenty against, and twenty-five abstentions. Comfortably more than the two-thirds majority required for the Japanese to get the seat. I keep my expression blank. She is fishing for our numbers; she wants to know how Patrick sees it.

"No comment?" she says.

None, I answer, that she would like to hear.

She smiles into her glass. She tells me that she has a suite at the Waldorf tonight. "Suite Twelve," she says, lifting her eyes to give me a look that is unnaturally, and very intentionally, direct.

"Ah," I say. The only thing I can think of.

"Eleven-thirty?" she suggests.

I study her a moment, my heart skipping lightly. And then I hear myself say "Eleven-thirty's fine" before we immediately turn away from each other. The Pacific Islander who has been hovering nearby quickly closes on Jennifer; as I move off, he starts in lobbying her for U.S. support on some greenhouse-gases resolution his country is pushing this session.

Elated by the unexpected appointment, I go drifting back through the suits, telling myself that it's okay, that I still have a handle on it, we are both grown-ups, we both know the rules, a late-night rendezvous at the Waldorf is absolutely fine. A minute later the glass doors swing open and people go pouring out of the lounge toward the General Assembly Hall. Shuffling forward in the crush, I finally detach myself from the crowd outside the Assembly Hall doors. For the next couple of hours we will have to endure welcoming addresses from the SG and the session president, both notorious windbags, so I want to leave it till the last moment before I venture in.

I take the opportunity to stroll up and down the concourse a few times while everyone else goes filing into the Hall. Suite Twelve, I think. Eleven-thirty. Then, glancing at my watch, I catch myself calculating the hours between now and eleven-thirty tonight. I purse my lips. Not good. The personal will not impinge on the professional: That was the vow we made back when this whole thing started, an honest intention that is proving harder than either of us ever imagined. Folding my arms, I bow my head and keep walking, stretch my legs, try to think of something else.

By this time all but a handful of the crowd have disappeared inside. The guard at the door signals to me with his hand: in or out?

I haven't taken two steps toward him before I'm stopped in my tracks by a cry of "Sam!" Turning, I see Mike Jardine charging over from the escalator.

"Sam," he calls again, breathing hard, barely slowing as he nears.

The guard at the door asks if everything's okay. Mike seems to remember himself then; he slows to a brisk walk and nods to the guard, gesturing for him to show the last of the delegates inside. Then Mike takes me by the arm, starts to lead me away.

"What's this?" I pull my arm free. "It's set to start," I tell him, tossing my head back toward the Hall.

This time when he grabs me it's higher up, near the armpit; he almost lifts me off my feet as he marches me toward the escalator.

"Save your ticket for next year," he says grimly. His brow is creased, his pale green eyes set straight ahead, unblinking. "We just found a frigging corpse in the basement."

2

IT IS TOSHIO HATANAKA.

Mike warned me long before we entered the room, but the shock, when I first see Toshio's familiar face staring up lifeless at the ceiling, staggers me. My heart thuds, my throat swells, I have to stop halfway across the room and steady myself. I close my eyes, muster myself a few moments, then go on. Mike moves to the far side of the body and we stand silent, looking down. The sight is truly awful. Toshio is on his back on the floor. His legs are twisted, his arms spread wide, splayed open like a crucifix. His tongue lolls loosely over bluing lips, and on the crotch of his pants there is a dark stain, and a smell—the bladder and bowels have clearly opened—but worse than this, far worse, are his eyes. Always dark, they are now simply dull. Always clear, strangely innocent, they now look like two painted marbles of glass. In death they have given Toshio's face an expression of imbecile vacancy; curiosity stilled, determination and courage both vanished. A peace of total emptiness.

Putting a hand to my mouth, I choke back a sound. Mike looks at me. Then he crouches and considers Toshio's jacket, which is draped over the chair by the body. Beside the chair is a tan leather briefcase I recognize as Toshio's. The shirtsleeve on Toshio's left arm has been rolled up above the elbow, and on the floor just beside him is an empty syringe, its long silver needle glistening. I have to look away a few seconds. God, I think. Sweet Jesus. When I turn back, Mike speaks.

"It had to be today," he says miserably.

Crouching, I reach for the syringe. Mike's hand suddenly shoots out and clasps my wrist. When our eyes meet, he shakes his head.

Standing upright, and trying to affect a normality I most definitely do not feel, I ask, "Overdose?"

"Possibly."

"Self-inflicted?"

"Ask me another."

I lock my hands behind my neck. "God almighty" is the best I can manage as the ramifications begin to sink in.

"Yeah," Mike mutters. "Ain't we just in the tulips."

But his wise-ass manner is no cover for his real feelings, Mike is absolutely furious. He calls for the lone guard at the door to come in.

"Let's have it again," Mike tells the young man who enters. "For Mr. Windrush."

The young man, Latino by his looks and speech, recites his story over Toshio's body. It doesn't take him long. With everything going on upstairs, the guard says he'd been left alone to do a regular patrol down here, a sweep of the corridors at fifteen-minute intervals, a no-brainer that he swears he's been carrying out diligently for the past two hours. The doors to the rooms here were all locked; as far as he's aware, they have been since yesterday, and no one could have any real reason to be down here today. He says he got bored. On his final pass, just to keep himself busy, he brought along the ring of keys. He holds them up for me to see.

"So you opened this one," I say, indicating the door behind him.

"Others too." He nods, his gaze going down to the body. "He is like this. I touch his neck, he is cold. I know he is dead."

From his eyes, his whole manner, in fact, there is no sense of the tragedy that has happened here. His prevailing emotion seems to be one of unease, in Mike's presence, that he might not have handled the situation correctly.

"Wait outside," Mike tells him.

Once the door closes, Mike rests his hands on his hips. "We got lucky." When I make a sound of disbelief, he jerks his head toward the door. "The kid didn't panic. Called in the code red. I came."

I turn that over. "No one else knows?"

Mike crouches, inspecting Toshio's arm without touching it. "Right now it's just you, me, and the kid." His head drops. He peers at the arm closely. After studying it awhile, he asks, "What you seeing?"

Gesturing to the door, I tell Mike that the detective work can wait. Right now this has to be reported. He reaches up, grabs my sleeve, tugging me into a crouch beside him. Then he points to Toshio's bare arm. "Look like a junkie's arm to you?"

Straight out of law school, I did some pro bono work in the projects. The bruised, pulped-up look of a junkie's arm is one of those things you don't forget, and now I admit to Mike that no, this does not look like a junkie's arm at all.

"See here?" Mike touches the air above the arm three times. "Three stabs. Only one on the target."

Tentatively, I lean closer. And I can see that Mike is right. Toshio's California-tan skin has grayed, but the deeper shadow of the bruise is unmistakable. In the center of the bruise are three puncture marks, one to either side of the vein, one bang on the target.

"You suppose," Mike asks, glancing across at me, "he was just practicing?"

I remark somewhat hopefully that Toshio was under a lot of pressure lately, that people do strange things. Mike pulls a face.

"Sam. If Hatanaka was a user, I'm a horse's ass."

He reaches, gently pushing back Toshio's straight fringe of black hair. Finding nothing, he does the same with the hair over both ears.

"What are you looking for?"

Ignoring me, Mike continues the careful examination of Toshio's head. And then his hand pauses. He grunts. "Lump back here size of a goose egg." He brings his hand up and looks at it. "No blood."

"Maybe he fell."

"Yeah. And maybe he did a double somersault before he landed just to get the great pile-driver effect." He looks at me. "This one's not going away just 'cause we want it gone."

Standing, I put my hands over my face. Mike rises beside me.

"Sam," he asks, "have you got the first fucking idea what it is we're meant to do here?" When I drop my hands, he reads the answer in my eyes. "Jesus," he says. Then, as I go to step past him, he lays a firm hand on my chest. "Unh-unh. You're the diplomatic rights and privileges man. Do us both a favor. Give this little problem"—he gestures to the body—"a few minutes of your undivided attention."

With that, he fetches a black marker from the whiteboard at the rear of the room and begins sketching an outline on the floor around the corpse. Cop instinct. Meanwhile, I attempt to do what Mike has asked me. Toshio Hatanaka, either by his own hand or with assistance, has been killed. Apparently right here at UN headquarters. Think, I tell myself, like a lawyer. But my mind keeps skimming over the scant few legal principles that could possibly have any bearing here and, finding no purchase, returning to the one irreducible fact. Toshio Hatanaka is dead. After a lifetime's devotion to the cause of peace, after more than ten years hotfooting it around the globe at the behest of two successive Secretaries-General, years in which he has visited some of the worst hellholes on earth and dealt with some of mankind's worst miscreants, Toshio's own number has come up, in this shockingly unexpected way.

Crouching, Mike gingerly touches a finger to Toshio's face. When he withdraws the finger, a pressure dimple remains on Toshio's cheek; all pliancy has drained from the body. A sound rises in my throat. Mike glances up.

"You all right?"

When I nod, he frowns. Then he indicates that I should turn around, step away. "See what you can see," he says. "And don't touch anything."

Relieved, I move back, turning my attention to the disposition of the objects in the room. Anything to take my eyes off Toshio.

There are two rows of chairs, six chairs to a row, each with a small tray-desk attached. The rows aren't neat, but there's no sense of any tussle; it looks as if whoever used the chairs last simply left them like this, vaguely askew. At the rear there is a whiteboard. On the whiteboard there are numbers, letters, and arrows, the arrows going left to right, directing the numbers and letters into various boxes, the whole thing done in black marker. By the whiteboard there is a table, Formica-topped, with no drawers; to the left of that, a trash can. The only trash seems to be a few candy wrappers. Lifting my head, I scan the faded, out-of-date UNICEF posters publicizing some god-awful disaster of a decade ago—children with black skin, imploring eyes, and distended bellies, staring up vacantly at whoever shot the picture. Normally, my glance, like the glance of just about everyone else on the planet, skates right over these all-too-familiar scenes, but this morning I am appalled. Death, and the imminence of death, crowd the room.

Higher up the wall, just past the poster, there is a grille. And immediately below the grille sits the last chair in the back row. I look up from the chair to the grille, gauging the distance, by my guess no more than six or seven feet. From there my gaze drifts back to the corpse.

Upstairs in the General Assembly the speeches will have started. The hopeful but never fulfilled affirmations of goodwill, the empty blandishments to peace and brotherhood throughout the world, a raging cascade of abstract nouns that will be punctuated by applause from the delegates, more than half of whom come from nations where wrongful imprisonment, confiscation of property, torture, and murder are the common currency of political life. And down here—Toshio Hatanaka.

"So where are we?" Mike says, turning in my direction. "What's the procedure?"

Pointing, I ask if he's noticed the grille.

"Ah-ha. You touch it?"

"No."

He steps around the body and comes over. "So what did you figure?" He pulls up a chair and stands on it, rising on tiptoe to look through the plastic grille into the duct behind. After a few seconds he glances back over his shoulder. "Sam?"

It looks big enough to crawl through, I tell him.

"Not this." He screws up his face. "The legal shit. Who gets notified about Hatanaka. What we're gonna do about an investigation. The stuff you been nuttin' out."

"We'll have to tell Patrick."

"Right," Mike mutters from the corner of his mouth. Taking some keys from his pocket, he turns back to the grille. He levers a key behind the catch and pops it open. Using the same key, he lifts the grille back and takes a good look inside. "Almost be worth it just to see the smug smile wiped off his face," he says. Then he lowers the grille and faces me. "Maybe we drop it on him, he has a heart attack, you get to be the new legal counsel."

"What's up there?"

"Zip."

I draw Mike's attention to the scuff marks on the chair beneath the grille. He snorts.

"Shoe marks, you're thinking?" When I nod, Mike shakes his head and gets down. He bends over the chair, inspecting it. "Without forensics, Sam, it's just scuffing on a goddamn chair." Then, rearing upright, he turns back to the room's center of gravity, Toshio Hatanaka's corpse sprawled on the floor midway between the whiteboard and the chairs. Mike bites his lip. "The only thing we got for sure," he says, "is a body."

Liberally, he swears. Then he goes and kneels by Toshio, searching the pants pockets before turning out the jacket pockets on the chair. A tan leather wallet, a key ring with half a dozen keys attached, and a clean white handkerchief. Mike searches the wallet. I cannot help myself. Slowly, I feel myself drawn across the room till at last I am standing right over the corpse. The initial shock, the wave of nausea, has passed, and now my gaze lingers on the ghastly sight.

I have seen dead bodies before, usually singly, sometimes in numbers, on one mind-numbing occasion in Rwanda a huge, tangled heap of them piled in a mass grave that no one had bothered to cover. But this is not remotely the same. This is Toshio Hatanaka. I knew him. His office is just down the corridor from mine; it was part of my everyday routine to put my head in, chew the fat, part of his routine to drop in at my office unannounced with some problem of law. Half an hour ago Patrick told me to speak to him. And now here he is, a corpse.

"He got family here?" Mike asks.

A sister, I answer readily. Moriko. Occasionally I went to Toshio's apartment for dinner; Moriko was often there.

"He wasn't married?"

When I shake my head, Mike drops the wallet on the chair, then crouches to close Toshio's blank eyes. Go get Patrick, he tells me.

But I linger a moment. And a strange thought comes to me then, quite distinctly. This is how it was, I think. This is just how it was three years ago on a hillside in Afghanistan, with Toshio standing by a corpse. How did he feel? I wonder. The first impact over, the natural revulsion overcome, how was it for Toshio Hatanaka? Was he stunned? Stricken with grief? Or did he feel as I do now, overwhelmingly grateful simply to be standing here, alive? I never asked him. One more piece of the tragedy I will never know or understand: how it touched him. How Toshio felt when he stood there on a barren hillside in Afghanistan, ankle-deep in snow, over the dead and mutilated body of my wife.

3

"Suicide," Patrick O'Conner says as we step outside. "Right?"

The remark is so unexpected that I balk, but Patrick continues on over to the giant metal sculpture of a pistol, its barrel knotted, a gift to the UN from the people of Luxembourg. When I join him by the sculpture, he has both hands braced on the pedestal.

"You heard Mike," I say.

"I heard him."

"He thinks it's murder."

But Patrick doesn't seem to hear me, and when I say his name, he simply lifts his head and takes a few deep breaths of air. His jowls hang heavy and there are tension lines across his brow that could signal the onset of a migraine. He stares past me across the North Lawn.

After getting him away from the Assembly Hall I took Patrick down to the basement, where we've just spent ten minutes with Mike. Mike told Patrick the same thing he told me. That he thinks it's murder. That we need a forensics team. Patrick's response was to ask me to accompany him outside, a request for which I admit I am grateful. Unlike Mike, neither one of us seems to have the kind of cast-iron stomach needed to think straight in the presence of a corpse, but Patrick's look now, as he stares out over the lawn, is not so much one of shock as dismay. He is pondering the effect of Toshio's death on the vote. And after reflecting on Patrick's opening remark, I wonder if perhaps I might be missing something here.

"Why suicide?" I ask.

"Because it fits."

"That's not how Mike sees it."

Patrick looks at me. "What about you? How do you see it?"

I state the obvious, that I'm no expert but that Mike's judgment seems fair. Toshio was no user, I say.

"User, my ass." Patrick pushes away from the pedestal and I follow him across the terrace, down the steps and onto the graveled path across the lawn. Usually this area is crawling with tourists. Today, thankfully, they've been kept out because of the opening. "Jardine's just guessing what was in the syringe," he says, thinking out loud. "He's guessing some kinda dope. Someone set it up to look like Hatanaka was injecting. Accidental overdose."

"You don't buy that?"

"Whoever did it would end up on the tapes. Who's that stupid?" The security tapes, he means. There are cameras on all the basement corridors; Mike has just gone to check the tapes from last night. "Suicide fits," Patrick says again. "Coulda been anything in that syringe. Straight in the vein, some poison, be as good a way to do it as any."

We toss the idea back and forth a minute; Patrick seems absolutely convinced he is right. And the idea is not outrageous, God knows. Toshio spent his career visiting parts of the world most people catch only in glimpses from the safety of their armchairs on the TV nightly news. Sarajevo. Sierra Leone. East Timor. More recently Kabul. Sometimes as a special rapporteur gathering information for the Secretariat, sometimes as a special envoy representing the Secretary-General at cease-fire negotiations, putting the reasonable view to men whose only real interest was in slitting each other's throats.

And Toshio was never one to confine himself to the boundaries of the inevitable cordon sanitaire decreed by the local authorities. He went out into the field, tried to see firsthand what conditions were really like, what was actually happening to the people whose tragic fate it was to be born into the front lines of hatred. Twenty-five years a Secretariat staffer, he had heard all the lies. He had seen more evil than any man should be asked to see, maimed and suffering humanity in all its wretched forms, and who could blame him if after this he had finally given up on the world? Down in that unlit basement room, surrounded by those posters of starving children, doesn't that seem possible? That he reached for a peace that life couldn't offer?

And yet I just don't see it. Not Toshio.

"How does suicide square with the Council vote?" I ask. "One minute he's campaigning against the Japanese seat, the next he just offs himself?"

At the end of the path Patrick stops suddenly.

"You don't see any connection there?" he asks me.

"With the vote?"

But Patrick's look is suddenly abstracted; a thought has just occurred to him. "You're sure there was no note?"

"Nothing."

Patrick ruminates awhile; in the end, I have to ask him what he's thinking.

"How much would Hatanaka have sacrificed to screw Japan's chance at a Council seat? That's what I'm thinking."

It takes me a moment. Then I get it. "You're not serious."

"Why not? Part of Jap tradition, isn't it? Bushido, whatever they call it. Who was that guy? Mishima? Like a grand protest thing. If Hatanaka did that, then left a note saying what a bad idea he thought a Jap seat was, Christ, can you imagine the headlines?"

"There was no note," I say firmly.

"Check his office," he tells me. "And his apartment."

I suggest that we should first wait and see what Mike finds on the tapes, but Patrick waves that aside as if I am simply being obtuse. He has decided on the answer. The answer is suicide. And this is, frankly, the worst example yet of just how badly Patrick's judgment is being impaired by his preoccupation with the vote. There is just no way Toshio committed suicide to make a political point, I don't care how much he might have wanted to derail the upcoming vote. But confronting Patrick head-on, I know, is useless, so I don't even try. As we turn and head back down the path, I wonder aloud about notifying the Japanese consulate.

"No need," says Patrick.

I glance at him.

"He's on a UN passport," Patrick reminds me.

"He's a Japanese national."

"Is this Japan?"

At the top of the terrace steps I touch Patrick's arm, and we both stop. "Patrick, he's dead. It doesn't matter how he died, we have to notify the embassy. His relatives have to be contacted. This isn't something you can keep under wraps."

"We just need two days."

"If you believe you can keep this secret until the vote. If you think you can get Mike to go along with that—"

His fantasy deflated by this quick reality check, he looks down at his feet. What he is thinking about, I suspect, is not Toshio Hatanaka but Patrick O'Conner. How to handle this disastrous situation, how to limit any damage it might do to the campaign for the Japanese seat. How to protect his own career.

"There's probably no note," I say. "And I really don't think it's suicide anyway."

"Suicide, murder," Patrick mutters. "Once the word gets out that the opponent in chief of the Jap seat's dead in the bloody basement, all fucking hell's going to break loose. First thing they'll do is make a play to shuffle the agenda."

From Patrick's point of view, a catastrophe. A delay in the vote, the way the momentum is running, would be a certain prelude to defeat for the Japanese. Patrick swears.

Right then Mike emerges from the Assembly building. He sees us immediately and jogs over, one hand resting on the walkie-talkie at his hip. "No tape," he reports, coming to a halt in front of us. "The camera in the basement corridor was turned off."

Oh, Jesus, says Patrick.

"Ten last night through to six this morning," Mike tells us, his voice strained. "Maintenance. Getting ready for today."

"Maintenance," Patrick moans, screwing up his face.

But last night there was a reception held in the public concourse, cocktails for the nongovernmental organizations. I ask Mike about that. The concourse is just one floor up from the basement; I can't believe the NGO event wasn't taped.

"Sure, we got that. But nothing in the basement. They're telling me the work on the cameras was scheduled days ago. I got someone chasing up the maintenance crew."

"Someone could have strolled down from the NGO reception, we wouldn't know?" says Patrick.

"We'll check the concourse tapes. See if we can spot anyone disappearing downstairs who shouldn't be." From Mike's tone, a long shot. His face is red now, an equal measure of embarrassment and fury.

I turn to Patrick, expecting some decision, a plan of action. But Patrick seems overwhelmed by the steady escalation of the problem. He stares right past us, lost in some private thought.

"One call," Mike suggests. "I can have a Homicide forensics team here in twenty minutes."

Patrick's head snaps around. "You don't call anyone. No one. Not Homicide, not NYPD Forensics, no one. This isn't Harlem, for chrissake. The New York cops come in here, half the bloody delegations will up and walk out. You feel like explaining that upstairs?"

"We need some help here," Mike protests. "Professionals."

"No one," Patrick repeats.

Mike pulls a face, but Patrick is right. The legal fiction that these few acres at Turtle Bay are not part of the U.S. is treated as divine law by most of the delegates. Any intrusion into these grounds by U.S. officialdom, whatever the reason, would set off major diplomatic fireworks.

"Isn't there a coolroom in back of the basement canteen?" Patrick wonders aloud.

"What about it?" Mike returns, deadpan.

"You could put him in there. Just for now."

"No forensics?"

Patrick doesn't reply.

"And then what?" says Mike. "Go home?"

Patrick starts to move off, telling me that he's going to speak to the SG. But Mike lays a hand on his arm.

"I'm reporting this to Eckhardt as a murder." Eckhardt, Mike's boss, the head of UN Security. "And I can tell you now, he's gonna flip if he finds anything got done without him hearing about it first."

So tell him, Patrick says.

"And I'll be telling him that unless we get an investigation started now, we got no chance of nailing this."

"An investigation?"

"Homicide," says Mike.

Cornered, Patrick turns right, then left. A full-blown investigation, the kind of unpredictable political currents it might stir up in this place, at this time—it is the very last thing Patrick needs so close to Thursday's vote. And Mike senses that.

"Put Sam on it with me." I shoot Mike a look, but he ignores me and continues to press his case with Patrick. "I'll do what I can with the detective work, let Sam play prosecuting attorney, keep it legal. I mean, look at it. What's the alternate plan?"

A fair point. Patrick considers. "What are the chances you can actually find out what happened down there last night? Given that you don't get your NYPD buddies involved."

"Not great," Mike tells him. "Doesn't mean we shouldn't try."

Not great, Patrick echoes. He strokes his throat a moment, then faces me.

What I would like to do, of course, is pass right on by, let the nightmare fall on someone else. And for a moment I consider doing just that. Sorry. Too busy. Try one of the junior legal officers from the department. But even as I consider this polite but firm refusal, I realize that I am not going to get that choice. Because this is not some draft proposal for an obscure UN committee, the kind of thing I delegate daily by the truckload down the line. This is murder at the UN. Toshio Hatanaka, everybody's favorite special envoy. And Mike wants me on it. And Patrick knows he has to do something. After fourteen years of practice, I can protect my bureaucratic butt as well as the next guy, but this just isn't one of those things I can safely palm off, watch explode in someone else's lap. Patrick is nodding to himself now, coming around to Mike's suggestion. A weight like lead settles in my bones. The legal point guard in the investigation of Toshio Hatanaka's death has just been selected.

Mike gets a call on his walkie-talkie; apparently Dr. Patel, the resident UNHQ medic, is waiting for Mike down in the basement.

"Patel?" Patrick is appalled.

"If you won't let a real forensics team in," says Mike, "Patel's what you got." Patel, needless to say, is a guy you wouldn't trust with any medical instrument more sophisticated than a thermometer. He does the occasional routine medical checkup, hands out aspirin, and spends the rest of his time sleeping in the sanatorium. Moving away from us, Mike calls over his shoulder that Eckhardt should be down in the basement any minute. "If you got a problem treating this as a homicide, come down and tell him."

The moment Mike is out of earshot, Patrick turns to me. "Check Hatanaka's office. If there's a note, bring it straight to me. Don't show Jardine. Or Eckhardt."

I repeat my opinion that there will be no note, that like Mike, I do not believe Toshio has committed suicide. But Patrick is not listening.

"If there's nothing there, go check his apartment. And see if you can't do something about Jardine. Settle him down. If he thinks he's going to have no problems running a homicide investigation in this place, he's just plain wrong. And I don't want to be picking up the pieces, cleaning up after him just because he's too bloody gung ho to listen to reason."

"He's a professional."

"He's your mate," says Patrick. "And I'm telling you to settle him down."

Today's second big edict. Speak to Hatanaka. Settle Mike down. Inside, we part at the escalators, Patrick giving me a few final instructions before heading grim-faced toward the Assembly Hall to inform the Secretary-General of the tragedy. I break into a jog down the corridor, hurrying to Toshio's office in the Secretariat building, feeling suddenly light-headed and nauseated, but glad to be moving, relieved to have something to do, something to think about other than the shocking sight in the basement. I am going upstairs to carry out my instructions: to look for a note that I do not believe exists. Twenty-nine floors up to Toshio's office. Thirty floors clear of the corpse.

4

AFTER SEARCHING TOSHIO'S OFFICE FOR FIVE MINUTES AND finding nothing that remotely resembles a suicide note, I retreat three doors along and across the passage to my own office and close the door.

The shelves in here are jammed with books and papers and files. At least once a week somebody will come to me checking up on the whys and wherefores of the Headquarters Agreement, generally the maintenance managers, who deal with things like the electricity and water we buy from the State of New York. So that booklet, though I almost know its contents by heart, is close at hand. But the *Geneva Convention on Diplomatic Privileges* is buried deep somewhere among the rest, and I twist my neck to read the vertical labels on the spines.

Gathering information and writing reports, you will learn from the PR handouts, is the work that takes place in the Secretariat building. More than thirty floors of worker ants busy gathering information and writing reports, and though I deal with only the apex of the legal pyramid, that is more than enough to keep me permanently wading through paper. I curse the system as I move along the shelves.

The door opens behind me.

"Elizabeth? I'm looking for Geneva dip rights and privileges, sixty-one. Any clues?" On my knees now, I shuffle along by the bottom shelf. "I thought it was down here."

No answer. When I look up, it is not Elizabeth, my secretary, peering down at me over my desk.

"Dad?" Rachel smiles and shakes her head, her bob of shiny black hair swaying from side to side. "Get a grip," she says.

My gut clenches. Quickly turning back to the shelves, I tell my daughter that I thought she had the whole day off from her job as a UN guide.

"What's lost?" she asks me.

I shoot her a dark look. She pulls a face and crosses to the window, remarking that most of the sightseers have left First Avenue. "How come you're not down at the opening?" she says, turning back.

"How come you're up here?"

"I'm a spy."

"How about you do your spying someplace else."

"Dad?" She leans right over, watching me through the opening beneath my desk. "What is it, some book?"

Yeah, I say. Some book.

In fact, if I can find the damn thing, it is the only document I can think of that might give us some guidance as to the legal situation arising from Toshio's death. Not something I want to get into with Rachel. Standing, I brush the dust off my knees. Rachel takes a tub of yogurt and a plastic teaspoon from her purse. She commences to eat, ruminating over each mouthful, her gaze directed to the Tibetan monks across the street. Watching her, I think, What do I tell her? How do I tell her? Remember Toshio Hatanaka, the guy who went to Afghanistan to negotiate your mother's release and failed? Guess what happened.

"Hello?" Rachel waves her plastic spoon, her singsong voice bringing me back to the present.

I nod to the yogurt. "I hope that's not lunch."

"Are you nagging me?"

"That's what I'm doing." I move along the shelves.

"And I really look like I'm shrinking away?" She pinches her cheek as she sits down. "Skin and bone?"

But she looks fine, a slimmer-than-average eighteen-year-old kid who probably hasn't slept as much as she should have since moving out of the family home last week. And I recognize the veiled warning too—what she eats, her weight, are not subjects she likes to discuss. When her mother died, Rachel was your normal, healthy adolescent, no more hang-ups or neuroses than any fifteen-year-old girl. Within a year she was in a special-needs ward at Bellevue, being fed a cocktail of nutrient-enriched liquids through a tube in her nose. Anorexia nervosa. Words that can still fill me with helpless terror.

"So what's the big deal with this book?"

Just some procedural thing, I tell her, facing the shelves again, wondering how to get rid of her. For one of the committees, I say. No big deal.

"I don't know why you bother."

"It's a job."

"I mean, why you bother lying, Dad. Really. You are the world's absolute worst."

Locating the diplomatic rights and privileges file, I pull it from the stack, then face her. She has her feet apart now, her knees clamped together. She leans forward, trying hard not to drip yogurt onto her blue skirt. Her blue blazer is draped over her purse behind the door.

"This isn't a good time, Rache."

"Two minutes," she says.

Two minutes. I've got a dead man in the basement and my daughter needs two minutes to finish her yogurt. I flip open the file and pull up a chair behind my desk.

"I'm a chaperone for the day," she tells me.

"Good for you."

"All the guides got landed with different delegations."

Nodding into the file, I turn a page.

"Guess who I'm doing."

"Amaze me."

"The Philippines. Argentina and Spain too, just the junior delegates."

"Excellent."

"You're not interested, are you?"

"Rachel." Lifting my eyes, I tap the file with a finger. "Won't the Philippines be missing you by now?"

She informs me that she's got another fifteen minutes. Then she flips her empty yogurt tub into the trash can, licks the spoon, and flips that too. She slumps back in her chair; she obviously has no intention of leaving.

I could tell her, I think. Maybe I even should tell her. Sooner or later the news about Toshio will get out; sooner or later Rachel will have to know, wouldn't it be better for her to hear it from me? But just now, as so often with Rachel these past three years, I simply cannot find the words. In the end I bow my head over the file and lose myself in the arcane region of the law that dictates the behavior of nations toward persons of credentialed diplomatic standing. On the page here it is clear as crystalline water. The rights of the individual, the responsibilities of the state. Totally clear. Completely transparent. But what happens, say, if the government of a country falls, revolutionaries seize power, and the U.S. embassy is besieged for over a year? What happens, say, if a diplomat from a rogue regime leans out of an embassy window in London and shoots a local police officer? What happens, say, if a UN special envoy is found murdered in the basement at UN headquarters? What happens, of course, is that politics takes over, and after years in UN Legal Affairs I have learned that politics has a way of turning the crystalline waters of the statute book into mud.

"Juan says the Japanese won't get onto the Council."

"Where'd he get that from?"

"Around," says Rachel.

Around, I tell her, keeping my head down, is not normally considered to be a source of high repute. But it is so much a measure of how deeply this vote is affecting all of us that I find myself making a mental note of Juan's opinion. Juan is Rachel's new landlord and roommate, a twenty-four-year-old with a bee in his bonnet about the state of the world. A senior figure at Lighthouse, one of the increasingly numerous NGOs that have UN accreditation, Juan could possibly be picking up signals that we're missing from some of the smaller delegations.

"He's not the only one saying it," she says.

"Mmm?"

"The guys from the *Keisan Shimbun* think Hatanaka's sunk it too," Rachel asserts confidently.

A sound rises from deep in my chest. After eighteen years, my daughter still has the most amazing capacity to surprise me. She has been giving Joe Public the tour and PR gloss for barely three months. And she got the job not because she was turned on by politics and diplomacy. Far from it. She got the job because for the first time in my career I stooped to pull a few strings. And here she is, I now discover, shooting the breeze with journalists from the leading Japanese business daily about who's hot and who's not in the world of big-time international diplomacy.

"Rachel." My hand traces a bewildered circle in the air, then I point to the door. "Out."

"You brought my stuff, yeah?"

Her stuff. A suitcase full of clothes from home. It's down in the trunk of my car. I told Rachel I'd drop it off at her new apartment tonight, but now I make a face.

"Oh, Dad, you promised."

"What's this, blackmail?"

She smiles sweetly. It is not as cute at this moment as she thinks it is.

"Okay, Rache. I'll try. No promises."

"Great."

She goes to pick up her purse and blazer from behind the door. And this is the moment that Mike chooses to arrive. He puts his head in and speaks before I can stop him. "Hatanaka died about eight hours ago, way Patel sees it. I wouldn't take that for gospel."

I wave a hand, my look is severe. His voice trails off. Then Rachel steps out from where she has been hidden from view; she has an arm in one sleeve of her blazer.

Mike makes a sound. I drop my head into my hand. Finally Mike nods to her and says "Rache," then with an apologetic glance in my direction he tells me that he'll be in Toshio's office. He quickly withdraws.

Rachel turns to me, her mouth open. "Hatanaka, Dad?"

"You didn't hear that."

"Toshio Hatanaka?"

Moving smartly around the desk, I close the door. "Okay, so now you've heard. In a couple of hours it'll be out anyway." My finger rises in warning. "But I don't want you telling anyone. Not Juan. Not anyone."

"How? What did he have, a heart attack?"

"Look, I haven't got time to discuss it, Rache. And for the time being, you forget that you heard. Okay?"

She glances at the file on my desk. "Is that why you needed the diplomatic rights thing?"

"Rachel," I say sharply.

Maybe too sharply. Startled, she jerks her head back.

"I'll bring your stuff tonight, okay? Any questions, ask me then." I toss my head toward the door. "Now go."

She sees at once that I am not kidding. She shrugs her shoulders into her blazer, comes around the desk, and pecks me on the cheek. Her look of curious astonishment lingers on me a moment longer, then she leaves without a word. Teenage daughters. Quantum physics could not be more unfathomable.

5

"ZERO POINTS FOR FUCKING SECURITY," MIKE MUTTERS WHEN I join him in Toshio's office. He gestures to the door behind me. "Wasn't even locked."

"Does Patrick know you're up here?"

Mike shrugs; the answer, I presume, is no. Then he starts apologizing for accidentally spilling the beans to Rachel, but I wave that off, explaining that I've told her to keep it quiet. Mike accepts that with a rueful nod, then we stand a moment, contemplating our surroundings.

"I've already had a quick look around," I admit, lifting my chin toward the desk and shelves.

"Yeah? For what?"

"Suicide note."

"No joy?"

When I turn my head, Mike's eyes sweep the room. "Don't tell me. Suicide's Patrick's theory, right?"

When I concede that it is, Mike grunts. Between him and Patrick the chemistry has always been bad, any contact between them abrasive. And Mike does not seem in the least inclined to put whatever differences they have aside in order to deal more effectively with this disaster.

"Patrick tell you to leave the door unlocked?"

"I left it like I found it, Mike. It was unlocked when I came in, I left it like that when I went out. Nothing to do with Patrick."

He steps a little farther into the room. In size the office isn't much different from mine, and the same shelves are stacked with books and files. But there are no family photos on the desk and there isn't even a poster to break those blank expanses of white wall that aren't covered by shelving. There are no windows either; that more than anything gives the room a cramped, somewhat claustrophobic feel. This isn't, frankly, the kind of place in which you would expect a UN special envoy to spend his working day. And in truth, though Toshio has had this office for at least five years, it was never more than a convenient base to him; unlike everyone else on this floor, he has never spent much time at his desk. My own impression of this room when I first saw it some years back was that it was ostentatiously austere for someone so senior. Over the years, however, I have come to see that Toshio's indifference to the trappings of power was absolutely sincere and not, as more than one resident cynic believed, a calculated front that concealed a vaulting ambition.

Mike's eyes run over the piles of paper, the notebooks, and the other everyday jumble on the desktop.

"So whadda we seeing here?" he asks me.

Nothing out of the ordinary, I tell him. It looks just like always: Toshio's innate tidiness and sense of order fighting a losing battle against the workload overflowing his optimistically small in box.

"Like always?"

Nodding, I thumb through the tray. Mike asks me how often I come in here.

"When Toshio's around? Once or twice a day."

"Work?"

"Mostly." Toshio, I explain, got VIP treatment from my department. Normally the requests for legal opinions that come to me are matters of no real importance. We have scores of lawyers in UN Legal Affairs, yet I still find myself signing off on proposed wordings of nonbinding agreements that will probably never even make it to the peripheral committee meetings for which they are putatively intended. But the legal problems of UN envoys I have always taken seriously, handled personally whenever I could. Out getting their hands dirty in the world, dealing with intractable problems of large and deadly consequence, they need our help, a need that is often all too real.

Mike starts rifling through Toshio's desk drawers. "I took another look at that grille downstairs. No way someone used it. Dust all the way back in the chute, and it's too small."

"So if it's murder, whoever we're looking for came through the door?"

"If?" says Mike.

I ask him about the security tapes. What are the chances, I wonder, that Toshio's murderer knew he wasn't being recorded?

"I got someone out trying to round up the maintenance crew, three guys. I'll be interviewing them soon as they come in."

"Do we know who had keys to the basement rooms?"

"Apart from the guards?" Mike shakes his head no. "Any good reason you can think of Hatanaka was down there anyway?"

I admit that I can't. Mike goes back to the papers in the drawer.

"Whoever left the body there locked the door," he says. "So whoever left him there had a key. If Hatanaka didn't have regular business down in the basement—"

"He didn't."

"Okay. So our man didn't steal the key from Hatanaka."

"The guy had his own key?"

"Seems like."

Mike closes the top drawer, crouching to open the next. When I came in here earlier, I checked what I thought were the most likely places for a suicide note: desktop, drawers, the corkboard where a UNESCO calendar hangs askew. I even looked in the trash. Rather than go through all that again, it occurs to me that it might be useful to know what Toshio was working on. Mike nods at my suggestion and points at Toshio's in box. So I settle myself in the chair and lift the whole pile of paperwork into my lap.

"What should we be looking for? Anything particular?"

"Nope," Mike answers without glancing up.

We carry on our respective searches in silence.

Toshio Hatanaka did not have what you would call a regular working day. He was, as much as anyone can be within the confines of this hidebound institution, a free agent, someone to whom many of the usual bureaucratic rules and customs did not strictly apply. The paperwork I am studying now reflects that. There is a stack of memos from UNHCR, the UN High Commission for Refugees, relating to logistical problems in the field: tents that should be in Pakistan currently caught up in a dockers' dispute in Singapore; field-workers wanting to know if they can still use the rehydration sachets for children with diarrhea, which arrived in Somalia three months late; an ongoing dispute with one of the aid agencies about joint use of telecommunications facilities, this one with an attached note from Toshio suggesting a senior figure in the agency who might be able to help. But free agent or not, Toshio's official assignment with UNHCR ended over two years ago, and this evidence of just how much time he was devoting to matters beyond his current remit is unexpected. I find myself frowning. I flick through the rest of the memos, most of which, I am relieved to see, concern Afghanistan.

"Geneva," Mike says suddenly. He pulls the stub of a plane ticket from the drawer and places it on the desk. He points to the date. "Last week."

We study the details. Toshio Hatanaka evidently took a Swissair flight to Geneva at the beginning of last week, spent three days there, then returned.

Mike remarks that Geneva, as he remembers it, is a hell of a long way from Afghanistan.

"Could have been a routine meeting," I suggest.

But Toshio, we both know, would have been working his butt off this past month just to prepare for the General Assembly session. Last week was not the time for a three-day meeting on the shores of Lake Geneva.

Mike pushes the ticket aside. "What have you got?"

When I show him the memos, he glances through them quickly. "Give it to me again," he says, puzzled. "Hatanaka was special envoy to Afghanistan, right?"

"He was with UNHCR till two years back." That, I explain, was a large part of the reason he ended up as special envoy to Afghanistan: Afghanistan has one of the worst refugee problems in the world.

"But it wasn't his job, was it, refugees? Lookit this." Mike flicks the memos. "Special envoy to Afghanistan? Where'd he find the time? The guy was doing everything but."

There was some talk, I remark absently, that Toshio might make a run at the UNHCR's top job, high commissioner for refugees.

A cynical weariness spreads over Mike's face. "Ahh," he says.

"Come on. He wasn't like that, Mike, this was a dedicated guy." I gesture to the memos. "If he thought he could help, he helped."

"Dedicated."

"Dedicated," I say.

The desk offers up nothing more, so we turn and face the shelves. There are files, hundreds of them, not all of them labeled. Shaking his head, Mike goes out in search of Toshio's secretary while I prop my ass against the desk and wait.

The last time I saw Toshio alive was yesterday morning. He was leaning against these same shelves, arms crossed, one shoulder against the files, trying hard to look relaxed. Half a lifetime he'd spent in the U.S., and he still couldn't manage the trick. The effort it cost him was visible in every stiff angle of his body; I never saw a man look less relaxed or more Japanese. Now my eyes run down the shelves to the tatami on the floor. And I have to blink away a sudden vision of Toshio's corpse.

A minute later Mike returns with Toshio's secretary, Mei Tan, in tow.

"So where'd he keep this report?" he asks her as they enter.

Mei Tan looks relieved to see me. A Singaporean, she is something of an institution here on Floor Twenty-nine. She worked with my deputy, Gunther Franks, for years before promotion to Toshio's office. Now she pushes her horn-rimmed glasses up the bridge of her nose and tells us that she's not sure about this. She says she would like some formal authority before allowing us into Mr. Hatanaka's office.

"We're already in the goddamn office," Mike mutters, going to the far side of the desk.

Mei Tan turns to me. "You must speak with Mr. Hatanaka."

"What report?" I ask her.

"Did he say for you to come in here?"

"Listen," Mike breaks in impatiently, but I raise a hand.

"Mei Tan," I say evenly, "we're here because Patrick O'Conner sent us. If you need to call him to confirm that, go right ahead. We'll wait."

She considers that. You can see that the idea of risking Patrick O'Conner's wrath does not appeal. And when I volunteer to take full responsibility for this, she finally gives up. She shrugs and gestures to Mike.

"I was telling him that Mr. Hatanaka was working on this report for the General Assembly. Like a five-year review. We've been working on it for months now. Is that what you're looking for?"

Mike and I exchange a glance. This could be something.

"Let's see it," I say.

Mei Tan takes down a box from a shelf and places it on the desk. "Officially it's for the Secretary-General and some of the committees."

Which committees? Mike wants to know.

The Third Committee, she tells him: Human Rights. And the Fifth Committee: UN Administrative and Budgetary Affairs.

The report, when I open the box, is inches deep. The cover page says Afghanistan, Status Report, then the year and Toshio's name and rank, special envoy. Turning to the chapter headings, I delve into the body of the thing.

"How long's he been on this?" Mike asks Mei Tan.

"Writing?"

"Putting the whole thing together."

"Since last year."

"You were working with him the whole time?"

Nodding, she asks what it is we're hoping to find, why we can't speak to Mr. Hatanaka directly.

"When was this due to go upstairs?" I ask.

"Tomorrow."

"It's finished?"

She nods again, so I pull out the whole wedge of pages and lay them beside the empty box. This time I search the pages more carefully. According to the table of contents, Toshio has broken his report into four sections: the general report, then three detailed sections: one for the Third Committee, one for ECOSOC—the Economic and Social Council—and one for the Fifth Committee. This last section, clearly listed on the contents page, is missing.

"He must have taken it home," Mei Tan says when I draw her attention to the omission. She screws up her face. "Actually, you really will have to ask Mr. Hatanaka about that. He was doing that section himself. He hasn't let anyone else see it yet."

I ask her if she has any idea what it might contain. Mei Tan shakes her head.

"He's got this pink file he keeps it in," she remarks, her eyes wandering over the desk, then up along the shelves. Edging past Mike, she checks the desk drawers. "No," she concludes, completing her unsuccessful search for the missing pink file. "You'll have to ask Mr. Hatanaka."

If only, I think.

Then Mike casually inquires, "Where is he?"

There is no sign that Mei Tan finds the question strange. "Down at the opening, I guess. I haven't seen him this morning."

When Mike asks her where we can find Toshio after the opening, Mei Tan goes to fetch the appointment calendar. When she's gone, we discuss the missing section of the report. Mike agrees that it's odd but warns me not to get too hopeful. Odd, he tells me, is not the same thing as important, but he assures me that he will be taking another good look in Toshio's briefcase down in the basement.

Mei Tan reenters with the calendar, an oversized book with a hard black cover. She flips it open and slides her finger down the page. Apart from three words at the top, "General Assembly opening," the page is blank.

"Busy man," Mike murmurs. Reaching across, he flicks back a few pages before Mei Tan can protest. Then he stabs a finger down. "What happened here?"

The dates are the first two days of Toshio's excursion to Geneva.

Across both pages the word *Canceled* has been scrawled over a list of appointments, and when Mike turns to the next page, it's the same there too.

"The trip to Geneva a last-minute thing?" he asks her.

"Geneva?" she says.

We both look at her, then at each other. Mike picks up the ticket stub and indicates the matching dates and Toshio's name on the ticket. Mei Tan studies it, becoming perplexed.

"This isn't right," she says finally, her brow puckering as she touches the ticket. "He wasn't well then. Those three days Mr. Hatanaka stayed at home. He called me. Gastro or something, you ask him."

"Who normally makes Mr. Hatanaka's travel arrangements?"

"Me," she says.

"Always?"

She nods, but there is a touch of hesitancy now, a flicker of doubt. The ticket. Our presence. These questions.

"Can't you come back later and see Mr. Hatanaka?"

Mike asks her if she has her own key to this office. She shakes her head. Then he flicks forward through the calendar and stops at Monday. Yesterday. Half a dozen appointments. He trails a finger down the page and stops at Toshio's penultimate appointment of the day: five-thirty P.M. Mike glances up at me to make sure I have registered the name: Patrick O'Conner.

"Hmph" is all Mike says. Then his finger moves on to Toshio's final appointment yesterday. Moriko. Seven-thirty P.M.

"Toshio's sister," I tell Mike.

Mei Tan confirms that Toshio kept the appointment with Patrick, but about the one with Moriko she's not sure. "I went home just after he went up to see Mr. O'Conner. Anyway, that's personal, his family." She is becoming distinctly uncomfortable now. And when Mike asks her to fetch us the most recent editions of some obscure journal from down in the Dag Hammarskjöld Library, it is hard to tell if Mei Tan is more surprised or relieved by the request.

The moment she's gone, Mike hands me the calendar and slips the Geneva ticket stub into his pocket. Then he reaches into one of the desk drawers and produces a bunch of keys. Toshio's keys, which Mike must have noticed during his earlier search. He pockets them.

"Sound to you like she was lying?"

I shake my head.

"Me neither." He lays a blank sheet of paper on the desk and writes. Large letters, black felt pen. DO NOT OPEN. LOCKED BY

ORDER—UN SECURITY. Then his name and signature. Next, he finds some Scotch tape, and while he tears off a piece, I ask him what he makes of the trip to Geneva.

"Nothing yet. Don't even know if he went." He takes his sign over to the door and tapes it up. He nods to the calendar in my hands. "Bring that."

After locking the door, he leads the way to the elevators. "Let's see if that pink file's anywhere in the basement. I wanna make sure the body's secure in the coolroom too."

"Then what?"

"His apartment." Mike gives me a sideways look. "I'm guessing Patrick told you to get over there to search for the suicide note. I figure while you're wasting your time with that, I can take a look around the place, maybe get some clue why the guy was murdered."

6

THE JOURNALISTS HAVE DESCENDED. NORMALLY IT'S JUST THE UN
regulars idling around the corridors singly or in pairs, looking
hangdog, complaining about lack of access to delegates and wondering when their editors will recall them from this journalistic waste-
land. Young hacks shunted here into the slow lane of advancement.
Old hacks wearing their stints of salaried idleness at Turtle Bay like
lusterless crowns to inglorious careers. But for these few days each
year, even the terminally embittered among them come to life, galva-
nized by the alluring possibility that they might actually find something here to report that their editors back home will call news.

Add to these regulars the incestuous packs that swarm around the
presidents, the heads of state, and foreign ministers, and what you
get is what Mike and I meet when we hit the concourse outside the
General Assembly Hall: indecorous shoving, microphones and cameras being brandished like weapons, and people swearing at one another in about twenty different languages.

Mike adds his voice to the chorus. "Assholes," he says, shouldering his way into the pack as I slide right along in his wake.

We have almost made it to the escalators, when I feel a hand on
my shoulder. Turning, I find Lady Nicola Edgeworth looking up at
me; she asks if she might please have a word. "Just one minute," she
adds, sensing my reluctance. When I look back, I see that Mike has
plowed on; he is waiting for me at the head of the escalators. I signal
him on. I will have to catch up later.

"A very quick word," I tell Lady Nicola, unable to conceal my
impatience.

"Somewhere a little more private," she suggests.

The private place we enter is a small room off the Delegates' Lounge. The room is hung with collages and oil paintings, social realism from the fifties, framed in pine.

"Special Envoy Hatanaka," Lady Nicola says the moment we're alone.

I cannot pretend to be surprised. Lady Nicola, the British ambassador, one of the Security Council's Big Five, is also the president of the Security Council this month. Once Patrick had given the news to the SG, Lady Nicola would have been his next port of call.

"Patrick's told you?"

"Yes."

I look at her. I am not quite sure what she expects me to add.

"It's rather about Mr. O'Conner that I wanted a word," she says, and with the slightest of touches she guides me away from the door.

Lady Nicola has been a fixture at Turtle Bay for most of my career. When I was working as a rapporteur on the Sixth Committee, Legal Affairs, she was the committee chairman. My job was to compile and paraphrase the debate that took place among the committee members: what to put up to the General Assembly for a vote, what to hold back and redraft, and what to discard as totally ridiculous. And though in those days I was just one of many lowly gofers from the Secretariat, Lady Nicola went out of her way to make me feel that my work was appreciated. She astonished the entire Sixth Committee by asking for a round of applause for me at their final sitting that year. Since then she has become her country's ambassador. The British ambassador, a big UN name.

"What can you tell me? Suicide?"

"We don't know that."

"I see."

"We don't know anything," I add quickly. "Suicide's possible."

" 'Possible' wasn't quite the word Mr. O'Conner used," she remarks dryly. "From memory, the word Mr. O'Conner used was 'likely.' "

I shrug the distinction aside. "Toshio's dead. And I don't mean to be rude, Lady Nicola, but me standing here with you, talking about it, isn't helping us figure out how he died."

"You're aware Toshio opposed a permanent Japanese seat on the Council."

"I'm aware that some people thought so." I cast a glance toward the door. I really do not want to be having this conversation.

"I've spoken briefly with each of the other perm five ambassadors," she says. "They all share my concerns as to the impact this might have on the vote."

"The vote?" I cannot help myself from blurting it out. "Toshio's dead, you're worried about the vote?"

"Please, Samuel," she says, lifting a hand.

But I don't apologize. I am pretty sure now that I am not going to like what is coming, the reason for this private word in my ear. The politics have begun. And to her credit, Lady Nicola broaches it directly now.

"I suggested to my perm five colleagues that I might approach you with a view to establishing an informal channel of communication about the investigation. Mr. O'Conner tells me you're leading it." When I don't say anything, she goes on. "It's an impossible situation. This vote—"

"Informal?" I break in.

She inclines her head.

"So what's wrong with the formal channel? I report to Patrick, you ask him what's going on."

"We prefer our information unfiltered."

Unfiltered. Meaning, I take it, that they do not believe they can get that from Patrick. And knowing Patrick as I do, I would have to say that the Big Five's fears are very well founded; but I can't admit that, of course, certainly not to Lady Nicola. She has obviously persuaded her ambassadorial colleagues that I can be trusted, that I am someone who will understand the awkward position they find themselves in. And I do understand; in some subtle way I am even flattered by this approach. But that just isn't enough, because in the end I am what I am, a Secretariat staffer, an international civil servant pledged to hold myself above the political fray.

"I can't do that," I decide out loud.

Lady Nicola presses her lips together, her disappointment plain. "You couldn't be persuaded?"

"No." My tone is firm and unequivocal. I want to cut this dead. "If that's all," I say, glancing doorward.

She studies me a moment, then seems to decide that it would be futile at the moment to press me further. "Of course," she says. Not an admission of defeat, more a tactical retreat. Her pale English skin wrinkles tightly around her mouth. As we move toward the door, she expresses a desire that this conversation should remain a private matter, a suggestion to which I diplomatically concur.

Out in the Delegates' Lounge the French and Chinese ambassadors are both hovering and Lady Nicola moves toward them, presumably to report the bad news that she has failed to tap a purer source of information than Patrick O'Conner. When word of Toshio's death gets out, when the storm breaks, the perm five will be navigating their way through the tempest with a compass they do not completely trust. Their problem, I think. Right now I have more than enough problems of my own.

Weaving my way swiftly through the posse of journalists outside the Delegates' Lounge, I cross to the escalator. I am already halfway down, when I become aware of some woman behind me, saying my name.

"Mr. Windrush," she says again.

When I turn, my heart sinks. A journalist's microphone. Then I raise my eyes to the woman, a vaguely familiar face, probably a regular on the UN beat.

"No comment," I say, nodding to the mike, trying to make it sound like a joke. But my heart is in my shoes. I am first deputy in Legal Affairs; about three times a year I am wheeled out to give the press a background briefing on some incomprehensible piece of legalese that might or might not have implications for some forgotten war in a distant quarter of the world. On these occasions the journalists tend to help themselves to the press release and skip my recondite lecture. Even after my fifteen minutes of fame as the poor son of a bitch whose wife was taken hostage and murdered by crazies in Afghanistan, there wouldn't be one in ten of the UN-accredited journalists who knows me by sight. Not one in twenty who knows me by name. But this woman riding down the escalator behind me has apparently made it her business to find out. Half the world's political big hitters upstairs, and here she is, trailing after me. Toshio? I wonder. Already?

"Aren't you headed the wrong way?" I ask her.

"It is possible." A French accent. She looks up over her shoulder, then back to me. *"Alors,"* she says.

I turn just in time to stumble awkwardly off the escalator.

Stepping off behind me, she says quietly, "Most dangerous."

I take a breath and compose myself. "Is there some question that you wanted to ask me?"

"You were with the ambassador. Monsieur Froissart?"

Relief. She is fishing for a story on the French ambassador. I was with Lady Nicola Edgeworth, I tell her, not Froissart. She has made a mistake.

"A long meeting?" she asks.

"It wasn't a meeting."

"No?"

I turn and walk, but she stays at my side.

"Three of the perm five ambassadors left the Assembly Hall during the opening speeches," she says. "That is strange, no?"

My glance skitters down to the mike she is holding low by her side. She follows my gaze down. Then she unplugs the thin black wire and crams it with the mike into her purse.

"Ambassador Edgeworth did not tell you why she left the Hall?"

No, I say.

"But she needed to see you?"

"We had a few words on a private matter. End of story."

"I interviewed Monsieur Froissart. He seemed anxious. He did not say to you why?"

"To me?" I point a thumb at my chest, but the act is overdone. Her look turns skeptical.

"You do not remember me, do you?"

I glance at her as we walk. An attractive woman, early thirties, dark hair, her skin faintly freckled on either side of her slender nose. And familiar too, but she sees that I still can't place her.

"Journalists and the Secretariat?" she prompts.

Journalists and the Secretariat. A series of seminars I conducted last year, part of a PR campaign cooked up by Patrick to get the Secretariat some decent press coverage. About a dozen journalists showed up at the first seminar, half that number at the second; by week three there were just me and two female journalists, so I called the whole thing off. One of those last two, the stayers, wasn't one of them French?

Memory triggered, I point. "Radio France."

Smiling, she reintroduces herself. Marie Lefebre. As we near the stairs, she takes the opportunity to remind me of just what I said in those high-minded seminars, my earnest endorsement of the journalists' right to question and the Secretariat's responsibility to respond.

I pull a face. "You were listening?"

"*Oui.* I have notes."

"Well, maybe you could show your notes to Ambassador Froissart," I suggest. "He seems a reasonable man."

At the head of the stairs a security guard steps aside to let me pass, but when Marie Lefebre tries to join me, he plants himself in front of her. He puts out his arm, telling her that the concourse and basement are temporarily off limits. I give her a curt parting nod as I descend.

"You were not discussing the Japanese vote?" she calls after me.

I concentrate on the stairs, hoping that I can walk right out of her sphere of curiosity just as easily as I walked into it. On the ground floor I meet Mike coming up from the basement.

"No pink file in the briefcase," he tells me.

"Let's go."

"You don't wanna see where we got him?"

"Monsieur Windrush?"

Mike's eyes dart upward, my own head lifts slowly. Marie Lefebre is leaning out from the cantilevered balcony above us, looking down at the guards Mike has stationed on the stairs to the basement. "What is so important down there?" she says.

Mike shoots me a look. He is not pleased with the curiosity I seem to have invited. Taking his arm, I guide him toward the exit while from up on the balcony Marie delivers a short burst of French at our retreating backs. The one word I hear quite distinctly is *merde*.

7

"JESUS, CAN I CHANGE MY MIND?" MIKE SAYS QUIETLY.

The subway across to Roosevelt Island is temporarily closed, so we have chosen the fastest alternate route, a choice that Mike seems to be regretting already. When the cable car lurches out from its station into the air, Mike's grip on the silver railing tightens, his whole body goes stiff. He watches the two uniformed attendants over by the controls as if he expects them to hit a button at any moment and send us plunging earthward.

When I tell him to relax, his eyes skate past me out the window.

"This ain't my best thing, you know."

I guess I did know that in the abstract, but this is the first time I have actually seen Mike in thrall to his fear of heights. People are so strange. Mike Jardine would not think twice about taking a bullet for the Secretary-General, yet now, elevated just fifty feet off the ground, perspiration is suddenly beading across his brow. It seems like a valiant effort to distract himself when he picks up our conversation again, telling me about the call he made earlier to an acquaintance from his previous life at City Hall, a pathologist at one of the city morgues.

"I told him it was some old delegate who croaked. Terminal fossilization or something. I asked him how long we could keep the body in the coolroom, what we needed to do."

Mike braves another glance out the window, then turns straight back. It's not just his knuckles, his whole fist around the bar has gone deathly white. Down below, a surreal landscape of flat building tops doubling as parking lots reveals itself as we climb; the cars look like toys from up here.

"How long?" I ask.

"Ten days max, unless we can freeze him. After that we'll be needing gas masks. Just to get near the body, that's what he said."

The Roosevelt Island cable car shudders as we hit maximum altitude and plane out for the haul across the water. Mike moans and closes his eyes. Across the tram car a young woman, the sole passenger apart from us, rearranges the shopping bags at her feet and regards Mike curiously. When I advise Mike to look at the bridge, he does that for a while; it seems to help.

"I took a few samples," he says, glancing back to me. "For Forensics."

"Samples?"

His gaze drops. "Like from the syringe. Like that."

I regard him closely. "That's all?"

"I figure, how else we gonna know for sure if we don't get it tested?"

"Mike."

He looks up.

"Don't bullshit me," I say.

He swipes a finger across his perspiring brow.

"I took a couple of bloods too," he concedes. Blood samples, he means, from Toshio Hatanaka's body. "Who cares what's in the syringe if it wasn't injected?"

I let my look linger, he knows I'm not pleased. Not so much with what he's done but with his apparent intention to keep it to himself.

"They've gone for analysis?"

He nods.

"Patel?" I ask, knowing in my bones that this is not the correct answer.

"I got a guard on it," he admits. "He's taking the samples down to a pathologist on Second, some guy I know. Might even be there by now." He checks his watch, then notices the look I am giving him. "Listen. If I'd told you, you woulda had no choice, you woulda told Patrick. Once he knew, I'd spend a week filling out forms while he dreamed up a million reasons not to do it."

"So you did it anyway."

"Give me a break. It had to be done. I did it."

I ask Mike when he expects the results back. Tomorrow morning, he says, first thing.

I guess now that it's done there isn't much point in recrimination. And in truth, I am not totally displeased with Mike's unauthorized action; at least this way we get reliable results from the analysis, not something that could have been guaranteed from Patel's tiny and ill-equipped lab. Patrick, when I tell him, will be livid.

"Then I'd like to hear the results," I say, "first thing."

Mike gives a brittle smile. He has just caught a glimpse of a barge passing way, way below us on the gray East River, and for the rest of the journey he sits rigid, staring at his feet.

———

Roosevelt Island is a few acres of land located smack in the middle of the East River, its whole southern shore clearly visible from UNHQ over on Manhattan. Alighting from the cable car, Mike and I turn northward, walking up into what you might call Roosevelt Island downtown. There is a post office, a bank, a few restaurants, and even a wine bar, but weirdly, the exteriors all look the same: glass-fronted and signed with standardized lettering. The place is not even pretending to be an organic civic growth, the planner's fingerprints remain annealed to its entire structure. A toy town. Urban life as every city bureaucrat would like to see it lived. It occurs to me now what this place reminds me of, what I'd never quite pinned down on previous visits here. Toshio Hatanaka, international globetrotter and cosmopolitan twenty-first-century man, when he chose his apartment, instinctively reached for this place, a pale simulacrum of where he came from, the territory in which his roots were inescapably embedded. That's what this place reminds me of: urban Japan.

While Mike looks around the lobby of Toshio's apartment building for the manager or super's room number, I go on up. Toshio's door is the last in line down a long corridor on the sixth floor. I'm thinking the place has the feel of a midpriced hotel. Mike joins me with the keys a minute later. He cannot find anyone.

"Feels real homey, don't it?" he remarks, gesturing along the corridor.

I point to Toshio's door, 612. Mike tries a few keys.

"You been up here lately?" he asks.

"About three times this year."

"Social?"

"The last two."

"The first time?" he asks idly. When I don't reply, he glances up.

"About Sarah," I say simply. Sarah, my wife. Mike's face falls, his eyes flicker down, an expression of awkward embarrassment that I have seen on so many faces so many times these past three years. Finally Mike finds the correct key. He pushes the door open and waves me in.

A regular apartment, much what you would expect from the exterior. Furnished a little on the spartan side, and neat, nothing much in the way of personal touches. It is immediately recognizable as the place of a bachelor.

"You wanna try the study?" says Mike.

"Through here." If there is a suicide note, which I very much doubt, the study seems the likely place. And the pink file Mei Tan mentioned, the missing section of Toshio's report—the study seems the most likely repository for that stuff too. But instead of following me, Mike drops into an armchair. He pulls some mail from his jacket and starts tearing open the envelopes. Then he catches my look.

"Letters for Hatanaka." Mike runs his eyes over the first one and drops it on the floor. "I picked them up from his mailbox in the lobby. Might be something, who knows?"

"You opened his mailbox?"

"Smallest key in the bunch."

"Just force of habit?"

Regarding me from beneath his brow, he says levelly, "Sam, you're standing in a fucking dead guy's apartment. Unauthorized entry, for starters. You want I don't tear the envelopes?"

He tears another. I turn on my heel and make my way to the study.

In here there is something of a monastic feel. The walls are white and there's just the one picture, that iconic photograph of Nagasaki after the bomb, the skeletal frame of a church and its dome the only thing left standing. Positioned alone in the middle of the white wall, it seems almost religiously emblematic; and knowing what I do about Toshio's past, the sight of the picture so prominently displayed is somewhat disturbing. Both his parents were killed in that blast. Not radiation; their house simply disappeared, taking a generation of Hatanakas with it. I never asked Toshio the details, but the story seems to be that he and his sister Moriko were out of town with the grandparents, who ended up raising them. Toshio never blamed the U.S. The event undoubtedly turned him to pacifism as he grew older, but I had never thought that he blamed any side for the catastrophe. The last few months, however, have proved me wrong; I realize now that he blames the Japanese military. This is the emotional engine powering his opposition to a permanent Japanese seat on the Security Council: He still does not trust the Japanese authorities to act in the best interests of either the world or the people of Japan. And this picture in his study must have been a daily reminder of that. Glancing around, I see a cupboard, built-in, floor to ceiling, but the desk is bare apart from the blotter and a neat line of pens. On the side table, a phone and fax. No suicide note. Through the window behind the desk I can see some kids horsing around with a football on a stretch of municipal grass.

My search of the single desk drawer turns up nothing but stationery, so I wander over to the cupboard. Mainly books, though God knows why he keeps them behind sliding doors, some mania for order maybe. Behind the third door I find what appears to be the mother lode: three bundles of paperwork, a stack of files, and a laptop PC.

"Any luck?" Mike asks, putting his head in.

Hauling the bundles from the cupboard, I dump the lot on Toshio's desk.

"Guy was neat, I'll say that," says Mike, crossing to the window. He stops to watch the kids down below with the football. Unlike me, he seems completely relaxed, as if searching a dead man's apartment is just part of the daily routine; a dubious legacy, I guess, of his twenty years in the NYPD. He whistles some old Sinatra number and turns to search the cupboards while I flick through Toshio's papers. The missing report is not among them. No pink file. Just loads of personal accounts; in his methodical way, Toshio appears to have kept every bill and receipt for the past several years. But at the bottom of the bundle I turn up a piece of correspondence that gives me pause: the letter, the one that had Patrick bristling this morning. It is a turgid and uncompromising rebuttal of every argument currently being advanced in favor of a Japanese Security Council seat. And the next page is a surprisingly long list of names, mostly public figures from the U.S. and Japan, to whom Toshio has apparently sent this letter of dissent. The few replies attached are all anodyne one-liners acknowledging receipt.

Finishing his unsuccessful browse through the cupboard, Mike eases into the chair.

"One note, three bills." He produces the trove he has stolen from the lobby and places the three bills on the desk. "Gas, phone, and AmEx. The note was just slipped in the box, no envelope."

He turns the note through his fingers. Curiosity roused, I ask him who it's from.

"Stab in the dark?" He lays it faceup by the bills. "Someone Japanese."

The note is written in kanji, Japanese script, with purple ink.

"And if you're thinking suicide note, forget it. You don't slip a suicide note into your own mailbox."

"Female," I declare.

"How do you figure that?"

When I point to the pair of powder-blue butterflies at the top left-hand corner, Mike frowns. "You're reaching, Sam."

That I am. But having failed to find any suicide note, this whole expedition is now no better than an extremely hopeful cast of the net. I take a glance at my watch. Twelve-thirty. More than two hours since we found Toshio's body. The major opening day speeches will have finished by now, the rumor mill will be sliding into action like a well-oiled machine.

"Get the translators to take a look at it," Mike says, referring to the note. "Phone bill might give us something. I'll try in the morning. Should get an itemized listing for the last quarter anyway." He folds it into his pocket along with the note. I decide not to inquire as to how Mike intends to extract this information from the phone company. Picking up the gas bill, Mike makes some ghoulish crack about Toshio putting his head in the oven. Then he takes up the AmEx bill, another single page.

"The guy was no big spender, that's for sure. Two hundred fifty dollars the whole month. No carryover from the month before. What was he living on, air?"

"Maybe he used cash."

"Cash," Mike says as if he finds the notion simply incredible. He inspects the bill a moment more, then hands it to me.

There are only three items: a meal in a restaurant called the White Imperial, presumably Chinese; a thirty-dollar dry cleaner's bill; and a hundred and eighty bucks to a store called Barney and Hunt's. When I hand the bill back to Mike, he pockets it.

"What you got?" He indicates the bundles I have retrieved from the cupboard.

I show him Toshio's letter. When he's read it, I ask what he thinks.

"I think Hatanaka was playing politics, is what I think." Mike considers the letter. "I don't get this guy. Who was he trying to impress? So he fires his letter off to every big wheel he knows, so what? I mean, I'm no politician, but where's that get him? Twenty-one-gun salute?"

Maybe, I suggest, it was simply an act of conscience, a stand that Toshio believed he had to make.

Mike passes the letter back over the desk. "Guy was puffing himself up, way I see it. Something for his résumé, for when he throws his hat in the ring for the big UNHCR job."

Way too too cynical, I say. Toshio Hatanaka, I tell Mike, just wasn't that kind of guy.

"One thing I learned down at City Hall, Sam. When you're talking politics, ain't no such thing as too cynical. Hatanaka was up the greasy pole same as everyone else."

"Ever heard of public service, Mike? Altruism?"

"Ah-ha. Right up there alongside Santa Claus and the tooth fairy." He goes out, telling me he's going to take a proper look around.

Deflated somewhat by Mike's world-weary judgment, I reexamine Toshio's papers. But there is nothing more of interest, so I switch on his laptop and do a quick search of the files on the loaded disk. Again nothing stands out, so I pop the disk and pocket it, thinking I might have time to go through it more thoroughly later. But I'm not hopeful. Not hopeful at all.

On my way to the living room I pause by the dining table and touch its shiny waxed surface with my fingertips. Mike is wandering around the far end of the room. When I catch the faint smell of wax, the memories rise: memories of this place, where I have spent some of the worst moments of my life.

It was at this table that Rachel and I heard from Toshio the details of Sarah's capture. We sat side by side, sick with fear, and listened as he talked us through what had happened to my wife, Rachel's mother. The whole medical team at the camp in Abatan had been taken, Toshio told us, all six of the UN volunteers who had flown out there just a week before. He mentioned the names of several warring tribes in the area, assured us that he had dealt with the local warlords on other occasions, that he was hopeful of a speedy resolution. We asked him what the Afghan tribesmen wanted. He did not know. He told us that it might be days before any demand was made—probably money—but that he would call us from the Afghanistan-Pakistan border when he arrived there the following night. He promised us that the word he was getting from Kabul was that Sarah and the rest of the medical team had not been harmed. After an hour of this, we rose from the table, numbed; Rachel gripped my arm like a limpet as we walked down to the car.

Then we waited. Endured the silent torture of not knowing, two weeks of it, irrational soaring hopes plunging into moments of total despair, both of us hovering by the phone each evening, waiting for Toshio's regular nightly call. I wanted to fly out there. Toshio said that it would not help Sarah, that he was doing everything that could be done, that I should stay in New York and look after Rachel. I complied with some reluctance.

The end, when it came, came suddenly. And I knew it was the end, the very worst, the moment the Secretary-General himself appeared for the first time in my career at my office door. I remained in the chair. I have a hazy recollection of a hand on my shoulder, of totally inadequate but well-meaning words.

When Toshio returned to New York, he asked Rachel and me up to his apartment. He rested his elbows on this same waxed table, hung his grief-roughened face over his notes, and tried to explain to us the unexplainable. How the life of the woman we loved had been extinguished for no fathomable reason, how his every effort to save her had failed.

Three years ago. Swaying forward now, I press my fingertips hard against the shiny waxed surface. At this same damn table.

"Sam?"

Stepping back from the table and moving across the room, I find Mike with his finger poised over the answering machine. Two messages, he tells me, then he hits the play button.

"Toshio" is the first and only word we understand of message number one. It's in Japanese, a woman's voice, not young.

"The sister?" Mike asks.

I shrug. It could be Moriko, but who knows? There is a beep, then message two begins.

"*Hello? Mr. Hatanaka? Lucy Frayn jus' callin', let you all know I done that freezer, be right you usin' it now. But I be needin' that bucket like I tol' you.*" Mike grunts. Toshio's cleaning lady rambles on, outlining her requirements. When she's done, there's a double beep and the machine resets. On the display panel there is a number, presumably Lucy Frayn's.

I suggest that it might be worth our while calling her, but when I reach for the phone, Mike's hand suddenly shoots out to block me. He turns his head, studying the machine. Then he hits rewind, leans over, and waits for it to finish, then hits play. The message in Japanese begins again. He hits the stop button immediately. Then rewind again.

"What's up?"

"Shh," he says. Pressing an ear against the machine, he hits play.

And this time, just before the woman's voice begins, I hear it: a faint click. Lifting his head, Mike stabs the stop button. He stares at the phone.

"That noise?" I say.

Mike picks up the handpiece, deftly unscrews the mouthpiece cover, then places the handpiece on the bench and peers into the electronic innards. A second later his eyes close, he silently mouths the word *fuck*. Beneath my shirt collar the hair on my neck begins to prickle. Without a word Mike turns the exposed handpiece toward me. He picks up a pencil and points to a little gray silicone square inside.

We look at each other. He does not need to tell me what he has found.

I follow him into the study and he repeats the procedure with the phone in there. Another square of gray silicone identical to the first. Swallowing down the sickening tickle in my throat, I ask quietly, "What the hell's been going on here?"

Stepping past me, Mike whispers, "Other phones?"

We find a third bug in the kitchen phone. Eventually we end up in Toshio's bedroom. It's bare but not quite as bare as his study. Three brightly colored Kabuki prints are hung along one wall. On the bedside table there's a reading lamp and a book but no phone. While Mike takes a look in the bathroom, I pick up the single slim volume from the bedside table. Bashō. *The Narrow Road to the Deep North,* Japanese with the English translation on the facing pages. On the flyleaf there's an inscription in kanji. When Mike returns, he quietly asks me what I've found.

"Nothing, some poetry."

Mike raises a finger to his lips. Though we have instinctively been talking in whispers since Mike found the first bug, this is the first concrete indication he has given me that he believes our conversation might be flowing down some hidden wire. Now he sits on Toshio's bed and opens the nightstand drawer. Finding nothing, he reaches for the lower drawer while I flip through the Bashō. There is more kanji on another page of the book, the corner of which has been turned down. A marker. Possibly the last page Toshio was reading when he put the book aside. In the middle of the page, a short poem.

A clump of leaning grass in the summer wind
Is all that remains of the great schemes and bold strategies
Of departed generals and buried politicians.

"I thought Hatanaka was some kind of a pacifist," Mike whispers.

When I raise my eyes, Mike crooks a finger, beckoning me over. I move around the bed, then bend and peer into the drawer where Mike points. The thing is just lying there, uncovered. A pistol. I make a sound. Mike gently pulls out the drawer an inch more, and two rounds of ammo in brass casings roll, clinking against the barrel of the gun. We are silent a moment.

"Makes you wonder, don't it," Mike says thoughtfully, "what coulda made the man change his mind."

8

TURNING IN TO THE UNHQ BASEMENT CORRIDOR, WE SEE people, a small crowd, milling outside the room where Toshio's body was found. Word, quite obviously, is out.

"Oh, great," says Mike through clenched teeth.

A guard stands by the door. Weyland. An old black guy, one of the cops Mike brought with him when he moved from City Hall, someone Mike trusts. Weyland seems unperturbed by the moron in a suit who is jabbing a finger near his face and shouting. Mike breaks into a jog, calling Weyland's name, and a dozen faces turn in our direction.

"What do these people want?" Mike asks.

From farther back along the corridor I begin to recognize the faces: senior delegates from the Organization for African Unity, the Arab League, ASEAN, people like that, but it's too late to warn Mike that he is facing what appears to be a handpicked gang from the General Assembly. He goes on pushing his way right through them. Then he addresses Weyland again, asking what this is all about.

"Seem like these people are expecting to get in here," Weyland replies. "Seem like they think they got a right."

Mike turns and points to the ringleader. "Okay, let's hear it, what's your problem, pal?"

Instantly, silence falls. Nobody can quite believe it. The guy Mike has addressed so curtly is Tunku Rahman Kabir, the Malaysian ambassador. Renowned for his interminable speeches, his ability to get himself onto any committee, and an unbroken twenty-year career of troublemaking at Turtle Bay, the Tunku, as he's universally known, is a UN institution. A minor member of one of the Malaysian royal families, he has a job here for life. Nearing seventy, about five feet four inches tall, he has an inflated sense of self-importance that is legendary, and the look he gives Mike now is pure acid. When Mike does not flinch, the Tunku finally condescends to explain the situation.

Toshio's death, it seems, has become public knowledge. The president of the General Assembly session, inspired by the Tunku, has appointed an ad hoc committee to investigate and report the facts of the case to him tomorrow morning. So here they all are, the committee members—some of them from countries where open and impartial justice occurs about as frequently as a four-leaf clover—and they are outraged, positively outraged, the Tunku tells Mike now, at this denial of access to the scene of Toshio's death.

The Tunku is still talking when Mike casts a despairing glance in my direction. I signal him over; he comes across and we turn our backs to confer.

"Suggestions?" he says.

"Let them in."

He squints, incredulous.

"Mike, you can't stop these guys. They can go over your head all the way up to the thirty-eighth floor."

"I'll call Eckhardt." Eckhardt, Mike's boss, the head of Security.

"Eckhardt can't help."

"O'Conner?" Mike wonders aloud.

"When Patrick sees the political firepower lined up here"—I toss my head back behind us—"there's no way he'll get himself involved."

"Backing us right down the line, huh?" Shaking his head, he calls Patrick a name. Then he lifts his eyes. "Way you see it, we got no choice?"

I tell him it hardly matters anyway; if we've got no forensics team, there's not much point keeping these guys out of the room. Mike takes a moment with that, trying to get used to the idea that the Tunku and his ragtag posse will be given the access they demand. He does not like it.

"Shit," he says finally, and goes back to push a path through the mob.

I drop into a corridor chair, my legs sprawled in front of me, my head resting against the wall. I am drained, the emotional strain of the morning finally catching up with me. I feel heavy and tired, as though I have been battling the consequences of Toshio's death for weeks instead of hours. Then, from the corner of my eye, I register the familiar purposeful gait of Jennifer Dale; she is heading in my direction. At this moment, the last thing I need.

She takes the chair next to mine. "Quite a surprise," she remarks at last, an opener to which I can only nod my head in weary acquiescence. "And I presume that when you reported Hatanaka's death to the U.S. legal counsel, she was quite surprised too?" The U.S. legal counsel, of course, is Jennifer.

"I'll write you a memo."

The crack is misjudged; she rounds on me. "You knew about it this morning, for Pete's sake. Why didn't you tell me?"

"When we spoke this morning, I didn't have a clue."

"You've known for hours. And I had to find out about it from a junior member of the Fijian delegation. How do you think that felt?"

I assure her that every perm five ambassador was informed by Patrick. Including the U.S. ambassador, James Bruckner. "If Bruckner didn't pass it on to you, I'm sorry, Jennifer, but you'll have to take it up with him."

"You're passing the buck."

"I'm giving you the facts."

"Finally." Her fingers work the small pearls of her necklace as if they're worry beads. Her expression borders on the severe, a look she'd already perfected in those far-off days at Columbia. Even then she seemed to have a direction that so many of us lacked, some sense of purpose about what she was doing at law school beyond the mere acquisition of a degree. Her father was a judge, I guess that was part of it, but there were plenty of others from the same high WASP background who were happy to coast along, collect their pieces of paper, and move straight into lucrative careers as if by right of birth. But Jennifer, somewhat aloof and high-minded, seemed to have her gaze fixed on a more distant prospect, a lone eagle soaring over the valleys of worldly ambition down which the rest of us were inexorably sliding. But now, here we are, twenty years later, sitting in the same corridor, contemplating the same death.

"Where's the body?" she asks me.

Gesturing toward the room into which Mike and the others have disappeared, I remark that she seems to be missing the show.

"That wasn't the question, Sam."

"He died on UN territory. And he wasn't a U.S. citizen. This whole thing's an internal affair."

"Secretariat eyes only?"

"It doesn't impact on the Host Country Agreement." The agreement that regulates UN headquarters business with our geographic host, the U.S.

"And you're sure he died on UN territory?"

Surprised by the question, I hesitate before nodding. It doesn't get past her.

"Christ." She rises to her feet. "I want to see the body, Sam. Right now."

There are, of course, a hundred legal quibbles I could raise to obstruct her, and she knows that. But she also knows that being the host country to UN headquarters and by far the biggest contributor to the UN's stretched budget, the U.S. has sufficient clout to brush these quibbles aside. And for my part, I am aware that if I make things difficult for her, she will respond in kind, refusing any request I make to carry the investigation of Toshio's death onto U.S. territory. So we stand here, eyeing each other and doing the calculations, then at last I lead her to the cafeteria.

The guard stationed outside the coolroom is the same kid who found Toshio's body; when I give him the okay, he tells Jennifer his story while I unpadlock the coolroom door. She doesn't just listen to him, she grills the kid. Times. Keys. How many doors did he try? It is like a lesson in cross-examination. The kid gets confused, but Jennifer keeps pushing. Who did he call first? Why?

This is just like her law school persona, a facet of her character I haven't seen much these past six months. Brilliant, certainly, but there can be a harsh lack of proportion to Jennifer's legal jousting, though it has been, needless to say, no impediment to her career. She made the Law Review and went on from there to clerk for Donald Winslow on the Supreme Court, the kind of high-octane start to a career that every law student dreams of. From there she could have moved on to the fast track to a partnership in any law firm in the country, but what Jennifer did instead was join the Department of State as a junior legal officer for twenty-five thousand bucks a year. A sense of civic duty, I think that was the phrase used by the Columbia alumni magazine. Karl Kampinski, one of the few guys I still stay in touch with from those days, shook his head in disbelief as he showed me the announcement.

Can you believe the waste? he said, stunned that anyone could have passed up the glittering spoils of corporate law because of something so intangible as duty. Do you suppose, he said, she might be nuts?

But now here she is, three-quarters of the way through the career plan she tells me she had mapped out before she was twenty. Jennifer, whatever else she is, is not nuts.

Yanking up the metal bar, I pull. The coolroom door swings open stiffly and the kid, the guard, reaches in past me and flicks on the light. Jennifer steps up by me, we peer in a moment, our breath steaming silver in the refrigerated air. A single bare bulb throws a dim yellow light. Then slowly, gingerly, we step inside to view Toshio's chilled body.

————

"Basement, my ass," says Patrick when I suggest that he make a trip downstairs to speak with Jennifer Dale, the Tunku, and the sundry host of rubberneckers I have left wandering the basement. Tugging at his collar, he barrels past me out of his office, explaining that he has an appointment with the Secretary-General and the Japanese ambassador, Asahaki. "Upstairs," he adds, pointing to the ceiling. As we walk to the elevators, he asks me again if I'm sure that Toshio left no suicide note.

"I went through his office and his apartment. No note."

This would be the appropriate moment, of course, to inform him that we have discovered three listening devices in Toshio's apartment. But I hold off. Because Mike, for some reason, asked me to. He would not tell me why, but Mike is not a guy for unnecessary mystery; if he wants it this way, he has his reasons.

"Mike's interviewing the maintenance crew," I tell Patrick. "He's getting his surveillance people to run through the other tapes from the NGO reception."

"Anything?"

I explain that Mike has only just started. Then I ask about Asahaki. "If he's upstairs now, he might be able to help us."

Patrick looks at me.

"Maybe he can give us some idea what was going on with that private campaign Toshio was running against the Japanese seat," I say. "Asahaki must have been monitoring it. He'd likely know whose toes Toshio was stepping on."

"Asahaki's, for one. You leave Asahaki to me."

"Mike wants to ask him some questions too."

"I said, leave Asahaki to me."

From which I infer that Patrick wants to retain personal control over any part of the investigation that intrudes into the big league, the upper reaches of the UN family. Now I mention Toshio's missing file; Mike has rechecked Toshio's briefcase, the basement rooms nearby—the file is definitely not there. The file, I tell Patrick, contains some private report that Toshio was doing, something for the Fifth Committee, Budgetary Affairs, we believe.

"You checked with the committee?" Patrick asks me.

I am seeing the committee chairman in half an hour. Patrick makes a face. He does not hold out much hope of a lead in that direction.

In the elevator I elaborate on my encounter with Jennifer. "Under the Headquarters Agreement she thinks USUN has a right to be kept informed." USUN, the mission of the U.S. to the United Nations.

"Bullshit," says Patrick.

"If we don't meet her halfway, she won't play ball. If this spills onto U.S. territory, she won't help. They might even obstruct us."

"She said that?"

"Implied."

Patrick considers a moment. "Clear it with me first, anything you tell her. And make sure she understands she doesn't go poking her nose into this. She's got the same rights here as any other delegate. Fuck all."

Once we've made our way past the aides and security guards on thirty-eight, it becomes apparent that Patrick has no intention of inviting me into his meeting with the Secretary-General. Secretariat politics is essentially feudal, only one step removed from a medieval baron's court: Access to the SG is power. Which is why Patrick leaves me in an outer waiting room, cooling my heels, while he disappears into the inner sanctum, the SG's dining room, for a private conference with the boss. The Japanese, evidently, have yet to arrive, so I sit myself down and while away a few minutes, distractedly turning pages in one of the UNESCO brochures that lie fanned across the table. By the third brochure Patrick has still not reappeared; I get up impatiently and cross to the window.

From here, the view on a good day is grand. But today there is smog; the East River looks gray and sluggish as it ribbons past below. On the far shore you can see the thin line of dead and dying industry near the water, the neighborhoods of Queens up beyond. The southern tip of Roosevelt Island is visible too, its most prominent feature a derelict mental asylum—the uninhabited twin, so the jokers will tell you, of its sister building over here. Leaning forward, I crane my neck a little, but the view up toward Toshio's apartment is obscured by the Queensboro Bridge. Then a sudden swell of voices rises behind me. I turn to see the Japanese arriving, Ambassador Asahaki himself and three of his minions.

While one of them goes on ahead to announce the ambassador's arrival, Asahaki and the other two wait. They talk together in Japanese, their tone somber, the name Hatanaka surfacing a few times from the babel. I look over to the SG's door. No sign of

Patrick. I ponder a moment. Nothing to lose. Then I go over to the Japanese and introduce myself as Patrick O'Conner's deputy.

"We're doing everything we can," I answer blandly when one of the minions asks me what's happening.

They pump me for more details, but I politely turn each question aside. One of them mentions suicide.

"Our security people are treating it as a homicide."

Blank looks all around.

"Murder," I say.

Ambassador Asahaki's head goes back.

"Mr. Ambassador, if you can spare me a few minutes—"

He turns his back on me. Ignoring my presence now, the three of them confer in Japanese. Crass behavior, but then, Bunzo Asahaki has never been on anyone's list of favorite ambassadors. He isn't the type to be much concerned with any bruises he raises, and over the past few years he has raised plenty. When the push for a vote on a permanent Japanese presence on the Council was first gaining momentum, Patrick tells me that the SG actually considered asking Asahaki to stand aside temporarily in order to help smooth the way. Nothing came of the idea. And in any event, Bunzo Asahaki has proved to be the major asset of the Yes campaign, a real success, an unstoppable force whose vigor and persistence have easily outweighed his evident lack of subtlety. Too successful for some. Toshio, for one, had a real thing about the man, frequently referring to him as Banzai, the tag first conferred by the peaceniks back home in Japan. Banzai Asahaki. Unfair maybe, but with his silver hair, his haughty manner, and ramrod stance, the Japanese ambassador would not look out of place in a sharply pressed military uniform, definitely something with epaulets.

Fearing Patrick's imminent return, I finally butt in on the conversation.

"Mr. Ambassador, would it be possible to arrange a time for me and maybe one of our security people to come and speak with you?"

He grunts.

"This afternoon?" I suggest.

He shakes his head emphatically. Patrick, I would have to concede now, had a point. I just don't carry sufficient weight to warrant a guy like Asahaki putting himself out for me. But still hoping for something useful from this encounter, I bring out the note Mike found in Toshio's mailbox. Asahaki has already turned aside, talking with one of his minions. I show the note to the other and ask him for a translation. He frowns. He is not sure if he should help me. Then he looks over my shoulder and I turn to find Patrick bearing down on me. He does not look pleased. He jerks his head toward the door, indicating that it is time for me to leave.

As I repocket the note, the Japanese confer intently. Patrick arrives at my side and gives me a long, hard look from the corner of his eye. Then, before I can make my exit, the youngest of Asahaki's colleagues steps up to Patrick and bows. A deep bow. Patrick, unlike me, is Secretariat top-drawer.

"Ambassador Asahaki," says the young man, rising, "respectfully request the body of Toshio Hatanaka."

Patrick cannot hide his surprise. "The body?"

"Yes. Ambassador Asahaki respectfully request the body."

"That might be difficult."

"Impossible." I correct Patrick beneath my breath.

But to my amazement, Patrick appears to actually give the idea some thought. "Where would the body go?"

"It must be returned to Japan."

"Mike won't buy that," I blurt out.

"Excuse us," says Patrick, then, taking me by the elbow, he walks me over to the wall. We stand beneath the latest statesmanlike portrait of the SG. "What is this?" Patrick hisses. "You want to give me a few pointers, tell me how to do my job?"

"This is way out of whack, Patrick. You know it is. They want the body back in Japan? Just like that? Come on. They just want this whole problem out of the way during the buildup to the vote."

"Of course they want it out of the way. Where do you think we are here, grade school?"

"Toshio was murdered."

Patrick touches his forehead. For chrissake, he mutters.

"Patrick, you can't seriously think it's all right for them to take the body. What happens if we give it to them? Say they take it back to Japan, say the vote goes fine, they win their seat on the Council. You don't think some pretty uncomfortable questions are going to be asked when it gets out what we did? That we just played along with the Japanese because they asked us to? We'll be crucified."

Now Patrick glances over to Asahaki. "What the fuck did you say to them?"

"Nothing. I asked Asahaki if Mike and I could speak with him later. Ask him some questions."

Patrick faces me. "You dopey shit."

Directing my gaze to the SG's portrait over Patrick's shoulder, I count my way slowly toward ten. At five, Patrick leans close.

"So they don't get the body. But when we get back over there"— he tosses his head—"I need you to do something for me." He taps a finger lightly on my lapel. "Keep your fucking mouth shut. Not one more word."

We rejoin the Japanese. Patrick tells Asahaki as diplomatically as he can that it is not legally possible for us to hand over Toshio Hatanaka's body. Not yet. But Patrick assures them that we will hand it over as soon as we can. Asahaki speaks with one of his minions.

Patrick gestures toward the SG's dining room. "He's waiting for us," he says, referring to the SG, trying to move on. But when Patrick takes a step in the direction of the dining room, the Japanese stand firm.

That same young guy who spoke earlier speaks again. "Ambassador Asahaki regrets he is unable to attend the meeting with the Secretary-General."

Patrick faces Asahaki. "Unable?"

Asahaki remains silent, aloof. Unable, the young man repeats.

Then, without the courtesy of a parting nod, Asahaki turns his back on Patrick; he retreats with his colleagues down the corridor. A deliberate and very pointed snub. When they disappear from sight, Patrick turns on me.

"You." He holds up a hand, cutting off my protest. "I don't want to hear it. You've got the body. You've got the investigation you wanted. But if you speak to another ambassador about this without clearing it with me first, in fact, if you do anything on this without clearing it with me first—"

"I've got the picture."

"You'd better have."

We look at each other.

"I want to speak to Moriko Hatanaka, Toshio's sister."

"She an ambassador?" Patrick shoots back.

It is going to be quite a while, I see, before I am forgiven for screwing things up with Asahaki.

"Oh, go on." Patrick waves a hand, banishing me from the thirty-eighth floor, dismissing me from his sight.

But I have a question. "What did you think I said to Asahaki?"

Patrick waves that dismissive wave again, then turns sharply and retreats to the safety of the SG's dining room. I study the door behind which Patrick has just disappeared. Something is not right. If I had not been present when Asahaki made that request for the return of Toshio's body to Japan, Patrick, I am certain, would have given it very serious consideration. Possibly even complied. And the same question comes to me now as came to me earlier this morning when Patrick gave his wildly premature verdict of suicide. The question that comes to me is why.

9

"S HE HASN'T BEEN TOLD YET?" MIKE ASKS, GLANCING across the passenger seat at me. "Those assholes, the Tunku and his buddies, they all know, but no one's told the sister?" When I redirect his attention to the street up ahead, he swerves around some maintenance workers, then turns to me again.

So I give him a two-minute rundown on the state of play. Mei Tan, Toshio's secretary, contacted the Japan Society, where Toshio's sister, Moriko, works. Moriko was not there. Her colleagues informed us that she was over at the Isamu Noguchi Garden Museum, arranging to borrow pieces for a forthcoming Japan Society exhibition. They gave Mei Tan the number of Moriko's cell phone, but the phone seemed to be temporarily disconnected. I instructed Mei Tan to keep trying.

"And then I came to get you."

"So maybe this Moriko knows, maybe she doesn't?"

I nod. Mike breathes out a long breath.

"When we get to this gallery," he tells me, "there's no way I'm going in first."

We swing left, cruising past a banged-up Pontiac; loose newspaper sheets go scudding up from the gutter. We have had the note we found in Toshio's mailbox translated; it says, *I will see you tonight.* Nothing else. No date and no name. The translator told us it looked like something someone had just scribbled quickly, which leaves us with some obvious questions like who and why. Given the entry in Toshio's calendar, Moriko seems the most likely candidate. Something we'll be able to clear up with her, provided, of course, she's in any state to talk once we've broken the news.

"Oh, yeah," says Mike. "Did I say about those bugs from his apartment?"

I look at him. He knows that he hasn't.

"Funny thing," he says. "They're the same make as ours."

Ours? I ask.

"UNHQ Extra Security."

I have, naturally, heard of this secret cabal, but from Patrick, not Mike. And from Patrick only infrequently, oblique references from which I was meant to infer my peripheral position in the organizational power scheme. UNHQ Extra Security, from what I understand, is a tripartite body involving only Patrick O'Conner, UN Security, and the SG. It keeps tabs on a very small number of delegations and delegates perceived to be a security threat to UNHQ. Just the crazies. People who in a sane world would be committed to an asylum or a jail instead of representing their countries at the parliament of man.

Mike's gaze remains fixed on the road, but he looks uncomfortable. My guess is that he has turned over the information for quite some while before telling me.

"The same make?"

"Right."

"Rare?"

He screws up his face. "Standard issue for every law enforcement agency in the U.S. From the Bureau on down."

Then why, I ask him, has he stuck his neck out to tell me?

"I checked our inventory. Then I checked Security's requisitions book. See if any of our guys had something on."

"Any luck?"

"Now, there's a question." He glances at me. "Remember how many bugs we found at Hatanaka's place?"

"Three."

"Three." He holds up three fingers from the steering wheel. "And how many bugs at Extra Security do you guess I found missing? Missing, unaccounted for, not signed through the book."

"Three?" I venture.

"No," he says, lowering one finger. "Two. Two missing."

We sweep left past the local cash-and-carry. Two bugs missing, three bugs found. I state the obvious. Those numbers don't add up.

"No, sir."

"Someone stole two and supplemented them with one of their own?"

A screwup in the records, Mike suggests, is the most likely answer. The Extra Security team apparently has a deliberately distant acquaintanceship with the regular procedures. He is not saying the bugs came from UN Security, and he is not saying they did not. Something to chew on, Mike adds.

"Greek area," he remarks then, circling a finger above the steering wheel, and like a guide on some strange urban safari, he singles out the finer points of decay. This is one aspect of the city, I confess, that I have never gotten used to even after living in the place for more than twenty years. Among the Turtle Bay cynics there is a constant stream of jokes about it, the divisions of New York City as a microcosm for the divisions of the world. Question: How do we solve the Chinese problem? Answer: Bomb Mott Street. Question: How do we put a stop to economic migration? Answer: Close the Brooklyn Bridge.

Mike's mental map of the city seems to be drawn on these ethnic divisions. He is the perfect guide to such urban mysteries as where a Korean shopkeeper will do a thriving business in this great city and where he is very likely to have his life's work and savings burned to the ground. He talks of these things so casually that I'm sure they must appear to him as facts on a level with the borders between nations. But for a son of Cyrus, Kansas, the splintering of the American people, the sectioning off of quasi-independent urban territories filled with mutual loathing, cannot help but feel a little strange. And it is not lost on me that Mike's patter, as he drives, has cut off any further questioning from me on the subject of the bugs.

The museum is some kind of converted industrial building: cinder block painted dark chocolate, the name Isamu Noguchi an artful scrawl across the banners flapping loosely from poles high up the wall. We park by the entrance, and Mike points me in ahead of him. While he pretends to check out the postcards and leaflets, I ask at the front desk for Moriko. They direct me to another part of the museum. I look back to Mike; he folds his arms and turns his head. I am on my own.

The area where I eventually find Moriko is more like a garden than a room; the place is walled but open to the sky. A few sculptured stone pieces, Oriental abstract, are visible beneath long, waving palm fronds. Moriko is there by herself. A clipboard propped on one knee, she is crouching to examine a polished sphere of granite by the wall. Touching the stone, she makes a note. And I know at once that Mei Tan has not yet reached her. Her brother is dead and Moriko has not heard.

I take a moment with myself. Then I speak.

"Moriko?"

She looks up and takes a moment to recognize me in these unfamiliar surroundings.

"Sam?" she says, rising.

As I move toward her, she faces me squarely, and curious now, with friendly surprise, she offers me her hand. "Sam," she says again, and she smiles.

———

"You wait much longer," says Mike, taking in the situation at a glance when he comes up from the basement, "they'll be closing the gates."

He has joined me outside on the terrace, where I have been lingering for the past quarter hour. At the far end of the North Lawn, settled in the relative privacy and seclusion of the Eleanor Roosevelt memorial bench, Moriko Hatanaka sits alone. Since coming out from seeing her brother's body, she has not moved from that place, and though I told Mike I was going to ask her our questions, I haven't yet had the heart to intrude on Moriko's grief. She sits absolutely still there, weeping.

"You want me to do it?" Mike asks me.

I tell him that I've just been giving her some time, that I'll go down and speak with her now, but I make no immediate move to do that. We watch her a while longer, a lonely figure partially obscured by the trees.

"Seems like they were close. She could have something. You sure you don't want me?" Mike gestures toward her.

No, I tell him again. Waving a hand back to the building, I suggest that Dr. Patel might have his report ready by now, then I descend the steps to the lawn.

Moriko doesn't even glance at me when I join her, and after a moment she raises her handkerchief to her eyes. Barely an hour since we found her at the museum, and she seems to have aged years. Her shoulders are hunched, her head bowed. Most of her makeup is now on her handkerchief, and her cheeks glow moist and red. There are lines around her mouth; her eyes seem swollen.

Words, I think. What can anyone possibly say?

"Moriko. I am so sorry."

She wipes her eyes and nods with an incongruous formality.

"You don't have to stay here."

"Your friend," she tells me haltingly, "he said that I could help."

Mike. Before I intervened, he had actually started quizzing her in the car on our way here from the museum.

"It's possible. You might be able to pin down a few things."

She makes a fist around her handkerchief. "I want to help."

"Are you sure you're up to it just now?"

She nods firmly, but I am not convinced. She looks dreadful.

"Okay, Moriko. But if you want to cut it short, go home, just say the word." Leaning forward, I rest my elbows on my knees and clasp my hands. God, this really is so damn hard. I collect my thoughts a moment.

"There was an entry in Toshio's calendar for last night. The Japan Society, seven-thirty. We don't know if he got there."

"He was there."

"You wouldn't know when he arrived or when he left?"

"Seven-thirty he came."

"You're certain?"

Moriko nods without hesitation. She explains that an exhibition was being opened, she was taking tickets at the door. Toshio was the first guest to arrive.

"Did he stay long?"

"Before nine, he left."

"How long before?"

Moriko stares at the ivy that has begun a slow encroachment up the base of the carved slab in front of us. Eleanor Roosevelt's memorial. She trawls her memories of last night.

"We were screening a movie," she says finally. "Kurosawa. It started at nine. Toshio had left his briefcase in my office. He came and picked it up while the others were going in to the screening."

"So just a few minutes before nine. That's when he left."

Moriko nods. She asks me if that helps us.

"Right now anything helps. Did Toshio say where he was going?"

"There was a function. The NGOs?" She casts a hand toward the UN buildings. "He said he was coming here."

"Not home first?"

She shakes her head.

"Were you around his place at all yesterday?"

"No."

I take out the note we found in Toshio's mailbox. I ask if it means anything to her.

" 'I will see you tonight,' " she translates.

"Not your note?"

She shakes her head, she is obviously lost.

"Did he have a particular reason to go to the NGO function?" I ask, repocketing the note. "Anyone he mentioned he wanted to see?"

"He didn't want to go. He was very tired. Always this last year, so tired." She lowers her eyes; tears well again, and she raises her handkerchief. She really is not up to this. "What your friend thinks. Drugs. That is not Toshio."

"That isn't what Mike thinks. It's not what any of us thinks, but we had to ask. How we found Toshio, the way it was laid out down there, Mike just had to ask you."

"Toshio did not kill himself. He did not."

An emphatic protest. So emphatic that for a second my lawyer's reflex takes over. I find myself considering the possibility that Patrick's initial theory—suicide—might be correct after all. But then, where is the missing pink file?

"Did Toshio give you anything for safekeeping recently, Moriko? Some papers or maybe a file?"

She shakes her head again.

Too much to hope for. But at least now we have a decent fix on one part of Toshio's movements last night. Once Mike's surveillance guys have finished running through the security tapes, we should have some idea of when Toshio arrived at the NGO function. The walk from the Japan Society premises on East Forty-seventh across to UNHQ takes less than five minutes. So if Toshio arrived much later than nine, it will mean he went somewhere else first. Around nine and he probably made his trip direct. A picture is at last taking shape.

"This might seem a little strange, but did Toshio ever give you any indication that he thought he was being watched?"

Moriko squints. "Here?"

"Anywhere. I mean, he never mentioned anything about surveillance, did he? Or any fears he had about anything he was doing?"

Moriko is silent.

"Had anyone threatened him?" I ask straight out.

"About his work, what he did, what he saw, those things—he never talked to me. You know, he was my big brother. He always thought he must look after me. Even now." Her face tightens. A professional woman in her early sixties, married with grown children, grandchildren even, she remained a kid in the eyes of her brother. The strange and lifelong currents of a family. "I told him my problems. Always. He never wanted to bother me with his. To make me worry."

"Outside of his work." I gesture vaguely. "Was there anything—"

"All Toshio's life was his work. You know how he was. Once a month he would come to dinner with my family. Sometimes to the Society. The rest, every day, it was his work. His whole life." Her head drops, she covers her face. An unexpected chord. Regret. For Toshio's all-absorbing commitment to his work, for the thousand daily sacrifices he made, and the lack, in the end, of any real private life of his own.

"Was he lonely?" I ask, a question that never crossed my mind when Toshio was alive.

"Sometimes, I think." Moriko presses her handkerchief to her cheek. "I think he would have liked a family. A family of his own. With my sons he was always so good when they were boys." She puts out her hand, indicating the height of her sons as children. And then memory takes hold. She tells me about Toshio and her sons; it seems she needs to do that, so I don't interrupt her. Toshio, she says, was a favorite uncle. In the years when Moriko's husband, a Texan, was frequently away on business, working his way up the ladder in the accounting firm he now runs, Toshio filled in, taking the boys to ball games, supervising excursions into the city. Happy times. Fond memories that quickly become too much for Moriko. She drops her head and presses her hands to her face again. "Oh, Toshio. Toshio," she says, and when I lay an arm across her shoulders, she leans in to me, a gray-haired woman weeping as inconsolably as a child.

Sarah, I think. It comes on me that suddenly, some deep and painful echo tolling like a bell. Three years a widower and yet now my eyes moisten. I blink back tears. Sarah, I think, my wife.

For a minute, maybe longer, I hold Moriko tight.

At last she lifts her head, tries for no understandable reason to apologize for her tears, and I squeeze her shoulder, I speak soft words. When she has finally regained some measure of self-control, I help her up from the bench and guide her over to the guardhouse by the gates, where I slip one of the guards forty bucks. I instruct him to radio Mike for authority, then to hail a taxi and go with Moriko. The only thing I can think of. To get Moriko back to her family. To see Toshio's grief-stricken sister home safely.

10

"IS JUAN AROUND?" I ASK RACHEL, LIFTING OPEN the trunk of my car.
"I didn't tell him," she replies, instantly defensive. "I didn't tell
anyone. He just seemed to find out. It's like everyone knows already,
not just Juan."

One hand on the bulging suitcase, I tell my daughter that it's okay,
that I'm not blaming her. Word of Toshio's death was probably
spreading through Turtle Bay even as I was issuing my stern warning
to her up in my office this morning. Grunting, I heave the suitcase
out onto the sidewalk.

"So he's here?"

"Practicing," she says, taking a hand from her parka, waving
across the street to the No Name bar from which she emerged to
greet me. The exterior of the No Name is lit by a single strip of scar-
let neon. The security grille is up but the doors, covered in graffiti,
are closed. "So what all's the story with Hatanaka?" she asks. "Has
anyone figured out what happened?"

In response, I transfer a pile of folded dresses from the trunk into
Rachel's arms. Then I close the trunk, pick up the suitcase, and stagger toward the No Name bar as Rachel shoots more questions at me
that I continue to ignore.

Juan Martinez, Rachel's new landlord, has been identified from
last night's security tapes as one of the people Toshio Hatanaka
spent time conversing with at the NGO reception. A few others have
been identified, but not many; without laboratory enhancement, the
definition on the film isn't clear enough to recognize most of the
faces. But when Mike showed me the tape, the figure of Juan

Martinez was unmistakable. A tall, rangy type. Lots of hand-waving when he speaks. And the clincher: a white linen suit, a sartorial affectation Juan adopted a year ago to get himself noticed. After viewing the tape, I volunteered to come down here to Alphabet City to deliver Rachel's stuff and to pick Juan's brain and find out what I can about the last hours of Toshio's life.

Besides, I needed to get away from the office. All through the afternoon, people have been stopping me in the corridors, phoning me, asking me if it really is true. Between turning aside the intently curious and the genuinely shocked, Mike and I have somehow managed to interview nearly all the UN guards who were around last night or early this morning, and most of the Secretariat staffers who attended the NGO reception. We have come up dry. A big zero. When I glanced out my window half an hour ago and saw the evening drawing in, I had an overwhelming desire to get away. I told Mike I'd be back within the hour.

"Just leave it here," Rachel tells me now, shouldering open the door into a poorly lit passage. She continues on to the stairs at the rear, and when I suggest that it might be easier if I take the suitcase straight up, she tells me not to. So I deposit my burden in the passage and watch as she climbs the stairs with an armful of clothes, up to her new home, a sanctuary into which I have not yet been invited. "Juan's in the bar," she calls back over her shoulder. "Go on in."

The bar is even darker than the passage, the brightest light coming from an overhead spot that illuminates the tiny stage in the far corner. At the edge of the stage, an acoustic guitar propped on one thigh in the classical manner, sits Juan. He is wearing his white linen suit. He has his head down, concentrating hard as his fingers flicker across the strings. He hasn't seen me come in, so I cross quietly to the bar and sit down. Music fills the place, something restrained but filled with yearning. I feel the tension in my shoulders slowly ease as I lean back against the bar.

Juan Martinez has a gift. The first time I heard him play was at the memorial concert, the fund-raiser Juan arranged as a tribute to his father. Juan's father, José, was the senior doctor in the medical team of UN volunteers who were abducted from the refugee camp on the Pakistan-Afghanistan border, then slain. José's body was found next to Sarah's. At the time, Juan was just twenty-one years old, a recent graduate of Juilliard. You couldn't help but be impressed by the kid. He put together that concert from scratch, raised about twenty thousand dollars, and used the money to found

Lighthouse, the anti-drug-trade NGO he still runs. And all that while dealing with the loss of his father. In those days it was all I could do to get Rachel off to school each morning, myself in to work. Juan played the final piece at the concert alone onstage, head down, just as he is now. Like so many others there, I had to bow my head to hide the tears.

But now the music stops abruptly.

"Hi," says Juan, peering at me through the gloom, one hand resting on the strings. "I think Rachel's upstairs."

"I've seen her."

He nods, then cocks his head, so I explain that I have just dropped off the last suitcase from home. "Not letting yourself get rusty," I remark, indicating the guitar.

He shrugs. He knows my opinion: A guy with his musical gift should not be wasting his time on NGO campaigns, however laudable the cause. He rests the guitar on its stand and comes down from the stage.

"What's the latest on Mr. Hatanaka?" he asks me. "Unbelievable, isn't it?"

Unbelievable, I agree.

"I mean, they're saying it happened like right there in the UN basement."

"We don't know that yet."

"Jesus." He goes behind the bar and reaches into the display refrigerator. I refuse his offer of a drink, and he takes out a Perrier, rings it up on the cash register, and drops some coins into the drawer. "I keep waiting for it to hit me," he says. "You know. Like it's not quite real? Like someone's gonna come along, say how it was all some big mistake or something?"

"I wish I could."

He takes a swig, then replaces the bottle on the bar and stares at it, his glance finally cheating up to me. "There's a lot of rumors."

"I can imagine."

"Some people are saying it was suicide."

"That's possible."

"Some others saying maybe not suicide. And maybe not natural causes either. Wild stuff."

"You want to just ask me, Juan?"

The corners of his mouth turn down, he lifts his goateed chin. And he asks me, "Was he murdered?"

Looking him straight in the eye, I tell him the truth. That we don't know. That we're still trying to figure the whole thing out. "And right now that means pinning down what Toshio was doing last night. Last night after nine."

Juan's brow creases. "He was at the reception. The big NGO thing. You didn't know that?"

"You saw him?"

"Sure. Even talked with him for a while. I guess that's why it seems so crazy, him being dead. I mean, we were talking about the session, what was on the Assembly agenda. Resolutions that seemed like they might be important, stuff for like in the future?" He shakes his head. "Jesus, the future."

"How did he seem?"

"You mean like his state of mind?"

When I nod, Juan recaps the bottle of Perrier and returns it to the refrigerator.

"Okay." He shoots a glance at the crates stacked on the floor, then asks if I mind if he does a few things while we speak. "Some of the senior NGO reps are coming over shortly. For a kind of strategy meeting about the UN Assembly session. Put our heads together, figure out where we might be able to push things along some. Now"—he lifts a hand—"now, you know, I guess it'll be more like a wake."

Juan lifts a crate of beer and proceeds to restock the refrigerator behind the bar. I trail a finger through the circle of water on the counter.

"Toshio seemed okay," I prompt.

"Far as I could tell. The vote for the Security Council seat, that was driving him nuts."

"He mentioned that last night?"

Juan considers. "Not last night. But, you know, it was like no secret the way he wanted it to go. End of last month he was even asking around, seeing who had what on Asahaki."

Asahaki, the Japanese ambassador to the UN. I lift my head.

"Actually, I don't know who else he asked, maybe it was just us," Juan says.

"Lighthouse?"

"Right."

I ask Juan to elucidate, to tell me what Toshio said.

He takes the empty crate to the end of the bar and returns with a full crate and begins transferring more bottles into the refrigerator. "It was a couple of weeks back, we were at some ECOSOC thing. Mr. Hatanaka just came out with it, wondering aloud to me if we ever had any problems with Asahaki. Like if Asahaki had ever put any pressure on us over the reports we were doing on the drug trade in Afghanistan." Looking at me over his shoulder, Juan makes a face. "It was nothing really, I guess."

I turn that one over. "You thought Toshio might have been digging for dirt on Japan? Something to use against them?"

He shakes his head, dismissing this whole line of conversation. "It wasn't just Asahaki, he was asking about some others too. Honestly, it really was nothing."

"So what were you discussing with him last night?"

"At the reception?" Juan smiles crookedly. "That was just me being a pain, trying to get him to speak to some people on the Third Committee." Juan mentions some names, big hitters who have the power to set the committee's agenda. This kind of last-minute lobbying is the only real influence the NGOs can exert now that the General Assembly is in session. "He was pretty good about it," Juan says, referring to Toshio's response. "Anyway, he said he'd do it, you know, speak to them."

We look at each other across the bar. Toshio Hatanaka's unfulfilled intentions seem to fall between us like a ghostly shadow.

"God," says Juan, leaning back to elbow the refrigerator door closed. "What's that song? 'Turn Back Time'?"

"He seemed okay? He didn't say anything about meeting anyone later?"

"No."

"Did you notice who else he spoke to at the reception?"

"The place was crammed, I mean wall to wall. Once Suzi Yomoto buttonholed him, I drifted off. I never saw him again all evening."

"Who's Suzi Yomoto?"

"She's with Greenpeace, I think. Someone like that."

I ask if she is Japanese. I am wondering about that note we found in Toshio's mailbox.

"Japanese-American," Juan tells me. "From Hawaii. Why don't you check the security tapes to see who he was with? Like from the cameras."

"We are."

"Cool."

"Where can I find this Yomoto?"

"You won't find her tonight. Not unless you feel like doing the dance clubs. If you wanna get ahold of her, there's some protest tomorrow morning up at the Waldorf." The Waldorf-Astoria, where the U.S. ambassador, James Bruckner, and his entourage are in residence. "She'll be there for sure."

He makes a wry face. I ask if there's something about this Yomoto woman he does not like.

"Not much about her I do like. She's been in here a few times. Big mouth. Last time she was in I had a friend here, he's going to college out in Hawaii. He recognized her. Seems like her father owns most of the chemical industry over there. All kinds of pollutants being dumped at sea. Rich as hell on it, the whole family. She runs around playing like the black sheep." He shrugs a shoulder. "Maybe some weird Freudian thing. Weird anyway."

"How did Toshio know her?"

He shakes his head. He has no idea. I make a mental note of the name, Suzi Yomoto. One to check out on the security tapes, and maybe I might go see her in person tomorrow.

"Did you notice if Toshio had a briefcase with him last night?"

"Yeah," Juan says after a moment, gesturing to the floor. "He had it kind of clamped between his feet while we were talking."

"Did he open it? Maybe give someone some papers or a file?"

"Not that I saw. But hey, that doesn't mean much. I only spoke with him five minutes. Maybe he opened it someplace else. Is that important?"

I shrug. Probably not.

Rachel enters, comes to the bar, and asks Juan what she can do. When he hands her a stack of coasters, she moves off to distribute them around the empty bar while I ask Juan some more questions. It is pretty clear that he saw nothing last night apart from the Yomoto woman that could help us. After a minute our conversation runs into the sand. When Rachel calls to Juan asking for ashtrays, he excuses himself, then digs the ashtrays out from beneath the bar and takes them over to her. He gives her half of them, then they part, distributing them among the tables. A pair of busboys. Juan and Rachel.

After that memorial concert Juan put together, some of the kids who'd lost a parent in the tragedy started hanging out together under the unelected leadership of Juan. One by one the others have gone off to college, moved, or simply lost touch, but Rachel and Juan remain close. The bond between them goes deep. When Rachel slipped into the nightmare world of anorexia and was finally hospitalized, Juan was the only one apart from me whom she would allow to visit. And though I cannot pretend to be overjoyed that Rachel has chosen Alphabet City as her first place of residence outside the family home, I am immeasurably reassured that Juan Martinez will be her first landlord and roommate. Twenty-four years old, but courtesy of his father's life insurance he already controls the lease on the whole building: the living quarters upstairs and the two ground-floor sections, the No Name bar here, and the office of Lighthouse, the anti-drug NGO he runs next door. Though he has the organizational instinct of a born entrepreneur, so far he seems happy to direct that instinct toward greater ends than his own material gratification. A good kid.

Now, as Rachel places the last ashtray, Juan comes back to me. "There'll be plenty of people here later. You know, the NGO crowd. Guys who liked Mr. Hatanaka a lot. I could put the word out, see if we can't do some digging, maybe turn up something that might help?"

A well-intentioned proposal, but frankly the vision conjured by Juan's offer is alarming. Every NGO from the hard-line eco-warriors to the Red Cross blundering through the same territory that Mike and I have to traverse, stomping across whatever faint trail of evidence might still remain.

"I'm not ungrateful for the offer, Juan, but I think we can manage."

Rachel pipes up. "Juan just wants to help."

I shoot her a look. She comes to stand beside me at the bar. "So have the police found anything yet? Clues like fingerprints and that?"

"The police aren't involved. Mike's handling the investigation."

"Mike?" Acute surprise. Mike Jardine's friendship with me has evidently stripped him of all credibility, in Rachel's eyes, as a cop.

"Mike and me both," I say, sliding off the barstool as the first few of the night's customers come filing through the door. Juan waves them to a table, they call across for beers.

Flipping over a coaster, I scribble down Mike's phone and room numbers back at the Secretariat. Then I hand this coaster to Juan. "Mike wants to record statements from everyone who spoke with Toshio at the reception. We need to build a clearer picture of Toshio's last hours. Call and make yourself an appointment."

Juan considers the coaster. "Strange, isn't it. How it's all worked out like this." He looks up. "You know, someone even asked me if I was thinking about doing a memorial concert?" He makes a sound and shakes his head. A memorial concert. For one of the chief mourners at the last memorial concert Juan arranged.

When I glance across at Rachel, her gaze is fixed on the bar. And I decide that this is a conversation that would be best to avoid.

"Tomorrow morning." I pistol my fingers at Juan.

He nods sadly and raises the coaster.

Rachel walks me out to the car, her hands thrust deep in the pockets of her parka. She is pensive, not unusual for her these days, and when I stop and lean against the car, ask her how she's doing, she simply smiles awkwardly and dips her head.

"Is that 'okay'?" I ask. "Or 'not okay but I'm not going to tell my old man'?"

She doesn't answer.

"Rache?"

"People were crying," she says, lifting her head. "At work. I went to see one of the translators, she was in like floods. Like it was her best friend had died or something."

"Toshio was admired by a lot of people."

"Yeah, admired, but he wasn't her best friend, was he? I mean, I'm sorry too, but I'm not going to cry my eyes out."

"No one expects you to."

Looking down, she scuffs her shoe on the sidewalk. In the past three years her mother has died a violent death, she has been stricken with anorexia, and she passed through late adolescence. Somewhere along that tortuous path her thoughts, the desires and fears that were once so clear to me, have become a closed book. But I am her father. I keep trying to understand.

"Not everyone's the same, Rache. Not everyone's lost someone they love, but you can't hold that against them." When she shrugs, I lay a hand on her shoulder. "Let them cry. If you don't think they have that much to cry about, so what. Maybe one day they'll see that too. But that's not for anyone else to judge, we all have to get through these things our own way, the best we can. You know that."

No response. I could be talking to myself, to the air.

"Maybe this is something you might want to talk over with Dr. Covey," I suggest finally.

But at the mention of Dr. Covey, the psychiatrist who undoubtedly saved her life, Rachel dips her head again and steps back. My hand slips off her shoulder.

"Thanks for bringing my stuff."

Hands in her pockets, eyes on the ground, she wanders back across the street to the No Name bar. More people are arriving now, young people mostly, converging on this off-off-Broadway venue of the diplomatic circuit. And Rachel disappears into their midst, just one more kid struggling to find her own piece of light in the world.

11

Nighttime, the Dag Hammarskjöld Library. The desk lamp casts a white light across the stack of papers spread out in front of me, part of the big report Toshio has been working on. For the past two hours I have been cross-referencing it with the field reports Toshio deposited here in the UN library after various missions abroad this past year. Mike hoped that I might turn up some obvious suspect, someone Toshio riled badly in the course of his work; a long shot, as I told Mike, and I have come up dry. The story of the day.

Mike has finally spoken to the guys on the maintenance crew. It turns out they were working virtually side by side the whole shift; none of them could have gotten to the basement without being missed. And the camera maintenance, they tell Mike, was simply on their worksheet for last night, just the regular routine.

Rocking back in my chair, feet up on the trash can, I drum a pencil on the desktop. Whatever other qualities Toshio had, he was certainly no master of the English language; and I would have to say that after forcing myself through page after turgid page, my efforts have been largely a waste of time. I pick up the title page of one field report, the only one of any real interest, and read again the few words that gave me the deepest sense of unease when I first saw them. The Drug Trade in Afghanistan, an Evaluation, the title says.

The rest of it gives the details of tribal involvement: the Baluchis and the Pathans, primary routes of export, the influence of the Taliban, cooperation or lack thereof from the government of Pakistan. All of this, naturally, has the same effect on me as the probing of an unhealed wound; this whole subject became more familiar to me than I ever wanted it to be at the time of Sarah's death.

But even this field report has offered up no candidate as Toshio's murderer, so I put it aside, then rise from the desk and move along the aisle of shelves.

It has been years since I spent any time in the library. In the early part of my career I was down here several times each week, checking wordings on international agreements for which the Dag Hammarskjöld is a primary repository, advising my seniors in Legal Affairs on where to find what in the UN archives. These days I send Elizabeth, my secretary, who loathes the chore. And it isn't even those early times that are foremost in my mind now as I wander between the shelves, searching. What keeps playing through my mind is that week I spent buried here two months after Sarah's death.

By then, of course, I had heard the whispers. Nothing official. Loose remarks in the corridors, awkward silences from the others present when Toshio and I were together in the same room. The word was that Toshio's handling of the negotiations with Sarah's kidnappers was not what it might have been. Though I tried to shrug it off, discount the rumors as idle scuttlebutt, the doubts once raised were not easily suppressed. They gnawed at me.

Finally I did what I had promised myself I would not do. Each evening I left my desk early, came to the library, and ordered up the paperwork on the whole affair. Statements from the UN field-workers at the camp in Abatan. Letters to Toshio from the Pakistani commissioner of police. Other notes from a Pakistani army officer advising on a military-style rescue, and two offers of assistance from the U.S. ambassador to Pakistan. In addition, there was a file full of useless advice from different branches of the Secretariat. Last of all, Toshio's final report. I buried myself in this paperwork night after night for a week.

The conclusion I came to was that Toshio had done all he could. There were mistakes, sure, but nothing serious, certainly nothing that led to the slaughter. There was simply no way it was his fault that they died. But the gossip still surfaces from time to time. A month back I heard that Asahaki was raking over these same coals, reminding anyone who would listen that Toshio's UN record was not unblemished. But for me, that week's sojourn in the library laid my doubts to rest for good.

Now I move along those same shelves, pausing by a small line of box files. UNHCR. Refugees. Subheading, Camps. Subheading, Afghanistan.

"Sam."

Startled, I turn. Two guys are moving toward me down the aisle,

Dieter Rasmussen and Pascal Nyeri. The odd couple. A pugnacious late-middle-aged German and a quiet-spoken young man from the Cameroon.

"We have your message," Dieter says.

"I didn't need to see you. Just Pascal."

Dieter waves that off. In fact, I left the message hours ago; I'd given up expecting to hear from Pascal tonight. As I lead them back to the table where Toshio's report is laid out in sections, I apologize for the misunderstanding. I had no intention of wasting Dieter's time.

"This past month you were seeing Toshio every few days," I remark to Pascal, picking up Toshio's calendar. "And there are quite a few other entries where he's just written Internal Oversight. Would they be meetings with you too?"

I locate the most recent entry of this kind and show Pascal. He glances at Dieter, then nods. When I ask Pascal the obvious question—what all these meetings were about—he turns to Dieter again.

"Is it a secret?" I say jokingly, but neither of them smile.

I flip the calendar onto the desk. I look at Dieter and wait for some explanation as to why he, the head of Internal Oversight, the UN's financial police, is here.

"You are investigating Hatanaka's death?" he says.

"That's right."

"And this has been cleared with O'Conner?"

"Dieter, it's an investigation into a suspected homicide. What do you mean, cleared?"

"Has he told you yet why Toshio was working with us?"

I feel the muscles of my shoulders and neck begin to harden. On more than one occasion I have heard Patrick refer to my own liberal faith in open dealing as flaky; if Patrick had his way, all UN business of substance would take place behind unbreachable walls of silence. But here he seems to have bypassed me, his deputy, entirely. Toshio and Internal Oversight?

"Let's assume that he hasn't. So how about you just tell me, Dieter. I'm all ears."

Dieter chews on his lip. Pascal studies the floor.

"Has Patrick specifically forbidden you to tell me?"

"No," says Dieter, but his tone is qualified.

It takes me no effort to picture the scene. Patrick with all the bluff authority of his position insinuating that the whole matter, whatever it is, should be kept under wraps.

"When I called him at lunchtime he said it was being looked into," Pascal volunteers.

The muscles in my neck are not just hard now, they are suddenly bunched tight. Internal Oversight called Patrick about Toshio several hours ago, and this is the first I have heard of it. The vibe here is way wrong. Leaning forward, I plant my hands on the table.

"How about you just tell me what you were working on with Toshio. Or if you prefer, we can go upstairs and have this out with Patrick."

"Tell him," Dieter finally tells Pascal.

Pascal hefts his briefcase onto the table and pops it open. "We were contacted by the Audit Department earlier this year. They thought they had found something. They needed our help."

"Nothing new," Dieter puts in.

"Found what?" I say, but Dieter just points to Pascal's briefcase and studiously avoids my gaze. Which unsettles me somewhat. Because though he is probably the most feared man at UNHQ, certainly the most vilified, I have a real regard for Dieter Rasmussen. Blunt in the usual German fashion, he carries on his work, makes his decisions, with a very un-Germanic lack of regard for the bureaucratically stipulated boundaries.

One time I accompanied him on a trip to Somalia. I was meant to be observing conditions in what is laughably described as that country's judicial system; Dieter's task was to discover how ten million dollars' worth of food aid went missing from the port at Mogadishu. Upon our arrival at the airport, it was immediately apparent that reports of peace breaking out in the area had been greatly exaggerated. Two mechanicals—stripped-down vehicles mounted with artillery—were parked near the runway. They were pumping shells into a nearby warehouse, each explosion greeted with roars of delight from a crowd of weapon-waving Somalis. Dieter took one look at all this and turned me around and walked me back to the plane. He ordered the UN pilot to refuel and fly us straight out. Two nights later the hotel where we were meant to be staying took a direct hit; three of our local people were killed. Dieter is a man whose judgment and character I have good reason to trust, and it is more than a little disconcerting to find now that he cannot look me in the eye.

Pascal hands me some papers. UNDCP headings. The UN Drug Control Program. I flip through the pages.

"Minutes from a meeting of the Special Committee," Pascal tells me.

"Special Committee for what?"

"It was overseeing the UNDCP's activities in the Golden Crescent." Pascal speaks softly, his voice so mellifluous that the words "Golden Crescent," the source of an endless supply of heroin and grief, come out sounding like some brand of rich dark chocolate. "The Special Committee was responsible for a substantial budget."

"How substantial?"

"Twenty million, annually."

A substantial budget, I think. And Pascal had been called in from Internal Oversight to assist Toshio, special envoy to Afghanistan. Afghanistan, the center of the Golden Crescent.

"Someone was skimming it?"

"The auditors could not make the numbers add up," Dieter interjects. "We were called in."

But that does not explain the secrecy in which this has been shrouded. The defrauding of UN budgets by UN appointees is a regrettably frequent occurrence.

"How much went missing?"

"Hundreds of thousands." Pascal lifts a shoulder. "It is possible up to a million."

"U.S. dollars?"

Pascal nods. But again, a million dollars, though a substantial sum, is not earth-shattering in the context of a UN budget that runs into billions. I remain puzzled.

"So who was on this Special Committee?"

"Three people."

I make a crack about this being the smallest UN committee I've ever heard of, but Dieter looks pained.

"Senior people," he says.

"Who?"

"Wang Po Lin and Lemtov."

I make a sound. Two very big names. Wang Po Lin was number two on the Chinese delegation until his recent recall to Beijing. Nobody seems to know if he was recalled to be promoted or kicked in the pants, and the Chinese just aren't telling. Lemtov is a rising star in the Russian delegation, one of the new breed that emerged after the collapse of the Soviet Union. A fluent English speaker, he made his reputation as the Russian Central Bank's front man in numerous crisis negotiations with the International Monetary Fund before making the switch into diplomacy. I am beginning to understand Patrick's involvement, the veil of secrecy.

"Number three?" I ask.

Dieter passes a hand over his mouth. Pascal stares into his briefcase.

"A three-man committee, right? Po Lin, Lemtov, and who's number three?"

"Asahaki," Dieter says.

I remain very still. Ambassador Asahaki, Japan's number-one man here at the UN. The guy who has been leading his country's charge for a permanent seat on the Security Council.

"Where does Toshio come in to this?" I ask them.

"He gave us access to the documents for Afghanistan," says Pascal. "When we found the defrauded money had been returned to a private account here in New York, he came with me to the bank."

"So this wasn't some arm's-length thing. He wasn't just oversee-ing it. Toshio was actually working with you?"

Pascal nods.

"And did those three on the Special Committee know that?"

Pascal tells me that Toshio spoke to all three of them. Surprised, I turn to Dieter and wait for some explanation as to why in the world a guy as senior as Toshio was doing that kind of donkeywork.

"O'Conner did not want us calling those three into the Oversight office," Dieter says. "It would look bad for them. But for Pascal they would make no time to be interviewed. None of them. I agreed with Patrick that someone must speak to them, someone they couldn't ig-nore. I was too busy."

"Toshio," I say.

Dieter opens a hand; it almost seems like an apology.

So in the last few weeks of his life, Toshio was deeply involved in the investigation of a fraud against the UN. Was actually interview-ing suspects. And Patrick was aware of that, yet neglected—even af-ter Toshio's death—to tell me.

"So which of the three had his hand in the cookie jar?" I ask.

"When Pascal told me you had called earlier," says Dieter, "I called O'Conner. He was in a meeting. He has been in the same meeting for three hours now."

Dieter has not answered my question. I keep my gaze fixed on him. At last he lowers his eyes and admits that the culprit really had begun to look like the Japanese ambassador. Bunzo Asahaki.

———

"I should have been told, Patrick."

"Why?"

Glancing at the clocks on the wall, he brushes past me down the corridor. I dive out after him.

"Why? Are you serious? Toshio just pinned a fraud on Asahaki, for chrissake."

"Keep it down," Patrick mutters.

"Did that just slip your mind?"

"You're getting way ahead of yourself, Sam." He shoots me a dark look. "Way ahead."

"I'm chasing the goddamn game here. We've been busting our balls looking for a motive, and you didn't even mention this."

"Wait." He raises a finger as he turns in to the Operations Room and goes to confer with Dwight Arnold, tonight's duty officer, a bearded Canadian with the hulking stature of a grizzly bear. While they bend over a PC monitor to examine the latest status report from some UN mission in God knows where, I stand in the doorway, steaming.

Patrick O'Conner is going to dinner with some very important people. Players, he would call them. Big wheels, guys with clout on the diplomatic scene. He hasn't told me that, of course, but I've been working for him long enough to recognize the signs. Black bow tie, gold cuff links. The single line across his brow that is meant to denote the serious and thoughtful mind beneath. And this, the mere fact of his descent here to Operations, a place referred to with self-mocking despair by those who work here as UN Central, the supposed nerve center of UN peacekeeping operations worldwide. The office is pathetically small. For the night shift, just Dwight Arnold and two assistants. It used to be telexes chattering away in here; now it's PCs humming and faxes disgorging paper, giving updates on crises, daily accounts of wars and cease-fire violations, and the thousand other infractions of civil order that the UN is obligated by Security Council resolutions to observe and police.

Folding my arms impatiently, I lean against the door frame and watch Dwight Arnold and Patrick confer. God, I am a fool. Suicide, Patrick's seemingly inexplicable call this morning; now I have the explanation. And now I also understand the strange crosscurrents at this afternoon's brief meeting with Asahaki outside the SG's dining room. Patrick's anger. Asahaki's request for the body, then the hurried retreat.

You would think I might have learned by now. Three years his deputy, you would think I might have learned not to take Patrick's words or actions at face value, to always look one layer deeper to find his real motives. Like this visit to the Operations Room, for example. He will, without fail, pay the place a visit immediately prior to attending any major social occasion. Then at the ensuing grand dinner he will wait for a pause in the conversation before casually mentioning that there has been a shooting across the UN line in Cyprus. Or a bomb blast in Kinshasa. Or that tonight's polling in Laos has ended in riots. From these gleamingly fresh scraps of information his fellow guests are tacitly invited to infer Patrick's high and central place at the table of world affairs. And they do. Depressingly, his ruse invariably works. Patrick is on the A list of every New York hostess who matters.

At last he finishes with Dwight and rejoins me in the hall, but my questions go unanswered until we are alone together in the elevator. He hits the button for the ground floor, then faces me.

"Toshio never pinned the fraud on Ambassador Asahaki. Who'd you hear this from anyway?"

"Dieter says it was Asahaki. He says Toshio knew that too, that Toshio was involved in the investigation. Why the hell didn't you tell me that?"

"Toshio wanted it to be Asahaki, that's not proof. There was no evidence."

I frown. This sounds like blarney.

"Jesus, Sam, use your head." Patrick taps his own head. "What was Toshio's big mission lately, what was he trying to screw up?"

I suggest the obvious, the Japanese seat on the Security Council.

"In one. And can you tell me a better way to do that than by sandbagging Asahaki? Hang a fraud charge around Asahaki's neck at the last minute, he'd be a lame duck. He's leading the last big push for votes on this thing; if he gets sunk, the vote's probably dead in the water too. With Asahaki out of the game, chances are the Japanese don't get the Council seat. You follow?"

I follow. And I also follow the unstated corollary. Patrick must have been as keen to keep Ambassador Asahaki in the game as he claims Toshio was to close Asahaki out. And I don't buy Patrick's take on Toshio's motives anyway.

"Toshio wouldn't have done that. He wouldn't have put Asahaki in the frame for the fraud unless he believed it was true. And it wasn't just Toshio, Pascal says the same thing."

"Pascal," Patrick murmurs, pinching the skin at his throat. "He and Dieter both came to see you?"

"Well, they didn't seem to be having much luck getting hold of you."

Before he can decide whether I am taking a shot at him, I remind him that I've worked with Pascal Nyeri before. That Pascal Nyeri knows what he's doing. Not something you can automatically assume in the Secretariat; the place is stuffed with deadwood employed solely to fill the geographic quota.

"Dieter wouldn't be handing an investigation like that to a jackass. And Pascal agreed with Toshio. It looked like Asahaki was skimming the committee budget."

"You think Nyeri doesn't know what's good for him?" Patrick says. "He was working under a special envoy, for fucksake. Toshio puts the finger on Asahaki, you're telling me some wombat from Oversight's going to object? If Nyeri had made any trouble, Toshio'd have him on a plane back to wherever he came from." He snaps his fingers. "Like that."

"The Cameroon."

"Wherever."

The elevator door opens, and we step out across the black-and-white checkerboard marble floor toward the exit. The delegates' exit, which Patrick frequently makes a point of using just to show that he can. The guard at the door nods us out. I wait till we are down the steps before I say it.

"I have to speak to Ambassador Asahaki."

"You can't."

Patrick straightens his cuffs and runs a finger over his jacket collar as we walk on toward the gatehouse. Times like this it is hard to believe that when his appointment as Undersecretary-General for Legal Affairs was announced, I went out with several other senior guys from the department and celebrated. Just before Sarah died. Since then there has been ample time to get to know the man behind the reputation. Ample time to have taken more of his bullshit than I care to remember. Now in the center of the UN forecourt, I angle myself in front of him, forcing him to stop.

"Do you even want to know how Toshio died?"

"You're not going to find that out speaking to Asahaki."

"That's for me to decide, Patrick. Or do you want me to pass the ball to Mike, let him handle the whole thing?"

The thought of UN Security wresting control of the homicide investigation away from Legal Affairs strikes Patrick into appalled silence a moment. Then he speaks.

"You want to see Asahaki."

That's what I want, I tell him.

"Well, you bloody well can't. You can't, Sam, because he's not here."

My glance slides across to the Assembly Hall.

"Not here at Turtle Bay," Patrick goes on. "Not here in New York. Not even here in the U.S. The man's gone back to Tokyo."

I am astounded, stunned.

"Officially for last-minute talks on their push for the Council seat," says Patrick. "Unofficially Asahaki got the feeling he was being set up. First he had Toshio asking a lot of questions about the fraud. Then Toshio dies. And then you crash in like a bull in a china shop this afternoon, telling Asahaki you want to interview him. Jesus Christ, how did you expect him to react?"

Buffeted by his evident anger, I sway back.

"How about you do like I tell you from now on," says Patrick, stepping around me, waving to a cluster of men in dinner jackets and women in evening dresses alighting from cabs across First Avenue. All laughing. Everyone set and ready to give their expense accounts the first five-star belting of the UN session. "Show some tact," Patrick tells me, buttoning his jacket as he walks away. "Act with a little diplomacy."

He passes out the gates, head held high, and joins his friends and disappears up the street. Off to my right the spotlit flags, all one hundred and eighty-five of them, flutter gently, shackles clinking. The wondrous UN family. Across First Avenue the Tibetan monks are rolling out their sleeping bags. Turning back to the Secretariat building, I find that my fists are clenched, my stomach knotted. I am so fucking angry.

Mike is up in Surveillance. Once I've finished explaining the situation to him, calming him down a little, I go up to my own office and sit brooding awhile. What was it Moriko said? Toshio's work was his life. This place. People like Patrick.

Then at last I do what I know I should not do. I make a call.

A young woman answers. "Waldorf-Astoria," she repeats when second thoughts make me miss a beat.

"I want to be put through to one of your suites," I say, lowering my forehead into my hand. "Suite Twelve."

12

WHEN WE'RE DONE, JENNIFER JUST LIES THERE BESIDE me, breathing hard, staring at the ceiling, the back of her hand resting on my chest while her chest rises and falls beneath the rumpled sheet. Her upper lip is beaded with sweat. From outside, there come the distant sounds of traffic, an occasional siren.

"Is this"—she asks finally between broken breaths—"is this where I ask for a cigarette?"

I pinch her thigh and she rolls away, swinging her feet to the floor. My finger traces a slow arc from her shoulder blade across her spine to her hip. We are in an executive suite at the Waldorf, in the biggest bed I have ever seen, and if this were any other night, I would not consider leaving before daybreak. But when Jennifer asks me now to stay, I tell her no, that I have to be getting home.

"Hmm," she says, then, rising, she slaps her butt lightly and makes some ribald remark about modern romance. She catches a glimpse of herself in the dresser mirror and frowns critically as she disappears into the bathroom. In truth, she has very little to be critical about. For a woman nearing forty, her body remains remarkably firm and unlined, the result of ten years of hard labor, half an hour per day, in the local gym.

She calls to me from the bathroom. "I wasn't really expecting you to call."

"You got lucky."

"Huh." And then after a moment, "Hatanaka's death still off limits?"

"Yes." It was the first thing I told her when I arrived, a direct warning. "Was the sex meant to addle my brain, make me weaken?"

Her face reappears in the doorway. "Usually works."

I make a weak pretense of tossing a pillow in her direction, and she jerks the door closed. "How did Rachel's move go?" she asks.

"Fine."

"Nice place?"

"I'll tell you when she's let me see it."

"Want some advice, Sam?"

When I don't answer, Jennifer seems to take the hint. Anyway, a moment later the shower is running and I ease myself over to the edge of the bed and sit up. There is a half-empty bottle of champagne on the side table, two half-empty glasses. Picking up one of the glasses, I take a sip, studying my own reflection in the dresser mirror. Unlike Jennifer, I have not availed myself of the opportunities for self-improvement afforded by gym membership; the daily workout has never held a place in my routine. And somewhat regrettably, the consequences have now started to show. Once, the muscles on my shoulders and arms had firm definition, but now there is a slackness, a lack of tone that if I am not careful will soon pass beyond the point of no return. My stomach muscles that I still think of as hard ridges are showing signs of settling into three distinct and heavy rolls. Drawing myself up for a second, I suck in my gut. My penis flops drunkenly, comically, sideways. Breathing out, I let the natural slump of middle age fall back into place. I sip my drink. I consider the man in the mirror and the woman in the shower.

There have been other women since Sarah died. Not many, just a few. Friends allowed me to wallow in the slough of despond for six months before trailing an assortment of divorcees and late-unmarrieds across my path. For a while, messages on the answering machine at home were a source of dread, invitations to meals the only purpose of which was to introduce me to women I did not want to meet. A couple of times I tried to play the game, ended up in some lonely woman's bed, but emotionally I wasn't even trying to make it to first base. After a while I simply refused all invitations. Then, during the eighteen months of Rachel's battle with anorexia, I was too worried, too helplessly distraught over my daughter's condition to be giving serious consideration to anything beyond her desperate need.

But Rachel had been out of the hospital for months by the time Jennifer reentered my life. The timing worked. The searing flame of grief over Sarah, the heartrending anguish over Rachel, both had at least partially receded. Time—everyone from the Secretary-General on down had platitudinized—would heal. And now to a greater extent than I ever believed possible, time has done that. Three years from the death of my wife, I am finally able to look to the future with hope. And the reason for that, quite simply, is Jennifer.

She wants me in her life. A woman who knows her own mind, she told me that early on, the second or third time we slept together. I made no serious response, and whenever the issue has risen since, I have always turned it aside, but I know that we cannot go on like this much longer. She deserves an answer, at least to know what I'm thinking, and I guess what I'm thinking is that all the hurdles don't appear as insurmountable as they seemed even three months back. But I cannot kid myself; some hurdles remain. Because in the way of those who find themselves unexpectedly dating in their middle years, neither one of us has arrived at this point unencumbered, free of obligations or, for that matter, wounds.

For me, the big two are obvious: Sarah's death and Rachel's illness. With Jennifer it is her ex-husband, another lawyer, Stephen Morrelli. She refers to him infrequently, she can hardly speak his name without spitting some venomous epithet. Their marriage lasted barely a year before imploding upon Jennifer's discovery that Stephen had carried on an affair from the time of their engagement and on through their marriage. A regular Wednesday-night appointment, apparently, when Jennifer was led to believe he was doing pro bono work for a group of Pentecostal churches up in Harlem. Four years later the pain of this betrayal remains raw. The memory of her ex-husband still prowls the shadowed regions of Jennifer's emotional life like some dark nocturnal creature, one she keeps hidden from the light. Though she can turn her ready wit to most anything, about Stephen Morrelli, and infidelity, she does not jest.

And she has one major obligation too: her son, Ben, now four. He was born three weeks after her marriage crashed.

Swirling the champagne in my glass, I fix my eyes on the eyes of the man in the mirror. Her son. Another man's child. Jennifer has never pushed the point, but she never shirked it either. Over the summer the three of us went on a few picnics together, lately some kid things like the zoo. Last week we went to see *Fantasia;* walking down the street afterward, Ben reached up unprompted and took my hand. A strange moment that Jennifer pretended not to notice. The boy has dark hair, dark eyes, and olive skin; he looks nothing like his mother. He doesn't smile much or speak often; he couldn't be less like what Rachel was at that age, but a likable kid just the same. And I sense that he wants me to like him. A son. Could I cope? Is the man in the mirror ready for that?

Finally rising, I cross to where my jacket is draped over a chair, dig in the inner pocket, and pull out the letter from Professor

Goldman, the leading light in the Department of International Affairs at Columbia. The letter is a job offer. A job offer for me. After idly rescanning it, I toss the thing onto the bed, then I refill both glasses with champagne and wander in to join Jennifer in the shower.

————

"What's this?"

"Read it."

"I have," says Jennifer. Swathed in a white bathrobe, the Waldorf-Astoria logo embroidered on the pocket, she sits with one leg drawn up beneath her on the bed. The letter from Goldman is open in her hand. Toweling off, I stroll from the bathroom to where my clothes are piled on the chair beneath the window. "Goldman wants you at Columbia?" she says.

"If I want to go, sure, he wants me."

Tossing my towel aside, I pull on my shorts.

"And do you? Do you actually want to go?"

I lift a finger. "Ah," I say, then step into my pants.

"What's that mean, 'Ah'?"

"It means I was hoping you might have some opinion."

"On whether you should give up your career?"

"Call it a change of direction."

"Honestly, Sam." With a despairing gesture she lets her hand and the letter fall back to the bed. "Sometimes I just don't get you, where you're coming from. You want to make a decision like this now? You can't do that."

I raise my eyes from the buttons on my shirt. My fingers keep working. "No?"

"Jesus," she mutters. She considers the letter, then asks, "What brought this on anyway? Hatanaka?"

I draw her attention to the date on the letter. The offer was made to me last week.

"You didn't ask me for my opinion last week," says Jennifer, the razor-brained USUN legal counsel. When she looks at me, I turn my gaze in the direction of the giant television screen by the dresser. It is tuned to BBC World, the volume turned down. Some flak-jacketed journalist is standing in front of a pile of twisted metal wreckage, possibly a bridge, and talking soundlessly. "Sam?" says Jennifer.

"If I took the job at Columbia, it might make things easier."

"Who for?"

"Us."

Silence. When I face her, she is looking at me hard. Storm clouds gathering.

"That is such crap. If you've got a problem with your career, you can't put that on us. If you don't like your job, leave. But don't kid yourself it's anything to do with us. With me." She jabs a finger into her sternum. "Because that's a lie."

I pull on my socks. I wriggle my feet into my shoes. Don't hold back now, I say quietly. Speak your mind.

"I'm serious. I'm fed up with it, Sam. Maybe our careers don't make it straightforward, but what does that matter if you really want this to work? Don't keep blaming your career, it's too easy."

"Well, what do you want?"

"I want you."

I raise my eyes. She regards me steadily.

"And sometime soon," she says, "I'd like to hear that from you too. Plain and simple. No hiding behind your job or pretending that Rachel still needs all of you."

Bending, I do up my laces.

"And your wife's been gone three years," she says, looking away. "That's about long enough for you to be letting go there too."

I keep my head down. I study my fingers and the laces on my shoes. Though we have talked about Sarah several times, Jennifer has never once pushed me further than I wanted to go. Those conversations, I thought, had brought us closer, helped Jennifer see where I am. This is the first indication she has ever given me that where I am is somewhere she doesn't much like.

"I was right the first time, wasn't I?" she says after a moment. "It's Hatanaka, isn't it?"

"Partly."

"Not partly. Mostly. Seeing him laid out like that. A guy you knew, and suddenly he's dead. I mean, it's made me think too."

Mortality. Now I see where she's coming from with the mention of Sarah. The sands of time are running for us all.

"I bumped into Goldman last month. We had a drink, got to talking."

"Talking," she says.

"I guess I gave him the impression I wasn't totally satisfied with spending the rest of my career as Patrick's bag carrier," I admit. "Goldman must have figured I'd be open to an offer."

"And you weren't last week, but today you are?"

Moving to the chair, I collect my jacket. By this time, of course, I am aware that I have made a mistake. This was not the opportune time to signal the depth of my discontent with Patrick, or to trail any thoughts of a possible alternate future.

"What's wrong?" Jennifer asks suddenly.

I roll my eyes. After the events of the day, some question.

"You weren't like this this afternoon," she says. "This afternoon you were on the case, a man with a mission. And now you're moping around, wondering about a career change?" Her eyes take on quickened light. She tilts her head. "Is someone trying to interfere with your investigation?"

"No."

"No one's trying to lean on you?"

"Apart from you?"

Her look hardens. She sweeps a hand around the suite. "Nobody forced you up here. If I'd known it was going to be an issue, I wouldn't have asked you."

I raise a hand in apology. Stupid crack, I say.

Jennifer pulls the robe tight around her waist and retreats up the bed. Resting her back against the headboard, she points the remote at the TV and cranks up the sound. Could I have handled this any worse? I wonder. For a while I chew the inside of my cheek and watch the U.S. vice president wave and launch his sound bite for today into a crowd of cheering Cuban refugees. Then my glance cheats across to Jennifer. Stupid crack maybe, but her reaction is overdone. She remains silently, furiously, focused on the TV. And I find myself wondering if my gibe maybe cut a little close to the bone. Is that possible? Not a premeditated plan, of course, but in some hidden chamber of her mind, where the USUN legal counsel never sleeps, was Jennifer hoping that in the comfort of one of the Waldorf's finest suites, after half a bottle of champagne and sex, I might become loose-tongued and indiscreet?

After Toshio's death, James Bruckner, the U.S. ambassador, will be working desperately to keep the vote for the Japanese Security Council seat on track. And Jennifer, his chief legal counsel, will naturally be doing everything she can to assist him in the cause.

My glance slides around the room. Around the goddamn suite. A suite paid for by the U.S. State Department, at the Waldorf-Astoria, for chrissake. Shrugging my shoulders into my jacket, I make a suggestion that I really should have made on my arrival. Or, even better, by phone.

"While this is going on, till Mike and I find out what really happened with Toshio, maybe you and I should take a few steps back. Just stick to our jobs."

She looks down at the pillow beside her, then back up at me. "Nice timing."

"That's not how this is, Jennifer."

"No?"

"Give me a break."

Her look continues to smolder, so I cross to the bed, pick up the remote, and zap the TV. Silence as I sit down beside her.

"Okay. Give me your word that absolutely nothing I say to you gets back to Bruckner." I am looking straight at her. She is steady for a moment, then her eyes flicker down. "That's right," I say. "You can't."

"What is this, a loyalty test?"

"Ask me the same thing. Can I promise you if you let something slip I won't take it back to O'Conner?"

We look at each other.

"Right. I can't either."

"So what's that prove, that we can't trust each other?"

It proves, I tell her, that Professor Goldman's offer is worthy of very careful consideration.

"Mmm," she says, one corner of her mouth rising. Then the phone rings. She rolls across the pillow and takes the call. She signals for me to wait.

I fetch my watch from the side table, then wander over to the life-size portrait on the wall, some European lady dressed in Renaissance finery, lacework and ruffs. I study the face, the sloe eyes, as I strap on my watch. All the while, I cannot help hearing Jennifer talking on the phone behind me. And though I can hear only one side of the conversation, the name of Jennifer's interlocutor and the subject under discussion are immediately clear to me. It is Ambassador Bruckner. He is telling Jennifer that Asahaki has removed himself back to Japan.

"He's definitely gone?" she says, lowering her voice further. "Oh, Christ, you're sure?"

My stomach sinks. This is the first she has heard. And when she finds out that I already knew, and that I chose not to inform her, all hell is liable to break loose. I consider taking my leave. But before I can, Jennifer hangs up the phone. My gaze fixed on the portrait, I wait for the eruption. Nothing happens. No object comes flying at me, no voice is raised in recrimination. Eventually I dare a glance over my shoulder. Jennifer is standing disrobed by the bed, pulling on her panties.

"Bruckner," she says. "Some damn crisis."

"Serious?"

Her back turned to me, she puts on her bra. "One of our guys just took unexpected leave. Bruckner wants to see me."

I study the nape of her neck. Jennifer Dale, whom I have never known to lie, has just lied to me.

"Someone important?"

"Where are my shoes?"

I pick them up from by my feet and take them to her. She steps into her dress and places a hand on my shoulder for balance as she puts on her shoes.

"I can't hang around," she says then, grabbing her laptop from the floor and turning for the door. When I step over to join her, she puts a hand on my chest. "Give me two minutes," she says, "then let yourself out." She rises on tiptoe, presses her cheek against mine, then goes.

I stand staring at the closed door a long while. Then I turn and go back to the bed and dig through the sheets till I locate the letter from Goldman. I slip it into my pocket, and two minutes later I am wandering down a wide, empty hallway in the Waldorf-Astoria, feeling strangely torn open. Bloodlessly wounded in the silent battle of international politics and diplomacy. The world Jennifer and I both chose. Secrets and goddamn lies.

WEDNESDAY

13

"BIG-TIME," SAYS MIKE AS HE ENTERS MY apartment laden with brown paper bags that emit the salty odor of two three-ninety-nine breakfasts from a diner up on Jolimont. "Made the front page of the *Post*," he tells me, and I pull the folded newspaper from where he has it clamped beneath his arm.

He goes to the kitchen while I scan the headlines with a sinking heart. DEATH OF SPECIAL ENVOY AT UN OPENING. It's in the bottom story inside. But the report, to my relief, is strictly factual. Toshio is named, and though it mentions speculation about the cause of death, there is a quote from Patrick saying that natural causes are assumed and that confirmation should be forthcoming by the end of the week. The rest of the piece centers on the opening speeches, certainly the last time this session that anything from the General Assembly will be given space in the *Post*. There is no mention of Ambassador Asahaki's precipitate return to Tokyo.

In the kitchen I lay out knives and forks. Mike gets the coffee going. Every Wednesday, holidays excepted, this has been the routine for almost a year. Wednesdays, Mike's wife, Deborah, goes to visit her mother, who lives alone on the other side of Queens. Deborah takes the Jardine family car, so Mike rides in to work with me.

Cops, it would be fair to say, have never been my most favorite people. But like so much else of my being, over the years I have come to recognize this reflexive antipathy as a legacy from my parents, two children of the dust bowl whose own parents stayed where they believed the Lord had planted them while so many other families were uprooted, driven westward before the rolling sand. They watched helplessly while the sheriff's office was called in to evict bankrupt neighbors from their homes, folks whose only crime was their poverty. The injustice of those times remained with my parents all their lives, finally coming down to me in fragments, gossip about neighboring farms, the fireside talk of winter nights. Sheriffs, cops, all secular authority was to be quietly but firmly avoided. A God-fearing life on your own piece of earth and the good book to guide you. Raise a hand against no one, the Friends' creed, supplemented by the more practical creed of the Kansas farmer. You still see it nailed to farm gates right across the state. PRIVATE PROPERTY—KEEP OUT.

But with Mike Jardine, somehow, I connect. The reason, I suspect, is that beneath his tough and brassy New York City exterior, there is a man who still holds, however despairingly at times, a real belief in justice.

"Ketchup?" Mike says now.

"Should be there."

Shaking his head in disappointment, he closes the refrigerator. "One for the shopping list." He flicks on the portable TV and sits down. "I got results from the bloods," he tells me.

The blood samples he took from Toshio. I look at him.

"Heroin," he says. "In the syringe too. A match."

"Recreational dosage?"

"Only if Hatanaka got his jollies whacking horses."

"Ahh."

"Yeah," he says, stabbing his fork into home fries. "Something else you're gonna like. My friend down at the lab says it's the purest stuff he's seen for years. Says he wants to keep it for an exhibit, like. For his students."

He chews on his potatoes, head turned to the TV. The morning news.

"Can he tell if it was the heroin that killed Toshio?"

Mike nods and speaks around a mouthful of breakfast. "I took the bloods from the veins and the arteries. Mix of heroin was the same right through the circulatory system." He taps the fork to his chest. "Heart was still pumping when he croaked."

I push a slice of sausage through some egg yolk in desultory fashion. Mike's appetite seems unimpaired. After a moment I venture another question. "How long does this friend of yours think it would have taken Toshio to die?"

"Once the junk went into him?" Mike shrugs. "Few minutes at the outside. Way my buddy tells it, anyone using that stuff is gonna blow a head gasket soon as it hits the brain. Fried. Oh, yeah," he says, turning from the TV to face me, "and where do you think it came from?"

I take a second. "Afghanistan?"

Mike laughs. "You ever think about taking this up as a job?"

The dope that was used to kill Toshio came from Afghanistan. We bat this fact to and fro a few minutes as we eat, then Mike decides that it's taking us nowhere. Half the dope going into the arms, thighs, and groins of junkies right across the country, he tells me, comes from the Afghanistan-Pakistan crescent. It might mean something, but shooting the breeze about it over breakfast is not going to produce the answer.

"More legwork required," Mike concludes, reaching for a last shot of coffee.

A key turns in the front door. Mike looks at me.

"Rachel," I tell him. She rang earlier to say she was coming over to pick up some dress.

As she waltzes in, Mike says "Hi," but all Rachel does is screw up her nose.

"You can smell it out in the hall," she says, glancing at the remains of our breakfast. "Honestly, you guys. You never heard about calories?"

She glides on past us toward her room. Mike knocks back his coffee, his glance sliding to the hallway where Rachel has disappeared.

"How's she taking this?" he asks me quietly.

"Okay."

"Just okay?"

"Mike, she's moved out. I can't watch her every second of the day even if I wanted to. Which I don't. She's okay, all right?"

Mike considers his empty mug. Clearly he has had the same thought as I have, that Toshio's death might have knocked Rachel hard, brought back memories. Though Mike never saw Rachel in the hospital, he saw me often enough after my daily visits there. One time when the doctors seemed to be losing her, when I'd sat holding Rachel's fragile, bony hand for two hours and watched her breathing with barely the strength of a sparrow, I returned home and called Mike.

She's dying, I said.

He assured me that my daughter would not die. I gripped the phone, white-knuckled, and to the embarrassment of both of us began to cry.

Now I push my car keys across the table, asking Mike to go and gas up while I shave. I tell him I'll meet him downstairs in ten minutes.

When he's gone I wander down the hall, pausing outside Rachel's open door. She is holding a long black dress, still on its hanger, against her body. She considers the figure she cuts in the mirror.

"What's the occasion?"

"A party." Eyes fixed on the mirror, she turns left and right. "It's not me, is it?"

I remark that she must have thought it was her when she bought it.

"It's not too young?"

Too young. She is all of eighteen years old.

"Dr. Covey called," I tell her. No response; she continues to examine the dress. "He wanted to know why you hadn't made it to your last three appointments."

"I'm not a minor anymore." Her brow wrinkles in vexation as she faces me. "That's private. Why'd he tell you that? Did you ask him?"

"He just wants to know if you're going to see him again. If you're not, he's got other patients who need that time with him."

"Well, he should tell me that, not you."

I raise my hands in surrender. I have learned by now not to argue. But I say that I told Dr. Covey she was moving out, that I gave him her new number so he could call her direct. Rachel is somewhat assuaged. She pulls a face and slips the dress off the hanger. The talk of appointments reminds me of something else.

"Has Juan contacted Mike?"

"Oh, yeah." She points. "Juan wants to show you something."

I lift my head. Show me what? I ask.

"He just said if I saw you, I should tell you that." She rolls the dress into a Macy's bag. "About Hatanaka, I guess." Her eyes are averted now, and her whole manner brings Mike's earlier question forcefully to mind. How is she taking this?

"Rache."

"Hmm?"

"You don't have to move out just because that was the plan. If you'd rather wait, you know you can stay here awhile longer. As long as you like. It's your home."

She looks up at me. "Why?"

"No reason. Maybe just let things settle down."

"Things?" she says.

Will I ever again, I wonder, get back the daughter with whom I could truly communicate?

Somewhere out on the street a musical car horn blares crazily. Rachel clutches the Macy's bag as she rushes by me. "That's my ride," she says, turning to face me as she reverses down the hall. "And, Dad, don't worry, okay? I'm not the only kid in the entire world who ever left home." Exiting out the front door, she calls over her shoulder, "Call Juan."

The musical horn blares again, another two bars of *"La Cucaracha."* Don't worry. In the bathroom I sneak a look out the window, but there's no immediately identifiable young lunatic leaning from any of the parked cars.

Shaving, I retune my thoughts, get myself focused on the day. Finding Toshio's murderer, of course, is priority number one. While I'm trying to do that, someone will have to fill in for me at the office. Gunther Franks seems the obvious choice. Danish, a fifteen-year veteran of Legal Affairs, he is supremely reliable, the office workhorse; I can trust him not to screw up. And I will have to speak to Patrick too. I want to sit down with him for ten minutes, straighten out the ground rules on this investigation so that I don't get left the way I was yesterday, chasing my butt in the dark. First up, though, I have an appointment with Pascal Nyeri from Internal Oversight; we are meeting at a bank uptown. The Portland Trust Bank, so Pascal assures me, is the repository of the money Asahaki defrauded from the UN. Ambassador Asahaki. Who is now quaffing sake in the far-off safety of Tokyo.

In the bedroom I check my calendar. A dinner appointment with the Cohens that will have to be canceled. A professor of obstetrics, David Cohen was a close colleague of Sarah's; the two of them coauthored a paper on preeclampsia that launched them onto the medical conference circuit for a time. Every few months since Sarah's death, David and his wife have invited me over for supper, and I go, but Sarah's absence on these occasions seems to coalesce into something almost solid. We seem to spend the entire evening talking around someone who isn't there, though on my last visit David was bold enough to remark that Sarah was still remembered and missed down at Bellevue.

Buttoning my shirt, I stand looking at the family portrait propped on the dresser. Sarah with me and Rachel after Rachel's junior high school graduation. A regular family. Mr. and Mrs. Normal and their child. And that is what is most remarkable to me now, just how unremarkable, how ordinary, our lives seemed when Sarah was alive. A professional couple with a teenage daughter, an apartment in Brooklyn Heights, and an annual two-week vacation on the West Coast. Our lives were firmly entrenched somewhere in the lower reaches of the professional urban elite, and when I got up each morning, when I went in to work, I thought about ordinary things, day-to-day hassles. I did not think about life. Or love. And now? Now I find I think about them all the time.

Remembered and missed. An epitaph that does not begin to sound the depth of longing that can still well in me at unexpected moments for the life we have all lost. I wonder about Moriko, Toshio's sister. By now she will have contacted friends and relatives in Japan. By now the shock will be receding, the long, slow ache of life without her brother begun.

As I pull on my tie, I hear someone in the living room. Rachel, I think, in her rush to leave, has left something behind. Turning down my collar, I go to her, phrasing in my mind a delicate warning about the kind of young men who have car horns that play *"La Cucaracha"* clear across the neighborhood.

"Rache," I say, passing from the kitchen into the living room. And then I freeze. The person standing there by my phone is not Rachel. Or Mike. The person standing in my apartment is not anyone I have ever seen before in my life. He looks as surprised as I am. For a split second we both simply stare. Asian, ponytail, casually dressed but his hands are gloved. And then he runs.

"Hey!" My legs finally move just as the door slams behind him. "What the hell?"

Jerking the door open, I rush into the hall in time to see him disappear down the stairwell. I shout, then go sprinting after him, but my apartment is only four flights up; within seconds I hear him race across the lobby below me and out the main door. Charged with adrenaline, I ricochet down the stairwell, leap off the last stair, and go skidding across the lobby to the main door. Out on the street I turn left and right. Parked cars by the curb; an empty sidewalk. The guy is gone. I jog up a block toward Jolimont. No sign of him. Eventually I stop, my hands resting on my hips as I lift my head and suck in air.

"Son of a bitch," I say, breathless.

Turning back toward my apartment, I try to hold the memory. Five ten. A hundred and fifty pounds, a hundred and sixty tops. Early thirties.

Just ahead, Mike eases my car up to the curb. He rolls down the window. I turn my head to him, addressing him as I walk by.

"I've just had an intruder."

"What?"

"Upstairs."

Mike's face falls.

By the time he joins me up in the apartment, I've checked my wallet. It was lying where I always leave it, on the hall table. A hundred bucks cash, all my cards, still inside.

"You get a good look at the guy?" Mike asks, casting his glance around the room as he enters. My living room. Suddenly a crime scene.

Pocketing my wallet, I explain the circumstances of my brief confrontation with the intruder. Mike chews on his lip.

"Asian, you think."

I nod.

"Korean? Japanese?"

I hitch a shoulder. I really have no idea.

"So you're walking through there, out of the kitchen." Mike points. "And this guy's where?"

When I lift my chin in the general direction, Mike wanders over that way and I sit myself down. My legs have started to tremble. Breakfast, heavy in my gut, begins to burn.

"Rachel gone?" Mike inquires calmly.

"The guy came in a few minutes after she left. I even heard the damn door open. I thought it was her coming back for something."

Mike bends, inspecting the coffee table. "This ever happens again, don't go chasing the punk down the street."

"He broke into my goddamn apartment."

"You happen to notice if he was carrying a gun?"

The burning in my gut climbs into my chest. I shake my head and Mike continues his inspection.

Physical reaction to the shock and the sudden exertion have set in. I am perspiring freely now, my chest is tight. I go out to the kitchen and slug back a couple of glasses of water. Then I stand by the sink, brooding. Son of a bitch, I think. Goddamn son of a bitch. Five minutes earlier, it would have been Rachel instead of me who walked right into the guy. And if I wasn't here? Suddenly I am every hang-'em-high type you have ever seen ranting on daytime TV. An unbridled redneck, zealous in defense of territory and family. Goddamn son of a bitch. I go back to the living room.

"What was I meant to do, direct him to the door and wave goodbye?"

Mike has his hands on his hips, looking down.

"What do I do next time?" I ask. "Give him my wallet?"

"Your wallet ain't the problem here," says Mike quietly.

And then I see what he has seen. I stare down at my phone. It has been unplugged. The mouthpiece has been removed and the inner electronics exposed. Mike points a pencil at the little gray silicone square that lies on the polished mahogany table.

"Like the three at Toshio's?"

"At a guess," says Mike. He peers closely at the miniature miracle of electronics, then pins the silicone square on a pencil point and holds it up between us. The hair prickles on my neck. "Real question you wanna be asking yourself," he says, "was this thing on its way in when you disturbed the guy, or on its way out?"

I make a sound. We have to tell Patrick, I say.

Mike looks at me askance as he hands me the pencil. "I wouldn't be telling Patrick anything just yet." He rescrews the mouthpiece, repositions the phone on the table and plugs it in, then takes the pencil. He studies the silicone square awhile. He finally lifts his gaze. "At least not till we find out just how much that slippery fuck already knows."

14

PASCAL NYERI IS WAITING FOR ME OUTSIDE THE Portland Trust Bank, loitering between an enormous pair of Corinthian columns. He shakes my hand soberly.

"I have made the arrangements," he says, turning to signal through the closed glass doors.

His suit is gray flannel, a couple of sizes too large, and he looks down, fidgeting with the cuffs. Pascal is a worried young man. Career advancement in the Secretariat is too often a reward for keeping well clear of trouble, and Pascal knows he is far enough down the pecking order and deeply enough involved in this to be scapegoated for any kind of debacle. Patrick's failure to return his phone call yesterday was just a prelude. If the situation gets too much worse, Pascal could be the first man off the end of the plank. Now, as the giant glass doors open and we go in, I clap a hand encouragingly on his shoulder.

Inside, the bank looks like something from the Gilded Age. A high-vaulted ceiling and a dark marbled floor, the sound of our footsteps echoing across the cavernous space. Behind a counter of oak paneling the tellers are at their PCs, preparing for the day. But the man with whom Pascal has made the arrangements, a Mr. Dixon, is not in his usual place, and while Pascal wanders off to find him, I take a seat on a padded green leather bench. Dixon, I think. Then I take Toshio's calendar from my briefcase and find the half-remembered entry quickly, a morning appointment last Friday. Dixon, PTB, 10:30 A.M. Less than a week later, I have the morning appointment with Dixon. I close the calendar and slide it back into my briefcase. I have the morning appointment, I think, and Toshio Hatanaka is dead.

After a minute Pascal returns with Dixon, an old guy with a deep tan and improbably perfect white teeth. Dixon continues to smile as we cross the hall and descend the stairs to the archives.

"Mr. Hatanaka not coming today?" Dixon inquires over his shoulder.

Pascal reads my glance. Not today, he tells Dixon.

In the basement we are shown into a room that resembles a private library. Countless leather-bound books are arrayed on neatly aligned shelves around the walls, surrounding a broad table in the middle of the room with a row of green student lamps down its center. Pascal, familiar with the procedure, flips his briefcase open on the table. He hands Dixon a list of the paperwork we want to see and Dixon retreats through a rear door.

"Secure vault," Pascal remarks when he sees my eyes following Dixon. "Bank officers only."

While Pascal signs himself in at the visitors' ledger by the door, he explains that he hasn't ordered up every piece of paperwork that he went through with Toshio. "But what I have asked for, it will show you how the fraud occurred. And I have brought some other papers." He indicates his briefcase.

"What if I want to see something else?"

"Ask. I will have Dixon bring it."

I look around. "Did Toshio spend much time down here?"

"He came with me five or six times. One, maybe two hours each visit."

"How long was the investigation running?"

"Toshio became involved in July."

"No, I mean right back from the start."

Pascal considers. "The auditors queried a Special Committee payment in May. That is when they called me. By the end of June we knew there was a problem."

"We?"

"Internal Oversight."

"By the end of June," I say, lowering my brow. And he knows what I am thinking. By the end of June, under the regular Secretariat procedures, I should have been informed.

"It was not my decision." Coming back to the table, he gestures to the ledger. I will have to sign myself in. "It was between Mr. Rasmussen and Mr. O'Conner," Pascal says. "If you were not told, that was their decision."

The enormous visitors' ledger rests on a pulpitlike stand; after printing my name, place of work, then signing, I fold my arms and lean against the open pages. "From the end of June till now, Patrick and your Oversight colleagues were the only ones in on this?"

"And Toshio."

"What about the audit guys?"

"After they gave it to me, their work was finished. They did not want to know if they had found a real problem or if it was a mistake. They think that is our job."

"They must have wondered."

Pascal shrugs. If the audit people are still concerned, he tells me, they have not mentioned it to him. That figures, I guess. A kind of battle-fatigue apathy is the UN bureaucrat's usual response to the endless burdens dropped on him from on high. There is no reason for this to have been treated any differently from the thousand and one other problems dumped on Audit daily.

"Did Patrick come down here when he knew?"

"At first nobody came. Only me. I am not sure Mr. O'Conner believed there was a fraud. It was August before Toshio came down here. Mr. O'Conner, never."

Mr. O'Conner. Plain Toshio. A clear indication as to how each man is, and was, regarded by Secretariat sherpas like Pascal. I remark that Patrick must have been kept informed.

"A weekly memo. That is what he wanted."

Pascal hauls a stack of paperwork from his briefcase, and I suggest to him that we get started before Dixon returns. He switches on the nearest lamp, takes out his pen, and we begin.

Right from the start I am in trouble. Numbers. In columns, across rows, down pages. Reams of them. Payments and invoices, accounts being opened and closed. It is like one of those terrible nightmares I had before my math SAT, a sense of being rigorously examined on a subject in which only my ignorance is profound. But to Pascal this stuff is second nature; he appears to have no idea how hard I am working just to keep up with what he is telling me. It is at least ten minutes before the dim outline of what has occurred finally shimmers into view like some mirage on a lonely desert horizon.

"So all these invoices," I say, laying a hand on the pile of slips Pascal has set to one side. "All these are bullshit?"

"Yes."

"No money changed hands?"

Pascal makes a face. To his consternation, I have still not grasped this at all. "The money changed hands. That is what was stolen. But what the Special Committee was paying for, 'management services,' that is the lie. The money was going out but paying for nothing."

The mirage seems to steady, become solid. "It's like a public service salary."

Smiling, Pascal directs me back to the paperwork. And listening to him, it occurs to me that he is our one piece of good fortune in this investigation so far. He cares. He wants to do this right. And it's not just because of the ramifications in his own career. I know that because I have seen him in action before.

Eighteen months ago we flew out to Cambodia on the same plane. I was standing in for Patrick, giving my blessing to some recent election results that our observers declared were relatively clean and free of violence. Pascal was going out to give evidence against Lok Nol, a local UN field agent who it turned out had been stealing UN vehicles and reporting them as destroyed by brigand remnants of the Khmer Rouge. With time on my hands, I went to watch Pascal lay out his extensive dossier of evidence before the Cambodian judge. Pascal's presentation of the case was exemplary. Concise and direct. The judge, however, was belligerent from the outset; he treated the evidence with something like contempt. Lok Nol sat off to one side of the courtroom with his lawyer; throughout the hearing neither one of them said a word. When the judge pretended that the translation of Pascal's English into Cambodian left the case unclear, Pascal switched to French. We had both heard the judge speaking fluent French in the hall earlier, but now suddenly the judge's only French vocabulary was *non*. Knowing by then that the case was lost, Pascal nevertheless pressed on grimly. An hour later on the courtroom steps, Pascal and I stood and watched Lok Nol drive away in a brand-new Mercedes. That a judge can be bought was not a new lesson for Pascal. What hurt him, what actually made him flinch, was when the judge emerged from the courtroom, strolled past us down the steps, and casually tossed over his shoulder the word *nigre*.

Now Dixon reenters. The stack of files he is carrying is so heavy that he stoops. Pascal helps him unload the mountain of paperwork onto the table while I watch in despair. I simply cannot do this. When Pascal said that he would talk me through the paperwork, show me what Toshio's investigation was all about, I had no idea he intended this huge expedition through the numbers. My aim was to review the investigation, not relive it.

"How much of that is relevant, Pascal? Really essential."

Pascal sweeps his hand over the pile: all of it.

I shake my head. This is not going to work.

When Dixon seems about to settle himself at the far end of the table, I touch Pascal's sleeve. "Is he staying?"

"Security," Pascal whispers back. "While the bank documents are here, he must stay."

I look to Dixon, then back to Pascal. "We need another file," I say.

Dixon locks the files he has just brought into a wall safe, then goes to find the unnecessary paperwork that Pascal requests. When Dixon is gone, I tell Pascal, "I don't have two months to do this. I don't have the time to look through every file. Just keep it simple and tell me, in your own words, what you and Toshio found down here."

"You should see everything."

"I don't have the time."

An accountant, and schooled by Dieter in a kind of thoroughness the rest of us would call pedantry, Pascal cannot conceal his disappointment with my broad-brush approach. "I did a final memo for Toshio," he reluctantly volunteers, gesturing to his briefcase. "But it does not give you everything."

The memo, I say, will do just fine. He digs it out for me, three stapled pages, and I take a turn around the table, reading.

Though I have to pause a few times to ask Pascal for elucidation, the memo eventually yields up everything I really need to know. Those invoices Pascal has already talked me through are evidence of the fraud obtained from the paper trail within the UN. They gave Pascal the start he needed to track the destination of the payments. It seems the Special Committee held a perfectly legitimate account here at the Portland Trust Bank, but through a series of spurious "management services" payments, funds from the legitimate account have regularly been siphoned into a different account, designated BB7. And BB7 is the personal account of an unnamed private citizen.

I place the memo on the table. "So how much is in this BB7?"

"We cannot tell." Pascal nods to the invoices. "We know what went in from the Special Committee. It is possible other money went in too."

"So a few hundred thousand bucks at least. And maybe a whole lot more."

"Maybe less. We know the account is still open. But it is a private account, unconnected with the UN. We cannot look. The money could have been withdrawn."

"The account might be empty?"

"It is possible."

I ask him to show me the other documents mentioned in his memo, the ones directly implicating Asahaki as the guy responsible for the fraud. Pascal digs in his briefcase again.

"These are the copies." The originals, according to Pascal, are stored in a different vault across the street.

What Pascal hands me is incontrovertible, three letters authorizing release of UN funds for "management services" rendered to the Special Committee. All three letters are signed by B. Asahaki. Documentary evidence that the Japanese ambassador to the United Nations is a thief.

"Did Toshio confront Asahaki with this?"

"You should ask Mr. O'Conner. I gave Toshio my final memo. After that, Mr. O'Conner and Toshio decided what to do."

"Which was?"

Pascal lifts a shoulder. He does not know.

My eyes return to his memo, dated August 15. Three weeks ago the Secretariat had ample evidence upon which to act against Ambassador Asahaki—and did not act. This is not the situation that Patrick described to me on his departure from the Operations Room last night.

"I am sure that Toshio wanted to do something," Pascal says.

"And Patrick didn't?"

Pascal looks down at the table.

"I'm not going to hold you to it, Pascal. Come on, I need everything I can get. I'm just asking for your opinion."

"It is only an opinion."

I nod and wait.

"Toshio did not want Japan to get the Council seat. When I showed him this"—Pascal indicates the paperwork—"I knew he wanted something done immediately."

"But nothing happened?"

Pascal inclines his head.

"And you didn't like that either, but you stayed out of it," I say.

He nods again. No one's fool, Pascal was not about to step into whatever disagreement Toshio might have had with Patrick. I ask him if Toshio ever mentioned why he thought Patrick was dragging his feet.

Pascal shakes his head no.

I pause a moment. Pascal looks very uncomfortable now. Telling tales against the Undersecretary-General for Legal Affairs is definitely not how he intended this visit to go.

"Did Toshio ever give you any indication he thought he was under surveillance?"

Pascal's head rocks back.

No? I prompt.

"What surveillance?"

His evident surprise is all the answer I need. Waving his question aside, I remark that Toshio's failure to disclose what he knew about Asahaki seems somewhat surprising. If he was getting no satisfaction from Patrick, why not tell me? Or why not go public? Toshio wasn't known for allowing his voice to be smothered by higher powers in the Secretariat, not even by guys as far up the totem pole as Patrick.

Pascal concurs.

"Then why didn't he do that?" I wonder out loud.

Pascal speculates that it might have something to do with the family trouble Toshio was having. "He has a cousin in the hospital in San Diego," he explains. "Toshio went to see her last week. After he came back I called him. He did not want to speak about Asahaki then."

I take a moment with that. "Can you recall exactly when he took this trip?"

Pascal reaches into his briefcase. "He canceled an appointment with me. It was the day he left." Consulting his calendar, he finds the canceled appointment and gives me the date. The same day the airline ticket stub gives for Toshio's departure for Switzerland. And Mike has confirmed with the airline that the trip took place, that the ticket was used.

"You're sure he went to San Diego?"

"He said so."

"Not Geneva?"

Pascal eyes me curiously. He clearly has not the slightest idea what I am talking about. Then Dixon returns with the unneeded file.

Another question occurs to me. "If you had everything three weeks ago, all this evidence, why did you and Toshio bother to come back here last Friday?"

Pascal frowns. "We did not."

I go to the visitors' ledger and flip back the pages to last Friday. Toshio's name and signature both appear in the middle of the page. There is no entry for Pascal Nyeri.

"Toshio came here?" says Pascal, turned in his chair now to face me.

I nod.

He knits his brow. "Why?" he says.

I turn to Dixon. "Would you be able to tell us what our colleague Mr. Hatanaka was looking at last Friday?"

Dixon comes over and directs my attention to the next page in the ledger. There are entries for files requested by each visitor listed on the previous page.

"These files are from the vaults here." He points to a dozen or so numbers. Then his finger moves on. "And these are from across the street."

Pascal joins us at the ledger, and the three of us stand contemplating the list of files Toshio requested Friday. Too many. More than twenty. I ask Pascal if he recognizes any particular file that Toshio might have needed to review.

"No. He never told me. He never said there was any more he wanted to see down here." He is puzzled, maybe even a little put out by Toshio's independent foray into the paperwork.

Whatever it is that has been going on here, endless hours spent wading through papers will not help us. Not me anyway. What I really need to do now is get back to the office, hand the departmental reins to Gunther Franks, then go and see Mike. Maybe he can figure out who has been lying to whom, and why. Alone, I really have no chance.

When I turn back to Pascal, his eyes remain fixed on the ledger. Our visit to the bank, our excursion into the paperwork, has not worked out as he might have hoped. He has not been able to extricate himself from the whole affair, to distance himself from the swelling whirlpool of trouble.

"He should have called me," he says like a man unjustly condemned.

I decide it can wait till we're back at Turtle Bay before I break the news to him that I want him to go through Toshio's office drawer by drawer, file by file; that I am relying on him absolutely for some brilliant insight into what the hell has been going on. For now I just instruct him to make a note of everything Toshio requested Friday. Then I lay a hand on his shoulder.

"Some connection might occur to you later," I say.

15

T HE UNITED NATIONS SECURITY COUNCIL IS IN PERMANENT session; this is an obligation decreed by the Charter. The permanent five plus the ten nations elected for two-year terms by the General Assembly must each have a representative present at UNHQ at all times, ready to attend the Council Chamber. So when Patrick sticks his head in at my door and says "Look sharp. Lady Nicola's called the Council in," what he means is that these fifteen are about to converge on the chamber. "She wants you down there," he adds, withdrawing his head.

"Why?"

Patrick's face reappears. "Well, I doubt she needs your advice on a nuclear strike." He slaps the door frame. "Come on. Something's going on with this Hatanaka business."

Grabbing my jacket, I shoot some final instructions to Gunther Franks, who sits at my desk, taking notes. Then I hurry after Patrick down the hall.

Mike has asked me not to mention the morning drama at my apartment to Patrick. In fact, he wanted me to steer clear of Patrick till he'd had a chance to check with his own boss, Eckhardt, about any operation UN Extra Security might have in hand that Mike is unaware of. So I have spent my first quarter hour at work sequestered in my office with Gunther, bringing him up to speed on my appointments and the problems he will have to handle while I am off playing prosecuting attorney in the investigation of Toshio's murder. Mostly management hassles, dealing with the heads of the various Legal Affairs departments, and ensuring that their regular battles for turf don't flare into open warfare in my absence. Gunther has worked in nearly all the departments at one time or another. He knows the sensitivities and personalities involved; he should cope.

Patrick gives an impatient flick of his hand when I tell him that Gunther Franks will be filling in for me. "Whatever. Just make sure he's not on my back every ten bloody minutes, wanting instructions. Keep an eye on him."

I bite my tongue. I withhold the cheap sarcasm about all the free time I've got for purposeless supervision.

"So what do we know?" Patrick asks me. "What's new?"

"We've got another face from the security tapes, someone Toshio was talking to at the NGO reception. Suzi Yomoto."

The name means nothing to Patrick.

"Japanese," I tell him. "Mike's getting me a blow-up from the tapes. She'll be at some protest uptown later."

"You're thinking about that note you found at Hatanaka's apartment."

When I incline my head, Patrick nods. I might have something here. I do not tell him that I have not yet discounted the possibility that the note is Asahaki's. Instead, I mention my visit to the Portland Trust Bank, the fact that Toshio does not appear to have been completely open with Oversight.

"Toshio lied to Pascal about that trip he took to Geneva last week. As far as Pascal knew, Toshio was out in California."

"Hatanaka didn't have to report his movements to every prick in the building." Patrick shrugs it off. "It was a UNDCP committee he was investigating. So maybe he went to Switzerland to check it out with their people there. Who knows? He didn't have to tell the world."

I remind Patrick of something I am sure he already knows: The UN Drug Control Program is headquartered in Vienna. Vienna, Austria, not Switzerland. He shrugs again.

"Nothing else?" he says, referring to my investigation in general.

Nothing, I tell him. But I'm thinking of the bugs, my intruder, and Mike's injunction to silence.

Our journey down through the Secretariat building and across to the Council Chamber is punctuated with bursts of instructions from Patrick on what I am and am not authorized to disclose to the Security Council. After five minutes we are approaching the chamber doors and he has still not addressed the big question.

"What have we heard on Ambassador Asahaki?" I ask at last.

"Unless you're asked directly, don't mention him."

"And if I am?"

"Asahaki's gone back to get instructions from the Jap Foreign Ministry. The truth," he says.

I look at him. That is not the truth. And I very much doubt that the Security Council will buy it.

"What do you want, Sam, a script? They'll ask some questions about what's happening generally. They won't get into specifics unless you lead them."

"And you don't want me to do that."

"That's the message."

Down on the floor of the main chamber a few Secretariat stenographers and clerks are setting up at the horseshoe table where the fifteen Security Council ambassadors and their seconds will sit. There are more chairs behind for advisers. Rows of seats rise and fan out from the table like theater seating. Behind the table a giant mural is fixed to the wall: a darkly abstract representation of the phoenix rising from the ashes of war.

There is a scattering of early-arriving delegates in the Public Gallery; two Africans laugh and call to each other across the empty seats as we go by. The General Assembly and the main committees won't be commencing their work for at least an hour; these guys must have heard word of trouble afoot and come along for the show. There will not, of course, be much to see. In the public arena of the main chamber it is not the real workings of international relations that are on view, merely the PR facade. A parallel universe where nations are not motivated by self-interest, where jealousy and wounded pride do not figure. In this PR projection of our world, sweet reasonableness is the defining tone. Statements are read calmly, for the record. Contrary views are presented. The president of the Council calls for a vote, and the vote is made. You would never know that during the preceding hours, in the smoke-filled side chamber, these same ambassadors were conniving, lying, hurling abuse, and getting lowdown and dirty in the never-ending battle not to emerge the dejected screwee.

"Side chamber," Patrick mutters, and I feel my heartbeat flutter as we descend the stairs through the main chamber.

The Security Council side chamber. In the course of my UN career I have not once been summoned to the place. I have been consulted by Patrick on points of international law, advised him on advice he has subsequently given to the SG down there during various crises. I have even assisted with the preparation of draft resolutions and suggested wordings for compromise statements, but no one has ever thought it necessary to request my presence in the holy of holies.

Reaching the floor of the main chamber now, I notice two senior members of the Japanese delegation sitting in the "interested parties" section. This area is set aside for nations and NGOs directly concerned with the issue currently under consideration by the Council. The two Japanese whisper to each other when they see us pass.

"Did you see them?" I ask Patrick as we leave the main chamber.

"I saw."

"Asahaki's two and three man."

Patrick's mouth is tight. The presence of those two indicates that there will definitely be questions raised in the side chamber about Asahaki.

"Play it straight," he advises. "If it gets rough, I'll step in. Save your ass."

I shoot a glance at him. He will save my ass, the guy who has put me directly in the firing line. Striding on, he nods to the guard at the side-chamber door. The guard leans inside and announces us, and the next moment I am standing at Patrick's side, facing Lady Nicola down the length of a long, narrow table. The room is windowless and surprisingly small. Paneled with mahogany veneer, no pictures on the wall. Here we are, I think distinctly. Here I am.

"Samuel Windrush," says Lady Nicola, opening a hand in my direction by way of introducing me to her colleagues, "is running the investigation into Special Envoy Hatanaka's death."

I take a second with the faces down either side of the table. The French ambassador, Froissart. The Russian, Gradavitch. Chou En, the Chinese ambassador, and Bruckner from the U.S. Just the Big Five. Each ambassador has brought along one sidekick: Ambassador Bruckner, his chief legal counsel, Jennifer Dale. My heart is pumping hard now. Jennifer meets my glance briefly, then leans back and doodles on her pad. Beside me, Patrick promptly claims the single spare chair and I am left standing, for all the world like a man about to be judged. Lady Nicola smiles pleasantly.

"Mr. O'Conner has explained to you that the Secretary-General wishes all of us here fully informed?"

"Within the remit of the Charter," Patrick cuts in. An unsubtle warning to me. Don't let them railroad you.

Lady Nicola doesn't miss a beat. "Perhaps if you would outline the position for us, Samuel. Tell us where you are."

Right to it. No messing around. So I do as she asks; within the constraints laid down by Patrick, I summarize the events of yesterday as well as I can. A lightly edited version, from the discovery of Toshio's body till now. The one truly awkward moment comes when

Jennifer wonders aloud why the U.S. authorities weren't informed before Mike and I visited Toshio's apartment. On U.S. territory, she reminds me pointedly. Confessing to my misjudgment, the press of time, I move right on to conclude my summary. Though my performance really does not seem too bad to me, by the time I'm done, Lady Nicola has long since ceased to smile. Like the rest of them, she is visibly unimpressed with my report. An uncomfortable silence ensues. When I look down the two rows of faces, Jennifer is doodling in her pad again. Her boss, Ambassador Bruckner, finally speaks.

"Ambassador Asahaki left last night. Do you have any idea why?"

Great, I think. Question number one. I glance at Patrick, but he is staring into space.

"We were told he was recalled by the Japanese Foreign Ministry," I say. "For discussions."

"On what?"

"We weren't told."

"I understand you wanted to speak to him."

Where did Bruckner get that? I wonder. The Japanese delegation? "I would have liked to. Sure."

"Why?"

I turn to Patrick and let my glance linger. Lady Nicola takes the hint.

"Mr. O'Conner?"

"There was some question about misappropriated UN funds," he admits. "It turns out Hatanaka was looking in to it with Oversight." It turns out. This is vintage Patrick O'Conner. Depending on how this thing breaks, he will claim as much or as little foreknowledge as he pleases. If it turns into an even worse disaster than Patrick clearly fears, Pascal Nyeri will be left to carry the can.

"And what would that have to do with Ambassador Asahaki?" Lady Nicola asks.

"It turns out," says Patrick, "Ambassador Asahaki was one of those Hatanaka was investigating."

James Bruckner drops his head into his hands. "For chrissake," he says loud enough for everyone to hear.

The other ambassadors confer with their assistants, no one bothering to whisper.

"Hatanaka was investigating Ambassador Asahaki, so Asahaki bumped him off?" Bruckner asks now in disbelief. He looks down the table at Patrick. And Patrick, the son of a bitch, gestures to me.

"We have to consider all the possibilities," I venture finally.

"All the what?" Bruckner's voice is suddenly full of scorn; he is furious at what he is hearing. Something the Japanese have withheld from him. Two days from the most important General Assembly vote in decades, his own political reputation riding on a Yes vote, and I have inadvertently driven the chief campaigner for the Yes vote into exile. For no good reason that James Bruckner can see.

When Froissart attempts a question, Bruckner speaks right over him. "Show them the statement," he tells Jennifer, tossing his pen on the table, pushing back in his chair. "All the goddamn possibilities," he mutters to himself, rubbing his forehead.

Jennifer hands Patrick and me copies of the statement. It is from the Japanese Foreign Ministry, two brief paragraphs. The first paragraph protests Ambassador Asahaki's treatment at the hands of the Secretariat; my name, incredibly, is mentioned as Asahaki's chief persecutor. But the second paragraph is worse, a bald declaration of Japan's intention to revive their dormant territorial claim over the Spratly Islands, an uninhabited archipelago in the South China Sea. A claim no one has heard since the Second World War.

I reread the statement, shaking my head.

"I take it you're familiar with the Spratlys," Bruckner remarks acidly.

I look up at him, then return my eyes to the statement. Every freshman in every international law faculty in the world is familiar with the Spratly Islands; the archipelago is a standard case study of territorial disputes. It has been under claim by China, Taiwan, Malaysia, Vietnam, and others for decades, everyone hoping for an offshore oil bonanza in some indeterminate future. The dispute gets airtime at the occasional UN-sponsored conference, but in recent years it has slipped off the main agenda, just one more unsolvable problem in a world that has thousands of more immediately pressing concerns. The threat here from the Japanese, though not directly stated, is clear: Either we ease up on Asahaki or they will throw a match into the international tinderbox that is the Spratly Islands.

"Something there you don't understand?" says Bruckner.

"They're blaming me?" I look up again. "For what?"

Lemtov, the Russian number-two man, the guy who sat on the UNDCP Special Committee with Asahaki and Wang Po Lin, speaks up. "The Japanese have not been pleased with your treatment of Ambassador Asahaki."

"We never even had the chance to question him," I protest. "I hardly spoke to the man."

"You refused to give him Hatanaka's body," Bruckner says.

Confirmation, if I still needed it, that he is getting his information directly from the Japanese delegation.

"We couldn't surrender the body. The request was out of line. And they haven't dragged up this claim on the Spratlys just because of that."

"What evidence do you have that Ambassador Asahaki was in any way involved in Hatanaka's death?" Lady Nicola asks me.

"Look, no one's accusing him of that," I tell her somewhat ingenuously. "Internal Oversight has found some accounting anomalies involving Ambassador Asahaki. Toshio was assisting Oversight, helping them look in to that. If Ambassador Asahaki wants to come back here and answer some questions, no one's going to be happier than me."

Froissart, the French ambassador, points an unlit cigarette in my direction. "If you do not insist on questioning Ambassador Asahaki, the Japanese will not press this claim on the Spratlys. You understand that?"

An unnecessary crossing of t's and dotting of i's. In some embarrassment, Lady Nicola drops her gaze to her notes.

Yes, I tell Froissart. I understand.

"But you continue to insist?"

"Yes."

He looks at me as if I am an imbecile. And then the condescending asshole actually begins to lecture me. The Spratlys, of course, are not really the issue here, and Froissart does not pretend that they are. It is Thursday's vote that is causing the ulcers, and Froissart hammers the well-rehearsed arguments hard, as if he believes an aggressive assertion of the perm five's position will somehow persuade me to relent, persuade me to give Ambassador Asahaki a clean bill of health so that Asahaki can return to Turtle Bay and do the necessary final lobbying for the Japanese seat. Froissart elaborates grandly, but the essence of the Yes case is simple: Japan must be given a place in the international political arena commensurate with its economic stature. "You must see," Froissart says several times in the course of the oration, as if he is addressing an idiot. "You see it?"

This lecture, frankly, would be much easier to stomach from any other one of the ambassadors present. The U.S. has never made a secret of its support for a Japanese seat; Kissinger was pushing for it as long ago as the seventies. And though the Russians and Chinese have not been as active as the U.S. in promoting the Japanese cause, both Gradavitch and Chou En have been instrumental in keeping the spoilers back in Moscow and Beijing in check. And Lady Nicola would not think of talking to me in this hectoring tone in the first place.

But Froissart is a lot like his country: a little dog with a big yap.

Until last year, France was adamantly opposed to any change in the Council's composition. Fearing the inevitable long-term diminution in their own power, they instinctively blocked every recommendation put forward for reform. The old world order, ossified into place by the UN Charter, has always suited France just fine. It was Bruckner who finally managed to convince the French of the necessity for change—a monumental achievement, and part of the reason that Jennifer signed up with him when Bruckner asked her. Anyone who can move the French, she has told me not altogether jokingly, must have more than enough political smarts for a successful gubernatorial campaign. Thankfully Froissart now concludes his harangue before I become riled enough to break in and say something regrettable.

Then Lady Nicola addresses me.

"I'd like to inform the Japanese that the Secretariat won't interfere with Ambassador Asahaki in any way should he wish to return here immediately. Does that seem fair?"

"Sure."

She smiles.

"Provided," I say, "he answers the questions we need to ask him."

Instantly Lady Nicola's smile evaporates.

"Toshio's been murdered," I tell them. "The very least he's owed is a proper investigation. And I mean to give him that."

The eyes around the table are all on me now. I hold Lady Nicola's gaze.

"Then would it be too much to expect the perm five to be fully informed and consulted on the progress of your investigation?" she asks curtly.

"No problem," Patrick assures her.

My head swivels. No problem? These people have no interest in discovering the truth; it is blindingly obvious that their sole concern is a smooth passage onto the Security Council for the Japanese. Yesterday I flatly refused Lady Nicola's overture on behalf of the perm five, and now Patrick has committed me to consult with them. No goddamn problem?

But before I can voice my dissent, Patrick is on his feet, nodding reassurances all around. He looks stoical enough, but I am sure he is raging. Furious at me for not rolling with Lady Nicola and Froissart's suggestion, for not dropping Asahaki from my investigation. Somewhat frostily Lady Nicola thanks me for my time, then she signals Patrick over to her side for a private word. Conversation and argument break out across the table; they appear to have forgotten my presence already. Now that they're done with me, I am invisible. But as I move to the door, Jennifer rises, file in hand, and comes over.

"Ms. Dale?"

My tone is caustic. I make no attempt to disguise how angry I am. The first time I am called into the side chamber and it is not legal advice they want from me but a whitewash. Their one big hope, it seems, was that I would do the diplomatic thing, roll over and play dead while Asahaki returned unquestioned to secure the Japanese their seat. She doesn't bat an eye. Opening her file, she invites me to peruse a blank page.

"Do you expect your investigation might take you outside UNHQ again?" she says, her voice low.

"Possibly."

"Likely, isn't it?"

I look up at her and wait.

"We're willing to bypass the Headquarters Committee," she offers. We. The U.S. State Department. Relations between UNHQ and the host nation, the U.S., are overseen by the Headquarters Committee, a notoriously bureaucratic body. One legendary dispute over a parking fine rumbled on in this committee for two years before the malefactor inadvertently cut the Gordian knot by getting himself killed on a peacekeeping mission to Bosnia. There is nothing I would like better than to bypass this committee. "If the Secretariat's agreeable," Jennifer adds.

"What's the catch?"

She doesn't bother to deny that there is one. The Council side chamber is not a place where people do favors from the simple kindness of their hearts.

"You report your actions direct to my office. To me. If we have any problem with what you're doing, I'll take it up direct with you."

"No State Department committee? Just you?"

"Just me."

Now I see it. The U.S. jumping on their perm five colleagues. Jennifer would have a feeler extended into any part of the investigation that occurs on U.S. territory. She is pushing against Article 100, my responsibility to remain impartial. Above influence. Then again, I won't have to deal with that god-awful committee. Glancing over Jennifer's shoulder, I see Lady Nicola and Patrick deep in discussion. Gradavitch, the Russian ambassador, is jabbing a finger in the air, emphasizing some point to Froissart across the table, while the Chinese are conferring between themselves. Bruckner, who has undoubtedly put Jennifer up to making me this offer, is reexamining the Japanese statement.

"All right, no committee," I agree. Then I lean closer. "But this arrangement doesn't change what I said last night. In fact, it goes double. Okay?"

"If that's how you want it."

"That's how I want it."

She nods to herself.

"You knew he was gone last night," she says then, referring to Asahaki, to our ill-advised rendezvous at the Waldorf.

"Yeah, I knew he was gone," I say. "And you lied to me."

I close the file in her hand sharply. She studies me a moment before reaching past me to open the side-chamber door. As I exit, she leans toward me.

"Your choice, Sam. From here on in, you're on your own."

16

THE GUN FROM TOSHIO'S APARTMENT HAS NO FIRING PIN.
"Kind of restores your faith in human nature," Mike remarks
dryly as he hands the gun across his desk for my inspection. He
points out where the missing firing pin should be. "Guy from Barney
and Hunt's, the gun place, he called soon as I got in this morning.
He says he remembers the sale. The customer asked for a replica. He
says the guy settled for a secondhand real one when they told him
the thing couldn't fire."

"The ammo?"

"Get this. They're telling me they always throw in a couple of free
shells every sale. For luck."

I ask him if Toshio told them why he wanted the gun.

"He wanted a replica," Mike corrects me. "Guy at the gun shop
says he got the idea Hatanaka needed to show someone he wasn't
gonna be messed with. But that was it. Just show."

I place the gun on Mike's desk and we both consider it awhile.

"The betting's gotta be someone like Asahaki," he says. "Or whoever it was bugged Hatanaka's apartment."

"That could have been someone working for Asahaki."

"Could have been," Mike agrees without conviction. He picks up
the gun and turns it over in his hand. "What's for sure is Hatanaka
was spooked. Not spooked enough to do something smart like get
himself a real gun, maybe telling Security what was going on. But he
was worried, all right. Worried enough to go and get himself this
useless piece of shit."

Mike drops the gun into his desk drawer and shoves the drawer
closed. But unlike Mike, I find myself strangely heartened by this

turn. I am relieved to have Toshio's pacifist credentials reestablished: The man I knew is once again the man I knew.

Going out to the hall, we discuss the bugs, our voices low. Mike has not gotten hold of Eckhardt yet, and he looks pained when I tell him that I have been unable to avoid Patrick. When I mention my visit to the bank with Pascal, and Toshio's lone inspection of the bank paperwork, Mike asks a few questions, then returns to the subject of Patrick and the bugs. This preoccupation with Patrick is starting to worry me. I wonder if personal antipathy isn't beginning to distort Mike's judgment. Besides, I have had time to reconsider Mike's verdict on the intruder.

"You said the guy must have seen you going down to my car," I remind him now. "That the guy must have thought you were me, that's why he broke in after you drove off."

"Okay."

"So how does that square with any involvement from Patrick? Anyone working with Extra Security would know what you look like. And someone doing it for Patrick would have a description of me."

"Hey, don't flatter yourself. I ain't no oil painting, Sam, but from across the street, you and me, we're just two middle-aged guys in suits. Guy on the stakeout looks away, looks back, Windrush's car's moving. What's he gonna think? Joyrider?"

"Why would Patrick want to bug my place?"

Mike smiles to himself. "Funny thing. You never asked that about the bugs at Hatanaka's."

We walk on in silence. At the door of the Surveillance Room I catch Mike's arm. "I have to tell Patrick sometime."

"Sure." He disengages my hand. "Sometime later," he says, and turns in to the room. He comes out after a moment with a six-by-nine blowup, the still he has promised me from Monday night's surveillance tape. "Here's your girl." He hands me the picture. As we move down the hall again, I study the black-and-white headshot.

Suzi Yomoto. She is not a girl but a woman, late twenties, I would guess. The pose is odd, her head tilted back, her mouth open and possibly laughing, but it's really quite hard to tell. Her black hair is cut into straight bangs and shaped around her elfin face. Her face is colored a ghostly white. Some kind of makeup, maybe powder. Her eyebrows are two slashes of black, more heavy makeup, and her lips are if anything a shade or two darker. A nightclubbing sprite. Not the kind of look you see too often here at UNHQ. I glance up at Mike.

"Twenty-four-carat fucking kook," he says. "You wanna go see her, take Weyland."

Weyland, the big guard, the ex-cop Mike trusts. I remark that I am probably capable of handling a hundred-pound woman all by myself. Mike takes a folded page from his inner jacket pocket and hands it to me. A long list. I read two lines. Alleged assault. Resisting arrest. Then I look up at Mike curiously.

"Suzi Yomoto's rap sheet." He points at me and veers away toward Eckhardt's office. "Take Weyland," he says.

———

The protesters have gathered outside the Waldorf-Astoria. They look like the usual cross-section of NGO activists: concerned senior citizens and college students skipping their politics classes for a morning's entertainment, just regular folk. A cluster of maybe a dozen stand near the entrance, while most of the others loiter back along the sidewalk, gathered in small groups, talking. An old man in a camouflage jacket is moving among them, handing out sandwiches from a box. The demonstration hasn't started yet; the placards denouncing the U.S. and the Security Council are propped against the hotel wall or lying on the ground.

"Worse kind," remarks Weyland, handing me back Suzi Yomoto's picture and the rap sheet he has been perusing. "But a face like that, one thing for sure, only a blind man gonna miss her."

I slide the paperwork into my pocket, then we get out of the cab and walk over toward the Waldorf. I have had time to look through the rap sheet properly and I have come to pretty much the same conclusion as Weyland: Suzi Yomoto is the very worst kind of trouble. In the past five years she has been arrested in five different states, most frequently California, although the Washington, D.C., and New York police holding cells have seen more than their fair share of her too. The pattern of arrests has a certain monotonous regularity. Suzi has what you might call a modus operandi, a firmly established pattern of behavior that is designed to cause maximum inconvenience to everyone else without landing herself in a real jail. You would not find her protesting the closure of a local public library. She goes—as her kind always does—for the big ones. World trade. Defense and armaments. World peace. Her method is to place herself in the front line of any march, the front row of any sit-in, then join in any action short of violence to provoke her own arrest. Nominally she has some connection with Greenpeace, but I would guess she is on some more personal crusade. That would fit with what Juan told me about her last night. A rich lady with time on her hands, searching for a cause.

Now I wander down the sidewalk with Weyland, scanning the faces. No luck. When we reach the cluster near the door, the ring-leaders, I step right up and ask about Suzi Yomoto. Weyland's uniform draws some attention, but when they see he's UN and not a cop, they loosen up enough to ask me who's asking. So I tell them who, the deputy to the Undersecretary-General for Legal Affairs.

"She'll be along shortly, five minutes," some guy tells me. He has wire-rim glasses, a full red beard, and a Greenpeace sticker on the lapel of his coat. "She's bringing the coffin," he says. "What's the problem?"

Ignoring his question, I ask one of my own: What coffin?

The guy looks faintly embarrassed as he explains. The coffin is just a prop, a bit of street theater for the TV cameras to focus on. It is meant to symbolize, so he tells us, the death of the new world order. "I mean, that's what's happening here, isn't it?" He waves a hand upward, presumably toward the suite of the U.S. ambassador to the UN.

But I am not here to debate the rights and wrongs of U.S. policy, so I simply ask him from which direction he expects the coffin to appear. When he nods southward, I set off with Weyland down toward Forty-ninth. Weyland suggests waiting, letting her come to us.

"She's coming with a coffin," I say. "You want to wait till she's sitting outside the Waldorf with that, the TV cameras all running, before we try to question her?"

Weyland sticks out his lower lip. He sees my point.

About a hundred yards down Park Avenue seems far enough; we stop and linger. Weyland goes and gets himself a hot dog from the stand, then comes and rests his back against the wall beside me. He is in his mid-fifties; his tightly matted head of curls is already gray. Like so many older guys in uniform, he has a careworn and sad-eyed look; it's as if he has seen a little more of the underside of life than he would care to remember. He chews on the hot dog and tilts his head back, enjoying the sun on his face. He is making the most of his unexpected excursion beyond the boundaries of UNHQ.

"Take you back to the good old days?" I inquire after a minute, just making talk.

"Not my beat." Weyland gestures with a finger up and down Park. "My beat, there weren't no good ol' days. Just a lot of no-hope gangbangers doing crime."

I ask him how long he was a cop.

"Nigh on fifteen years. Too long. Shoulda stayed in the marines, have my ass retired by now instead of standing here waiting for some freak with a coffin." He finishes the hot dog and brushes his hands together. "Make any kinda sense to you, that new-world-order blah?"

I tell him that the NGOs have been pushing their own proposals for a more comprehensive reform of the Security Council. The proposals have never made it to first base in any place that mattered.

"So they don't get what they're crying for, they just spit," Weyland remarks.

Not quite how the senior NGO people would see it, but I tell Weyland that he has the general idea. He shakes his head.

"Makes you kinda wonder how it's gonna be when they all grow up and take over the zoo."

Then his head swings south and I hear the same sound a moment later. A rhythm of voices above the traffic, a faint chant rising. The pedestrians going by us pick it up, heads begin to turn. After a few seconds the words of the chant become audible.

"Insecurity! Insecurity! Insecurity Council!"

Weyland turns to me, his eyelids droop.

The coffin comes bobbing and weaving toward us through the pedestrian traffic, carried by six pallbearers shoulder-high. The pallbearers are wearing black body stockings printed with X-ray-type skeletons, the features of their faces obscured by white greasepaint. Ahead of them three guys in long black cloaks carve a path for the coffin. One of them has a bullhorn; he walks by us now, leading the chant. A leaflet is shoved into my hand as I search the faces, afraid that we've missed her in the sidewalk crush.

"Back behind," says Weyland, nudging me.

And then I see her, ten yards behind the coffin, forcing leaflets on the indifferent citizens of New York. She is wearing a black cloak that reaches down to her ankles and her face looks just like it does in the still from the surveillance tapes: elfin, powder-white with black trimmings, and a wide-open mouth.

"Insecurity! Insecurity! Insecurity Council!"

She thrusts a leaflet into Weyland's hand as she goes by. I turn to walk beside her. She comes up to my shoulder; I have to stoop as I speak.

"Miss Yomoto, my name's Windrush. I'm from UN Legal Affairs. We've been trying to get hold of you regarding the NGO reception Monday night."

"From where?"

"UN Legal Affairs. The Secretariat."

She carries on handing out the leaflets.

"Do you mind if we just step aside a minute?"

"Ah-ha."

I turn aside but she does not follow me. When I catch up to her, she continues distributing the damn leaflets. By now there is a snow-drift of the things on the sidewalk; the Park Avenue pedestrians do not seem overly concerned with the proposed change in the Security Council's composition. I touch Suzi Yomoto's arm.

"I said, do you mind stepping aside?"

"Ah-ha," she says again.

So now I get it. A smart aleck.

"Miss Yomoto, this isn't a joke." I beckon Weyland; he steps up and walks beside me, giving the Yomoto woman a clear view of the uniform. "We didn't just happen to be passing. We came here to speak to you. And you could make this easier by stepping aside for a few minutes and talking to us."

She throws back her head and laughs and skips away from us. A kook, all right. But more than that, a real pain in the ass. Weyland nods up ahead to the Waldorf. A TV broadcast truck has pulled up at the curb; some guy is on the roof connecting the satellite dish. I walk on fast, catching up with Yomoto, who is now immediately be-hind the coffin. She pretends not to notice my arrival. The leaflets disappear from her hand like cards for a croupier, left and right. I bend and speak into her ear as we walk.

"Here's your choice, Miss Yomoto. You step aside with me now, or your friends up front will be hearing exactly how it is you fund your life of outrage."

She darts a surprised glance at me.

"Chemicals at the Hawaiian seaside. Should make some impres-sion, shall we see?"

I tap the nearest pallbearer on the shoulder. He turns awkwardly, still holding on to the coffin. And then Yomoto reacts. She stops in her tracks and watches the coffin move away from us toward the Waldorf. Then she turns to give me a mouthful, but before she can do that, Weyland wraps his huge hands around her biceps and ef-fortlessly guides her through the pedestrians into the relative privacy of a doorway.

"Get off!" She pulls away, rubbing her arm when Weyland re-leases her. He stands with his back to the sidewalk, penning her in the doorway. "Whatta you want?" she says. "So I was at the thing Monday, whatta you gonna do, arrest me? Who are you?"

I take out my wallet and show her my United Nations ID.

"So?" She looks up at me belligerently.

"Were you invited?"

"Yes."

"Who invited you?"

"It wasn't a personal invitation. Can I go now?"

"Why were you there?"

"Look, I was there, whatta you want? Everyone was there, a few of us gate-crashed the thing. I don't see that it's any big deal. What are you gonna do, send us a bill?"

"Who did you speak to?"

She laughs. Not the kook laugh but a real one, low and short. She leans out past Weyland and hands someone a leaflet. Weyland turns her back into the door.

"Miss Yomoto," I say, "if you can't be a little more cooperative, I'm not going to waste any more time. I'm going to talk to your friends, and they're going to know how your family makes its money. How you can afford to swan around to protests in the middle of the week and not worry about your job. I'm not saying this again. Who did you speak to?"

"I don't know." When I turn away, she clutches my arm. "No, I mean seriously, I don't know. It was full. I spoke to lots of people, I don't know who most of them were. NGOs. Secretariat people."

I look straight at her. "Special Envoy Hatanaka?"

She nods.

"What did you discuss?"

Her eyes go from me to Weyland. "He never asked me to leave," she says, referring to Toshio. She is still talking about the gate-crashing thing.

At the Waldorf the protest seems to be getting into its stride. The chanting is loud now, the placards raised, everyone joining in. The coffin is making its way up to the Waldorf entrance. I repeat my question.

"We didn't discuss anything," she says. "I just told him what I thought about all the refugees and things."

"You didn't discuss the vote on the Council seat?"

"Why would I?" She frowns. "He did Afghanistan, yeah?"

It takes me a second to understand. Suzi Yomoto is no Juan Martinez. She is so self-absorbed, so directed at her own personal mission that the real political game is totally outside her field of view. Toshio's campaign against the Japanese seat has quite simply passed her by. He did Afghanistan.

"How well did you know him?"

"I didn't. I just met him Monday night, we spoke for a couple of minutes, that's it."

"You were never at his apartment?"

She shakes her head. By now she really does seem perplexed by the questions. It could be a front, but I have an uneasy feeling that it isn't.

"Did you see where Toshio went when he left you?" I ask her. "Who he spoke to?"

She peers at me. "Hey, didn't you guys put out some statement saying he died of natural causes?"

Suddenly a siren sounds on the street; all three of us turn to see an NYPD van race by. It stops near the Waldorf and about a dozen armed cops pile out. In fact, they are more than just armed, they're wearing helmets and bulletproof vests. Half of them stay out with the placard-waving protesters, the other half go charging into the Waldorf lobby, where the coffin and its pallbearers have disappeared. Several wild-eyed youths run past, pulling kerchiefs up from their necks to cover their faces as they close on the Waldorf. The protest has evidently been more meticulously planned than it first seemed. The TV cameraman is going in after the cops and the coffin.

Yomoto dives out of the doorway. Before I can even react, Weyland has her by her cloak collar. He hauls her back and plants her against the door.

"You can get your ass busted later. Just now Mr. Windrush is talking to you."

She says something to him in Japanese; it does not sound too polite. Now I reach into my jacket pocket.

"Can you translate this for me, Miss Yomoto?"

I open the note we found in Toshio's mailbox. She glances down at the note, then back up.

"Are you trying to be funny?"

"Is it yours?"

She doesn't answer.

"You never left this at Toshio's apartment? You never had an appointment with him Monday night?"

She looks from Weyland back to me. She smirks. "You can't really be the best the UN's got."

"Listen—"

"Oh, screw off. I never knew Hatanaka. I was never at his apartment. And I never had any damn appointment with him Monday or any other damn day. Now, if you don't let me go, I'm going to report this as harassment." She looks at Weyland, her brow creasing. "What authority have you got here anyway?"

When I tell her I will be needing a handwriting sample from her, she flicks the note in my hand and laughs. More a hoot really.

"Could be tough. I don't write kanji. I can't read Japanese."

"You just said something in Japanese."

"Oh, I can swear in Japanese fine. I can even speak a little. But I can't read or write it." Her smile is smug. She realizes now just as I do that we have made a mistake here, that we have gotten the wrong person. She really did not know Toshio. The note is not hers. "And if you don't let me go now, I'm gonna call the cops."

I look down at my feet, then up at Weyland. His eyelids droop sadly. Finally I nod and he steps aside and Suzi Yomoto bolts out past us up the street. If she hurries, she might still be in time to get herself arrested.

17

JUST DOWN FROM THE SECURITY COUNCIL CHAMBER THERE is a room set aside for press conferences. A sterile gray space lined with chairs, it has a small podium up front and behind that a giant UN plaque decorating the wall. When I arrive, this room is packed, the chairs all taken, people standing crammed in the aisles, the journalists up front crouching to give the cameramen at the rear a clear view. And there are more than the usual journalists here. Senior figures from the Secretariat stand discreetly in the audience, most from Political Affairs, but these are far outnumbered by the General Assembly delegates who have abandoned the tedium of yet another plenary speech on the evils of capitalism and come down here to catch up on life in the real world. Lady Nicola, center stage on the podium, is fielding questions. My eyes sweep the room for Patrick. After the dead end with Suzi Yomoto, I simply cannot put this off any longer.

"I reiterate what I have already said," Lady Nicola says now. "This isn't a question that has been put to the Council."

"But it's true, isn't it," her inquisitor presses, "that Japan has revived its claim on the Spratlys?"

Oh, Lord, I think. Already. Word of the Japanese statement must have leaked. How long now before my own name gets a dishonorable and very public mention?

"Is it?" Lady Nicola lifts a brow in gentle mockery of the questioner. "Your contact with the Japanese prime minister would appear to be more intimate than mine," she tells him.

Normally this verbal backhander would be greeted with amusement by the assembled company of professional cynics. Today it does not go down well at all. Someone not far from me hisses softly.

I finally locate Patrick sitting to one side of the podium, a forefinger crooked over his chin, a study of intense thoughtfulness. But the crush of bodies is too thick for me to get to him without attracting attention, so I have to wait. And now the Tunku—the chairman of the UNHQ Committee, the guy who screwed up any chance of proper forensics down in the basement—gets to his feet. A general groan runs over the room. The Tunku smiles left and right, then proceeds to read from a prepared statement. Some people near the doors make their escape; evidently they have better things to do than listen to yet another state-of-the-world address from Tunku Rahman Kabir.

Unfortunately I really do need to see Patrick. So I steel myself.

The Tunku touches all the usual high spots: Zionism, neocolonialism, the exploitation of the poorer nations by what he refers to as "the grotesquely overdeveloped countries of the world." Then he departs from the prepared text to give us further reflections on various weighty matters of the day, till eventually a burly South African journalist intervenes, shouting at the Tunku to ask his question and sit down. This is greeted by applause. The Tunku's wrinkled face puckers.

"What is the truth of this matter, then?" he continues rhetorically. "I ask you. Is the General Assembly not the parliament of man? But we can see here what is the practice of unaccountable power in the Security Council, that the General Assembly is not informed of what is taking place not only in the world, but here"—he points theatrically at the floor—"yes, here in the United Nations itself, which, as we know, was established for the swords to be beaten into plowshares, as the saying goes, and to defeat the scourge of war."

"Mr. Ambassador—" Lady Nicola puts in wearily.

"Yes, yes." The Tunku flourishes a hand. "And so when is the General Assembly to be informed of what is being done in the matter of the death of the special envoy? And other such questions, such as why the General Assembly committee is not receiving proper cooperation from the Secretariat? And what is the true situation with Japanese intentions to the Spratlys, which every international legal expert has stated in black and white belong to Malaysia?" So concludes the Malaysian ambassador.

Across the room the journalists are talking to one another, some of them laughing openly at the Tunku's performance. Lady Nicola repeats the agreed public line on Toshio's death: assumed natural causes, all questions to the Secretariat. But the Tunku is not listening. His oration over, he is heading for the door, the Malaysian delegation trailing after him studying the carpet.

In the general shuffling of chairs I raise a hand and catch Patrick's eye. He tips his head left, to the exit.

"Bloody man," he says when I join him in the side corridor. He screws up his face at the memory of the Tunku's display.

Gesturing back to the room, I ask him why the press conference was called anyway. Publicity on this is surely the last thing we need.

"Journalists got wind of that note from the Japs," he tells me. "Bruckner wanted Lady Nicola to slap the whole thing down before it turned into a story."

"You think it worked?"

"Christ knows." He turns on his heel. "So what are you after? Come to explain what got into you down in the side chamber?"

My failure to bend to the Big Five, I see, still rankles. I tell him about the blank I have drawn with Suzi Yomoto: She did not leave the note at Toshio's apartment yesterday. And then I return to the subject of my early-morning visit to the Portland Trust Bank with Pascal. I am trying to get Patrick to give me some hint as to what was going on with him and Toshio. He hears me out in silence.

"Pascal doesn't know why Toshio went back there Friday," I conclude.

Patrick regards me from the corner of his eye. "You're still mad at me, aren't you? Just because Hatanaka was investigating this stuff and you weren't told."

"Pascal showed me all the evidence you had on Asahaki. And he told me when you had it too."

"So?" Patrick veers aside, disappearing into the john.

But I have no intention of letting him off the hook that easy. Going in after him, I stoop and check beneath the two stall doors. Both empty. Patrick unzips at the urinal.

"You had that stuff three weeks back, Patrick. It's not just that you didn't tell me. You sat on it. Deliberately kept it from me. You knew it was a fraud, and you sat on it to protect Asahaki's butt. And last night you told me there was nothing concrete against Asahaki, that you'd only just heard. You lied to me."

"That's one interpretation."

"You want the Japanese to get this seat. You want it so bad you don't care if I find anything, do you? Maybe you might even prefer that."

Patrick studies the wall above the urinal. Then, rezipping his fly, he informs me that I am going about this all wrong.

"Well, I'm open to suggestions."

"Look," he says, turning and stepping up to me. "You think I don't have enough worries without you jumping on my back? How about you get off your fucking high horse and get on with your job. Properly. How I tell you to. Can you do that?"

Our faces are inches apart. His aftershave smells like musk.

"You mean, now that I've got the blindfold off?"

His eyes narrow. Just do your job, he mutters, crossing to the basin, flicking a hand toward the door.

But I don't leave. I stand and watch him. At last he pauses, one hand resting on the soap dispenser button. He regards my reflection in the basin mirror. "So are you going to spit it out, what's really eating you?"

Mike will not like this, I think. Then I speak.

"The phones in Toshio's apartment were bugged. Our security people are missing some bugs of the same make. And this morning I had an intruder at my apartment. When I walked in on him, he was busy with my phone. Planting or removing the same kind of bug we found at Toshio's."

Patrick makes a sound.

"I just thought you should know that."

He sticks his tongue into his cheek, his color rising as he continues to consider me in the mirror. Then he rinses his hands and puts them under the dryer. When he finally faces me, his look is severe. "You went to Hatanaka's apartment yesterday. And you waited twenty-four hours to tell me it was bugged? And you had this intruder at your place, what, six hours ago? What did you think I meant when I told you to keep me posted?"

"I'm keeping you posted now."

"The fuck you are."

"Would you prefer I took all this to Lady Nicola?"

He lowers his brow.

"Or the Security Council?" I say.

"Don't play the smart ass. You had the rules from the start. Keep me informed. Instead of that, it turns out you've been dicking me around. You expect me to put up with that?" He points. "Now, just get yourself off Asahaki's case. You get back to heel."

I wince. Back to heel, as I recall, is a command that masters use with their wayward dogs. Most of my illusions about Patrick have long since dissolved, but this one—that he regards me as a colleague, that he genuinely respects my opinion—this one has always been a great consolation to me, a personal reward for Sisyphean labors. But now I wonder. The thousand times we have disagreed and subsequently reached what I thought was a mutual compromise, the flexibility I have shown—did he take these all along for signs of weakness? Back to heel. God, I am furious. With him. With me.

Turning my head, I back away toward the door. "If Ambassador Asahaki returns, the second he gets back, I'm going to question him. When you next speak to him, you might want to tell him that."

"Sam," Patrick says, his eyes widening as he realizes he has over-played his hand. "Sam!" he calls, but I take one more step back and nod stiffly as the door swings shut between us.

The journalists are pouring from the conference room down the hall, their session with Lady Nicola finally over. I skirt around them, seething. Back to heel. Back to goddamn heel.

"You did not ask Lady Nicola about the Special Committee."

Startled, I turn my head sharply. That journalist, Marie Lefebre, has fallen in step beside me. She taps her handbag.

"No microphone," she says, smiling.

We are well clear of the other journalists; no one has heard her mention the Special Committee.

"What questions were you expecting?" I ask.

"Oh, you could have asked, for example, if Mr. Hatanaka was doing an investigation into the Special Committee's activities."

I keep walking. I show no surprise. "Where'd you get that, Miss Lefebre?"

"Marie."

When I stop, she stops. "Where'd you get that, Marie?"

She waves a hand loosely. She gives me a phrase in French.

"If you're trying to get some half-baked story confirmed," I warn her, "try someone else."

"It is already confirmed."

"Sure it is."

"You do not believe me?"

I turn away, intent on extracting myself from this conversation. Then her next remark slams through me like a thousand volts.

"Now I need only the full information on the fraud," she says.

She nods good-bye and walks right on past me, going through the door that leads up to the press box in the Security Council chamber side wall. And I stand flatfooted a second. This I really and truly do not need now. If she broadcasts the story, whatever part of it she has, all hell is liable to break loose. Guys like the Tunku, with some justi-fication, will accuse the Secretariat of conspiracy to hide the truth. They will push for the General Assembly to override the Secretariat and take control of the investigation into Toshio's death, and if that happens, the whole thing will turn political. Any chance of actually finding out what occurred in the basement Monday night will disap-pear beneath a storm of paperwork, subcommittees, and bloc votes,

Toshio's death becoming just one more bargaining chip in the endless puerile games of the Assembly.

Christ.

By the time I catch up with Marie Lefebre, she is seated by the radio and TV consoles in the press box. The place is empty apart from her, all the screens are switched off. To my right, the long windows of smoked glass let in light from the Security Council main chamber, and glancing down there, I see a lone technician working away at the microphone cables. When I accidentally bump into one of the mounted TV cameras in the cramped space, Marie lifts her eyes from her desk. We look at each other.

"What fraud?" I say.

She rolls her eyes. I am going to have to do better than that.

"I can have Undersecretary-General O'Conner come and see you," I tell her, a somewhat crass attempt to bludgeon her with rank. "He might be able to clarify your position here for you."

"I understand my position."

"I'm not sure that you do."

She puts down her pen. "If you withdraw my UN accreditation, I will give what I know to a colleague. And because you have withdrawn my accreditation, my colleague will know what I say is the truth. Plus, he will accuse you of interfering with press freedom." She tilts her head, smiling pleasantly. She has me by the balls.

"I'd like you to hold your story."

"Yes?"

"I'm telling you to hold it. Whatever you have. Is that possible?" While she considers my request, an unhappy thought strikes me. "Does anyone else have it?"

"No." Instantly she corrects herself. "Yes." Laughing now, she crisscrosses her index fingers in the air. "Question number two, the answer is no. I think no one else has it. Question number one, if you can convince me to hold back the story? Maybe."

"You just said yes."

"Now I say maybe." She purses her lips, momentarily lost in a thought of her own. Then she reaches for a magazine at the far side of the console, her skirt riding up her stockinged legs. "This is the question you could ask me, Mr. Windrush—Samuel?"

I lift a shoulder: What she calls me is hardly the problem here.

"You could ask me," she says, "what you can do to help me."

"What I can do to help you?" I say.

Fixing me with a look that is almost feline, she hands me the magazine, the latest issue of *Time*. The Dalai Lama, robed in orange, is at prayer on the cover.

In a thoughtless stab at humor, I ask if she wants me to pray for her. Marie is not amused. Her eyes suddenly blaze, Joan of Arc in the twenty-first century. She snatches back the magazine.

"I have applied for a job there."

"*Time* magazine?"

"I am fed up with this." Her hand sweeps over the consoles, she does not have to explain. Radio, the third-class citizen of the media age. Audio journalists like Marie can never get the big interviews; the ambassadors who matter all insist on print or sound-bite TV. The job at *Time*, so Marie tells me now, is New York–based. She would be doing editorial on the European desk. She clearly covets the prospective job with every fiber of her journalistic being.

"And how is it I can help you exactly?"

"Special Envoy Hatanaka."

I nod. Still listening, I say.

"O'Conner's press release said natural causes," she goes on. "But he did not mention Hatanaka's investigation into the Special Committee. O'Conner did not say, I think, the full truth, the misappropriation of the Special Committee funds. I know there is a story here. It could be a big story."

"Would it be pointless to ask you how you came by this information? Which I am not, by the way, confirming."

"Here is my choice," says Marie, ignoring my question. "I report it today, what I know already. Then every journalist in New York will come here. I will have one minute of glory, then—poof." She makes an exploding gesture with her fingers. In that scenario, she means she will be merely one among hundreds, buried, as the UN regulars are always buried, by the big names sent in from outside: *The New York Times* and *The Washington Post*. *Time* magazine.

"Plan two?" I inquire.

"I wait for the whole story."

My eyes wander down to the copy of *Time*. I am beginning to get the picture here, what Marie Lefebre wants from me.

"When you've got the whole story, you give it to *Time*, they run a big splash on it, you're their new golden girl. They're so grateful, they offer you this great job you want." Glancing up, I ask, "Close?"

"You missed out where someone from Legal Affairs gives me the pieces of the story that I cannot find for myself."

"Ah."

"And also, if I have information that can help this person from Legal Affairs in his investigation of Hatanaka's death—"

"You'd be obliged to hand it over anyway. And who told you I had anything to do with the investigation?"

"This information I will share with him. But only if"—she raises a finger—"only if he gives me his word that I will have exclusively the full inside story when it is finished. And an interview."

"With me?"

"Of course."

"No chance."

She frowns in mock bad humor. She knows she can lighten up now; it has become obvious to both of us that I am going to have to agree to some kind of deal. Not just because I want everything I can get on Asahaki from any quarter I can get it. But because she has me over a barrel. I simply cannot risk Marie broadcasting whatever it is she has on the Special Committee. Or on Toshio's investigation. Or mine.

"Here's the offer," I say after giving it some thought. "You give me whatever you've got. You give it to me right now, then you leave this story alone. When this whole thing's cleared up—and it's cleared up when I say it is—I'll give you your exclusive. You can't quote me. No direct attribution. But you'll have enough to take your shot at *Time*. That's the deal. And it's nonnegotiable, so don't even ask."

She turns that over, then finally offers me her hand on the deal. But when I take her hand, I hold it firmly and look her dead in the eye.

"If you back out of this, if you broadcast one word before I give you the okay, I'll have your accreditation withdrawn. Then I'll speak to some friends in the State Department and they'll make sure any application you make for a green card gets turned down. Without that you won't be working at *Time* or anywhere else in the U.S. You'll be kicked out of the country. That's the deal."

She looks at me now as if reappraising what she sees. Her brassy front is shaken somewhat. She extracts her hand from mine. It is clear she did not enjoy my routine.

At that moment a door to the rear of the press box opens. Someone calls out, asking Marie if she is ready to go to lunch. I glance over. It is Mei Tan, Toshio's secretary. I look from her to Marie. Right, I think. Okay. Lunch. Just the girls. Marie's face now is a picture of annoyance and confusion. She tells Mei Tan to go on ahead. Mei Tan disappears. Then, reaching over the console, Marie begins fooling with some switches, unwrapping a large reel of tape.

"Your informant?" I venture.

"We have made the deal."

"If Mei Tan's all you've got—"

"She did not give me this." Touched in a sensitive place, her journalistic pride, Marie pulls a slip from her purse and slaps it down on the desk. A list of company names. Beside each name, a number. Some very large numbers, all with dollar signs in front.

I look up.

"American investments," Marie says, "made with the UN money stolen from the Special Committee."

My jaw slackens. I look down again. The numbers range from one hundred thousand dollars on up to a million. And there are more than a dozen companies on the list. Marie turns over the slip of paper. On this side there is just one company name, Jade Moon Enterprises, the number beside it one million dollars. And for Jade Moon, unlike the other companies, there is an address. When I remark on that, Marie tells me that Jade Moon is the sole company on the list that she has so far been able to trace.

I lay my finger on the street name. My brow flexes. "Chinatown?"

"Of course Chinatown. He would have many contacts there."

It takes me a few seconds, the meaning of her words creeping over me like a slow sea mist. The air becomes chilled; the light by which I have been guiding the undermanned ship of my investigation suddenly gutters low. There were three people on the UN Drug Control Program Special Committee. One of them was Chinese. I hang my head over the piece of paper. It is not the Japanese ambassador Marie is talking about here. These investments of the misappropriated UN funds were not made by Bunzo Asahaki.

Marie's hand brushes against mine. She lays a finger on Jade Moon's address down in Chinatown.

"Is there a better place," she asks simply, "for Wang Po Lin to invest the stolen money?"

18

M IKE IS WHISTLING "BLUE MOON" AS WE WALK out of the cop station down by Mott Street; he has been whistling it on and off
for nearly an hour.

"It's *jade* moon," I say, finally reaching the end of my rope.

He stops at the head of the steps. My car, illegally parked, is down
by the squad cars.

"The company," I tell him, pointing to the papers in his hands,
everything we have extracted from the local cops about Jade Moon
Enterprises. "The company's called Jade Moon. Jade's not blue," I
say. "Jade's green."

Mike looks at me blankly. Then, nodding to himself, he recommences his plaintive whistling and starts down the steps while I put a
hand to my eyes and rub gently, taking a quiet moment out.

Wang Po Lin, it seems, is not a name with which the precinct cops
here are at all acquainted. And after Mike's all-out friendly assault—
a quarter hour chewing the fat with the precinct captain about the
old days, ten minutes at the coffee machine slapping every uniformed back that came by, and a prairieful of bull dust to the ethnic
Chinese cops whom the captain ordered to speak with us—I am
pretty sure that these guys are not giving us the brush-off just because they are too lazy to check in their files. The name Wang Po Lin
genuinely rings no bells here.

More surprisingly, the name Jade Moon Enterprises sets no hearts
jumping either. From what they tell us, it's a long-established family
concern, a dry goods wholesaler and a movie theater, each place run
by one of a pair of twin brothers, the Kwoks, who are near retire-
ment age. Over the years there has been the occasional fracas at the

theater, but nothing to bring the SWAT team running, and the cops simply laughed when we raised the question of any Triad connection. So what goes on here? I wonder now. What, precisely, are we chasing?

When I ask Mike those same questions down in the car, he turns his head.

"Hey, don't believe everything you heard back there."

"I didn't. And what was all that crap you told them anyway? Since when did the Hong Kong police start knocking on your door for advice?"

"They bought it, didn't they?" he says, referring to how the local cops swallowed his improbable tale.

"They bought it because they couldn't believe a guy would be such a jackass that he'd go in there mouthing off like that if it wasn't true."

"Right." Mike hits the ignition and laughs. "What's your point?" As we pull out around the squad cars, he expounds on his theory about cops and their mistakes, why I shouldn't give up on Jade Moon Enterprises just yet. "Every station's the same. They all think they got their own precinct taped. Out on the street, things look like yesterday? Hey. No problem. We got the drop on it. One place I worked, guys bought their doughnuts from the same old fella every morning. A real character, you know. Black guy. Nobody notices he's selling more than just doughnuts till some unhappy customer goes in there one day flying and blows this guy's head clean off. I'm telling you, Sam. Cops are like everyone else. Most of the time they're just seeing what they saw yesterday."

I remark that it seems unlikely the Kwok brothers are masterminding an international criminal conspiracy from the back room of a dry goods wholesaler in Chinatown.

"Wait," Mike tells me. He says that we will see what we will see.

As we drive, he outlines our cover story, that we're doing a survey for the Bureau of Small Business. Only half listening, I browse through the paperwork the local cops have given us on Jade Moon. There isn't anything to hold my attention, and after a minute I find myself restudying the single sheet on Wang Po Lin that Mike pulled from the UN Security files.

There is a photograph, a headshot clipped to the top left-hand corner. Po Lin is an old guy, seventy-one according to the given birth date, and he looks every day of it. His hair is white. The lenses in his horn-rimmed specs are thick. And from the way his frown lines droop down either side of his chin, it is clear that this guy does not regard his passage through the world as a barrel of laughs.

That squares with his reputation too. The number-three man on the Chinese delegation, he gives the impression at times that he is personally out to right all the wrongs that have been done to his people over the centuries by foreign, primarily Western, aggression. He takes his retribution in the usual diplomatic manner, through the delivery of interminable and rancorous speeches. Whenever the opportunity arises, Po Lin can be relied on for a thirty-minute diatribe on imperialism and the West. The British are a particular target— Hong Kong, the Opium Wars. Rumor has it that Po Lin's recall last month to Beijing is somehow connected with a verbal attack he made recently on Lady Nicola. Patrick tells me he heard that Lady Nicola delivered a diplomatic counterpunch that caused Po Lin's recall.

But Patrick did not know the nature of Lady Nicola's weapon. And I wonder now if it's possible she had the same information that Marie has given me. When I run the idea by Mike, he screws up his face.

"How it sounds to me? Sounds to me like a wild-ass guess," he says. "How about we do the legwork first, leave the head work till we got a few facts."

When he parks the car, I hand him the Po Lin mug shot, then I shove the rest of the paperwork under the seat and get out.

Chinatown never changes. Though it gets a little bigger and plenty more crowded each year, its essential quality remains what it was when I arrived in New York half a lifetime ago. The restaurants are part of it, the smell of frying pork and vegetables that seem over the years to have impregnated the walls of the buildings; walking down the sidewalk with Mike now, I cannot help sniffing the salty air. And the old ladies loaded down with shopping, green vegetables and bolts of garish fabric sprouting from plastic bags—these could be the same people Sarah and I used to see when we came down here as freshmen, searching for a restaurant that wouldn't break the bank.

"Here," says Mike, turning right.

We see the signs immediately, twenty yards on down the street. The Jade Moon Theater is on the left, directly across from a shopfront that has the words *Jade Moon* emblazoned in dark green on its awning. Mike selects the shop as our first destination. Inside, the air is clotted and rich with spices. Cinnamon and nutmeg and God knows what all else. Open burlap bags stand in rows, knee-high along the back wall. A couple of elderly Chinese women are giving the goods a careful inspection, trailing their fingers through a sack of brown seeds.

"Imported," Mike says, drawing my attention to the labels on the sacks as we turn down the first aisle.

Taiwan, it would appear, is the Kwok brothers' major source. The shelves are loaded with bowls and jugs decorated Taipei style, cheap and shiny.

I have a question. I gesture along the aisle both ways. "What are we looking for?"

"A million bucks."

I lift a brow.

"Or something that looks like a million bucks," Mike tells me from the side of his mouth. "Anything to give us some idea we're not just down here chasing our asses."

He moves up the aisle, and I trail after him, chewing my lip.

I have an appointment with Jennifer Dale. When I phoned her earlier to let her know that Mike and I are making a brief excursion beyond the bounds of UNHQ coming down here to Chinatown, she naturally had some questions. When I turned those questions aside, her tone became distinctly frosty; she more or less ordered me to get myself to her office the moment I'm back in Turtle Bay. And Jennifer is not my worst problem. When I gave Pascal Nyeri the list of company names I got from Marie Lefebre, he took one look at them and told me not to hold my breath. The companies, he says, might be registered anywhere in the U.S. from Florida up to Alaska; a proper search of the corporate registers in every state will take him at least a week. He can probably get a good financial picture of Jade Moon Enterprises in four or five days, he tells me, provided I can convince the U.S. corporate affairs authorities to speak to him. I'm going to have to raise the subject with Jennifer when I get back. An unhappy prospect.

As I pause now by a stack of stainless steel woks, it strikes me that this investigation has wandered into rather strange territory. In truth, Dr. Livingstone himself was never more lost.

"That Martinez kid came in this morning," Mike tells me, picking up a box of joss sticks. "With Rachel."

"Juan's okay."

"Kid's got a frigging ponytail. Twenty-first century, we're still breeding hippies."

I ask Mike if he learned anything from the NGO types he has questioned, if their statements brought anything useful to light. He shrugs, replacing the box on the shelf.

"Seems like Hatanaka got to the reception around nine. He musta come straight from his sister, you know, the Japan Society. After that all we got is pieces. Martinez and a couple more guys spoke to Hatanaka. But nobody noticed anything strange."

"Do we know when he left?"

"No one saw him go. But that doesn't mean much. Those things, who notices? Hundreds of people coming and going. The duty guard says he thinks maybe Hatanaka left late."

"That's something."

"That's nothing. The guy's covering his butt. If we find out Hatanaka left early, he'll say he told me he wasn't sure. If we find Hatanaka left late, the guard's gonna say, sure, he already told me that. Covered both ways."

We move on down the aisle. Mike pauses to inspect the contents of an open crate.

"What about the security tapes from Monday night?" I ask. "Did you get any more out of the maintenance guys?"

"Another winner." He reaches into the crate and pokes around. "I've been through it ten times with the maintenance guys, the ones who were working on the camera gear that night. They don't see they did anything wrong. Scheduled work, they just did their jobs. And get this. I ask their boss—Blaveski? Blatski?—I ask him if he thinks it's smart doing maintenance a day before the opening. As if he hadn't had months to straighten it out. You know what he said? He said that's how it was on the works schedule. The fucking works schedule. Like it's set in stone, the goddamn eleventh commandment. I'm telling you. Brains?" Mike lifts his head from the crate.

We move on, stopping to peer through an open side door into the Kwok brothers' garage-sized warehouse. Sacks are piled high on pallets, dust particles drift through the air; a shaft of sunlight slants down through a broken roof tile overhead. Half a dozen pine crates in one corner. And the floor, bare concrete, is cracked.

"This look to you like a million bucks' worth?" I ask.

Mike agrees that it doesn't. Not remotely. Then, as we turn down the next aisle, I break the news to him that I have been holding back all this while.

"I saw Patrick. I told him about the bugs at Hatanaka's apartment."

Mike looks at me sideways.

"And the intruder at my place," I say.

"Jesus, you had to?"

"He's my boss."

"He's fucked us around. Right from the start of this thing." Mike broods awhile before speaking again. "So how'd he take it?"

"Mad as hell. He wanted to pull me off the investigation."

"Figures." Mike ponders a moment. "And now it figures too why he was so worked up when he came down to see me."

"This morning?"

"Sure. Barged right in when I was interviewing Rachel."

"My Rachel?"

"I told you, she came in with the Martinez kid. She was with him for a while at the NGO thing Monday." Mike dismisses it with a toss of the hand; then, as we approach the counter, he concludes with a few choice remarks on Patrick. "Guy's an asshole," he decides.

At the checkout, those two elderly women are emptying their baskets. They call out back and an old man shuffles out, blinking like some nocturnal creature surprised by the harsh glare of daylight. I lean toward Mike.

"Kwok?"

Mike takes in the old man at a glance. "Go take a look at the theater across the street," he tells me. "This guy ain't gonna talk to two of us, I can tell you that for nothing."

I don't argue. This is cop business, something Mike would know.

A minute later I'm studying the posters plastered to either side of the Jade Moon Theater entrance. The week's big features. Stripped to the waist, the next generation of Bruce Lee and Jackie Chan wanna-bes bare their teeth, frozen in athletic poses amid fantastic scenes of slaughter. When I go in, more of the same posters are displayed in glass cases, lit by a pale light that shines out from the ticket stall. The stall appears to be unmanned, so I take the opportunity to have a look around. The carpet is threadbare. There is no obvious sign of any recent one-million-dollar renovation.

When a chorus of rough laughter erupts from behind the theater doors, I turn. Then I move slowly up to the swinging doors, push the left one open a few inches, and peer into the darkened room. Up onscreen a bearded villain-type is being impaled on a spear. Another gale of laughter from the audience. Once my eyes adjust to the dark, I can see there are no more than twenty rows of seats. The place is surprisingly small, certainly nothing like the scale necessary to earn Po Lin a reasonable return on a million-dollar investment. I am wondering about that when the right-hand door swings back and I am suddenly face-to-face with what can only be Kwok number two. Apart from the clothes—a neatly pressed white shirt and black pants—he is a dead ringer for his brother across the street.

His head goes back in surprise, and I have just sufficient presence of mind to launch into my patter.

"I'm from the Bureau of Small Business," I say, but that is as far as I get. Kwok makes a guttural sound in his throat, shouting toward the ticket booth as he steps by me. The theater doors flicker closed. Trailing after him, I reprise my limp story, pointing out that the Bureau of Small Business might be able to render some assistance to his commercial endeavor. I ask him if he might be interested in helping us with a survey.

"Uh?" he barks. Then, from behind the ticket counter, a head appears. The surprised young man, Chinese, of course, looks half asleep. He rubs his eyes. And Kwok goes off the deep end. The kid cringes as Kwok leans over the counter, shouting; it is some while before Kwok returns his attention to me.

"Wha you want?" he snaps, facing me.

"We're doing a survey in this area—"

"No, no." He waves both hands at me. "Go. Finish."

"Could I speak to the owner?"

"Speak to nobody. I am the owner."

"Your investors?"

He blinks vigorously behind his eyeglasses, then shoots a mouthful of Chinese to the youth behind the counter. The young man stands up straight now, alert, and looks me over. The kid is small, but I have the impression that beneath the counter his hands are reaching for some hidden weapon. He has a chance to redeem himself. Whitey, I sense, is about to be thrown out on his ear.

"Go," Kwok says to me. Not polite, and not a request.

Then I hear a metallic clang beneath the counter. The kid looks down to his hidden hands, then back up to me. His eyes are glazed. I realize that he is tripping, that this probably is a very wise moment for me to make my exit. So, sidling past the ticket booth, I dip my head at Kwok, then depart quickly.

"Yo!" Mike shouts as I hit the street. He beckons me from the corner. "Anything?" he asks when I join him.

"The place is a fleabag. If Po Lin sunk a million bucks into it, he's lost his dough." I dab at my face with a handkerchief. "Oh, yeah, and did I mention I nearly got my head kicked in?"

"Like that."

"Yeah. Like that."

When I tell him about Theater Kwok's unduly aggressive response to my mere presence and few queries, Mike turns thoughtful.

"Dry Goods Kwok wasn't much better," he tells me.

"You got nothing?"

"Zip."

We look at each other. We have wasted almost two hours on this excursion.

"You go on back," Mike says at last. "I'll be along in a while."

Mike gazes back down the street toward the Kwok brothers' establishments; he has a certain glint in his eye. The last time I saw that glint he was removing a doped-up protester from the UN North Lawn. The protester was wielding a bottle. Mike's hand had to be stitched up later, but the protester was hospitalized for a week.

"Mike." He faces me, and I say, "Don't give Patrick any reason to take your balls off." When he smiles, I touch his lapel. "Or mine."

He nods and backs away from me down the sidewalk. As he turns in to the passing stream of pedestrians, I hear him whistling the first plaintive bars of "Blue Moon."

19

"DID SHE SAY WHAT SHE WANTED?"

"Just that she wanted to see you," Elizabeth, my secretary, replies, taking another bite from her pastry and chewing as she speaks. "Some guard brought her upstairs. He said she was Toshio's sister." She shrugs; she wants me to know that she is not to blame for this deviation from regular security procedure. A Brit, at least fifty pounds overweight, groomed like a bag lady, Elizabeth is, at forty-three years of age, resentfully unmarried. This could be her personal motto. I am not to blame.

Now I lean through the door to look down the hall to where Moriko Hatanaka is standing outside Toshio's locked office. She has a large scroll that looks like a map tucked beneath her arm, and she appears to be reading the keep-out message that has been taped to her brother's office door.

"How long's she been waiting?"

"Few minutes." Elizabeth goes on to inform me around a mouthful of pastry that I have had two calls from Jennifer Dale; apparently I have been expected over at USUN for an hour. "And this one's been calling too," she says, holding up her notepad for me to read. J. Martinez. Juan. I instruct Elizabeth to call Jennifer, let her know I have been delayed, then I gather myself a moment before stepping out into the hall.

Moriko smiles sadly as she takes my hand. An awkward moment, I'm not quite sure what to say to her. But then, recalling just how much I grew to dislike the endlessly repeated assurances of sympathy after Sarah's death, I simply return Moriko's sad smile and guide her into my office.

"Can I get you something? Coffee?"

"This won't take that long. I know you are busy."

She is, I am relieved to see, in control of herself. Her makeup has been meticulously applied, her gray skirt and jacket are both crisply pressed. Only her eyes give any hint of the depth of her sorrow. All other outward signs of grief have been temporarily erased. A gutsy lady.

"I want to make the arrangements," she tells me, "for Toshio's body."

Propping myself against the desk, I fold my arms. "You don't have to deal with that immediately. Give it a few days."

"Toshio wanted his body returned to Japan."

I nod. I tell her that shouldn't be a problem.

She offers to bring me a copy of Toshio's will to prove that this was Toshio's wish, but I wave the offer aside. If Moriko says that's what Toshio wanted, I believe her; besides, she is next of kin. And in truth I am not really surprised by this last wish of Toshio's. For all his internationalist credentials, Toshio remained at the core very deeply Japanese. Falling leaves return to their roots. The old saw.

"It'll take us a few days to arrange." Reaching for a pad and pen, I inquire if she has anyone lined up to handle things at the Japanese end.

"There is a funeral parlor."

Pen poised, I ask for the name. When Moriko hesitates, I look up. "Are you really sure you want to do this now?"

She smiles. "I was just going to say that the Japanese consulate has offered to do all this for me."

"At the Japanese end."

"Here too. Everything."

I take a moment with that. "The consulate offered to fly Toshio's body to Japan? To make all the arrangements?"

"When they called, they said that would be easiest. I came here only to see when you could let them take Toshio." She looks down. "His body."

When they called. They said. "They approached you?"

She nods again.

"When did they call?"

"This morning." Moriko looks at me askance now, suddenly aware that something is going on that she has missed. Is still missing. "I agreed to let them arrange everything. Won't that be all right?"

"And they asked you to come up here."

"Yes."

"To hurry up the release of the body."

"They said it would help."

I drop my gaze. These goddamn people. The Japanese Foreign Ministry. Asahaki. Whoever else is behind this cheap and tactless ploy. Even grief, the loss of a dearly loved brother, has not put Moriko off limits. They want Toshio's body removed from UNHQ, my investigation closed; and though Moriko does not know it, they have attempted to use her as the emotional lever to prize her brother loose. At last I raise my eyes.

"I'll make sure the body's released to the Japanese consulate as soon as that's possible, Moriko. But despite what they may have led you to believe, that's unlikely to happen before the weekend. More likely sometime next week."

"Not sooner?"

"I can't."

She is clearly disappointed, but she knows I would not be refusing her request without good reason. In the end she makes no objection, simply bows her head in acceptance. And then she seems to remember the scroll that she has been holding all this time. She takes it from under her arm.

"This is something Toshio did," she tells me, tugging at the red ribbon, unrolling the thing. "He did it Monday night. I thought there would be somewhere here at the UN to hang it. As a memory."

"A picture?"

"Calligraphy."

A hobby, as I now recall, of Toshio's. Four vertical lines of kanji in thick black ink trail down the fibrous handmade-paper scroll. When I glance at Moriko, she gives me an impromptu translation.

" 'Just like the grass in the wind, the same now are the hopes and plans of the ancient generals.' "

"Bashō," I say.

Moriko turns to me in amazement. And I am more than a little surprised myself. Crossing to the shelf behind my desk, I pull down a thin volume. *The Narrow Road to the Deep North.* By Bashō. Rejoining Moriko, I search for the page.

"We went to Toshio's apartment Tuesday morning. This book was on his bedside table." Locating the page, I open it out next to the scroll. "It's the same poem he's marked here, isn't it?"

Moriko inspects the page in the book. After a second she nods. "But that is not Toshio's writing." She indicates the purple ink jottings in the book.

I flip back to the flyleaf and show her the kanji there. She translates again.

" 'Two men may disagree yet not be enemies.' " She points. "And there is a date. July this year. It is a gift to Toshio."

"Who from?"

Her finger slides down the kanji. "Bunzo Asahaki."

My head rises. A gift from Bunzo Asahaki to Toshio. I do not get this at all.

"And it was Ambassador Asahaki who asked Toshio to write this," Moriko remarks, puzzled, touching the calligraphy on the scroll.

I look at her. "Monday night?"

She nods. No big thing.

"Monday night where?" I ask her.

"At the Society," she says. The Japan Society. "The ambassador was our guest of honor. He opened the Kurosawa festival for us."

Oh, God. How in the world did we miss this? Taking the note from my pocket—*I will see you tonight*—I hold it up by the kanji in the flyleaf. She squints; she remembers the unsigned note I showed her yesterday. And I do not even have to ask her my question.

"The same handwriting," she says. "The note is from Ambassador Asahaki."

Taking the scroll from Moriko, I lay it by the Bashō on my desk. Then I clasp her shoulders and ease her into a chair. "Monday night. Whatever you can remember. Anything you heard Toshio and Asahaki say to each other. Anything they did. This could be a huge help to us, Moriko."

Perplexed by my intensity, she frowns. "If I knew it was so important—"

"Just remember now. Whatever you can."

She thinks a moment. "Ambassador Asahaki was late," she says. "He didn't stay long. He spoke with Toshio five minutes, not more."

"Did they argue?"

She drops her gaze, trying to recall. "No. They were just talking. I remember I was annoyed at Toshio. We needed the ambassador to make the opening speech for the festival. Instead, he was talking with my brother."

"You didn't overhear anything?"

When she shakes her head apologetically, I gesture to the scroll. I ask her what that was all about.

"After the ambassador opened the festival, I asked Toshio to do some calligraphy. To hang in the lobby during the festival. Toshio was always happy to do that, he liked to make a show. When Toshio asked everyone what he should write, the ambassador made a suggestion."

"That poem?"

She nods. I fetch the book and open it at the flyleaf. *Two men may disagree yet not be enemies.* I speak the words aloud.

"Does that mean anything to you, Moriko?" I gesture to the scroll. "Any of this?"

"Ambassador Asahaki's family is well known in Japan. An old military family. Toshio did not like these kind of people. The Japanese military. Never." Not news by now. Not after the campaign Toshio was running against the Japanese seat. Moriko looks down at the kanji on the flyleaf. "Here I think the ambassador was asking Toshio for less hate. Disagreement, yes. But not enemies."

Back in July, I think. When they were already at loggerheads over the Japanese seat on the Council, when Toshio knew about the Special Committee fraud but before he had conclusively pinned it on Asahaki.

"And on Monday night?" I ask, nodding to the scroll.

"You must see," says Moriko, evidently surprised by my failure to connect the dots.

But frankly I do not see. While she has made the deduction instinctively, to me the barrier of an alien culture remains impenetrable. Two grown men exchanging poems is not a social act with which I can claim any acquaintance. At last Moriko spells it out for me.

"On Monday night Toshio wrote out this poem the ambassador suggested to him. The same poem from that book."

She sees that I am still lost, still floundering.

"On Monday night," she says, "Toshio accepted what Ambassador Asahaki wrote in July. 'Two men may disagree yet not be enemies.' " She lays a hand on the scroll. "On Monday night," Moriko tells me, choosing her words carefully, "Toshio and Ambassador Asahaki became 'not enemies.' "

———

Jennifer Dale is mad at me. It isn't just that the marine guard from the lobby has brought me upstairs, clearly under orders; there are other signs too. Like the look I get now from Jennifer's young personal assistant as he walks me to her office. He opens the door and announces me, then quickly retreats.

"You have a report for me?" Jennifer asks tightly as I enter. She carries on editing the page on her desk, her ire permeating the air around her.

"Verbal," I offer, closing the door at my back.

"Fine." She moves on to the next page in the stack. "Written copy by eight tonight."

"Jennifer."

"If it's an excuse, I don't want to hear it."

"Hey," I say softly. When she finally raises her eyes from her work, I make the sign with my hands: time-out.

She considers me a moment, then takes off her reading glasses, stylish lozenge-shaped steel frames, and eases her head back. With one hand she massages her neck. "What am I meant to do, Sam? Wag my tail?"

Leaning onto her forearms, she studies her glasses contemplatively. I know how she feels. Since last night at the Waldorf we seem to have been traveling a steadily downward slope, an uncomfortable journey that neither of us wanted and which is apparently not over yet. The interplay of our professional lives has turned serious, the playful frisson of the past few months sliding into real friction. I direct my gaze to the State Department eagle on the wall; the pair of crossed U.S. flags, banners half unfurled.

"The ambassador doesn't believe you're cooperating with us fully," she says. "And I agree with him."

"We're doing our best to be cooperative within the bounds of our own responsibilities."

She pulls a face: bullshit.

Bending forward, I press a finger down on her desk. "When we needed to cross into U.S. territory, I called you, Jennifer."

"I'm not an answering service. You don't just dump your message on me, then go off and do what you like. That's not how this was meant to work."

An unguarded remark, not like Jennifer. Which suggests that the numbers for tomorrow's vote might not be looking too good, that Bruckner is not too happy. She glances from her desk to the door, trying to focus on something other than me.

"No?" I say. "So how was it meant to work? You keep tabs on what we're doing, then interfere when we look like we're screwing up Bruckner's plans?"

"I don't have the time," she mutters. She puts on her glasses, pulls a blank sheet onto her blotter, then uncaps a pen. "The ambassador wants to know what you've been up to. And I need to know how often you intend to flit in and out of U.S. jurisdiction."

"I've just had Toshio's sister up in my office."

"Mmm?"

"Your friends at the Japanese consulate sent her over. A grieving woman. Just to hurry up the release of Toshio's body."

"Did it work?"

"No."

"Pity," she says.

She is even madder than I thought. But I am not exactly overjoyed with how this is going either, so I forgo any attempt at explanation. I simply take Pascal Nyeri's letter from my briefcase and hand it to her as I make my request.

"We need access to the financial records of these companies." The companies from Marie Lefebre's list.

Curious now, Jennifer reads the letter, then glances up. "Is this anything to do with the dirt Hatanaka was throwing at Ambassador Asahaki?"

"Is our request for assistance granted or denied?"

"It's under consideration," she decides, finishing the letter. She chews it over a second, then jots a note to herself. "Maybe when you're a little more forthcoming as to why you need the information, I'll reach a decision. Now, what were you doing in Chinatown?"

"Secretariat business."

"Not funny."

"It wasn't meant to be."

She swears beneath her breath.

"Are you mad at me personally, Jennifer? Or just at the job I'm doing?"

"There's a difference?"

"You seemed to think so last night."

"Don't give me that." Rising suddenly, she shoves back her chair and snatches her purse from the desk. "I've been waiting for you nearly two hours. Ten minutes ago I got a call from Stephen saying he couldn't pick up Ben like he's arranged. So here I am, the vote tomorrow, Bruckner going crazy, and I have to go explain to Ben why his father's not taking him to the movies like he promised. Believe me, Sam. Between you and Stephen, the man thing is not big with me right now." Moving toward the door, she adds, "And you better reconsider how cooperative you're being, or this arrangement is terminated. I'll redirect you to the Headquarters Committee."

I step back and lean against the door. "I want this to be over as much as you do. But when it's over, I'd like to be able to say I didn't regret anything I'd done. And that means not compromising myself. Not for anyone."

"You want to keep it professional," she says.

When I nod, she comes and stands right in front of me. She puts her face up close. "So when was the last time you felt you had the right to hold the USUN legal counsel confined against her will in her own damn office?"

"Listen—"

"Get out of my way."

"Jennifer."

"Get out of my goddamn way." Grabbing the door handle, she tugs sharply; the door strikes my back and I shuffle aside awkwardly as she pushes out past me. She gives Pascal's letter to her PA along with some instructions. Then she pivots, stalking past me to the elevators. We ride down together, the silence between us as solid as ice. On the ground floor the receptionist buzzes us through the reinforced plate-glass door to the lobby, where the U.S. marine guard comes to attention and salutes us out into the street. Still not a word.

"Pax," I say as we hit the sidewalk. "So I was out of line. I didn't mean to do that, I was angry."

"You guys are on notice," she says, turning on me fiercely. "The Secretariat gets its act together now, or we're not going to even try to hold the line against Congress. If Capitol Hill wants to withhold this year's UN dues, that's fine by us. State won't lift a finger to stop them. If O'Conner wants to play games, see how he likes this one."

"No one's playing games here."

"Last warning, Sam." She peels away to the left, repeating over her shoulder, "Last warning."

Stunned by the threat, I watch her retreating back. The U.S. is responsible for one-quarter of the UN's annual budget. And Jennifer, if I understand her correctly, is saying that the State Department, which has always fought in the UN's corner on this vital matter, will now let Congress do what it is always threatening to do and block the necessary appropriation. When he hears this, Patrick is going to flip. And not just Patrick, the entire thirty-eighth floor will come down on me like a ton of bricks. Jennifer turns in to East Forty-fifth; I set off after her, my briefcase slapping against my leg.

She has disappeared inside the building before I can catch her. I stop, in two minds now about whether to follow her in. By the entrance there is a sandbox, red and yellow plastic toys lying scattered in the sand. Monkey bars. On the glass wall the gold lettering says INTERNATIONAL SCHOOL KINDERGARTEN. And inside I can see a dozen or more kids sitting cross-legged on cushions arranged in a circle, clapping in time with their teacher. The smaller kids don't seem to have the hang of it; they just clap and watch the others in a vaguely puzzled kind of way. Asians. Africans. Europeans. It looks like one of those cornball posters the PR people scattered all over the Secretariat building during the UN Year of the Child.

Then Jennifer appears amid the circle of children. Still showing the strain of our encounter, she directs a smile at the teacher that is small and tight. Then she crouches, opens her arms, and a kid gets up off his cushion and rushes her. Ben, her son. He flops into her arms, laughing, and her expression is instantly transformed; she is momentarily radiant. All her worries—me, Bruckner, the vote—sloughed off in the sudden escape she feels at this touch from her boy. But only for a moment. Then she frowns, her brow creasing again as she takes Ben aside to talk. No Stephen. No promised trip to the movies.

Right then the teacher notices me looking in from the street. She rises, giving me a very direct look: I am not a father she recognizes. Before she can come out and confront me, or worse, ask Jennifer if I have anything to do with Ben, I turn on my heel and walk. But down at the corner on First, I pause and glance across to the USUN steps where Jennifer rounded on me. In some bafflement now, I recall what she said: If O'Conner wants to play games. A bureaucrat of international justice, I stand here bemused. Then I look back over my shoulder.

What in hell did she mean, "Last warning"?

20

"SMOKY, SMOKY, SMOKY," WHISPERS SOME DREADLOCKED WEIRDO OUT-side the local bodega. When he opens his palm to display his ready-rolled wares, I walk right on by to the No Name bar across the street. The bar is closed; a metal roll-up door covered in hellish Technicolor graffiti has been pulled down to shield the front door and window. The roll-up door is secured with a heavy padlock to a piece of iron embedded in the sidewalk. But the door beneath the Lighthouse sign a few yards down is wide open, the sweet, cloying odor of burning incense drifting out invisibly. An unexpected memory surges. Me with Sarah, naked, entwined on a pile of beanbags. A Bowie record on the player.

"Hi," says Juan Martinez when I enter.

The others gathered around his desk, all about Juan's age, turn and look me over. Middle-aged, in a suit. The enemy.

"Hi," I say, feeling like one of those college lecturers we used to laugh at, the guys who thought smoking dope with students some-how kept them hip. "You've got something for me?"

"It's upstairs." Juan directs a thumb to the ceiling, then gestures to his young colleagues. "You mind if I just finish this?"

I shoot him a look: Make it quick. While they conclude their dis-cussion, some dispute about which member of the UN's Third Committee, Human Rights, is likely to give them a hearing tonight, I take a slow turn around the open-plan office. Half a dozen desks, PCs, filing cabinets, and a coffee machine at the back. Plastered over the walls are the inevitable posters from a hundred NGO causes. From a recent Lighthouse campaign, black-and-white shots of dark alleys and empty syringes, tables of statistics, charts that show the increase in numbers of heroin addicts in various countries. These, depressingly, look like a great bull-run on the Dow. A corkboard alongside is covered with Polaroids that have been pinned up in anarchic profusion. Kids. Kids partying. Juan, recognizable in his white linen suit, is in many of the shots. In one he's been caught in close-up, staring at a can of Bud, clearly bombed out of his mind. In another, two lily-white butts protrude from the windows of an old Chevy, a mooning that appears to have taken place outside the No Name bar. Next to the Chevy three girls have been caught, hands raised, soaking wet and dancing, the dark shading of their nipples visible through their clinging white T-shirts. Kids, I think. But then, something about that girl on the left. I lean closer, squinting. Rachel?

"Let's go," says Juan, coming over. Mistaking my expression, he touches some Lighthouse poster as he goes by. "That's not the worst of it either. Sad."

Upstairs, my daughter's new home is laid out open-plan like the office below. But here there is a kitchenette at one end, a dining table with a Ping-Pong net slung across its center, and a couple of sofas that appear to have lost their legs. At each of the four corners of the place, cubicles have been partitioned off with plywood, the ply graffiti'd in the same hellish style as the roll-up door outside the No Name bar. From the ceiling a giant wagon wheel hangs parallel with the floor, four bare lightbulbs dangling from it like mutant jellyfish tendrils. Juan leads me in, apologizing for the evident disorder. It occurs to me now that Rachel might not welcome this unannounced visit.

"Rachel in?"

"Got called back to work," Juan tells me. "All the guides, everyone down in Public Information, they're back there answering more questions."

"I thought she did that with you this morning."

"That was about the NGO bash. Now they're talking to anyone working down at basement level. The bookshop, the cafeteria, all that. Down there's where they found the body, yeah?"

I nod, preparing to turn any further questions aside. But Juan doesn't pursue the line.

"Hey, you wanna see her room?" Shoving open the door to one of the corner cubicles, he wanders straight in. "She's made it real nice."

Curiosity defeats me, I put my head in. A mess. Just like her room at home. The closet door stands ajar, and the bed, piled with clothes, is unmade. Juan draws my attention to the abstract design on the walls. Stripes and circles.

"She did that last week. Took her only a couple of hours."

Looks like it, I think, but I keep the thought to myself.

Withdrawing my head, I ask, "So what have you got to show me?"

"In here." Juan wanders out by me and into another corner cubicle. This one must be Juan's room; there's a guitar case on the bed and a picture of his parents on the dresser. His father, José, I met when I put Sarah on the plane to the camp in Abatan. And I met Juan's mother a few months later at the memorial concert that Juan put together. Rachel tells me that Mrs. Martinez has hit the bottle in a big way since then, in and out of clinics all the time. But in the picture on the dresser she looks a lot like her son. Young and full of life. "It'll take me a minute to get it on-screen," Juan says, switching on his PC. He pushes his guitar case along the bed, inviting me to sit down. "So what have you guys found?" he asks, tapping at the keyboard. "Any luck with that hypocrite whatshername, Yomoto?"

Smiling at the artless inquiry, I explain that our investigation is a confidential matter, not an item for public debate.

"You got a debate anyway," Juan says simply.

I look at him.

"Internet," he tells me. "It's on all the NGO message boards, everyone's putting up any information they've got. Theories on what happened to Mr. Hatanaka. Comparing notes, like." At this piece of news, I groan. Juan finishes working the keyboard. "I'll show you after this," he says, swiveling the PC screen to face me. "Here."

I lean forward from the bed. And when I understand what I'm looking at, I raise my brow.

"You see where he went last week?" says Juan.

"I see you've just broken the law." He has hacked into the Secretariat computer system. The travel files. "Where'd you get the password?"

"Everybody's got it." He waves a hand breezily. Ignoring my stern look of disapproval, he points to the screen. We are looking at the Secretariat travel billings for last week. I could have checked here myself, but after Mike confirmed with Swissair that Toshio actually used his ticket both ways, I didn't bother. It seemed like there was nothing more to learn.

"He went to Geneva last week," says Juan.

"That's not news."

"It was news to me. He told me he was going to California."

I miss a beat. "San Diego?"

"Yeah."

"A sick relative?"

Juan regards me curiously. "He lied to you too?"

I shrug the question off. Unlike Pascal Nyeri or Juan, I was not seeing enough of Toshio lately to need an explanation for those few days' absence. But this reconfirmation of Toshio's deliberate deceit is nonetheless troubling. I ask Juan what he makes of it.

"Him lying? I dunno. He was always so straight with me. With everyone. I guess it doesn't seem right somehow." Juan pushes the mouse around; the cursor moves on the screen. "Anyway, that's what made me check this out. I mean, what was he doing in Geneva that he had to lie about?"

"You could have given me this on the phone."

"Yeah," he admits, disappointed that his revelation is not quite as revelatory as he'd hoped. Then he points to the screen again. "But I wasn't so sure about this."

Another flight: Geneva-Basel round trip. An unnamed passenger.

"I tried to trace what he was doing in Geneva," Juan tells me. "I figured visiting some UN agency. A conference or something. I kept drawing a blank, so I checked the accommodation billings. Nothing in Geneva. He didn't stay in Geneva. Turns out he stayed overnight in Basel."

I make a sound. Juan is pleased.

"That's news, right?"

I look at the Geneva-Basel-Geneva flight on the screen and the blank space where the name of the traveling Secretariat staffer is normally entered. Juan blithely admits that he has had the Lighthouse's best hacker bust into the Swissair records to confirm that the trip took place. And it did. The airline records confirm that Toshio was the passenger.

"The only time he spent in Geneva was an hour at the airport," Juan says.

Toshio lied to Juan and Pascal. And by leaving his name off the Basel flight billing, Toshio apparently intended to deceive anyone at the Secretariat who wanted to check on where he'd been. Why?

"You wanna see the Internet site?" Juan offers, producing a laptop from beneath the desk and plugging it in.

"You could be prosecuted. Hacking into the UN records. Swissair. That's breaking the law."

"We just peeked. Nobody changed nothing, I swear." When his glance slides across to me, there is the hint of a smile. "Anyway, it's not something they'd put me in jail for."

I recognize the allusion immediately. And before I can move the conversation, Juan comes right out with it. "Rachel says you did some time. You know. Like when you were young."

"She misled you."

"Uh-huh," he says.

When I was young. In fact, I was twenty-five years old and working at my first job as an assistant in the D.A.'s office. It was years before I was able to laugh about it with Sarah and Rachel, the incident becoming a cozily familiar piece of Windrush family folklore. Rachel and her mother kidding me about my criminal proclivities, reminding me of all the time I spent in jail.

"The time I did," I tell Juan now, "the sum total of my incarceration, it was seven hours. And I wasn't in jail, it was a police holding cell."

Juan smiles and asks me what happened.

"Then can we get on with this?" I ask, indicating the laptop.

He nods. He has obviously heard some embellished version of this from Rachel, so the sooner I put him straight, the better. This is one story I do not want doing the rounds in any version other than my own. I just stick to the facts. I keep it brief. Sarah and some med school friends, I tell him, had organized a march on the mayor's office in protest of the mayor's fervent headline-seeking support for the death penalty. At Sarah's urging, and with a degree of naïveté that is inexplicable to anyone who has not spent years buried alone in books working toward a doctorate, I agreed to join the march against my boss's boss. The one march I have ever attended in my entire life. When we got to the City Hall steps the TV cameras and the cops were waiting. The day was hot. The mayor would not allow a representative of the medical students to go inside and present a petition. The invective directed at the police line became unnecessarily abusive, and when one student threw a placard that struck a cop, the senior officer present took the opportunity to make a random arrest.

"You," says Juan, grinning broadly.

"Me," I concede.

"So you broke the law because of something you believed in. No death penalty."

"I didn't break the law."

When he continues to smile, I redirect his attention to the laptop PC.

"Mostly it's just junk," he says, turning back to it. "Like Toshio's not really dead, he's been abducted by aliens and the UN's covering it up. Seriously. These Net-heads, you gotta wonder sometimes." Then someone calls Juan's name. He leans back and answers "Yo" through the door. Glancing out, I see one of Juan's colleagues from downstairs. "Roommate," Juan tells me. He navigates his way onto the Internet site, then leaves it with me and goes out to see his friend.

The information on the Internet message board is just as Juan indicated, mostly junk; but scattered amid the junk are several items that give me pause. One of the NGOers Mike has interviewed, for example, has evidently taped the whole interview and posted a transcript here for general view. And there are several pieces speculating on reasons for Asahaki's sudden disappearance back to Japan; these are being treated skeptically; dismissive remarks about conspiracy theorists abound.

Finally I lean back and look out. Juan and his roommate are consulting over at the Ping-Pong table out of earshot. Young men with a cause. I cannot risk them returning while I am in the UN travel files, so I fold my arms and force myself to wait.

My time in jail, I think. Seven hours' custody and the whole course of my life was changed. When I went back to work at the D.A.'s office the next day, I was ostracized. Everyone took their lead from the deputy D.A., Randal White. An attorney of the old school, he had an atavistic adhesion to the death penalty as a cornerstone of justice. He took my unintended visit to the police holding cells as a personal affront. For a month I endured every kind of petty abuse that can be inflicted around an office. My work mysteriously disappeared. My opinion was drawn out as a target for mockery. My desk was relocated daily. In short, every childish form of retribution Randal White could dream up. And I endured all that because I believed that it could not last, that the storm would eventually pass. In the end, I did not wait to find out. I resigned the day I overheard Randal White wondering aloud to a young paralegal if it might not be amusing to wait till I went to the john, then go and spit in my coffee. A few months later I joined the UN. And Randal White is now the chief prosecuting attorney, one of the most respected lawyers in the State of New York.

Juan reappears in the doorway with his friend and introduces us. This other kid, Garth, is also twenty-something, wiry like Juan but shorter. He takes a book from Juan's shelf and heads back downstairs. Juan wanders out into the apartment.

"Just the three of you," I call through the open door. "You, Garth, and Rachel?"

"Yeah. I only got the kitchen and bathroom fixed up over the summer. Garth moved in sometime last month." Crossing to another cubicle, he pushes open the door. It is the bathroom: a shower and a toilet. "It's a big enough place," Juan tells me, closing the door behind him. "Three's fine."

I turn to the PC, quickly typing in a command, then my own password.

"I heard there was a press conference," Juan calls, his voice muffled. "Was it the usual, or did someone say something worth hearing?"

"The Tunku offered us a few words."

"That guy." Juan laughs. "He thinks we're like his new best friends or something. He thinks Lighthouse has got some kind of pull with Greenpeace. He wants to block this resolution they're pushing, anti–logging in the rain forest. He says if we help him, the Malaysian government's gonna give us a freebie office lease in Kuala Lumpur." He laughs again at the Tunku's hamfisted maneuvering.

The PC screen finally changes. I am out of UN Travel now and into Accounts; here I will be able to confirm which UN department authorized Toshio's irregular swing through Geneva and Basel. My money is on Internal Oversight. This I really should have been told. I cannot believe it has been kept from me. What stupid bureaucratic game is Dieter Rasmussen playing here? Clearly he never told Pascal. But Patrick? Thinking about it winds me up further; my fingers pound like hammers on the keys.

"If you want to get out of the system," Juan calls, "double-click escape."

Punching the final key, I wait, staring at the screen. Hot fury simmers in my chest. But the moment the screen comes up, my righteous, soaring anger comes crashing violently back to earth. The departmental authorization code for Toshio's trip, the letters and numbers in the top left-hand corner, they are not the ones I expected to see. Not IO, for Internal Oversight; but LA, for Legal Affairs. And the authorizing name is not Dieter Rasmussen's.

"Found anything?" Juan calls from the bathroom.

I stare at the screen, rocked into silence.

Then the john flushes, the bathroom door opens, and I reach out and double-click the escape key. Immediately the screen goes blank.

A moment later, Juan rejoins me. "Any use to you?" He nods at the PC.

I nod distractedly, still staring at the point on the screen where the authorizing name appeared. Shock seems to have seared the letters to my retina: S. Windrush.

21

L ISTEN UP!" MIKE CRIES OVER NOISE IN THE room. "Here it is."
He stands in front of the senior uniformed Security people,
clipboard in hand, and talks them through the duty roster for the
night. The General Assembly session is the worst time of year for
everyone here. Delegates are never where they should be; scores of
national secret services endlessly scream for reports on how their
people are being protected; belligerent journalists continually breach
security at the worst times and in all the worst possible places. And
this evening, of course, there is another matter that Mike's officers
want to raise: What progress has been made in the investigation of
the death of Toshio Hatanaka?

"Sam's running it," Mike answers when the inevitable question finally comes. He gestures over their heads to where he has just
caught sight of me by the door. "It's early days. What I can say is,
anybody pointing a finger right now knows diddly-squat. That right,
Sam?"

A few of the guards turn around, so I nod as firmly as I can.

But the tired eyes linger; there is an air of weary resignation here.
Bitter experience has taught these people not to put much faith in
the half-truths that trickle down to them from the upper floors of
the Secretariat. What they know for a fact is that the senior
Secretariat bureaucrats and the delegates generally treat them like
bellhops, not security professionals, and now that these same high-
handed pols are pointing the finger at them as responsible for
Toshio's death, their understandable response is an aggrieved closing
of ranks.

"Bullshit," someone mutters.

I pretend not to have heard, but Mike glowers darkly. He consults his clipboard again.

"Anybody hears anything, anything at all might give us a lead on Hatanaka, I wanna hear it. Not tomorrow. Not when-I-get-a-minute." He levels his pen at them. "You know, I know."

"Glad someone does," comes a lone voice. Grim laughter ripples through the room; even Mike manages a tight smile. When he dismisses them, they go filing out the door like a team of NBA rejects about to meet the Lakers.

"Not good?" I say when they're gone.

Mike comes over to the door. "Morale gets any lower, they'll be sending someone to the frigging ILO." The International Labor Organization. I take this as a joke at first, but Mike isn't smiling. "Some young idiots are actually talking about a strike," he says.

"How were the Kwoks?"

"Oh, yeah." Mike nods as we go down the hall. "They sent you a present."

"A present."

"Yeah."

"What kind?"

"Just a second," he says, turning in to the Surveillance Room.

Banks of screens line one wall, black-and-white pictures from security cameras positioned within the UN buildings and grounds. Two guards are monitoring the monitors, the remains of a family-sized pizza sitting on the desk between them. Beside the pizza lie several empty foam cups; there are candy wrappers on the floor by the trash can. Mike leans on the console, one eye on the monitors, and receives the senior guard's impromptu report: The General Assembly broke up early, the guard thinks the Assembly president looked badly hungover; the Third and Sixth Committees are still sitting, word from the door guards is they're expecting a ten P.M. finish; the grounds and the Secretariat building are quiet, as they should be, and the dwindling band of Free Tibet protesters across First Avenue has stopped beating the peace drum. Another day winding down.

Mike spends a few moments just shooting the breeze then, making sure these guys feel like they're part of the team. Appreciated. There isn't one window in this room; a ten-hour shift here, five days a week, cannot be anybody's idea of a good time. As Mike pushes off the console to leave, the guard says, "And Weyland had visitors."

Mike stops.

The guard flicks a switch and points to a monitor. The scene that appears is pre-taped; the time flashing in the bottom right-hand corner is from two hours ago.

Weyland, down in the cafeteria, is approached by two men in suits. He stands, barring their way to the kitchen and the coolroom where Toshio's body lies. Neither of the two visitors looks pleased. One of them is the Tunku. The other one, Patrick O'Conner. After a brief exchange, Patrick and the Tunku retreat.

The guard flips a switch, the tape freeze-frames.

"Just those two," the guard tells Mike. "We radioed down to Weyland. He said it wasn't a problem." He points to another monitor, the cafeteria again, real time. Weyland sits alone, reading a magazine.

Mike chucks the guard's shoulder, makes some ribald remark, then under the cover of the guard's laughter he leads me out to the hall.

"Patrick mention to you he wanted another look at the body?" Mike asks, his brow furrowing as we go down the hall to his office.

I shake my head.

"The Tunku?" he says.

The Tunku, I tell him, hardly needs my approval if he has a direct line open to Patrick. Besides, as chairman of the UNHQ Committee, the Tunku can roam pretty much where he likes. Mike sucks on his teeth. He asks me again about Patrick's reaction when I mentioned the bugs in Toshio's apartment. And I give him the same answer. Extreme anger.

"This is Patrick," I remind Mike. "He can't help sticking his nose in. If he's not doing something himself, it's not being done right."

"Well, he's sticking his nose in too damn far. Now I'm hearing he's been interviewing some of those NGO bozos we had in, like he's checking up on what I'm doing. He's screwing around. I don't like it, I'm telling you."

He goes in to his office. I go in after him and close the door.

"Toshio didn't have any business in Geneva," I say. "He just went through Geneva on his way to Basel."

Mike stops, one hand on his desk, and looks back at me. "Basel?"

I use his PC to log on to the Secretariat system. Then I take him through the Travel and Accounts files, pointing out everything that Juan showed me. Mike receives all this in silence.

"LA," I tell him finally, clicking onto the authorization. "Legal Affairs. We authorized Toshio's trip."

Mike lays a finger on the screen: S. Windrush.

"You."

"No, Mike, not me." I explain the different access levels in the Legal Affairs software, the electronic hierarchy. "And I didn't put my name in there, so that leaves Patrick."

"He knew Toshio went to Basel?"

"More than that. Patrick authorized the goddamned trip."

Mike looks at me. We have discussed Toshio's supposed journey to Geneva at least twice in Patrick's presence. And Patrick never said one single word about Basel.

"So what's in Basel?" Mike asks me.

I have no idea. Every UN agency in Switzerland that I am aware of is based in Geneva.

Mike ponders a moment. "Patrick got any reason he might wanna screw you?"

"I don't know about screwing me. But he's desperate for me to issue a clean bill of health on Asahaki. Clear him of any suspicion of involvement in the fraud."

"Which clears him of any suspicion in the murder."

"That's Patrick's take on it." I remind Mike of my summons to the Security Council side chamber this morning. "That's what they all want. The whole perm five. Asahaki back here lobbying for the Japanese seat. But Patrick especially. He needs that Yes vote to save his ass up on thirty-eight."

"And you told Patrick to go jump."

"I told him that if Asahaki comes back, I'd question the man."

Mike studies the PC screen. S. Windrush.

"Patrick's telling Eckhardt you're letting personal stuff screw up your judgment." Eckhardt, Mike's boss. "Personal stuff, meaning that girlfriend of yours."

Jennifer. Sighing, I squeeze the bridge of my nose. Patrick, it seems, remains determined to apply pressure on me from every angle possible. I ask Mike what Eckhardt said to Patrick in reply.

"Eckhardt said he'd tell me. So he told me." Mike shrugs. "Bunch of crap. I wasn't even gonna mention it."

He wasn't going to, but now he has.

"I've kept everything with Jennifer strictly on the level, Mike."

He studies my name on the screen. The authorization. Finally he pushes back from his desk and beckons me into the small side room off his office, where pieces of outdated security equipment are piled untidily on leaning shelves. Walkie-talkies the size of bricks. Earphones the size of saucers. The only modern equipment is the video recorder and the TV, and Mike pulls up a chair in front of them.

"We got something from the Kwoks," he says. "Don't ask me what, but it's something."

"Do you think Patrick's trying to screw me?"

"One thing at a time, okay? What big palooka was it dragged me down Chinatown anyway?" He pushes a tape into the VCR. "Here's the story. When you left me, I went back there. Had coffee in a place next to the dry goods shop, thinking it over. While I'm sitting there, I saw maybe five old fellas come and go from the Jade Moon Theater. Not staying long, coupla minutes, then out. They go in with nothing, come out with a bag full of Christ knows what. Spot the clue. Next old guy comes along, he's about eighty, when he comes out, I follow him."

I raise a brow. I ask Mike if I really want to hear the rest.

"He volunteered an item from his bag." Mike points to the VCR. "This tape."

When he hits the button the screen flickers.

Orchestral music rises, and there's a shot of footlights and a red-curtained stage. As the music crescendos, the title comes up: *Dance the Dance*. Beneath this, Chinese subtitles. Then the red curtain rises. Mike grunts in disgust; my own instinct, I admit, is to laugh out loud. There are six men onstage, three jock types, big and beefy, and three others as slender as reeds. It is some kind of ballet, the three big guys dressed as men, the other three as women, but not one of them is wearing a stitch from the waist down. The effect as they pirouette and leap around the stage is bizarrely comical; they appear to be taking themselves absolutely seriously, as if they really can dance, which they patently cannot.

"What's this got to do with Po Lin?"

"Watch."

A few moments later the dancers are shuffling together, forming a boy-girl-boy line center stage. Each "girl" bends and takes hold of the buttocks of the "boy" in front. Behind each "girl" a "boy" moves into position. The orchestra plays on. We get close-ups now of several well-oiled pink erections.

"Okay, I get the picture."

"It gets better," Mike says.

I press the button and the screen goes blank. "Po Lin was investing the stolen money in the gay porn industry?"

Mike flips out the tape and we wander back to his office. "When I found out what kinda stuff old Theater Kwok was selling, I went back to see him. We had a talk. Once he got it through his thick head I wasn't there to put him outta business but I could if I wanted to, he talked a little. He wouldn't tell me anything about the business, his investors, where he gets the porn, like that. But he says he never heard of any Wang Po Lin."

"You bought that?"

Mike flips open his wallet and hands me the mug shot of Po Lin from our Security files. "This guy," Mike says, tapping the mug shot, "this guy is someone Kwok knows."

"Po Lin."

"With Kwok he used an alias. Dong? Pang?" Mike lifts a shoulder. "Something."

"You said Kwok wouldn't talk about his investors."

"Po Lin wasn't an investor. He was a customer."

"Wholesaling Kwok's tapes?"

"No, Jesus. Not some kingpin-type customer. A customer customer. A Joe off the street. Po Lin bought a couple of tapes a week, personal use, that was it."

Personal use. A seventy-one-year-old anti-imperialist crusader. I take a moment to weigh this totally unexpected connection against what we have learned from Marie Lefebre.

"Either Theater Kwok's lying or the money went through the dry goods operation."

"He wasn't lying," says Mike.

For a few minutes we discuss the possibilities for recycling stolen money through the import-export business. Despite the down-at-heel look of the Jade Moon store, the dry goods operation seems to me to be where the answer must lie. But the Kwoks will be prepared for us now, another visit down there would be a waste of time. I remark, somewhat hopefully, that Pascal might be able to trace something in the registered accounts. But Mike has serious doubts.

"Can't you get this journalist to tell you where those numbers came from? The source?"

I make a face: extremely unlikely.

"Try," Mike says, then he looks down at Po Lin's mug shot in his hand. "If Po Lin was pumping money through Jade Moon Enterprises anywhere—dry goods, whatever—how come old Theater Kwok identified this? Don't you think he'd wanna speak to his brother about it first?"

A very good point. And while we're still trying to puzzle that one out, Mike gets a call. Eckhardt. Mike turns aside and lowers his voice, so to make things easier for him, I step out into the hall where I wander along to the water fountain and fill a plastic cup. My gaze drifts out through the window. There is a clear line of sight to the USUN building across First Avenue. The lemony evening light is fading, and on every one of USUN's eleven floors the white fluorescents are glowing. Late-night oil starting to burn. The big vote is tomorrow. From now until then the USUN phones will be running hot, faxes flying, e-mails zipping through the ether. Last-minute arm-twisting. Hourly updates to the Secretary of State down in Washington.

Resting one hand against the windowpane, I sip my water. I count up eight floors in the USUN building, then across two banks of windows. Jennifer's office. The lights, of course, are on.

And I am standing like that, pondering the strained state of my relationship with the woman I am seriously considering asking to be my wife, the heated words we exchanged down there on the sidewalk this afternoon, when Mike shouts my name from his office. Dropping my cup in the trash, I head back.

"Get upstairs," he says as I go in. "Go see Patrick right now. I have to wait here for Eckhardt."

He is standing behind his desk. He evades my eyes by staring down at the phone.

"What's up?"

"Patrick's detained a suspect for Hatanaka's murder. Get yourself up there fast, Sam."

"Who?"

Mike finally lifts his eyes. His look is strained.

It's Rachel, he says.

22

I DO NOT KNOCK. I SHOVE THE DOOR OPEN and barrel straight in. There is a crash behind me as the door swings back, slamming into the wall. My right arm is extended before I am two paces into the room. On the way up I have rehearsed a hundred possibilities, but now that I see Patrick's obvious alarm, register that he is unprepared for any act of violence, it crosses my mind for one wild moment that I should actually do what he clearly fears I am about to do and leap across his desk and pound him into the floor. But the moment passes and I am left standing on one side of his desk, arm still extended, finger pointing, trembling with rage. The words when they come are not those I have rehearsed but ones altogether simpler, the hard and essential core of what I intended to say.

"Let her go." Release her. Let my daughter go free.

The fear in Patrick's eyes slowly recedes when he understands that he is not about to be struck. "That's what I want, Sam," he says in a placatory tone. "That's what we all want."

"You've detained her, for chrissake!" My glance flickers around. "Where is she?"

Patrick opens his hands, inviting me back into the land of sweet reason. "You think I wanted this? You don't think I was surprised when I saw the evidence?"

"Evidence?"

"That's right."

"Patrick." I place my index finger in the middle of his desk and lean forward. "Tell me where my daughter is, or I swear to God I will take your fucking head off."

So speaks Samuel Windrush, man of peace, lapsed member of the Society of Friends. Fear rekindles in Patrick's eyes.

"There's a case to answer here," he tells me lamely, but I stare straight at him until he cracks. "Room Seven," he says finally. "And there's a guard in there."

Room Seven is a general purpose conference room for the thirty-fifth floor, the place where Patrick schmoozes the other Undersecretaries-General, bending them to his point of view on such globally vital concerns as who gets to shake the hand of the U.S. president when he visits and who gets to carry the Secretary-General's bags on the next fact-finding mission to the Middle East. I barge straight in and find Rachel and the guard sitting at one end of the conference table. They are, somewhat to my surprise, playing cards. Even more incongruously, Rachel looks up at me and smiles.

"Hi, Dad."

I point to the guard. I inform him that I wish to speak with my daughter alone.

The guard isn't much older than Rachel; he clearly hasn't got the least idea how to deal with this situation. He begins to ask me if I have Mr. O'Conner's permission, but then Patrick himself arrives and the kid looks as if someone has just saved his life.

"Out," Patrick tells him, leaning in through the doorway. The kid lays down his cards and goes. Fast.

Rachel looks from me to Patrick as though she has suddenly lost the drift of what is going on. When I ask her if she's okay, she seems baffled by the question.

"Sam," says Patrick behind me. "If you step outside here, stand still for five seconds, you might learn something."

"Dad?" Rachel lays down her cards and gets to her feet.

I signal for her to stay where she is. "Don't say another word to anyone," I warn her. "Not till we've talked."

She makes a face.

Stay, I tell her, raising a finger. Then I back out of Room Seven, close the door, and turn to face Patrick. "You haven't told her she's been detained."

"That decision's just been made," he says.

Moving away from the door, I keep my voice low. "Well, unmake it, Patrick. Unmake it fast. Because how I see this, you've infringed on so many of Rachel's civil liberties already, she's got about twenty grounds to sue."

"Oh? And which court would that be?"

"She's a U.S. citizen."

"She's a Secretariat employee. And she's on UN territory. If you want to get legalistic, the only court that could hear her is the ICJ." The International Court of Justice, he means, in The Hague. This court's fifteen judges bear the imprimatur of the UN General Assembly, and notwithstanding their protestations to the contrary, each judge is subject to all the usual political pressures from Turtle Bay. Patrick, a grand master of these games, asks me, "Fancy your chances?"

I should have hit him. Earlier there, in his office. I have not the slightest doubt, of course, that he would do what he is implicitly threatening to do and pull every invisible string radiating out from the General Assembly in order to suborn the judgment of the International Court. My blood boils. But I have worked for this man for three years, I cannot pretend that I do not know what he is like. I have slaved too often into the early-morning hours preparing position papers at his request only to see the fruits of my labors discarded without proper consideration or even acknowledgment. I have watched him bury my work, then resurrect it at an opportune later date, claiming it as his own. I have heard him chorus praise to the faces of his fellow Undersecretaries-General, then subtly erode the Secretary-General's confidence in every one of them. And I have borne all of that because Patrick O'Conner—despite his arrogance and his addiction to political games—is the finest legal mind I am ever likely to work with, a bright shining star in the firmament of international law. Years from now lawyers will still be referring to his commentaries on the law of the sea, trade disputes will still be settled through mechanisms for whose wording and forms Patrick is primarily responsible. Though daily working contact has abraded my initial starstruck rapture with the man, I have never doubted that he is one of the finest lawyers of his generation. And that has sustained me.

But now I look him dead in the eye. And I muster every ounce of suppressed contempt I have ever felt for him.

"Patrick. You're a prick."

He does not flinch. But even Patrick's eyes cannot lie. From me, his lieutenant of three years, the judgment stings.

I toss my head toward Room Seven. "This is about Asahaki. It's got nothing to do with Rachel."

"She's got a case to answer."

"Let her go."

He assures me, absurdly, that Rachel was treated the same as the other guides.

"You've detained her. You haven't detained anyone else, have you?"

"Listen. Your daughter went down to the basement Monday night. She says to pick up her coat. Got that? Monday night. And now I hear she was in the library last week requesting the paperwork on a hostage rescue attempt that went wrong three years back in Abatan." When he sees my surprise, he nods. "That's right. UN volunteers. Your wife. Hatanaka's big mission."

I stare at him warily. What in hell was Rachel doing?

"Surprised me too," he says levelly. "Now your professional opinion, Sam. Personal involvement aside. What do you think I should do? Let her walk?"

Son of a bitch. But I have the presence of mind to swallow back my anger.

Patrick toys with a button on his jacket sleeve. "Ambassador Asahaki's back in New York in an hour. I've assured him that he can expect every courtesy from us. No half-assed allegations. And no more bloody questions till after the vote."

There it is. Out in the open. The real reason for this charade.

"Asahaki'll bolt back to Tokyo the second the vote's over," I say. "And you know that."

Patrick doesn't answer. He keeps his expression blank.

"I'm going to speak to my daughter," I tell him, moving toward the door. "Alone."

"This isn't bullshit."

"Sure it isn't."

"Hey!" When I turn, Patrick looks at me searchingly. And I am momentarily shaken by what I see there in his eyes. Real doubt. He really is not sure I should be allowed to see Rachel. But then he seems to realize that only force will stop me. He lifts an arm and touches his gold-plated Rolex. "You've got five minutes," he says.

Five minutes. Turning, I shove the door. Five minutes to explain to my daughter that on the thirty-fifth floor of the UN Secretariat building she has just been taken hostage by the Undersecretary-General for Legal Affairs.

———

"Dad?" Rachel is on her feet, her arms folded in an instinctive pose of self-defense. "What's wrong?"

I take her by the shoulders and sit her down next to me. We are half turned to each other, my left knee touching her right. She is wearing her UN guide uniform; now she straightens the skirt apprehensively.

"It's okay," I tell her. "Some people have some off-beam ideas. I'm trying to figure it out."

"Why were you so angry?"

I touch a hand to my forehead. If there were any way to avoid this, I would. Gladly. But Rachel is eighteen years old, and suddenly, astoundingly, she is in this thing way too deep. I cannot treat her like a child.

"The investigation I'm running into Hatanaka's murder. Patrick doesn't like which way it's going. He wants me off it."

"Why?"

"What's he asked you, Rache? What have you told him?"

"Nothing."

"Juan said all the guides got called back."

"Ah-ha," she says. Then, seeing that I want something more, she tells me that most of the guides left after giving Patrick's secretary brief descriptions of their work Tuesday morning. Only those who attended the NGO reception were requested to remain. "Three of us." Rachel gestures to the closed door. "Mr. O'Conner wanted to talk to us separately so we didn't like start talking it over, imagining we saw what someone else saw." She mentions the names of the other two guides. "Did you see them yet?"

"They've gone home."

Rachel drops her head to one side. "Already?"

And then I just cannot help myself. I ask her straight out what she was searching for down in the Dag Hammarskjöld Library.

"How come they've gone home?" Standing now, she folds her arms and turns her back on me. "He hasn't even seen me yet."

I study her as she retreats along the length of the conference table. Trust, Dr. Covey told me, was essential. If I was not to lose my daughter to a lurching relapse into anorexia, I had to trust her and she had to trust me. For all the physical devastation wreaked by the condition, it was, in the end, Dr. Covey said, a disease of the mind. And lack of trust, he warned me, could eventually be fatal. So in the past two years I have made it a habit not to pry where Rachel does not want me. And now I tell myself that that is the reason I let my question about the library slide by.

"Patrick hasn't been in here to question you?"

"No. He said he was going to be along in a while; he had to speak to the others first."

Reaching the far end of the table, she turns, regarding me in a puzzled kind of way. Now I rise.

"Patrick's using you to get at me, Rache. I don't want you answering his questions. I don't want you even talking to him. Anything you've got to say, you say to me. Not to Patrick. Not to the guards. Just to me."

By now she has gotten the idea that this thing is way out of whack. The corners of her mouth turn down. She shakes her head, the shiny black bob of her hair goes swaying. Then she picks up her purse, slinging it over her shoulder.

"Can you take me home now, Dad?" As if I am being called to fetch her from some party that she's decided isn't much fun.

My hands rise helplessly. Christ, how do I say this? "You're going to have to stay here tonight, Rache. I'll bring you some clothes."

"Here?"

"You're being detained."

She stares at me, not quite comprehending. "Who's detaining me? Detained for what?"

"It's Patrick. And don't worry, it's not about you, it's about me. Patrick doesn't want me nailing an inconvenient suspect for Toshio's murder. He believes he might stop me if he lines up a suspect of his own first. One he can use to twist my tail."

She peers at me a moment. And then understands. "Me?"

"I'm trying to figure it out."

"I don't believe it." Aghast, she runs a hand through her hair, the sequence of events that brought her here suddenly falling into place. Her voice is choked with outrage. "He's detaining me to stop you? He can't do that."

"As soon as the vote's over tomorrow, there'll be no reason for him to hold you. You'll be out."

"Tomorrow?"

"At worst, Rache. I'll keep trying, all right? But that's the worst that can happen."

A sound of frustrated fury rises in her throat. As she turns away from me, I seem to glimpse the girl beneath the woman, the adolescent whose emotions I know from painful experience can so easily sweep her past the point of reason, beyond the well-delineated boundaries of my own emotional terrain. At eighteen years of age she has visited darker psychological regions than most of us will ever see. And now she hangs her head over the far end of the table, holding herself very still. She is furious. Absolutely burning inside.

After four months of hell while Rachel was at Bellevue, I got a call from Dr. Covey telling me that my daughter had requested that her feeding tube be removed.

Oh, God, I said. No.

Silence from the other end of the line, then an appalled and hurried elaboration. No, not that. I had misunderstood. The reason Rachel wanted the tube removed, he said, was so that she might eat something properly. As I drove to the hospital, I kept hearing Dr. Covey say it: She wants to eat. In the average life, a banality, an unregistered part of the humdrum daily round. And yet for me the words were more like the "Hallelujah Chorus," sweeping me upward. My daughter wanted to eat. Elation. Relief. And when I got to the hospital, it was true—a nurse sat by this frail skeletal figure, my daughter, feeding her some glutinous yellow liquid with a spoon. I stepped out into the hall with Dr. Covey and pumped his hand, babbling my gratitude.

He warned me immediately that this was only the hint of a possible recovery. I nodded politely. For the present, I did not care what it was. Rachel was eating. From a spoon.

Dr. Covey explained how he intended to proceed with Rachel's treatment. Slowly. Increasing the intake at Rachel's own pace.

I finally dared to ask if I could hope for a full recovery.

The pathology of eating disorders, he told me, as he had told me so many times before, was unpredictable, too deeply connected to the patient's mind for any crude reductive analysis. But he saw immediately that I wanted something more from him at that moment than the standard textbook opinion. We seated ourselves in two molded plastic chairs at the end of the hall.

Rachel's case is unusual, he said, taking off his glasses. So often the cause of onset for anorexia was indeterminate, but with Rachel no one doubted that it was brought on by her mother's death. From there a misplaced complex of emotions—guilt and self-blame—led her down the same horrific route taken by thousands of teenagers each year. But now, said Dr. Covey, inspecting his glasses thoughtfully, now this reversal with Rachel seems as definite as the initial cause.

It took me a moment to interpret. So you think she'll get better, I said.

Dr. Covey chose his words with care. I believe, he said, she has a good chance. Rachel would appear to have resolved her feelings of guilt over the death of her mother. Perhaps in some self-protecting corner of her mind, he speculated softly, your daughter has acknowledged to herself that someone else was responsible.

Now here in Room Seven, with Patrick loitering outside the door, another picture comes to me, the one pinned to the Lighthouse corkboard: Rachel dancing in a wet white T-shirt among people I have never met, living a life I was not even aware that she had.

And I think to myself, What else don't I know?

"Dad?" Lifting her head, she moves toward me along the side of the table. "He can't do that, can he?"

Pain. It is like someone has reached into the cavity of my chest, clutched my heart, and squeezed. Squeezed hard. Stepping up to her, I wrap my arms around her, but she leans back, holding me off.

"He's got no right. You're a lawyer, tell him."

"It's not that simple."

Her grip on my arms tightens. Her voice becomes hoarse. "Tell him," she says.

My courage fails me totally. I do not ask Rachel the question that I had not thought of until this minute: Who was it? When she resolved her irrationally misplaced feelings of guilt over the death of her mother, who was it that she decided was responsible? In that dark, impenetrable region of her troubled mind, who was it she decided to blame?

THURSDAY

23

ONE A.M., THURSDAY, AND I AM DRIVING SOUTH with Mike. After fetching the clothes and things Rachel requested from her new apartment, fending off Juan's questions, then returning to Turtle Bay and making sure that Rachel was, as Mike promised me, under Weyland's care, I finally went home. I did not sleep. My daughter is a hostage. The thought played over incessantly in my brain, lodged like some weird mindloop. Late-night TV, the usual Windrush family prescription for insomnia, was no help to me, so I sat there in the darkness with my back propped on pillows against the headboard and considered the kind of world I move in, the people I deal with on a daily basis. I pondered some big questions like just how far the human race has progressed since Babylonian times, when the giving and taking of hostages was accepted practice, an essential maneuver of diplomatic life.

Be patient. That is what we invariably tell the desperate families who appeal to the Secretariat for assistance. A brother missing from a package tour in Angkor Wat. A father abducted from an archaeological dig out in Lebanon. Sons and daughters, mothers and fathers, people whose curiosity or idealism has sent them venturing out from their homelands, many hoping to render aid to the wretched of the earth; innocents abroad, fated to discover firsthand that the world is a dangerous place. Good people. People like Sarah. And now that Rachel has so unexpectedly joined the lonely band of the taken, I find that my own patience, just as on that earlier occasion with Sarah, is a virtue in extremely short supply.

She did not do it. I hold fast to that belief. She is my daughter, I tell myself, I know her. And I know she can have played no part in Toshio Hatanaka's death.

"It's off the main drag," says Mike, seeing me holding Toshio Hatanaka's AmEx bill up to the dashboard light. "Brighton Beach Avenue. You know it, yeah?"

I do; at least I used to. When she was a kid, we would take Rachel to Coney Island on those hot summer weekends; occasionally we'd do the trek right up to Brighton Beach. Eating ice cream, the three of us would wander down the avenue while Sarah retold the stories she had heard about the place from her parents: Estonian immigrants, the Lebovitzes spent their first years in America living and working just off Brighton Beach Avenue. Septuagenarians now, they moved to Orlando years ago, where Josh, my brother-in-law, lives with his own family. Josh tells me that he can hardly bear to visit his parents these days. Since Sarah's death, they seem to have given up on life themselves; he says he can't take the silence.

In the decades since the Lebovitzes moved out of Brighton Beach, the whole area has changed. A big turn for the worse, as Mike reminds me.

"Last time I ever went there," he says, "it was like a street war. Mayor goes there to do some election speech. He finishes late, and as we're coming out of the hall, we hear this popping—bam, bam—like gunshots up the street. I turn to the local muscle, I say to the guy, Have we got a problem here? No problem, he says. Some gang from Moscow shooting up some thugs from Ukraine. But the mayor's totally safe, he tells me. He says the Brighton Beach locals think it's just great the way the mayor's cracked down on black crime. Black crime." Mike turns his head to look at me. "Fucking Russians. You believe 'em?"

I fold Toshio's AmEx bill and put it in my pocket.

At the White Imperial down at Brighton Beach tonight, Yuri Lemtov, rising star in the Russian delegation and third member of the UNDCP Special Committee, has booked a table. I discovered this when I called the Russian mission an hour ago. Unable to sleep, I phoned the mission with the somewhat forlorn idea that Lemtov was the only accessible point of contact remaining to me from Toshio's investigation of the Special Committee. At the Russian mission they were doing the same as everyone else must be doing, poring over the numbers and figuring which way the vote is likely to go. But Yuri Lemtov was not there. The junior delegate I spoke to, a guy I helped with some mission problems last year, told me in a voice of complaint that Lemtov had slunk off for a night of caviar and champagne at the White Imperial. The White Imperial. As soon as I hung up I checked the AmEx bill Mike found at Toshio's apartment. And then I called Mike.

Mike yawns over the steering wheel. "What's the strategy? Shout 'Hatanaka,' see who bolts for the door?"

"I couldn't just sit on my hands."

"Why not?"

I look at him.

"The way you're telling it," he says, "Patrick's hanging the sword over Rachel's head so he can get Asahaki back to do one last push for the Japanese before the vote. So the vote's tomorrow. Not even twenty-four hours. You ask me, sitting on your hands sounds like a pretty good idea."

"And if she was your daughter?"

The corner of his mouth rises. "So what's Lemtov's story? We know anything about him apart from he was on that committee?"

I take a couple of minutes telling Mike what I can. Lemtov is in his mid-forties, one of the new-breed Russians, a technocrat who emerged to prominence after the breakup of the Soviet Union. He made a name for himself working for the Russian Finance Ministry, reconstructing his country's debt, then he switched to the Foreign Ministry, and now his negotiating skills and fluency in the English language have marked him out as the coming man on the Russian delegation.

"All three of them crooked?" says Mike skeptically. "Asahaki, okay, you've seen the paperwork at the bank. Maybe Po Lin's in it somewhere too. But all three? Where'd you get all that on Lemtov anyway, the files?"

"Patrick mostly."

Mike looks across at me.

The same troubling thought, I admit, has crossed my mind. What I know about Lemtov I have picked up from comments Patrick has made this past year. Patrick has been liaising with the IMF and the WTO over a series of conferences to be held next August on international finance and globalization. With his background in trade law, Patrick has high-level contacts in the West that are extensive, but Lemtov has been extremely helpful to him in providing the same high-level contacts in the former Eastern bloc.

"He and Patrick have done some work together," I tell Mike.

"Lemtov and Patrick."

"It's no big thing."

Mike nods to himself as he drops down a gear and pulls out to overtake.

———

It is raining hard when we park. Mike tugs his jacket up over his head as we dash across the street. When we skid to a halt beneath the protective awning of the White Imperial, the two doormen, in dinner jackets and bow ties, do not look impressed.

Mike stamps his feet, rolling his shoulders into his jacket. "Guests of Mr. Lemtov's."

The doormen turn to me then, and I say the first thing that comes into my head. "UN."

Open sesame. They step aside and wave us through. After checking my coat, we pause on the threshold of the main room and peer in. Opulent in a brassy kind of way.

"Guests of Mr. Lemtov's?"

"We're in, ain't we?" Mike scans the room. "You see him?"

The huge room is laid out cabaret style, with a stage up front and most of the floor space covered by tables. A bar along the rear wall is lit by a slanting lightning bolt of pink neon. A tuneless thunka-thunka blares out from hidden speakers and the buzz of voices is loud. A fragment of Las Vegas magicked into the heart of Brighton Beach; anything touched by light here glistens gold and silver. But I don't see Lemtov. When a hostess approaches us, Mike steers me around her to the bar, where a minute later we're each cradling a five-buck glass of Coke. Glancing around, Mike speculates on the possibility that Toshio was simply down here availing himself of all the female company.

"I mean, take a look. Throw a quarter, how many Olgas you gonna hit?"

There are, in truth, an extraordinary number of young women in the place, at the tables and loitering near us at the bar. Slavic. Lookers. The music dies away, a line of women in spangled leotards files onstage. U.S. and Russian flags unfurl above them. Applause. The room lights dim, the stage lights go up, and the music is suddenly pounding, the dancers moving sinuously into their routine.

Mike touches my arm and nods toward the entrance.

Lemtov has arrived. And with him an entourage of at least half a dozen men in suits, some of whom I recognize. Tariq el Jaffir, the Syrian ambassador. Rahman Abdullah, a member of the PLO observer delegation. Bepe, a Brazilian delegate and ex–national soccer star with a playboy reputation. And behind him, God help us, the Tunku.

"Oh, shit," says Mike.

It is not the Tunku's presence that has brought on this remark. Mike has just noticed one of the doormen at Lemtov's shoulder, pointing directly across the tables at us.

"Stay or go?" Mike asks, sipping his Coke.

Lemtov sees us and nods to me. I raise my glass. "Stay," I say.

Mike groans. He really does not want to be here.

As Lemtov is escorted to a table up near the stage, he pauses several times to speak with other patrons who hail him; he seems to be a known face in this garish arena. At his own table he supervises the arrival of an ice bucket and a magnum of champagne. Three young women appear. Bepe, who looks drunk, runs a hand up a skirt.

"Look at that." Mike chews on the ice from his Coke. "One of ours?"

"Brazil."

"Figures."

Now Yuri Lemtov weaves his way through the tables. Arriving at the bar beside us, he turns and watches the girls onstage. Mike gives me a look: Get on with it, ask him what you want, then let's get out of here. The opening routine finishes; there is a round of applause and Lemtov finally turns to the bar.

"You will join us?" he says.

When I decline the offer, he speaks to the barman. Two more Cokes appear on the bar.

"For my guests." He is being ironic.

"That was a misunderstanding."

His gaze is direct but unfathomable. He has those broad, flat cheekbones of many Russians, a touch Asiatic. A generous wave of silver hair parted on one side. And presence. It is not difficult to see how he won his reputation as a hardball negotiator. He has another few words with the barman; this time three shot glasses appear. The barman fills them with vodka. Lemtov slides one along to Mike, passes me the second, and raises the third himself.

"To my guests."

"For chrissake," Mike murmurs, throwing his head back, draining the vodka in one hit. Then, replacing the glass on the bar, he heads for the john. He looks tired and fed up. He does not like Lemtov's friends. And now it is clear to me that he does not think much of Yuri Lemtov either. Lemtov watches Mike disappear through the swinging doors.

"You have come here to see me," he says, still watching the doors.

I guess I could horse around, broach it indirectly as I first intended, but somehow this place and Lemtov's manner do not lend themselves to subtlety.

"We wondered why Special Envoy Hatanaka was down here last week," I say straight out.

Lemtov lifts a brow but says nothing. So I take out Toshio's AmEx bill and hold it up to catch the pink neon glow. After inspecting the bill, Lemtov glances over to his table. More girls have arrived. No one seems to be paying any attention to us. The music starts up again, some strange Russian rap, and Lemtov knocks back his vodka. Then he touches his ear—too noisy—and gestures for me to follow him as he turns from the bar. I look toward the john. No sign of Mike. Stopping by the fire door, Lemtov glances back over his shoulder. I turn a book of White Imperial matches through my fingers; then I pocket the matches, down my vodka, and follow him out.

———

The corridor leads up a flight of stairs to a rear exit. When we step outside, a sharp gust of wind buffets us; the smell of the sea is strong. The rain has stopped but water runs in the drains, falling from leaking gutters in the darkness. We have emerged by a coffee shop onto the boardwalk. Wetness shines underfoot, the light trails into inky blackness out where the beach meets the sea. The music from the White Imperial is muted; you can hear small waves lapping gently on the sand.

"You should have called the mission," Lemtov remarks, moving down the boardwalk. The Russian mission to the UN, he means. "They would have arranged an appointment."

"For next month maybe."

He smiles.

Then a door opens behind us. Expecting Mike, I look back but it is not Mike. It is some guy with a dark square face and an expensive suit who is built like an ox. Lemtov exchanges a few words of Russian with the guy before turning to me apologetically.

"My bodyguard. He insists he must join us."

Lemtov is immediately walking again. I hesitate, then fall in beside him. His bodyguard, the ox, trails a few paces behind.

"Monday a week back, Special Envoy Hatanaka was down here at the White Imperial. I'm assuming he came to see you."

"Why did you let Asahaki go?"

I look at him. "Ambassador Asahaki was never being held."

"Why not?"

I raise a hand. "Can we stick to that Monday for the moment?"

"Was Hatanaka with me?" He shrugs, pushing his hands into his pockets. "Of course."

"Just the two of you?"

"Yes."

Lemtov seems unconcerned. But some minutes have passed since I showed him the AmEx bill; he has had time to determine his pose. And it is, naturally enough, the pose of the innocent party.

"Who asked whom down here?"

"He wanted to see me. I invited him for lunch."

"What did he want to see you about?"

"Not Secretariat business," Lemtov says, suggesting by implication that it is no business of mine.

"Toshio's been murdered, Mr. Lemtov. Murdered while he was investigating the UNDCP Special Committee of which you were a member. I didn't come all the way down here at this time of night to be jerked around."

Lemtov continues walking. He gives no indication that my words have touched him in any way. "We spoke about Asahaki," he admits at last.

"Something in particular?"

"The fraud."

I glance across but he looks straight ahead as we walk.

"It was not the first time," he says. "But the other times, Hatanaka was careful. He asked only general questions. Where the Special Committee met. What Po Lin said. What Asahaki said." Lemtov makes a face, remembering. "*Kuratz.* Nonsense."

"But you guessed he was looking into a fraud."

"It was not so hard. Always he had someone from Internal Oversight with him. A black," he says dismissively.

Pascal. When I ask him if Toshio's assistant from Oversight was down here last Monday for lunch, Lemtov shakes his head. He looks somewhat surprised. He does not have to say it. He can socialize with the likes of Bepe and the Tunku, but he draws the line at insignificant black men like Pascal Nyeri.

"So Monday you discussed the fraud with Toshio."

"He needed some confirmations," Lemtov tells me. "What Asahaki agreed to. Papers he signed."

"Was that the last time you spoke with him?"

"Yes."

"Did he ask about Po Lin too, or just Asahaki?"

Lemtov studies the boardwalk at his feet. For the first time, some hesitation.

"Toshio was murdered, Mr. Lemtov. And if there's something you know, anything that might throw some light on that, I'd like to hear it."

Lemtov lowers his head. We walk a good ten yards before he speaks.

"Tonight we had a report from our people in Beijing."

I nod and wait. It is another ten yards again before he slows, then stops.

"Po Lin has been executed," he says.

Struck speechless, I stare at him.

"Unconfirmed," he warns, raising a hand.

"Executed for what, the fraud?"

"Ah, that you will have to ask Chou En." The Chinese ambassador. Lemtov thrusts his hands deep in his jacket pockets, the jacket pulled tight around him against the cold sea wind. "I do not know what happened with Po Lin. But on Monday I could see how Hatanaka was thinking. He was thinking Asahaki was guilty of the fraud."

"Toshio definitely wasn't asking about Po Lin last Monday?"

"No."

"Did he say what he was going to do about Asahaki?"

Lemtov turns his head. Hardball negotiator though he is, I can see that he is not telling me the whole truth. But the whole truth about what, I'm not sure. One thing for certain, like Patrick, he knew the full nature of what was going on between Toshio and Asahaki; he knew it yet he said absolutely nothing when Toshio's body was found. Not only that, he was prepared to sit on this unconfirmed report of Po Lin's execution.

"It would have helped if I'd heard all this a little sooner," I tell him, my tone sharp.

Lemtov lifts a shoulder. Not his problem. Then, wandering to the edge of the boardwalk, he looks out over the dark water. His bodyguard suddenly speaks. Lemtov answers *nyet* over his shoulder. I go and join Lemtov at the edge of the boardwalk. Staring into the night, I consider the whole business awhile.

"Or am I just being dumb?" I say finally. "Tuesday, when Toshio's body was found, you never told anyone what you just told me?"

"Who would I tell?"

"You never told Patrick?"

"Ask him."

"I will. But right now I'm asking you."

He does not speak. Or move.

"I could take this up with your perm five colleagues," I say. A feeble threat. On this matter his perm five colleagues are unlikely to line up against him.

"*Kuratz,*" Lemtov responds calmly.

I seem to have reached a dead end here. Lemtov's diplomatic shutters are firmly up, secured against any further questions. So I take a last shot.

"You have discussed this with Patrick, haven't you? The whole thing. Toshio and Asahaki, the fact that you thought Toshio was about to pin the fraud on the Japanese ambassador. You and Patrick."

Lemtov turns to me slowly. "If my daughter was where your daughter is, I would take more care."

I stand transfixed a moment. Then he turns away, starts to walk, and I reach and grab his arm.

"My daughter—" I say, and then my stomach suddenly implodes. My feet leave the boardwalk, my internal organs driving hard up beneath my rib cage. The air rushes from my mouth; I land on my knees and keel over, clutching my stomach. The pain is like fire. I can't breathe. My cheek pressed against the wet boardwalk, I open my mouth and try to suck in air. Nothing. Nothing. Then finally it comes, a few strangled gulps, then I moan and roll over and cough a trickle of vomit onto the boards.

Next I feel a hand under my arm, trying to raise me. It is Lemtov, he is kneeling beside me. I become aware of the situation slowly, of Lemtov trying to help me to my feet while he hurls abuse at his bodyguard in Russian. The bodyguard, it seems, has struck me in error. And now someone, somewhere, is crying out, "Sam!"

Shaking off Lemtov's hand, I kneel, hands braced on the boardwalk. And I breathe. The shock of the blow is passing but the pain is not. Lemtov continues cussing out his bodyguard as someone comes jogging toward us down the boardwalk. When the footsteps stop some way off, I lift my head. Mike. He crouches now, peering into the darkness.

"Sam?" he calls.

I raise myself, holding one hand to my stomach. I try to speak, but nothing comes, so I lift a hand weakly and signal Mike over. Lemtov reaches down, apologizing for his bodyguard. This time I let him help me to my feet. When Mike arrives, I rest a hand on his shoulder, leaning in to him. My other hand stays on my gut. Mike frowns.

"You okay?"

I manage a nod. When Lemtov explains that my injury is the result of the bodyguard's misplaced zeal, Mike turns to the bodyguard and swears.

I squeeze Mike's shoulder. Just a stupid mistake, I tell him. Let it lie.

"Feel like anything broken?" he asks me.

I shake my head. Then Mike rounds on Lemtov.

"No fucking thanks to you. Where do you get these guys?" He waves a hand at the bodyguard.

"We have made our apologies," says Lemtov.

"Fuck off," says Mike.

Lemtov appraises Mike coolly; I feel too weak to intervene. But finally Lemtov decides not to push it. He dips his head at me with a last word of apology, then turns and heads back toward the White Imperial. His bodyguard, who has not said one word throughout, goes with him.

When they're out of earshot, Mike says quietly, "What's the big idea? What the fuck you doing walking off in the dark with those two?"

"We were talking."

"No, Sam. *You* were talking. *They* were hitting you."

I take my hand off his shoulder, straightening gingerly.

"Teach you a lesson," Mike says, satisfied now that I have suffered no permanent injury.

"The guy made a mistake."

"That guy?" Mike points after the retreating figure of the bodyguard. "Sam, that guy is ex-Spetnatz. When the Russian president comes to New York, that's the guy they get to protect him. He don't make mistakes. He watches you. He watches his boss. He gets the signal, he pops you." Mike faces me. "You made the mistake. Coming out here."

Turning aside, I hack bile up from my throat onto the boardwalk.

"So what got Lemtov so mad with you?" Mike asks.

I lift my head and look down the boardwalk to where Lemtov and the bodyguard with the sledgehammer fist are walking side by side. "That guy hit me deliberately?"

Mike rolls his eyes at my naïveté. I have a sudden giddy vision of an infinite recursion of Russian dolls, faces behind faces, deeply entangled mystery.

"We were talking about Asahaki. The Special Committee."

"And Lemtov didn't like it?"

"He didn't seem too bothered."

"You didn't get socked for no reason, Sam, I'm telling you."

"He says Po Lin's been executed."

Mike's reaction to the news is the same as mine was. Struck silent, he stares. I take a moment to try to recall the entire conversation with Lemtov. There was, I remember, a distinct change in his tone right before the implosion of my solar plexus. I bend, then come slowly upright. The bruising will be deep but nothing seems torn.

"Executed," says Mike.

"Unconfirmed. And that's not when the guy hit me." I look back along the boardwalk; Lemtov and the bodyguard disappear now through the rear door to the White Imperial. "Lemtov knows Rachel's been detained. The guy hit me when I suggested a tie-up between Lemtov and Patrick."

Mike looks at me a moment. "Don't tell me," he says. "No big thing, right?" And then he swears.

24

M R. NYERI?"
    "Who is it?"
"Sam Windrush."

Silence then, and I stand with one hand resting against the intercom, my back against the wall, and wait. It is not just lack of sleep that has made me edgy; this part of Harlem is not a safe neighborhood for a lone white man at any time. Back in my college days I would come here sometimes with the regular gang and descend into the Bebop Shop basement and drink beer and listen to black men play jazz. The familiar contribution of our wised-up, post-sixties generation to the problem of race relations in America: Treat the problem like it wasn't there and hope that might somehow help it go away. Nowadays we all live in the suburbs or gentrified urban areas like Park Slope, while Harlem, this part of it at least, is territory we warn our children to stay clear of. But I need to see Pascal, so I stand here, trying to look relaxed even as I gauge the distance from here on the doorstep to the safety of my car at the curb. And though no one is moving around the street at this hour, the buzzer when it comes is a welcome sound.

The face that finally greets me when I have climbed the three flights of stairs and stepped over and around the bags of trash left out in the hall is not that of the confident young man I have grown used to. Pascal Nyeri, wearing only pants, looks tired, and, it has to be said, somewhat annoyed at this unexpected seven A.M. intrusion. Behind this is a certain wariness too; he would like to know but is too worried to ask what further escalation of our problem has brought me to his home at this early hour.

He ushers me into the living room, where an ironing board is set up in front of the TV. He gestures to the kitchen with a halfhearted offer of coffee.

"Pascal," I say quietly, hearing voices in the kitchen, "I need the financial background on Lemtov."

He blinks; his eyes are still rheumy with sleep.

"The Russian," I say.

He pulls a face. As if Lemtov is a name he is likely to forget.

"I need whatever you can get on him."

"I haven't finished with Po Lin."

"Po Lin's on the back burner."

"Why?"

"Because Po Lin wasn't having a private talk with Hatanaka last week down at Brighton Beach. And because this is what I'm asking you to do."

The voices in the kitchen rise, and two guys emerge, each carrying a bowl of cereal. Their gray flannel suits have the same hand-me-down look as Pascal's pants, the telltale sign that marks these guys even in Harlem as born and bred Africans. They stop when they see me. Pascal speaks to them in French, and they immediately retreat into the kitchen.

"When you were working with Hatanaka," I ask Pascal when we're alone again, "did much come up on Lemtov? Anything dubious about his work on the Special Committee?"

"No."

"Nothing down at the Portland Trust Bank?"

Shaking his head, Pascal crosses to the ironing board to finish the task that my arrival has apparently interrupted. The wrinkled white shirt has the sheen of cheap rayon. Pascal concentrates hard on the creases; he is plainly uncomfortable with my presence. Glancing around, it's not hard to see why. There are no pictures on the brown walls and the furniture looks secondhand. Through the open doors off the living room, bunk beds are visible, three and four to a room. Clothes and towels hang over the open doors. Not squalid, but there is an unmistakable air of poverty in the place, overcrowding caused by necessity, the same kind of thing I saw on several trips to mining camps in South Africa back when that nation was the international community's number-one pariah. Immigrant labor huddled together in prefabricated huts between shifts, young men in temporary occupation while their hearts were someplace else. When I turn back to Pascal, he pulls on his shirt. A proud man, he has probably never invited any of his professional colleagues back here. He is embarrassed by what I am seeing.

"Toshio never said he was seeing Lemtov last week." Pascal buttons his shirt. "What is this beach?"

Brighton Beach, I tell him again. Center of the Russian émigré community. "Lemtov says they discussed Asahaki," I add.

Pascal catches my tone. "You do not believe him?"

"Let's say I'm not too sure what they were discussing."

Another of Pascal's roommates wanders out from the kitchen, cereal bowl in hand. This guy, another African, is in his pjs. Less accommodating than the previous pair, he ignores what Pascal tells him and sits down and proceeds to eat his breakfast as he watches TV. Grimacing, Pascal nods me toward one of the bedrooms.

"Who are all these guys?" I ask quietly as he closes the bedroom door behind us.

Pascal digs beneath one of the three beds. "UN people."

"From Turtle Bay?"

Pulling his briefcase from beneath the bed, he tells me that they are mainly clerks and technicians. I tilt my head, curious.

"We live together to save money," he admits reluctantly. "To send to our families back home."

I feel a disconcerting stab of first world guilt. Fortunately Pascal is even keener than I am to drop the subject. He flips his briefcase open and hands me a folder.

"Po Lin," he says.

The folder is thick. When I remark on that, Pascal says that he was up half the night preparing this for me, the implication being that the least I can do is look at it. I guess he is right. So I sit myself down on his bed and spread the folder open in my lap. I want to get through this fast, but Pascal talks me through it in his customary thorough manner. After ten minutes I have the gist of it. Pascal isn't expecting anything back on the interstate company searches for days, maybe weeks; but for one of the companies from Marie Lefebre's list he already has the names of the directors and major shareholders.

"There is no Po Lin," he says.

"So?"

He touches the page. "This company is capitalized at twenty million dollars. But only shareholders who own more than five percent of the company must declare their names. So if Po Lin has invested less than one million dollars, his name will not appear on the register." He draws my attention to the number for this company, the one I gave him from Marie's list: seven hundred thousand dollars.

"You can't trace him?"

"Not possible. And if he did that in every company on your list, there would be no trace anywhere."

I flip through the pages wearily. If Po Lin was involved with Asahaki in the fraud, he appears to have hit on a simple and foolproof way of closing down his side of the paper trail. And if Lemtov's story is correct, if Po Lin really has been executed, we will never get to the truth here. Everything we reach for down this Po Lin road seems to dissolve when we get near. Things of substance suddenly turn to smoke.

Pascal has a suggestion. "If I had dates for those transactions, that might help."

I promise to see what I can do. But when he offers to go to my source directly, I instantly wave the offer aside. I doubt that Marie Lefebre would appreciate a knock on the door from Internal Oversight. I hand back the Po Lin folder.

"I want you to turn your attention to Lemtov," I say. "Take a look at the UN committees he's sitting on. See if any of those have had problems with you guys at Oversight or Audit." I give him the book of matches I swiped from the White Imperial. He studies the picture of the palace on the front, then the name and address on the back. "You don't have to go down there," I tell him. "In fact, don't go down there, all right? But see what you can find out about the place. Owners. What references they gave to get their liquor license. Whatever you can get."

He asks me if the place is a bar.

"Nightclub. And Lemtov seems to treat it like some kind of home away from home. Mike's got a feeling Lemtov might be tied in to the place financially. I want you to find out."

Pascal slips the matches into his pocket, then, standing, he drops the Po Lin folder into his briefcase. "What else?" he says.

"Mmm?"

"You did not come here to give me matches."

I don't answer immediately and Pascal turns and reaches for a tie in the minuscule closet. He flips up his collar and commences knotting his tie in the mirror. My glance wanders to his bedside table, an upturned crate. Pascal's small collection of books is lined up meticulously. Montaigne. Balzac. Several volumes by Voltaire. Probably the most civilized reading matter for fifty blocks.

"I want you to take a look at O'Conner."

No answer. When I look up, his hands have paused; he is studying me in the mirror.

"Undersecretary-General O'Conner," he says, and I nod. His eyes return to the tie and he finishes the knot. "I cannot do that," he says.

"I'll take responsibility."

"I cannot," he repeats, reaching for his jacket. Then he faces me, turning his head. "No."

A firm refusal, even firmer than I feared. I guess it always was a long shot. Delegates, even most ambassadors, Pascal knows he can deal with and still receive Dieter's full support; but an Undersecretary-General? Pascal's manner now, the way he looks at me, everything tells me that argument or further attempts at persuasion would be a waste of breath. Before he agrees to go poking into Patrick's private affairs, Pascal Nyeri will require more from me than a polite, unmemoed request.

"What if I ask Dieter?" I ask him.

"He will not agree to it."

"If he does, would you do it?"

Pascal weighs that. "If he instructed me, I would have no choice."

"Set up a meeting," I tell him, rising from the bed. "Me, Dieter, and you. Soon as you get into work."

Pascal's shoulders droop.

By way of encouragement, and apology for my unwelcome intrusion here, I tell him that I really do appreciate his work on Po Lin. Pascal is still young enough to look vaguely embarrassed by the compliment.

Then, out in the living room, someone calls Pascal's name. Before Pascal can get to the door, it opens. A guy is standing there, dripping, a towel wrapped around his waist. The tight black curls on his head and his chest are matted and wet.

"The Chinaman's back," the guy says, laughing, then he sees me and his laughter dies.

Colleague, I say, flicking a finger between Pascal and me.

The guy smiles uncertainly; there is a quarter-inch gap between his front teeth. He turns to Pascal. "He's parked in that same place. You want to go down, tell them who you are?"

"Not now," says Pascal, attempting to steer his friend back out the door.

Who you are? I ask Pascal curiously.

Pascal gives his roommate a fierce look. The guy grabs another towel from the door and starts drying his hair.

"Somebody from the Immigration Department came here," Pascal explains finally. "I was at work, he asked some questions about me. Now when he comes he just parks and watches the apartment."

"Chinese?"

"Asian-American," Pascal tells me.

"He parks by the alley," Pascal's dripping roommate volunteers. "He doesn't know we can see him from the back bathroom. He sits in his car, playing with his ponytail, like he's too smart."

Pascal turns the guy toward the door, tries to bundle him out. But when Pascal leans against the door, I suddenly reach and hold it open. Water drips from the guy onto the linoleum.

"Where's the bathroom?" I say.

Pascal leads me there, stands in the empty tub, and points through the open window. The car is a white Ford. You can see the driver's arm crooked out the car window, but you can't see a face.

"I called Immigration last week," Pascal tells me, apprehensive about my sudden interest in his minor tangle with the U.S. authorities. "I told them I was at the UN. That I was not illegal."

"What did they say?"

"They never called back." Shrugging, he looks out the window again.

"Have you ever gotten a good look at this guy?"

"Only from up here."

"Could you take a guess at his age?"

"Thirty-five?" Pascal ventures.

Asian, with a ponytail. Mid-thirties. Jesus, I think. Then I face Pascal. "Where's your phone?"

He leads me to the hall outside the living room. A phone is fixed to the wall with three thick metal plates. Under Pascal's curious gaze, I unscrew the mouthpiece.

"Is the apartment ever empty? Is there ever a time when all of you are usually out?"

Pascal shakes his head. Days off, technicians working irregular shifts, somebody recently fired, one way or another, he says, there is always someone here. He lifts his chin toward the phone, more than a little curious about what I am doing.

I peer into the mouthpiece innards. Zip. No silicone square.

Rescrewing the mouthpiece, I keep my voice low. "Somebody bugged the phones in Toshio's apartment before he died. Yesterday an Asian guy, mid-thirties with a ponytail, tried to bug my phone. This isn't an Immigration problem you've got here, Pascal."

The skin bunches between his eyebrows. His lower lip probes forward, a flash of pink.

Hanging up the phone, I rest a hand against the peeling wall. And I try to think this through. I could call Mike, but it would take him at least an hour to get up here; the guy in the Ford might be long gone by then. If I called the police, what exactly would I say to them? Jennifer, I think, then dismiss the thought immediately. Too many complications. Pascal's roommates would probably be only too pleased to help, but the idea of involving guys who cannot afford to lose their jobs does not appeal. Which leaves me, finally, with a guy who cannot afford to lose his job but who is already involved anyway.

"Come on," I tell Pascal, moving down the hall. He moans and shakes his head. But when I pause in the doorway and look back, he is right there on my heels.

There is no rear exit.

"Fuck," I say when Pascal tells me. We stand together in the main hall downstairs, a cloying smell of disinfectant in the air, while an argument rages in the ground floor apartment. Two women, cussing.

Going to the main door to the street, I stick my eye up to the peephole. My own car is right out front. "How far away is the Ford?"

Just past the alley, Pascal tells me. Thirty or forty yards to my right.

Stepping back, I check which way the door opens. "Does this guy know you by sight?"

Pascal lifts a shoulder. Maybe, maybe not.

I turn it over. After the brief glimpse the guy got of me yesterday, I'm not sure I would be recognized either. But then, is it really just a coincidence that the guy has showed up here now, so soon after my arrival? Doesn't it seem possible that he's here because I'm here, that he followed me? Besides, a white man walking out of this building? At this hour?

"You go out first," I decide, facing Pascal. "Keep your head down, try not to let him see your face. Walk on past his car but get the license number. Make sure you get it. I'll watch you from back here. Any trouble, I'll be out."

Pascal looks doubtful.

"Wait at the end of the block. Once you've got the number, I'll come out and see if I can get a look at the guy, make sure it's him. The same guy from my place."

"What if it is?"

"If it is," I say, "then when he sees it's me looking at him, he'll be out of here."

I beckon Pascal over to the door. His doubtful look lingers.

"Get the number?"

Get the number, I say.

He steadies himself a moment, then I open the door and Pascal shuffles out. When the door swings back, I hold it open a crack with my foot. The white Ford is visible now, but its plates are just a blur from this distance. Halfway down the front steps, Pascal stops and speaks.

"He is moving."

My eyes shoot back to the car. It is moving, pulling slowly away from the curb.

Shit, I say. Shit.

"Can you see the number?"

"No." Pascal squints. "It is too far."

I rest my forehead against the door. Should have called Mike, I think. Then I yank open the door, leap down the steps, and shout at Pascal to get in my car. I am already getting my key into the ignition when Pascal scrambles in through the other door.

"Watch the guy," I shout. "Can you see him?"

Pascal bobs his head like some crazed jack-in-the-box.

Hitting the gas, I swing into the street, the tires squealing. When I look straight ahead, there is no white Ford. "Left or right?" I shout, careering toward the crossroad.

"Left!"

I swing left. Halfway into the turn, Pascal changes his mind.

"No, right!" he yells.

I pull right and we begin to slide. A graceful arcing sweep, the tail of my car drifting while I haul back desperately on the wheel. Too late. The slide goes on in slow motion; from the corner of my eye I see Pascal brace both hands on the dash. Then the rear left wheel strikes the curb, the whole car jars, jumping a few inches into the air. I grip the steering wheel tight. There is a loud bang. We're both thrown sideways, and then the car stalls.

I close my eyes. Then I open them and sit up and look back over my shoulder. We have not traveled a hundred yards.

"I did not see the number," says Pascal.

I look at him. "You okay?"

He nods, shaken, finally releasing his grip on the dash.

We get out to inspect the damage. The lamppost is embedded in the rear fender, the left rear tire has already deflated. An insurance job. Windows are opening above the boarded-up shopfronts beside us. Black faces appear, mainly kids; you can hear TV cartoons playing in the apartments behind them. We receive a rowdy mixture of abuse and advice. A minute later an NYPD squad car comes into view; it cruises slowly past us, then U-turns and parks up behind. The kids jeer.

When I reach in to retrieve my insurance papers from the glove compartment, there is a high-pitched squawk from the bullhorn mounted on the squad car.

"Get your hands in the clear," barks a disembodied voice, and I turn to see a cop getting out, one hand on his holster. I withdraw my own hand from my car slowly. The voice on the bullhorn orders me to step away from the vehicle and put my hands on the hood.

25

WHERE'VE YOU BEEN?" RACHEL ASKS ME, PUTTING HER Walkman beneath her pillow, then sitting up. "You said you'd be here first thing."

"I was held up."

"By what?"

"I'm here now, Rache, okay?" Moving around the Room Seven conference table, I bend over her bunk and touch her shoulder. I can see that she has hardly slept. Her eyes are glassy, there are dark moons beneath them, and when I squeeze her shoulder, she folds her arms and leans back against the wall.

"I'll just be stepping outside here a while," says Weyland, who has remained standing by the door after letting me in. "You need something, Rachel, you just call. I'm right here."

Rachel lifts a hand. Exchanging a look with Weyland, I nod gratefully. He winks at me, then scoops his paperback off the conference table and withdraws to the hall. Rachel stays on her bunk. It looks like something from summer camp, green canvas stretched over black tubing. Weyland brought it up yesterday from the sanatorium along with a pile of sheets and blankets, most of which are now heaped on the floor. I deposit my bag on the table, then pull up a chair.

"Has Patrick been in to see you this morning?"

"Yeah." Rachel crosses her legs and toys with a thread in the blanket. "But I didn't speak to him. Like you said."

"Good."

"Mike came in too." She yanks the thread. "Cracking stupid jokes, like that was gonna cheer me up or something."

"He just wants to make things a little easier for you, Rache."

"Well, he could make them a whole lot easier if he just let me go."
I drop my gaze to the floor. Anyone else? I say, glancing up.

"Only Weyland." She gestures to the door. Then she looks at me a moment, finally cocks her head. "You look awful."

I remark that I would have settled for a comforting lie. At that, she smiles. But the smile quickly fades, and a second later she is looking past me as though I am no longer present in the room. A distant look. One that I have seen too often before. And for one dreadful moment I am transported back to those dark days of her confinement at Bellevue, sitting by her bedside, waiting for some word or even acknowledgment of my presence as she gazes blankly out the window. Hoping and praying that we can somehow pass through this thing together, that somewhere in the future my precious daughter might return to me, healed.

"The vote's scheduled for twelve," I hear myself say.

"The vote," she echoes, returning to herself. Then she swings her legs off the bunk. "I wish I'd never heard of the damn thing. I wish I'd never heard of this whole damn place." Standing, she throws up a hand. This place, the UN. And I know she is not thinking just about herself. She is also thinking about her mother.

She crosses to the table. Before I can stop her, she looks in the bag.

"What's this?" she says, and then she sees what it is: a few pounds of apples and bananas. I bought them from a stall outside the precinct headquarters in Harlem; something for Pascal and me while we waited. Useless to tell Rachel that now. The look she gives me is withering.

"You need anything else from home?" I ask.

Her eyebrows take on a V shape. "If the vote's at twelve, I'll be out then, right?"

I nod.

"So why would I need anything else?" she says.

"It was just a question, Rache."

"Well, it was a stupid question."

I bite back a fatherly instinct to pull her into line. She is obviously, and understandably, finding this whole experience hard to cope with. Now she grabs a bar of soap from among the toiletries on the conference table. She picks up her toothbrush and toothpaste, then snatches a towel from the foot of her bunk. When she marches out, I trail after her across the hall, receiving a sympathetic look from Weyland as I pass. Seated outside Room Seven, he drops his glance back into the paperback as we disappear into the rest room.

Rachel sets her things up at one of the white porcelain basins. She puts in the plug and turns on the tap. "So have you got any proper suspects?"

"We've got a few leads."

"You mean like me."

I look at her. Letting her know that she is not the only one on the rack here. Not the only one who has had a bad night.

"What did Juan say?" she asks, soaping up her hands. "Did he laugh?"

"I haven't told him."

Her head swivels.

"I told him you were spending the night back at home."

"Why?"

"Because he showed me the NGO message boards," I say. "The Internet. Pages of it. Every fruitcake in the world speculating about Toshio. Who killed the special envoy. In a couple of days they'll have it in the goddamn Drudge Report."

"So?"

"So I didn't want your name up on the message boards as today's big feature, Rache. And I was afraid that might happen if Juan knew you'd been detained."

She makes a sound. She splashes water on her face, then reaches for her towel. "That is such a crock, Dad. What happened to open government, freedom of information, all that? Isn't that what you're always telling me? That half the problems you have come from people trying to cover things up?"

"Well, this is one of the other kind of problem."

Almost imperceptibly the corner of her mouth rises. A smirk. The smirk of youth, ever alert to the small self-deceptions by which every adult life is sustained. Right now it feels like a blade to the heart. I turn away from her, then back.

"Listen. If you want Juan to know you're here, I'll call him. But there's no way I'm getting into any details with him. Not with him or anyone else."

"Don't you trust him?"

"It isn't a question of trust."

"Yes it is."

"Do you want me to call him or not?"

She squeezes a finger of toothpaste onto her toothbrush. Thinks awhile, and finally shakes her head no.

"I'll be out of here in a few hours anyway," she says, her eyes lingering on mine. I nod immediately. Of course. No question. This was, after all, why I came here. Not to hold some debate, not to argue, but to reassure my daughter, to let her know that I am standing by her, that I will do everything in my power to get her out.

She puts her toothbrush beneath the tap and looks down. "Weyland says the Japanese ambassador—Asahaki?—Weyland says he went back to Tokyo straight after Hatanaka was killed."

"That's right."

"Weyland says they didn't get along, Asahaki and Hatanaka. And that's what the *Keisan Shimbun* journalists said too, remember? Like Asahaki's probably not too sorry Hatanaka's gone, and maybe it could help the Japanese in the vote."

She seems to be waiting for some response from me. So I give her one. I remark that Weyland seems to have been very free with his opinions on the matter. Don't believe all you hear, I say.

Rachel rounds on me, flourishing her toothbrush. "Well, if you didn't keep acting like I was eight instead of eighteen, maybe told me what's happening, I wouldn't have to ask Weyland."

"Okay."

"And he doesn't bring me bags of fruit, like I'm some goddamn hospital case."

I raise a hand. "Okay."

"Don't say that, Dad. It's not okay. It's just not." She turns and grips the basin, bowing her head. "I'm stuck here for no reason. I can't even go to the bathroom without Weyland sitting outside the door like I'm a dangerous criminal or something. Don't blame Weyland just for talking to me."

"I'm not."

"You were," she says hotly.

Stepping up, I lay a hand on her shoulder. Her collarbone feels as fragile as a sparrow's wing.

"Who else can I talk to, Dad?" She screws up her face, fighting back tears. "You weren't here. Who else even wants to listen?"

I stroke her shoulder, trying to quiet her, to comfort her. My child. But then her words hit me, and my hand freezes. My whole body is momentarily chilled.

"Rachel, you haven't told him anything?"

She looks up at me.

"Last night. This morning." Stepping back, I open a hand. "You never said anything to Weyland about what you were doing in the basement Monday night. Or why you went through that paperwork down in the library. You haven't discussed that with Weyland, have you?"

"He's Mike's friend," she says. And in that one second I glimpse the abyss.

She has told Weyland, I think. She has told Weyland and he is going to report it to Patrick, who will then have a case to pass to the International Court. And there, if Patrick so decrees, the judges of fifteen nations will spend several years debating what to do with my daughter while she rots her life away in legal limbo, permanently detained at UN headquarters. Jesus, I think. No.

"What am I going to tell him anyway?" Rachel says, making a face. "Come on, Dad. Get real."

When I close my hands, my palms are sticky with sweat. I wait for the hammering of my heart to ease. Weyland is Mike's friend. That is right, I think. Rachel is right. Get real and calm down. Rein in the runaway paranoia. But the sudden bolt of irrational fear has left me badly wrung out; in the aftermath of the sickening adrenaline rush, my muscles feel like Jell-O.

I lay a hand on her shoulder. I tell her that I am going to see Patrick now.

"That won't change anything," she says. "I mean, what's he gonna say? Sorry, big mistake, and just let me out?" She throws out a hand despairingly. "God, what a mess."

That it is. And with greater insight than I would have given her credit for, Rachel seems to have gotten Patrick's number. Until Asahaki has completed his lobbying, until the vote on the Japanese seat goes through, Patrick will not be lifting a finger to release her.

"We'll have you out soon."

"When?"

"Soon," I repeat, trying to give my voice some conviction. But in truth I feel emasculated; not a father but a fraud. If I hadn't tangled with Patrick, Rachel wouldn't have spent the night here. We would not now be holding a futile debate on possible times for her release. I take both her shoulders in my hands. "After the vote he won't have any reason to keep you here. Once it's over, he'll let you go."

She regards me closely; she has always been able to read me like a book. And something more than doubt appears in her eyes. A sliver of real fear.

"It'll happen," I say. A lump the size of a fist has risen into my throat. Rachel gently pulls free of me and turns her back. The bones of her shoulders make small sharp ridges in her shirt. "I promise."

She gives a choked sound and looks at me over her shoulder. "You

know, you really are the world's absolute worst," she tells me
quietly.

It takes me a second to get it. Then I do. Liar, she means.

————

When I enter Patrick's office down the hall, he is busy working the
phones. He has one handpiece tucked beneath his chin, another in his
right hand, and with his left hand he is attempting to dial a number.
He nods me toward a chair, an invitation that I ignore, and carries on
his interrupted conversation, a blatant piece of lobbying for the
Japanese, as if I am not present. So I wait. And I simmer. I know, of
course, that the world is not black and white, that corners get cut,
edges blurred, and that there is an inevitable falling off from all the
ideals dreamed up by mere mortals. I accept that. God knows, after
my years in this place I cannot claim that my own hands are entirely
clean. But what I am witnessing here, Patrick O'Conner working the
phones, ringing the delegations like some backwoods political fixer,
lobbying furiously on behalf of a UN member, is so far out of line with
the Secretariat's obligation of impartiality that even a man of Patrick's
conveniently flexible standards cannot have any doubt that what he is
doing is wrong. And he carries on doing it right in front of me.

At last I reach over and press a finger into the phone cradle, cutting the line.

Patrick falls silent. He lifts his eyes and looks at me.

"I've just seen Rachel," I tell him.

"Unless Rachel has some pull with the swing votes in sub-Saharan
Africa, I can't say you have my attention."

"Last night I saw Yuri Lemtov."

Patrick returns his gaze to the phones. He starts dialing again, and
again I cut the line. He keeps his eyes down.

"The second the vote's over," I tell him, "whichever way it goes,
Rachel's released. I don't want to be hearing how you need me to
keep some little secret. Or to do some little chore for you. You've
had the leeway you wanted, you've got Asahaki back here, you've
had your chance. So now when the vote's over, she's out."

"That's your idea of justice?"

I wave this aside. From Patrick O'Conner I need no lessons in
jurisprudence, no lectures on the sanctity of the law.

"She's a suspect in a homicide," he tells me. "A real suspect."

"Is that why you can't look me in the eye?"

He lifts his chin. He looks me in the eye. Which from a veteran
politician like Patrick, of course, means absolutely nothing. But when
I screw up my face and turn aside, it seems to crank his handle.

"Let's recap here." Belligerent now, he comes around the desk. "One. You were assigned to investigate Hatanaka's death. Within twelve hours Ambassador Asahaki was on his way back to Tokyo and several years' painstaking diplomatic effort was disappearing into a big black hole. Two. You go rampaging around the perm five like a bloody bull in a china shop, upsetting everyone so much that even the bloody SG's asking questions."

"Who's complained?"

"Who hasn't?" he says. "Yesterday the U.S. and China. This morning the Russians. Maybe I should just call Lady Nicola and Froissart, save time." He touches his forehead. "Christ. When I saw that fucking body, I knew there'd be problems. I just didn't figure the major one would be you."

This really is too much. I point to the phones. I remind Patrick that which way the vote goes is no real concern of the Secretariat's. "Which makes it none of mine. Or yours."

"Oh, spare me. You know, I swear, sometimes you act like you just stepped off the fucking *Mayflower*." He turns and hits the intercom, instructing his secretary to get back the line he has just lost. "And three," he says, facing me again, returning to the list of black marks against my name, "you neglected to take seriously the possibility that your own daughter was involved in this."

I turn my head. I am not going to listen to any more of his self-justifying crap.

"Please yourself," Patrick says. "But I'm telling you, she's got some serious questions to answer. And what have you done to help exactly? You've instructed her to clam up, not to say a bloody word. This morning I stuck my head in the door to make sure she's okay. I ask her if she's comfortable. 'Ask Dad,' she says. Dad, for fucksake. You." I give a thin smile. Score one for Rachel. But Patrick is not amused. "So are you going to tell me what's going on with your kid? Or am I just meant to guess?"

"Guess."

"Son of a bitch," he says quietly.

Taught by a master, I think, but I save the thought.

Retreating behind his desk, Patrick retakes his chair. He pushes back, rocking in a quick staccato motion as he studies me. "Tell me something," he says, "have you even asked her?"

"I'm not getting into that."

"Jesus." He stops rocking. He leans forward, placing his elbows on the desk. "You haven't, have you? Your own daughter. She's a suspect and you haven't even asked her what in the name of Christ she was doing in the basement Monday night."

"She went down to pick up her coat."

"Is that right."

We eyeball each other across the desk. Then the intercom buzzes. Patrick's secretary, Leila. She informs him that she has the ambassador from Liberia back on line three.

Liberia. A country that has spent the past six months lobbying Patrick to get its name removed from this year's list of nations that conduct their internal affairs with habitual disregard to the UN Convention on Human Rights. For the past six months Patrick has been using me to fend off their ridiculous plea: A stand, so Patrick told me as recently as last week, had to be taken against these guys.

But now Patrick needs votes for the Japanese. He lowers his eyes.

"Liberia," I say.

Patrick's hand pauses on the phone. He lifts his eyes and his look now is piercing. "If you don't have the stomach for it, Sam, now might be a good time for you to leave."

A brusque invitation to absent myself from his office during negotiations. And at a deeper level, we both know, the suggestion that I am not quite up to my job. That I should maybe consider a premature conclusion to my UN career.

26

"CRAZY," SAYS DIETER, THEN ADDS FOR GOOD MEASURE, "stupid, crazy."
When I begin to recite the list again, an itemized reckoning of
Patrick's poor judgment, negligence, and downright hostility to the
truth in this whole affair, Dieter raises his hand. "About Asahaki, I also
am not satisfied," he concurs.

"But it's not just Asahaki, that's my point. Patrick kept that evidence under wraps until it was too late, you know that. But he's
done more than that, hasn't he?"

Dieter's hand returns to the railing, an aluminum tube that
stretches the length of the low wall by the walkway that cantilevers
over the FDR Drive. The New York traffic thunders past below us.
"You are accusing O'Conner of lying."

"Yes."

"That is not all that you are accusing him of."

"Look, I'm not accusing him."

At this splitting of hairs, Dieter raises a brow.

"Okay, so maybe I am. But I've got reasons, haven't I, Dieter?
Come on. I mean, how straight has he been with you and Pascal?" I
wave a hand toward Pascal, who is hovering a few paces along the
railing behind his boss. Since bringing Dieter down to meet me,
Pascal hasn't said a word. But he is obviously relieved to have chan-
neled my request higher up the line. "Or with Security?" I add. "Or
with anybody?"

Dieter turns and wanders down the paved walkway, his hand sliding along the aluminum rail. When I step up beside him, his hand
disappears into his coat pocket. Pascal falls in a few paces behind.

"A thief?" Dieter says. "The Undersecretary-General for Legal Affairs?"

"It's the only thing that makes sense."

He walks on in silence. My theory, riddled with holes as it is, has not convinced him. But in my own mind I am absolutely convinced now that Patrick, in some way, is tied up with this. I really should have listened to Mike earlier. We have been screwed around from the start, and after my encounter with Lemtov and his bodyguard last night, and my brief visit to the thirty-fifth floor this morning, I am no longer inclined to give Patrick any further benefit of the doubt.

Now Dieter asks me if I have accused Patrick to his face.

"No."

"Good," he says, relieved.

"Listen, no one's accusing Patrick of murder."

Dieter snorts. I touch his arm and we stop. We are by the rose garden now; the rose stems are thorny and bare. Faded nameplates have been spiked beside each plant: names like Peace and Hope and Brotherhood.

"One question, all right?"

He inclines his head warily.

"Do you trust him?"

There is a long pause. "I did," he says finally.

"And now you don't?"

Dieter puts up a hand. "What are you asking me for, Sam?"

I look away a moment. At the far side of the rose garden the moms and pops from Peoria are strolling around the North Lawn; a party of Japanese tourists is having a group photo taken near a statue. What am I asking for? My daughter's freedom, I think. The world.

"I want you to open Patrick up," I say, turning back. "His personal finances. And take a look at any financial authorizations he's made this last year. Any connection he has with Asahaki, Lemtov, or Po Lin." Dieter, to my dismay, is already shaking his head in refusal. "What's the matter, are you afraid of what you might find?"

When Dieter shoots me a dark look, I rein myself in. "I'm not talking anything official. Just give Pascal the okay to poke around. At least make some preliminary inquiries."

"I went to see Patrick this morning," says Dieter. "He was not there."

"He's there now." I cannot keep the bitterness out of my voice. "Maybe he can fit you in somewhere between his calls to Liberia and the damn Congo."

"Your daughter was there. In Room Seven."

I look at him. I know at once where this is going.

"She is detained?" he says.

"That's just dirty politics, Dieter. A cheap ploy."

"Detained by Patrick, yes?"

"This isn't some stupid revenge thing. I'm not asking you to open Patrick up just to get back at him for Rachel. You think I'd do that?"

"She is your daughter."

"This isn't about Rachel."

"Then it doesn't matter if we wait. Perhaps next Monday we can see—"

"Monday?" My frustration erupts. "I'm not waiting till Monday while my daughter's being held goddamn hostage."

Dieter's eyebrows rise.

"So she's my daughter and I want her out of there," I concede. "But that's not why I'm asking you to flip Patrick over. I'm asking you because I honestly believe he's involved in this damn thing somewhere. The fraud or Toshio's murder, I don't know where, but he's in it. And I'm not going to find out where or how unless I get some help from you guys." I wave a hand back to Pascal, who has his own hands braced on the railing, listening to our conversation.

Dieter glances over his shoulder. And seeing something other than Pascal, he grunts. "Your friend," he says, facing me again.

I look over toward the building. And immediately see what Dieter has seen. Asahaki. Ambassador Asahaki. He has just emerged from the Secretariat building with Jeremiah Sekelele, the Nigerian ambassador, a senior figure in the Organization for African Unity and a major power broker in the UN General Assembly. His white robe billows as he walks with Asahaki across the walkway. Heads bowed, conferring, they stop and lean on the railing thirty yards from us while their respective entourages stay back near the building. A familiar scene. You see it every day in the Secretariat corridors and down on the floor of the Hall; by the committee rooms and out in the lobbies of any number of uptown hotels. Two men, representatives of their countries, locked in private conference, auctioning favors, cutting deals, lining up the numbers for any big vote. Normally I would not even notice. But today is different. Today I stare.

On my way down to meet Dieter I bumped into Tommy Yelland, ex-doyen of the regular UN journalists. A plum job at the CBC took him away last year, but nothing could keep him away from today's vote. And in Tommy's opinion the Japanese have blown it.

What I don't get, said Tommy, buttonholing me in the elevator, is why Asahaki went back to Japan.

I shrugged. Politics. Who knows?

He probed a bit more. I remained unresponsive. Then finally he dropped the bewildered-old-man act and asked me directly. What do you think was going on between him and Hatanaka?

I was still shaking my head, walking away from the elevator, when it occurred to me that this meeting with Tommy Yelland was not simply fortuitous. I looked back over my shoulder. And sure enough, Tommy was riding back up in the elevator to find himself a more forthcoming senior Secretariat staffer to buttonhole.

With his extensive network of contacts in the Assembly, and an impartial eye to the outcome, I would guess that Tommy Yelland's pre-vote verdict will not be easy to overturn. And the Japanese must know the numbers. So Bunzo Asahaki, though he does not show it now as I watch him conferring with Sekelele, must be worried. Extremely so.

"You know what he's doing?" I jerk my thumb in Asahaki's direction, addressing Dieter.

Dieter shrugs. Of course he knows.

"Asahaki's back in the game only because of Patrick. Asahaki's wandering around out here free as a bird, lining up the African vote, and my daughter, Rachel, she's upstairs with a goddamn guard on her door. And I'm meant to wait till Monday?"

"Nothing will change."

I turn from Dieter to Pascal in frustration. Though Pascal's look is sympathetic, he does not seem surprised by my failure to carry the case. It is just as he warned me: Dieter will not touch Patrick.

"Is that your last word?"

"I can't help you, Sam," Dieter says.

I shove off the railing. And as I turn, there is a stir among Asahaki's people; they have just noticed me. Fingers point. Then one of them hurries to report my presence to Asahaki, who immediately breaks off his conversation with Sekelele and looks over. Only a second or two. Just long enough to register that it is me, his supposed persecutor, and that I am making no move in his direction. Just long enough to ascertain that whatever promises Patrick has made to him remain good. Then Asahaki turns away and resumes his discussion with Sekelele, secure now in the knowledge that I will not be troubling him in the lead up to the vote. All inquiries in his direction have been temporarily suspended.

Dieter begins to speak, but I flick a hand over my shoulder. I do not have the time for his apology.

This is how it feels, I think, marching down the path through the rose garden, my eyes fixed on the ground. Patrick has delivered for the Japanese. And this is how it feels to be brought back to heel.

27

WHERE DID YOU GET THAT STUFF ON Po Lin's investments?"
Marie smiles at my question. She hits the button for the elevator, then pushes a loose strand of hair over her ear. She regards me with amused condescension.

"Do I have to beg?" I ask her.

"It would not help," she tells me. "And you know it."

Her eyes go to the numbers above the elevator door. It occurs to me how absurd I must have seemed to the journalists who attended, albeit briefly, my course on journalism and the Secretariat. Did I honestly believe that I could teach them something? That they might actually want to listen? It's not just the reflexive skepticism they exhibit on every subject under the sun; it's this attitude, exactly what I'm getting from Marie here—that questions are the things they ask and you answer, that any reversal of roles is tantamount to the overthrow of the laws of nature—that sets them irredeemably apart. The give-and-take of daily life is not for them a two-way street; some essential human quality seems to be missing.

So now I raise my voice quite deliberately. "Didn't we have a deal?"

Marie blanches. She turns to make sure no one behind us has heard my question, but the only people there are two young female staffers clutching brown paper bags. They have not heard, and would not care if they had.

"We agreed, private," Marie reminds me, her voice a whisper. "You agreed."

"I didn't agree to just take whatever you dished up without question, accept it, and shut my mouth. I didn't agree to that."

Her look smolders. When the elevator arrives, we get in; she jabs the button for four, then fixes her gaze above the door. The two young staffers pick up the vibe; they decide not to join us.

"Internal Oversight ran through the list of companies you gave me," I tell her when the elevator doors close. "Interested?"

"Why did you do that?" she says, turning on me. "Why must you shout it, 'We have a deal'?"

"Nobody shouted."

"You did."

"Nobody heard."

"*Dieu,*" she murmurs, lifting her eyes. She takes a breath and thinks a moment. Then her expression softens somewhat, her angry frown slowly disappears. To my surprise, her hand rises and comes to rest lightly on my arm. "Please," she says. "I took a risk to tell you anything. And it is the truth, you did agree. Private."

Her hair spills from beneath a blue headband. My eyes wander down her hair to her neck. Unlined. Paler than Jennifer's. Her red varnished nails slide down my arm, then away.

"I have just missed my deadline," she explains as we leave the elevator and head down the hall. "My editor in Paris, he wants to kill me. My colleagues are shouting in my ears, and I am pissed off with everything." She smacks her hand into an open door as we pass. "Everything," she repeats. "Not only you."

Some guy sticks his bald head out of the *Frankfurter Allgemeine* office; while Marie pauses to confer with him, I look down the hall. Not all the UN-accredited journalists keep offices here, but today it appears to have become the unofficial assembly point for anyone with a reporter's scratch pad, camera, or microphone. There is a real buzz of anticipation, journalists huddled together, speculating on the vote. I hear Asahaki's name mentioned more than once; evidently his conversation with Sekelele has been observed closely from a window up here. A correspondent from the BBC is waving fifty bucks in the air, trying to place a wager on a Yes vote but finding no takers.

When Marie rejoins me, we shoulder our way through the thickening ruck outside the *Keisan Shimbun* office door. Then someone recognizes me. An Australian Broadcasting hack, Drew Armitage, a man who has been known to receive more than his fair share of leaks from Patrick. I do not like the guy. He instinctively shoves a mike at my face and asks about Toshio. Brushing the mike aside, I repeat the official line. That we're still waiting for the postmortem results but in the meantime he should consult our earlier press release: death by natural causes.

"Natural causes," he calls after my retreating back. "Does that include some UN guide? Name like Windrush?"

It takes every ounce of self-control for me not to pivot. I fix my gaze firmly on a point between Marie's shoulders and follow her straight down the hall. Drew Armitage cannot have the full story, I am sure of that. But I am equally sure that what he does have comes from Patrick, that what I have just felt is a tug on my chain from the thirty-fifth floor.

The Agence France-Presse office is empty. We go in, and I lean my back against the closed door.

"Why did he ask you that?" Marie deposits her purse on a desk. Bending, she searches a drawer. "A UN guide?" she says, idly curious. It seems she did not hear the jerk announce my name, or maybe she heard him but missed the allusion.

I wave a hand vaguely. I disclaim all knowledge. "Someone's idea of a joke," I say.

"A joke on you?"

Yes, I tell her. A joke on me. Something like that.

She pulls out a long reel of tape, its ribboning tail dangles. Then she crosses to the reel-to-reel machine by the wall and clicks the tape onto a spool. Like every other journalist in the building, Marie has an opinion on the vote. Now she gives hers to me. According to Marie, the Yes and No votes are evenly divided but there remains a big question mark over Africa. Less than an hour to the vote and the journalistic consensus is that the Africans will decide which way it goes. Which explains, of course, Patrick's call to the ambassador from Liberia and Asahaki's whispered conference with Sekelele. The last frantic push for votes is on.

I ask Marie how Agence France-Presse is calling it: thumbs up or thumbs down.

"The Africans are poor." She shrugs. "The Japanese have money."

"The Japanese buy themselves a Council seat?"

"*Oui*."

Supremely cynical but by no means absurd. Soft loans, aid, investment in infrastructure, all perfectly acceptable weaponry in the modern power game. High finance. Diplomacy by other means.

"If Asahaki had not returned," she adds, "I am not so sure. I think then maybe the Japanese would lose." She points at me. "But we have not been told everything about Ambassador Asahaki. No? Him and Envoy Hatanaka?"

"You'll get your story."

"Oh, I am not worried. We have a deal." Smiling as she turns to the tape machine, she darts me a look from the corner of her eye.

"I need your source on Po Lin."

Her smile dies instantly. She turns her back on me.

"Is that a no?" I ask her.

She does not bother to reply.

I am naturally not thrilled to find yet another door being closed in my face, to find that I am butting my head against a solid slab of oak. But from the outset Marie has not pretended to be other than she is. She openly staked her claim on what she wanted, the job at *Time,* and pursued it according to the lights of her own code. How many others here at Turtle Bay could honestly say the same?

I glance around the room. A purely functional space: PCs and recording equipment on half a dozen desks, wires hanging down behind machines, then running in tangled loops across the floor. Above the door, a framed photo of the French president shaking hands with the SG. Finally I see what I'm looking for, three large filing cabinets lined up behind the door. I go over.

"Do you keep your files on the perm five delegations here?"

"*Oui.*"

"Delegation members?"

"Who? Po Lin?" she asks, looking over her shoulder.

"That's a yes, I presume."

"We have nothing on the UNDCP Special Committee." She nods to the cabinets. "This is not my source."

"Then you won't mind if I take a look."

She drops what she's doing and comes across to the gunmetal-gray steel cabinets. She opens the middle one and hauls out a file. "You are wasting your time."

I reach for the file but she shields it with her body. "What do you give me?" she asks.

"You?"

"Me," she says. We look at each other, two adults suddenly aware of an unexpected undertow.

"I thought I was wasting my time."

"If that is what you want."

I turn my gaze back to the cabinet. "I want to see Lemtov's file too. Give me that, and I'll tell you something you'll be interested to hear."

Marie makes a clicking sound with her tongue as she studies me. Then finally she pulls Lemtov's file from the cabinet and lays it with Po Lin's on the desk. Smiling now. Playful. I have not the slightest doubt that if I attempted to grab the files, she would tear my eyes out. She tilts her head and waits for my news.

"Once I've told you, you give me both files."

"Is it worth it?" she says.

"Po Lin's been executed."

Her head comes up straight. Her lips part and a sound rises in her throat.

"That's unconfirmed. And don't ask me if it's connected with the fraud or his investments," I add quickly, "because I honestly don't know."

"You heard this in the Secretariat?"

"From Lemtov."

She looks down at the two files. Wang Po Lin. And Yuri Lemtov. When she lifts her eyes, I pull the files quickly from beneath her hand.

Then one of her Agence France-Presse colleagues comes barreling in. When he crosses straight to the tape machine, Marie shouts and hurries over to stop him from ruining her work. She calls a warning to me over her shoulder. "The files must stay. You can read them here."

While she commences an argument in French with her colleague, I slide the files along the table and pull up a chair.

In the Secretariat, brief notes on the accredited delegates are kept by Protocol and somewhat more extensive pieces on the major delegations by Political Affairs. All this information is volunteered. Volunteered, of course, meaning anodyne or downright misleading. Idi Amin's appearance at UNHQ some years back, for instance, resulted in a glowing encomium on the dictator's contribution to human rights finding its way into the Ugandan files; rogue copies of this document still surface from time to time amid general hilarity. But on rechecking Po Lin's and Lemtov's files upstairs this morning, I found nothing outrageous, just the usual list of previous posts and qualifications. In Po Lin's case, a footnote relating to his temporary recall to Beijing.

My hope here is that Agence France-Presse, free from the political constraints placed on the Secretariat, has made a more thorough and critical analysis of the two men. After a few minutes' inspection, my hope slowly fades. Both files seem to be French translations of the documents I viewed this morning in English up in Protocol. I lift my head and glance across at Marie. She is leaning over the tape machine, her skirt riding upward. Her colleague hovers impatiently at her side, and when the guy looks my way, I rebury my head in the files. A minute later I come across the clippings.

Real clippings, not just some faxed sheet from a clippings agency. In each file there is a large envelope, buff-colored, crammed with bits of paper. I spread the Po Lin clippings on the table. A few are torn, others carefully scissored from various newspapers and magazines, maybe a dozen in all. In some pieces Po Lin is merely mentioned as one of a list of names, in others he figures more prominently, but there appears to be no particular method in the selection. Random scraps. Whatever caught the clipper's eye. Finishing the last piece, I reach for the Lemtov envelope just as Marie appears at my side.

"You are certain Po Lin was executed?" she whispers.

"It's what Lemtov told me."

"You are not certain?"

"You're the journalist, Marie." I nod toward her colleague at the tape machine. "Put your heads together. Use your contacts. I'd be interested to hear some confirmation myself."

She rolls her eyes. "From Paris," she whispers, referring to her colleague. The implication being, I take it, that she has no intention of letting the guy in on her story. She points to the Po Lin clippings. "This is useful?"

"Not as useful as if you just told me your source."

She makes a face: No chance.

I hold up the Lemtov clippings. "Can I take these?"

"No." Unsmiling. Deadly earnest.

Then the big shot from Paris calls for her assistance and she curses quietly and goes over. Alone again, I spread out the Lemtov clippings.

Nearly all the clippings feature him prominently; unlike Po Lin, he is rarely bracketed by a list of names from his delegation. Some pieces mention Lemtov as the likely successor to the current Russian ambassador; a few go farther and speculate on a possible promotion to the post of foreign minister at some future date, speculation that I've heard myself from several quarters, notably Patrick, whose opinion on such matters is generally considered oracular. After wading through maybe fifteen or more clippings I notice a recurring motif, the seemingly off-the-cuff remark from Lemtov that passes directly into the journalist's copy as a quotable quote. Self-deprecating, wry, humorous; but seen together like this they present a picture of the not-so-loyal second-in-command carefully laying the groundwork for his run at the top.

Son of a bitch, I think as I come across yet another of his casual bon mots, this one a backhanded compliment directed at the current Russian ambassador.

And then three lines down, a single word leaps out at me from the page.

Basel.

I make a sound, something like a moan.

I sit up straight. Now my eyes scour the rest of the clipping, searching for the meaning of what I've found. But the word does not recur. There's just that one mention—a UN-sponsored conference in Basel that Lemtov attended—then the article moves on to the prospects of success in some long-forgotten disarmament talks. I turn quickly to the other clippings, searching, but that first mention of Basel seems to be all there is. Finally I pick up that clipping again, a scissored cutting, cheap paper, and study it carefully. It seems to be taken from some academic journal, one of those erudite publications that lie on the shelves unread in every college library. In the bottom left-hand corner someone has scribbled a date: April, three years ago. If I could take the clipping to the Dag Hammarskjöld Library I could probably find the article, cross-reference it with our files, and track down which UN-sponsored conference Lemtov attended.

"We are leaving," says Marie. When I look up, she is holding her notepad. Her colleague shoots a cartridge into the tape recorder that hangs like a purse from his shoulder. Outside in the hall I hear other journalists streaming by, smart-aleck remarks and laughter, cursing in a variety of languages. The migration to the General Assembly Hall, the jockeying for prime positions, has begun. Marie nods to the files. "You are finished?"

Not really a question. They want me out. So I shuffle the clippings back into the envelopes and reorder the files. I wait. After half a minute, Marie's colleague impatiently directs her attention to the clock, and they both look up. At that moment I bring my hands together, sliding the Basel cutting beneath my watchband. I tug at my sleeve. Then I rise from the table calmly, thank Marie for her trouble, and depart.

28

"WHO'S PLAYING HERE, THE YANKEES?"
Standing by me at the rear of the General Assembly Hall,
Mike runs a laconic eye over the milling delegates. Neither one of us
has ever seen the Hall so crowded. And there is no mistaking the
sense of occasion. It is like opening day all over again, clouds of ex-
otic national costumes moving like kaleidoscopic whorls through the
ocean of dark gray suits. Historic. Today the most abused word in
the lexicon of UN grandiloquence is absolutely appropriate. Only
the second time in the UN's history that a proposed change in the
Security Council's composition has made it to the vote, and no one
who has any right to be here has stayed away. Committee meetings
have been suspended, talks and conferences rescheduled; from every
quarter of Turtle Bay the delegates, Secretariat staffers, and NGO
observers have massed here on the plenary session, filling the Hall.
Down by the podium the Secretary-General and the session president are standing side by side, talking together as they scan the ranks
of delegates. From this distance they look like two small boys.

Mike whistles through his teeth and shoulders his way along the
aisle, searching for a pair of vacant seats. If he gets us seats, I have
told him, he can have a look at the thick bundle I am carrying beneath my arm. And Mike is curious.

After leaving Marie's office I went directly to the Dag Hammarskjöld Library, where, in the absence of inquiring journalists
and delegates who had already departed for the Hall, a holiday
air prevailed. Feet up on desks, paper balls lobbing into trash cans,
and the female librarians huddled together over the glossies. A
young Spaniard, clearly a newcomer to the ways of Turtle Bay,

seemed embarrassed by his colleague's lack of interest in my inquiry. Once I'd traced the source of the Agence France-Presse clipping, he led me down into the section dedicated to UN conferences—a labyrinth of shelves and cabinets and boxes—and loaded my out-stretched arms with papers and files. Five minutes' sifting and I had what I wanted, a manageable bundle that I have brought with me to the Hall.

"*Nada,*" Mike reports, coming up the stairs to rejoin me. Turning, he surveys the scene again. Words, talk, diplomacy's permanently debased currency, jangle loudly through the Hall.

I locate the U.S. delegation off to the left, halfway down the tiered chamber. Ambassador Bruckner is on his feet, glad-handing the neighboring delegates, smiling a smile that you can see from way back here. You would think he hasn't a care in the world, but his fellow U.S. delegates look distinctly apprehensive. Jennifer has her arms crossed, her back turned to Bruckner as she talks to someone across the aisle. Her body language is defensive and tense.

They don't know.

After all the arm-twisting, the years of lobbying and backroom deals, in spite of Rachel's detainment and Asahaki's recall, they still don't know. The U.S. has not been able to bed down the result. The upcoming General Assembly vote, for once, is not a foregone conclusion.

"Hey," says Mike, nodding down toward the front. There are two empty chairs between the podium and the exit. A guard standing nearby.

"Security?" I say.

"Two tickets, ringside." Mike brushes past me. "Or if you want you can stay up here in the goddamn bleachers."

———

The aisles are jammed, so we end up taking the long way, back out to the empty gallery behind the Hall, then around to the stairs. A few late arrivals go hurrying by, determined not to miss the big moment. As we walk, Mike fills me in on his morning.

"Guy comes up to my office, hammering on my door. Haven't even got my coffee yet. He's throwing a fit, telling me he's going to bust, tearing his goddamn hair out. I'm thinking like, Who is this guy? Turns out he's the caterer."

"The cafeteria?"

"Right." In the coolroom of which we have stored Toshio's body. "This guy," says Mike, "he's got the catering franchise down there.

Italian. He says we don't let him open up pronto, he'll be outa business."

"Does he know what's in his coolroom?"

"Public relations ain't my department." Mike glances across. "He started about suing someone. I gave him your number."

Grimacing, I turn for the stairs.

"So how's the gut?" Mike asks me.

My hand rises to my stomach, the place where Lemtov's body-guard connected. Sore, I say, but I'll live.

Mike gives me some advice on the treatment of internal bruising, cop tradecraft, but as we walk, I get the feeling that he's got something other than my state of health on his mind. Halfway down the stairs, he finally comes out with it.

"How come you never told me the full story on that Martinez kid, the hippie?" He continues down the steps in front of me. When he gets to the landing, he stops, one hand on the banister, and faces me. "You didn't hear the question, Sam, or you just thinking?"

"What full story?"

"How the kid's old man died out in Afghanistan. The kid's old man, who happened to be leading that medical team that Sarah was in."

I comment, somewhat ingenuously, that I don't see the problem.

"Could be a big problem," Mike tells me. "What if the kid blames Hatanaka for screwing up the hostage rescue that got his old man killed?"

"He doesn't."

"You asked him?"

"No."

He pauses a moment. Sensing the next question, I steel myself. Then it comes.

"You ever asked Rachel?"

I make no reply. Mike fills his cheeks with air, then blows. "I'm gonna bring the Martinez kid in again. And if I'm not satisfied with what he tells me this time, I might have to speak to Rachel too."

I cannot pretend to be pleased. But given the givens here, Mike has handled this as well as he could have. Straight. Totally up front with me. But now, as we make our way toward the Hall, I feel him glancing at me from the corner of his eye. Not so much mad at me as suddenly, and somewhat to his own surprise, touched by doubt.

Inside the Hall the talk is dying away, delegates who have strayed from their places hurrying to retake their seats. Mike has a word with the guards, who point us to the pair of empty chairs by the

NGO observers' box. Mike unbuttons his jacket as he sits; I catch a glimpse of the leather holster beneath his arm.

"I asked Dieter to check Patrick out," I whisper, sliding into the chair beside him. "He's telling me maybe next week."

"Guy doesn't have the balls to front O'Conner. Not next week. Not even next year."

But Mike, I am sure, has got Dieter wrong. On reflection, my encounter earlier with Dieter proves only one thing: that we have no real evidence against Patrick. On reflection, I feel sure that if we had something concrete, Dieter would not hesitate to act.

A gavel bangs down on the podium; it seems we have arrived just in time. The Secretary-General takes the rostrum over to our right, and the noise fades to silence as he looks out across the Hall. Caesar before the Senate. Lincoln at Gettysburg. A born showman, he milks the moment, arms braced and chin thrust forward. Silent strength seems to be the PR pose for the day. Then he begins his address, and right from the outset it is woeful. His voice rises at inappropriate moments. He gesticulates grandly. He expounds on three or four abstract topics without drawing breath, all the time swaying on the balls of his feet. It was Lady Nicola who pointed out to me that since its inception, not one great speech has issued from the main rostrum of the United Nations. We have had Khrushchev banging his shoe on the woodwork, promising to bury the West, and Castro grandstanding up there for hours, but this potentially great forum has yet to find its Pericles, and this speech we're hearing now from the SG is certainly not going to break the shoddy mold. Leaden platitudes come tumbling out like useless ingots off some haywire production line. It is truly, mind-numbingly, awful.

Mike nudges me, pointing to the bundle in my lap, the paperwork from the library. "Let's see."

I glance around. All eyes are on the SG. "Lemtov attended a UN-sponsored conference in Basel three years back," I whisper, sliding the ribbon from my bundle and passing four folders to Mike. "Somewhere in here we should find out which one. Maybe what else he was doing there."

"Basel," says Mike. "Hatanaka's trip?"

I tap the files. Get started, I say.

Fifteen minutes later the SG's speech is still going, and Mike and I are still reading. Conferences. Preconference conferences. Postconference conferences. Conferences on climate change. Conferences on aid. I have attended more than a few of these talkfests over the years, but the number and range of the events listed in these files is utterly farcical. Beside me, Mike has been alternately snorting and groaning as he turns each page. Now there is applause and we look up to see the SG stepping back from the rostrum. The applause is sustained; everyone is relieved at the unaccustomed brevity of the address.

"Praise the Lord," Mike mutters, stretching his back.

Then the president of the session, the guy who will oversee the mechanics of the vote, replaces the Secretary-General at the rostrum. We are not going to be spared. Within moments the president is launched on a speech of his own.

"Anything?" Mike whispers.

I shake my head. "You?"

"Unh-unh."

The speech continues. We drop our heads into the files again.

Psychoanalyzing the world, that's how Sarah described the conferences I was sometimes called upon to attend, and over time I came to accept a solid kernel of truth in the phrase. Swarms of highly paid professionals gathering in five-star comfort to discuss the suffering patient's latest symptoms, the cause of the moment—illiteracy, AIDS, refugees—swapping good intentions before picking up their ample paychecks and flying home. Having had a front row seat at this whole circus for years, I have grown weary of the endless prognostications of disaster, the act-now-or-the-world-ends-tomorrow brigade. But what I told Sarah, and what I still believe to be true, is that not every UN-sponsored conference is the same. Looking through the file spread open in my lap, I can see amid the welter of useless gatherings the occasional shining example of an event that was certainly worthwhile. A conference, for example, to establish the remit of the International Court of Human Rights. It did not, I notice, take place in Basel.

Registering a change in the president's tone, I lift my head. He is winding down. He concludes with a rousing admonition to the voting delegates, and a ripple of applause runs up through the Hall. And then silence. We have arrived.

"Sam?" Mike whispers.

I lift a hand sharply: wait. The one moment in my career when I will actually see history being made here. My one chance to see the parliament of man rise from its usual mundane and petty squabbles to make a decision that really matters. My gaze is riveted to the huge electronic display board suspended behind the rostrum. When the one hundred and eighty-five ambassadors have finished pressing their vote buttons, that is where the result will appear. Yes, no, or abstain.

The president reads aloud the official proposal for the amendment of the Security Council's composition, the inclusion of Japan as a permanent member. Then he calls for the vote. A rustle like wind over leaves passes up through the Hall as the ambassadors register their votes. Years of painstaking diplomacy telescoped into moments. Halfway up the Hall, angry voices suddenly rise; one of the African delegations has apparently seen their ambassador capriciously change their nation's intended vote. From the rostrum the president calls them to order.

"All votes registered," he intones grandly. Then he turns to look up at the display board. And there the numbers suddenly appear.

Yes—72

No—79

Abstain—34

The Nos have it. The Japanese do not get a permanent Security Council seat.

There is a second of silence.

Then somebody, a lone voice, starts to cheer. Others join in, then there is applause. Half the delegates rise, embracing one another and punching their fists in the air, their faces lit by victory. The entire U.S. delegation remains seated. They are not talking to each other or to anyone else. Bruckner is staring at the voting board as if reading the announcement of his own political demise. Jennifer has her head in her hands. And down near the front, the Japanese have risen as one and are now making for the exit after their leader, Bunzo Asahaki. Unable to endure the public loss of face, he is going to skip the official declaration.

Then my gaze falls on Patrick. Out of my line of sight till this moment, he has appeared from the far side of the podium. His face is set like stone. He stares up at the celebrating delegations as the president announces the official result. Immediately the SG descends from the platform and walks right by Patrick without even a glance in his direction. A snub that Patrick sees. His face glows with embarrassment and anger. He is hurt, I think. Patrick O'Conner is hurting and I am glad.

"Sam," says Mike, tugging at my sleeve. Then he shows me the stapled pages, what he has found. "This one was in Basel," he tells me soberly. "And that's him, yeah?" His finger stabs down on a name. Mr. Y. Lemtov, representative of the Russian Federation.

"That's him," I agree.

"And this one?" Mike's finger moves down the list to another name. Mr. P. O'Conner.

My head snaps back.

"Here's the good part," says Mike, flipping to the title page.

When I see it, my mouth opens, slack-jawed. Mike makes some wise-ass crack about thinking global, acting local. Then we sit amid the tumult of the post-vote celebrations and commiserations, two lonely travelers stranded by our own private shipwreck. We both stare at what Mike has found.

Money Laundering, says the title. The International Perspective.

A UN-sponsored conference attended by Yuri Lemtov and Patrick O'Conner.

"Food for thought," Mike comments dryly.

Before I can even begin to collect my thoughts, Patrick himself appears right in front of us. Mike flips the file closed.

"Happy now?" Patrick asks, leaning over me, his face still rosy with anger.

"The vote's over," I say, rising. I tell Patrick that I'm going up to get Rachel.

"Not yet you're not. You're wanted in the side chamber." Patrick gestures to the far exit through which Bruckner and Lady Nicola are disappearing. The French ambassador, Froissart, hurries to join them. "And when you're done explaining yourself and your cockass investigation to them, you can come upstairs and explain yourself to me."

"Give Mike the word, he'll have Weyland let Rachel go."

Patrick turns. "This is the word, Mike. You release the Windrush girl before this bastard comes to my office and I'll have you fired." With this final shot, Patrick pivots on his heel and goes.

"Man's full of shit," Mike remarks quietly. "Once he's cooled down, he'll let her go. Probably be out before you're even finished in the side chamber." He bundles together the files, handing me the one on the money laundering conference in Basel. "You take this. I'll dump the rest in the library." Then his eyes focus on something behind me, and I turn.

Lemtov. He is descending the steps to the main floor, deep in conversation with the wizened but irrepressible figure of the Tunku. The Tunku, the chairman of the UNHQ Committee, Turtle Bay's number-one troublemaker and pain in the neck. They remain locked in private discussion as they veer toward the exit. Lemtov and the Tunku. Not a combination I care for, and judging by his expression, neither does Mike.

"She'll be out by the time you're done," he says, hitching files beneath his arm. Then, moving off into the stream of delegates, he tosses me a few even more improbable words of encouragement. "Give 'em hell."

29

A SMOKY FOG IS BUILDING FAST WHEN I ARRIVE in the Security Council side chamber. I close the door behind me, then turn. The faces that greet me along either side of the table are grave. The perm five ambassadors again, each with one sidekick apiece. Lemtov is here. Jennifer is backup for Bruckner. Judging by the looks I am getting, this is not intended to be any kind of genial inquiry. When I nod to Lady Nicola, trusting in some human connection from that quarter at least, I receive a distinctly flinty stare. She gestures to the empty seat at the end of the table.

"When you're ready, Mr. Windrush."

Oh, Lord, I think. The air seems to thicken, as if the collective anger gathered in the room has found its true focus. I draw up the chair and brace myself. My role here is now clear to me. I am the whipping boy.

"Are you going to tell us," asks Froissart, gesturing with his cigarette, the smoke swirling upward, "that Ambassador Asahaki murdered Special Envoy Hatanaka?"

"I don't know that," I reply.

He moans. Cheap theatrics.

"It might help," I tell him evenly, "if Ambassador Asahaki could find the time to come and see me now that he's returned."

"Your investigation has been incompetent."

"I don't accept your judgment."

"I am not alone, Monsieur Windrush." Froissart casts a glance around the table. No one disagrees. Then he slides into French, making general remarks on my ineptitude, and I feel my temperature start to rise. When he utters the word *imbécile*, it soars.

"What?" I rock forward in my chair, unable to contain myself.

Lady Nicola intervenes. "The Council has a number of questions to put to you. Ample opportunity will be given for you to explain yourself, I do assure you."

Alone of the faces at the table, Jennifer keeps her gaze averted. Her forehead rests in one hand as she doodles in her notepad.

Walk out, I think. Walk out, go and get Rachel, then leave. Here I am in the Security Council side chamber, international diplomacy's holy of holies, a place in the service of which I have spent the better part of my career, and it is not respect I feel but something more like disgust. Lemtov I would not trust with a nickel. Chou En represents a regime that has probably had one of his own closest colleagues summarily executed. Bruckner is here at the UN solely because it might launch him as a serious gubernatorial contender, and Froissart has the usual Gallic chip on his shoulder about his country's steadily declining role in global affairs. To top it all, Lady Nicola has sensed the mood and seems content to preside over whatever drubbing the others wish to inflict upon me.

Rise, I think. Depart this Kafkaesque temple.

But, of course, I do not. Because I know that if I get up now and leave, that would finish the investigation; without my involvement, all support for a proper inquiry into Toshio's death would wither. The truth would never be uncovered. Most of them would be only too pleased to let Patrick draw a line under the whole mess with a verdict of suicide; at least one of them, I think, would be hugely relieved. But I do not intend to let Patrick do that. Forced back on the hard core of myself, the bedrock of my being, I find that Patrick was right all along: My essential self really has just stepped off the *Mayflower*. Like the Founding Fathers, I remain, in spite of every kind of assault on my faith, a believer, a seeker after that new world where truth and justice will finally prevail. A place where eighteen-year-old girls are not used as hostages, where the murder of a good man is not just an inconvenient political fact but an act of sacrilege fit to make the heavens weep. I want what I wanted when I first came to Turtle Bay: the dream of the sages, a fair and just world. And I see now what I guess Toshio always knew, that the path leading through the Security Council side chamber simply will not get us there.

That is why I do not rise and leave. Why I fold my arms and remain silent while Chou En, the Chinese ambassador, picks up where Froissart left off, venting his spleen.

After a few minutes of battering from the Sino-French tag team, with the occasional intervention from the Brits in the guise of Lady

Nicola, Lemtov leans his bulk forward. With his superior command of the English language, he has evidently been delegated by his ambassador to deliver the kicking I am to receive from Mother Russia. Lemtov rests both forearms on the table.

"Is it true you have been investigating Wang Po Lin?"

"Among others."

"And you have found?"

"It's been inconclusive," I say, surprised at this turn.

Chou En cocks his head, not sure that he likes this either. But Lemtov gives him no chance to interrupt.

"Is it true there is evidence Po Lin was defrauding the United Nations?"

An earthquake hits. The heavy pine table jolts sideways as Chou En lurches to his feet, pointing across the table at Lemtov and denouncing him in ripely abusive English. Untroubled, Lemtov glances at me and lifts a brow: It is just as he told me. Po Lin has definitely gone to the wall. When Lady Nicola finally convinces Chou En to sit down, she attempts to placate the man by offering him another free shot at me. He waves the offer aside and sits there brooding. So Lady Nicola turns to Bruckner.

"Mr. Ambassador?"

Bruckner touches Jennifer's arm and nods in my direction. She lifts her eyes from her pad, pursing her lips.

No, I think. Please, no.

She does hesitate, I must give her that. Jennifer Dale hesitates. But only a second, then she straightens the papers in front of her, steels herself, and faces me. All my internal organs seem to clench. I have a sudden memory of Myra Barclay, a student at Columbia who was playing state's witness when Professor Cranbourne invited Jennifer to do the cross. Myra ended the session in tears and dropped out of law the next week. Cranbourne gave Jennifer a distinction.

"Mr. Windrush," Jennifer starts right in, "we're not satisfied your investigation has been pressed with proper vigor or with due consideration to the circumstances. Would you like to comment on that?"

"No."

"You saw the vote?"

"Yes."

"No comment at all?"

"No."

"Don't you think the Secretariat owes the Japanese delegation an apology?"

"I'm sorry?"

"Ap-ol-o-gy," she mouths slowly, a touch of heavy-handed sarcasm appreciated by Froissart, who smiles.

Setting my jaw tightly, I ask Jennifer, "Apology for what?"

"You're not a fool, Mr. Windrush."

"I'm beginning to wonder."

Jennifer's eyes flicker down, the only sign she recognizes my remark as personal. No one else seems to notice.

"Unsubstantiated allegations were made by you people against Ambassador Asahaki," she continues. "Serious allegations. And you refused him proper right of reply."

"That's not true. I invited the ambassador to answer some questions. His reply was to get on the next plane out to Tokyo. That was his choice, not mine."

"You believe that he was treated fairly?"

"Under the circumstances."

"No regrets?"

"I regret that he chose to leave, if that's what you mean."

She fixes me with a look. "It wasn't."

Hard and pushy. Never give a sucker an even break. Her inquisitorial method has not changed since college days, a realization that brings a brief, baleful smile to my face.

"The situation amuses you, Mr. Windrush?"

At this cheap shot, our eyes lock. At last she glances down at her papers.

"You haven't established any connection whatsoever between Hatanaka's death and this fraud you're alleging Ambassador Asahaki perpetrated, have you?"

"Alleging," I interrupt, "on the basis of sound material proof."

"Which the Security Council hasn't seen."

"The Security Council isn't a court of law." I turn to the other faces at the table, aware that I am dealing with very large and touchy egos here. Aware that some measure of deference has to be paid. "Look, I'm not claiming we've been perfect, but considering the situation we were placed in, we haven't done too badly. My job, the way I see it, is to find Hatanaka's murderer. It isn't my job to keep the entire General Assembly happy. Find Toshio's murderer—that's my job. That's what I'm trying to do. And I'm doing it the best I can, and I don't think I should have to apologize for that."

The expressions around the table remain grim. After the debacle of the vote, no one here is in any kind of mood for a reasoned debate.

"So you're unrepentant," Jennifer presses.

I tell her, in carefully measured tones, that I don't believe I have anything to be repentant about.

"As usual, the Secretariat can do no wrong?"

"As usual, Ms. Dale, the Secretariat has an extremely difficult task to carry out with extremely limited resources at its disposal."

She looks at me as if she is sighting me down a gun barrel. "If you're not up to the job, maybe you should consider stepping aside."

"I don't think so," I say.

"You don't?"

"No, I don't." Then I ask her—and by implication everyone else at the table—if she has forgotten Article 100 of the UN Charter. "Or don't you think that applies here? You think you have some special immunity?"

"Mr. Windrush—"

I speak right over her, quoting from memory. " 'Each member of the United Nations undertakes to respect the exclusively international character of the responsibilities of the Secretary-General and the staff and not seek to influence them in the discharge of their responsibilities.' Each member," I repeat. "And last time I looked, the U.S.A. was still a member. Despite not paying this year's dues."

A low blow that makes Bruckner wince. The Russian ambassador smiles into his notes, but Lady Nicola immediately zeroes in on the quote.

"You're not suggesting that the Security Council has acted improperly."

Exactly what I am doing, of course. Contrary to their Charter obligations, they are attempting to lean on me. But I have been a Turtle Bay bureaucrat long enough to recognize a line being drawn in the sand.

"I'm not suggesting that at all. I was just pointing out that this whole thing hasn't been easy. It's been extremely difficult. Difficult for everyone."

Partially appeased, Lady Nicola nods as if I have made a concession. But Jennifer just shuffles her papers. I cannot be the only one who hears her mutter "Crap."

Then Jennifer lifts her head. "You're so interested in Article 100, Mr. Windrush, do you happen to recall the first paragraph?" Before I can respond, she reads it aloud from her notepad. " 'In the performance of their duties the Secretary-General and the staff shall not seek or receive instructions from any government or any other au-

thority external to the Organization. They shall refrain from any action which might reflect on their position as international officials
responsible only to the Organization.' "

"I'm familiar with it," I say, thinking: She had that prepared,
where is this going now?

"Really. You surprise me."

But Article 100 is drummed into everyone in the Secretariat, a big
thou-shalt-not of our world. The surprise would be if I didn't know
it, and I say so.

"What surprised me was your cheek," she says.

Bruckner dips his head in agreement; he seems pleased with how
his protégée is sticking it to me. I am stung, naturally, but more than
that, bewildered. Cheek?

"You're familiar with it," says Jennifer. "Presumably you understand what it means. Yet you sit there—your investigation, frankly, a
shambles, the necessary reform of this Council comprehensively
wrecked—and you have the cheek to quote Article 100 at us? After
the investigation you've led? I'm surprised you're willing to own up
to even a passing acquaintance with that particular paragraph of the
Charter, Mr. Windrush."

Her look now is direct and accusatory. My gut suddenly con-
tracts, my pulse races. Because at last I have gotten the unspoken
message. She is telling me that my position has been compromised,
and she is right, it has. By Patrick O'Conner. By the pressure he has
applied on me through Rachel's detention. But isn't what Patrick
wanted—Asahaki's return—what she wanted too? And how in the
world does she know what's been going on between me and Patrick?

"Can you honestly say the Secretariat has handled this investigation impartially?" she asks me.

"Yes." As if I could say anything else.

"Full and fair use has been made of all the information that came
into your hands?"

"Yes."

"No base left untouched?"

"I don't see what you're driving at."

"Then let me enlighten you." She clasps her hands together on the
table. All eyes are turned to her now; the persistence and aggression
of Jennifer's attack on me seems to have surprised everyone except
Bruckner. They summoned me here to vent their spleen, to kick the
dog, but Jennifer has upped the ante. If I did not know better, I
would say that she is gunning for my career. "Have you omitted,"
she asks me, "a proper investigation of any suspect in your inquiry

because you thought such a proper investigation might be impolitic?"

The air seems solid. My mouth, for a moment, refuses to open. Without naming names, she has found a way to ask me if I have soft-pedaled a part of my inquiry. And I have, the part that led to Patrick. Confronted by my boss, she is accusing me of acting contrary to the spirit of the Charter, she is saying that I intentionally stepped off the gas.

"I beg your pardon?" she says, touching her ear.

God is my witness, I have never hit a woman. Sometimes I argued with Sarah but nothing more than the occasional spats of a marriage, disagreements passing as suddenly as they flared. With Rachel my arguments these past few years have often been loud, but the real heat on these occasions has always been directed at me. But what I am feeling at this moment is something way different. I am not just angry. The blood sings in my ears, my eyes close. My daughter is a hostage. And this woman I made love to less than forty-eight hours ago is turning me on a spit, roasting me in front of this select audience for the crime of not opening fire on the man who has my daughter in his power. I see it there in my head: I hit Jennifer Dale hard.

"No," I say, finally opening my eyes.

"You mean," she says, placing her own lawyerly spin on my answer, "that you omitted a proper investigation of a suspect for some other reason?"

"I mean that you don't know what you're talking about."

"Well, one of us doesn't."

Her crack elicits a snort of assent from somewhere along the table. I feel, at this moment, about two inches tall.

I am saved by a rap at the door. Alfonso Hernandez, the Undersecretary-General for Political Affairs, the SG's new best friend since Patrick's fall from grace, puts his head in and informs the perm five that the SG has invited them up to thirty-eight for drinks and an informal postmortem on the vote. The SG, he says, can receive them whenever they're ready. When Lady Nicola thanks him, Alfonso glances at me: Patrick's number two in strife with the Council. The prick shoots me a smile, then withdraws.

"You're excused, Mr. Windrush," Lady Nicola tells me, rising. "But I trust we've been able to impress upon you the seriousness with which your investigation continues to be followed by the Council. Should we feel the need to call you in again, be assured we will."

She does not wait for a reply. There is a shuffling of chairs, everyone rising to their feet. Notepads are gathered up. Jackets buttoned as the ambassadors turn to consult their colleagues. I am painfully aware that I have been dismissed like some recalcitrant child. Jennifer studies an empty page in her pad; she doesn't even raise her eyes as I slip quietly from my chair and out the door.

Blank. My mind is blank as I stride from the side chamber, propelled solely by the urge to get as far away as possible from the place. Then the blankness is pierced by a single point of red light that explodes, and I see a thousand points of red light dancing before my eyes. How could she do that to me? And why? Just to keep Bruckner happy? Or was she trying to prove her mettle to me, to demonstrate that any personal connection between us will never stand in the way of her job? Before I know it I have blundered out into the glare of TV lights. A solid press of journalists sways forward, a jostling wall of microphones, voices calling for the perm five's first public response to the vote. Questions shouted at me before they realize that I am, in fact, nobody. Turning on my heel, I head back the way I came. And rounding the next corner, I walk straight into Jennifer. She is waiting for Bruckner, who is farther back along the hall, having a quiet word with Lady Nicola, getting the spin worked out before they meet the press. I step past Jennifer, then turn and step back.

"Thanks," I tell her through clenched teeth.

She makes a face. "You're not the only one with a job to do, Sam."

"You humiliated me. What was that for, your job?"

"Oh, come on."

"And you know what? You enjoyed it."

"Jesus Christ," she murmurs, glancing back over her shoulder to Bruckner and Lady Nicola.

"All that 'you surprise me' bullshit, don't tell me Bruckner primed you with that. That was you, Jennifer. Up there tap-dancing on my reputation. On me, for chrissake."

She faces me squarely. "You've been chasing your tail around New York for two days, Sam. Chasing your tail, wasting time, while the support for Japan has just crumbled. You saw the vote. Am I meant to be pleased?"

"You can't blame me for that."

"I can," she says. "And I do."

I look down at the seaweed-green carpet. I chew my lip. "So. None of this is personal."

"You set the ground rules," she reminds me, a reference to my little speech two nights back at the Waldorf. "It's a bit late to be changing your mind."

"You used me, Jennifer. First to try to get a privileged peek at my investigation. And now"—I gesture toward the side chamber—"now to score some big points with your boss. And you're telling me it's not personal?"

"Sam," she says, reaching to lay a hand on my arm. "Listen."

But I am way past the listening stage. Shaking her hand off, I step up beside her. Bruckner and Lady Nicola are coming our way now, both eyeing us curiously. After the encounter in the side chamber, they are understandably surprised to see us together at all. Now I lean toward Jennifer, our shoulders almost touching. My whisper, when it comes, is low and surprisingly mean.

"Next time you're feeling lonely, you've got a big empty bed available, do everyone a favor."

When she looks up, I catch the glint of alarm in her eye. Then I say it. And I say it like I mean it, which at this moment I really do.

"Go screw yourself."

She flinches. From a distance we are just two lawyers calmly debating our professional differences. Now I rest a hand on her shoulder and I nod.

"Jennifer," I say evenly. "Fuck you."

30

BACK IN THE SECRETARIAT BUILDING I MAKE DIRECTLY for Room Seven and Rachel. In the hall a radio is droning, the sportscaster giving the results for some game in Baltimore. Weyland isn't here, just that same kid, the young guard from the other day who was playing cards with Rachel. Right now he is alone in the hall, the droning radio at his feet.

He looks up warily.

"Rache?" I call, nudging open the door to Room Seven.

"Gone," says the kid.

My gaze flickers over the room. The bunk is gone. On the table where Rachel's toiletries—soap, toothbrush, toothpaste, deodorant—were neatly stacked, there is nothing. Everything has disappeared. My heart flutters. Patrick has freed her.

"Gone where?" I ask, going back out into the hall. "Did she say she was going up to my office? Or home?"

"She wasn't going home, I think."

Reaching down, he turns off the radio. And when I inquire if Mike Jardine is anywhere nearby, the kid shakes his head and tells me he hasn't seen Mr. Jardine all day.

I take a moment with myself. Relief is too weak a word. And it's not just Rachel either, because with Rachel free, I am suddenly released. If I wanted, I could now go public with Internal Oversight's evidence against Asahaki. But after the discovery of Lemtov and Patrick's joint attendance at that money laundering conference in Basel, I am loath to act too hastily. We seem to be missing something here, either not seeing it or not reading the facts we have correctly. More and more I am coming around to Mike's view that the three

Special Committee members are an extremely unlikely criminal troika. A double act between two of them? Maybe. But most plausible in my own mind is the notion that Lemtov, the politically adroit mover and shaker with the unsavory connections down at Brighton Beach, has manipulated Po Lin or Asahaki in some way that we have yet to fathom. Through Patrick? I wonder.

Then I lift my head. What was it this kid said? "You haven't seen Mike all day?"

"No." Registering my look, the kid adds tentatively, "That a problem?"

"So who told Weyland that Rachel could go?" The kid doesn't seem to get it, so I explain. "Weyland's orders were to not let Rachel out of his sight. Not till he got the all-clear from Mike."

"He hasn't," says the kid.

Bemused, I glance into Room Seven, then back.

"Weyland went with her," he tells me, pointing down the hall. "Five minutes ago. I got no idea where they're holding her now." *Where they're holding her now.* I sway unsteadily. His expression changes as he realizes at the same instant I do that we have had our wires badly crossed. "Oh," he says, "you thought—"

"Who came here?" I ask sharply, my stomach suddenly churning, relief splintering into alarm. "Who told Weyland to move her? O'Conner?"

"No, Eckhardt." Eckhardt, Mike's boss, the head of UN Security. Weyland really had no choice. Then the kid adds, "Just Eckhardt and some old guy. No one said where they were going."

"What old guy?"

He shakes his head, he didn't catch the name. "I think I heard Eckhardt call him Mr. Ambassador. I wouldn't swear to that, you know."

Mr. Ambassador. I grip the back of a chair to steady myself. Mr. fucking Ambassador.

"You didn't recognize him?"

"Unh-unh."

"At all?"

The kid tells me he has been working here only six weeks. "Like the big guys, Bruckner and those, I know them. But, God, there's hundreds. One little old Asian guy, I mean, does anyone know who all these guys are?"

A worm of fear suddenly moves in my throat. Chou En, the Chinese ambassador? Or Asahaki? Trying to stay calm, I ask the kid to describe this guy, the Asian ambassador.

"Small," he says, then thinks a second. "Gray hair. And his face."

He scrunches up his own face to show me. "You know, like a prune?"

That is not Chou En. Or Asahaki. That is the guy I saw less than twenty minutes ago in whispered conference with Lemtov. A face like a prune. Or a walnut. The guy who came to move my captive daughter to new holding quarters was that poisonous little bastard the Tunku.

The kid offers weakly, "I can try to find Mr. Jardine."

But Mike, I know, cannot help me here. Shoving off the wall, I go jogging down the hall to find Patrick.

———

His door is open. In shirtsleeves, Patrick is facing the window, fiddling with his tie and shouting for his secretary as I go in.

"Leila!" he calls. Glancing over his shoulder, he sees me and looks away swiftly. "Bloody woman. Give her my jacket to brush, she disappears." His tie finally knotted, he faces me. "You'll have to wait for your kick in the pants, I'm wanted upstairs."

"Where's Rachel?"

He strides across to the side door and leans through. "Leila, for chrissake!"

"The vote's over. There's no reason for her to be detained here."

Patrick returns to his desk and does some unnecessary rearranging of papers and pens. He keeps his eyes down. Contrition. Regret. These are outside this man's range of genuine feelings, but if I am not mistaken, there is a real hint of embarrassment now in Patrick's demeanor.

I step up to his desk. "The Tunku and Eckhardt showed up at Room Seven just now. After the vote. They moved Rachel."

"Mmm?"

"I'd like to know where." I lean on his desk, just my fingertips touching. "And I'd like to know why."

He holds my look a moment, then turns to the side door. If he calls for Leila, I will lose it. I will step around the desk and tear this man apart. But he turns back, smiling humorlessly.

"You know what's funny, Sam, what I can't get over?" He thumbs his chest. "I put you on this thing. Me. Christ almighty, it would have been easier if I'd just slashed my own wrists, got it over with. The fucking mess you've made."

The mess I've made. For Rachel's sake, I hold my tongue.

Then Leila, Patrick's willowy Indian secretary, comes in and hands Patrick his jacket. He pulls it on, instructing Leila to type up the memos from his Dictaphone. Picking up the vibe in the room,

Leila raises one eyebrow at me in sympathy as she takes the Dictaphone and wordlessly departs.

"What the hell have you been playing at, Patrick?"

He brushes some invisible lint from his sleeve.

"You tried to call Toshio's murder a suicide when you knew it wasn't. You kept me in the dark on Oversight's investigation of Asahaki. Then you make my daughter a goddamn hostage, and now that the vote's over, you're still trying to hold her?"

"It wasn't me who screwed up the vote," he remarks evasively and totally beside the point. He heads out the door; I catch up with him by the stairs.

"Where's Rachel?"

"No idea."

"Bullshit."

He looks left to the elevator, then right to the stairs. He goes right, shouldering open the stairwell door. He is not pleased when I follow him.

"You got an invitation?" An invitation, he means, from the SG. Patrick has evidently been summoned to the same informal gathering up on thirty-eight as the perm five ambassadors. When I arrive at thirty-eight, a guard will politely but firmly direct me back down.

"I've got a good story," I tell Patrick as we climb. "And if you don't tell me where Rachel is, I'll be telling that story to whoever wants to hear it."

"Me covering up for Asahaki? That's your big story?"

"Where's Rachel?"

"Well, you've got that one wrong too. Christ, what haven't you got wrong?"

"You detained her for no good reason. Just to yank on my chain. When the vote was over, she was meant to be released."

"I never said that."

I grab his arm, and he stops one step above me and looks back.

"She had the opportunity and the motive," he says, tugging his arm free. "And no one except you thinks her detention's unreasonable."

"So what's the Tunku, the goddamn deputy sheriff? Jesus Christ, Patrick. This is my kid. I'm not going to walk away from this. And why the hell did you bring the Tunku into this anyway?"

"The short answer is, I didn't."

We look at each other. Finally he leans back on the banister and blows out a breath. "What a fucking day," he mutters, putting a hand to his forehead. Then, seeming to reach some decision, he drops his hand. "Listen, she's not under my authority anymore, all right? You'll have to make your inquiries to the Headquarters Committee. It's out of my hands."

The Headquarters Committee. Of which the Tunku is chairman. For a second I am too shocked to speak. "You've given Rachel to the Headquarters Committee?"

"If you'd done as I'd told you—"

"Whether Rachel's released or not, that's up to the goddamn Tunku?"

"Okay," says Patrick, "here's what I can do."

When he actually begins to tell me, I just stare at him. Studying for my doctorate, I was obliged to read the memoirs of several secretaries of state, reading that cured me forever of the misconception that someone somewhere knows what makes the world of international affairs go around. Academic models of reality always supplanted the fluid and intractable world. Schemes for peace in the Middle East featured frequently. At the close of these books I was often left with the disturbing thought that the foreign policy of the most powerful nation on earth was, at times, being conducted with a willful blindness that bordered on the insane.

This disturbing thought, that there is a touch of willful blindness in the higher reaches of the political game, this thought comes to me powerfully now as I stand here in the stairwell, listening to Patrick O'Conner. He assured the SG that the Japanese were a shoo-in for the Council seat: He was wrong. He detained Rachel in order to put a leash on me, calculating that Asahaki would then see the Japanese safely through to a permanent seat on the Council: wrong again. Yet another woeful miscalculation has forced him to hand Rachel to the Headquarters Committee, and now I can hardly believe I am hearing him explain the intricacies of his next plot. It seems he has no sense that he is standing next to a man who would cheerfully sling him from the top of the building.

"Patrick," I finally break in. "I don't want your help, okay? If you hadn't detained her, this wouldn't have happened."

"There were reasonable grounds," he declares flatly. He even seems surprised by my rebuff. Then, apparently deciding that my mind will not be changed, he continues up the stairs. "If you don't like it, take it up with the Headquarters Committee."

"I might just take it up with Lemtov."

Patrick stops. Slowly faces me again.

"Lemtov's behind it, isn't he?" I say. No reaction from Patrick. "He's pulling the Tunku's strings. He's getting the Headquarters Committee to do his dirty work. That's why Rachel's still detained, because that's how Lemtov wants it."

Patrick frowns. "Why?"

"The same reason you wanted her detained. To put a leash on me."

At that, Patrick turns his head and swears.

"Where is she?" I ask again.

He repeats his improbable assertion that he does not know, his glance drifting up the stairwell. "But if you've got some real reason for accusing Lemtov, I'll come down to your office when I've finished upstairs and hear it."

In other words, he wants to discover what I know about Lemtov.

I climb a few steps and stand beside him. "You tell me where Rachel is. Because if you don't, I'll be calling Oversight. And I'll tell Dieter and Pascal that they might find something interesting if they make some inquiries about a certain conference in Basel three years back."

This hits the mark. He makes a sound.

"That's right," I say. "You and Lemtov."

Patrick studies me. Trying to assess what? How much I know? Whether or not my threat is real? At last he turns, lifts his gaze upward and climbs. My stomach sinks. The possibility that I am totally mistaken becomes real. Patrick does not care if I tell Dieter. The connection I am making between Patrick and Lemtov is illusory; Patrick is quite content for me to publicize his joint attendance with Lemtov at that money laundering conference in Basel. Above me Patrick climbs one flight of stairs. Then two. Then his footsteps pause on a concrete landing somewhere overhead. He knows that I have not moved. We both wait, listening to the silence.

"Try the basement," he says finally, then he climbs again, his footsteps slow now and heavy. "Basement Room B Twenty-nine."

––––––––

The basement room is bleak. White walls, two fluorescents, and cream linoleum on the floor. Rachel is lying on her bunk, facing the wall.

"Rache?"

No answer, not even a flicker of movement. I exchange a glance with Weyland, who stands beside me. His look is a mixture of apology and concern.

"They wanted Rachel moved," he says, and I nod quickly, telling Weyland that I don't blame him for this, that I'm grateful he's here. He seems reassured. He lifts his chin toward the bunk, then withdraws into the hall, leaving me alone with Rachel.

When I go and sit on the edge of her bunk, she does not stir. I lay a hand on her shoulder and there is still no response. I bow my head and I think, Not again, please God, not this. Not more.

It wasn't until months after Sarah died that I became aware of Rachel's illness. In retrospect, the signs were all there: her habitual absence at mealtimes, a certain listlessness, a growing touchiness about any remark directed at her personal appearance. But she was a kid who had just lost her mother. Her mood swings and all the rest of it did not seem that remarkable to me; for months I was really not much better myself. But as the months passed and I slowly resurfaced from the wave of grief that had engulfed us, I began to see that Rachel had not resurfaced with me. I gave it time. A few months. But by then the drop in her weight was too obvious to miss or ignore; food, what she ate, these were suddenly issues between us. Even as I got out of bed and went to set the table for breakfast, I found myself becoming tense, mentally preparing myself for the inevitable argument that would follow.

Then a morning came when she did not emerge from her room. I lingered around the kitchen awhile, shouted down the hall a few times, then finally went and knocked on her door and implored her to come out and eat. She did not answer. When I went in, she was lying on her bed, facing the wall. There was a muffled noise; it took me a moment to realize that she was crying into her pillow. My heart knotted painfully in my chest. I went and sat on her bed, put my hand on her shoulder, and felt for the first time what I had only seen until then, how fragile and wasted she had become. After a minute she lifted her legs and hunched over into the fetal position. When I squeezed her shoulder she curled up tight like a ball and I knew at that moment that if I did not get help for my daughter, I might lose her.

I got that help, I did not lose her. Yet here we are, in the UN basement, all this time later, reliving that awful scene. What help is there this time? Who will save her now?

Leaning over her, I stroke Rachel's hair gently. My words when they come are a whisper.

"Whatever it takes now, Rache. Whatever it takes, I'm going to get you out."

31

Park up here," mike instructs the cabdriver, and we slow. There is no NYPD box. I notice that every time I come here. Nearly all the important UN missions have one of the things planted on the sidewalk outside. Blue booths just big enough to allow a one-hundred-and-ninety-pound cop to slouch over a bench desk while he flips through the *Post*. Officially the boxes are there to ensure good relations between the city of New York and the foreign delegations. Unofficially the New York authorities find most everything connected with the UN a pain in the ass. They keep an eye on the missions to make sure that distant international conflicts don't spill out onto the fair streets of the city. One call from the police box and the squad cars can descend rapidly and in numbers.

But at the Russian mission there is no need for a police box because the NYPD 16th Precinct is headquartered right across the street. When our cab pulls up by the row of squad cars, we see some uniformed cops goofing off, drinking coffee at the top of the precinct steps. One of them recognizes Mike. He calls Mike's name and says something I miss. Smiling, Mike tosses an insult up the steps. The cops jeer at him good-naturedly.

But Mike's smile disappears as we cross the street to the Russian mission. He tells me again that he believes this expedition is not such a great idea.

"Well, I'm all out of great ideas."

"It ain't even a good idea. You forgotten last night already?"

The big punch. I shake my head.

"That was just a warning," Mike says. "You suppose Lemtov's

gonna be happy to see you? You're just gonna chat like old buddies?"

"Let's see what he's got to say about Basel."

There is an awning leading from the sidewalk to the front door of the mission, and a discreet plaque to the left of the door. There are flagpoles too, but no one has bothered to raise any flags. The gray building rises some fifteen floors; it looks like an aging office building or a crummy hotel.

Beneath the awning Mike touches my arm. "Don't threaten him," he warns me for the third time in ten minutes. "Not till we know what's going on with him and Patrick. Basel and money laundering. All that."

Inside, the light is dim, the veneer paneling of the low-ceilinged lobby is dark, the carpet a dirty faded green. At the reception window of bulletproof glass we go through the usual theater-of-the-absurd, spelling our names through an intercom that does not actually work. Eventually the receptionist guy wanders off to report our presence to Lemtov.

"Looks like one of those whatsits," Mike remarks, strolling into the adjoining room to the lobby. "You know. Crematorium or something." Hands in his pockets, Mike inspects the posters on the wall: poorly printed shots of Russian palaces surrounded by forest. "Did I say about your car?" he asks me. The incident up in Harlem. He tells me he has called some friends in the department but the paperwork is already too far along. "It's gotta go down the line. Official. Don't count on getting the car back for a week."

"Jennifer?"

"I tried," Mike apologizes. "But that paperwork's gone too. USUN were notified within an hour. Be on Jennifer's desk tomorrow."

I make a face. An incident involving two Secretariat staffers up in Harlem, one of them me. Jennifer is going to flip.

Now Mike sidles over to a rack of pigeonholes in the corner. "Patrick still pissed with how the vote went?"

"Wildly."

"It occur to you this isn't the greatest time to be sticking your hand in the cage?"

"What occurs to me is that Rachel should be out of there."

Mike glances at me, then casually reaches into the pigeonhole marked L, pulls out a handful of envelopes, and flips through them. He could be checking his own mail. When he finds nothing of interest, he shoves them all back.

"Windrush?" an accented voice behind us calls out, and we turn.

The receptionist is standing in the main lobby; he has clearly witnessed Mike's uninvited perusal of the mail. When I identify myself, the guy nods at me. "You come." Then he flicks the back of his hand at Mike. "You leave."

Mike moves toward a chair.

"You leave now," says the guy forcefully, and he eyeballs Mike from ten paces.

Mike faces me. "Any trouble," he instructs me quietly, "call me on my cell phone. I'll be across the street." Then he drops his hands into his pockets and wanders out past the receptionist without a backward glance.

————

The funereal atmosphere of the lobby carries to the corridors out back, a warren of passageways hung with faded scenes of palaces and dachas, the Russian dream of the good life before they discovered Miami. We twist and turn till I am totally disoriented, then I am eventually ushered into a white-tiled changing room.

"Towels," says the receptionist, pointing to a stack of them on a low wooden bench. He indicates the glazed door opposite. The door is fogged, dripping condensation. "Mr. Lemtov is steaming. You go there."

I look from the towels to the door behind which Mr. Lemtov is steaming. Oh, for crying out loud.

"Would you mind asking Mr. Lemtov to come out?"

The guy waves a hand at the sauna room, then saunters back out to the hall. Alone now, I give the situation a few moments' thought. Either this is one of those moronic power games, the kind of thing Patrick might dream up, or I have really arrived at an inopportune moment and Lemtov just cannot be bothered dressing to receive me. Either way, I do not much like it. But in the end I cross to the glazed door and push it open and a cloud of steam rolls out. There are two tiers of wooden-slatted benches around the walls, a pile of river stones in the middle of the floor. Next to these, a barrel and a long-handled scoop. On the bench to the right, alone in the small sauna, sits Lemtov. We consider each other a few seconds: me in my suit, Lemtov with his legs splayed in front of him, his loins wrapped in a towel.

"When you're finished," I say.

"Here is private."

"It's also very hot. And very uncomfortable."

Lemtov gets to his feet. He reaches up to the control panel and turns down the thermostat. Then he looks at me again. He is not coming out. So finally I reverse into the changing room, peeling off my jacket and my tie, cursing beneath my breath. I remove my shirt. It occurs to me then that there might be another reason he wants to speak to me in there. On a naked torso there is no place to conceal a wire. I am bending to take off my shoes, when the hall door opens and I look up. The Pavlovian twinge in my gut is instant. Him. Sledgehammer. The bodyguard, ex-Spetnatz, from down at Brighton Beach. Now I rise slowly, my cell phone still inside my jacket on the bench. But even if Mike got past the lobby, there is no way he would find his way back here. If this guy wants to hit me now, I am dead meat. So I do the only thing I can do. I stand and wait. After a moment the bodyguard simply nods to me, then he sits down by the towels and folds his arms.

I decide not to remove my shoes. Or my pants. I pick up a towel and enter the sauna.

"Your man just arrived," I tell Lemtov, sitting myself on the opposite bench.

Lemtov splashes some water onto the hot rocks, a puff of steam hisses upward, then he leans back. His silver hair is plastered to his scalp. Half-naked you can see he has the build of an aging athlete, his body accumulating fat, contentedly going to seed. His skin is a uniform sunlamped tan.

"I apologized," he says mildly, referring to the hit I took down at Brighton Beach.

"What you said was that it was an accident. That the guy made a mistake."

"Would you like for him to apologize?"

I wave the offer aside. Not why I came here.

"You believe me now," he asks, "that they have executed Po Lin?"

"I believe it. But I'm just not sure that's important right now."

He warns me, inconsequentially, that my shoes will be ruined.

"Mr. Lemtov, have you spoken to the Tunku about my daughter?"

"Your countrymen were not pleased with you."

My drubbing in the side chamber. I wave this aside too. "The Tunku and my daughter," I say.

"O'Conner was working hard for the Japanese," he says, ignoring my point a second time. "He is not happy with you also?"

"I want to know what the Headquarters Committee's doing with my daughter."

"I am not on the Headquarters Committee."

"The Tunku's the chairman."

Lemtov inclines his head and waits. He is not going to make this easy.

"And I hoped," I say, struggling to keep my suppressed fury from breaking through, "I hoped that you might be in a position to talk to him."

"Talk?"

"Reason with him." I gesture vaguely. "Make him understand that it's not in anyone's interests to go on with this. Could you do that?"

He considers. "Why?"

"Why what?"

"Why should I do that? Reason with him."

Wrung out and tense, dead on my feet through lack of sleep, I am in no mood for any kind of head game. I just want him to do what I want him to do. "Listen," I say, and then I pause.

Lemtov is very still now, his eyes focused on me intently. He is waiting, I suddenly realize, for an answer to his question: Why should he speak to the Tunku? Not a brush-off as I mistakenly thought, but a real question. The opening gambit to a trade.

"Because I believe it would be in your own best interests," I say, groping for the appropriately nebulous phrasing. In the back of my mind I recall Mike's warning: Do not threaten this guy.

"My best interests?"

"We're not going to stop till we nail Hatanaka's murderer."

He lifts a shoulder: So?

"Have you considered what that means?"

"It means you will be working hard to clear your daughter."

I make a face and turn aside.

"You have another—what? Suspect?" he says.

I turn back to him slowly. And I nod.

"But no evidence?"

"It's building."

Lemtov carefully ladles more water onto the stones. Another steam cloud hisses upward. The perspiration goes dribbling down my neck, and Lemtov pokes at the stones with his scoop.

Jesus, I think. This man. "On the Special Committee fraud," I say, looking straight at him, "we've got firm proof."

"Against Asahaki."

"He's not the only one."

He studies me intently. I have him out there now, suddenly doubtful about exactly what I know. So now I push it further than I intended. "And I'm not talking just about the fraud," I say.

Lemtov does not move a muscle. I have definitely hit something here, but what? Toshio's murder? Money laundering tied up with Patrick? Lemtov's stillness after several moments grows unnerving, but I am too far along now to turn back.

"My report's going to the Secretary-General," I tell him. "I couldn't stop it now even if I wanted to. Too many departments are involved, too many people. So it's going to happen, he's going to see it, what we've found. The only question now is when."

I have his full attention. Lemtov turns the scoop in his hand with studied casualness. "And you believe I should be concerned."

"I guess that's for you to decide."

"Hmm." He has not swallowed the whole hook and line.

"But you might want to consider how much you feel like explaining your attendance at a certain conference in Basel three years back. A conference you attended with O'Conner."

We look at each other. For a moment I think I have pushed him too far, that my bluff is about to be called. Lemtov's glance wanders to the door behind which his bodyguard is waiting. But at last he faces me again.

"What do you want?"

"You know what I want. I want my daughter. Now, I can sign my report and pass it upstairs immediately, or I might be persuaded to recheck the whole thing. That's really up to you."

He does not need the suggestion trailed across his path a second time.

"How long?"

"To recheck it? Maximum, forty-eight hours."

Lemtov squints. He does not like it.

"Maximum," I repeat. "After that, Internal Oversight would take it upstairs anyway. I couldn't stop them. Forty-eight hours I can do. But I'd have to be persuaded first that there was some very good reason for me to recheck it."

"Your daughter."

I dip my head. He leans back, chewing the whole thing over. "The Headquarters Committee meets tomorrow morning," he says, thinking aloud. "They might decide to release her." Meaning that he can do it: He can pull on the Tunku's strings and have Rachel set free.

When I suggest that the committee should meet tonight, Lemtov counters that a quorum cannot be raised at such short notice. I suggest that they convene at seven A.M. He suggests eleven. Like a couple of barroom lawyers, we bat the thing back and forth. Then he pauses to toss another scoop of water on the stones and I watch the steam rise, momentarily lost in my own cloud of desolate reflection.

I am forty-one years old. Against the advice of many people, I have stuck by the decision I made all that time ago, I have remained with the UN. God knows, it wasn't for the money. I could have gotten rich in any number of alternate careers doing something the brain trusts like Heritage think is useful: assisting in the dismantlement and reassembly of corporations, advising directors on their share option and figuring out how to lay off employees at zero cost to the boardroom. Most of the old crowd from Columbia are now senior partners in big firms, pulling in a million a year and still wondering who's getting their share of the cake. I have never envied them.

In truth, I have always regarded myself as lucky. Because even in my most despairing moments about the UN's well-documented failings I have been secure in the knowledge that I have not had to sacrifice the best part of me, my conscience, just to earn my daily bread. My conscience. My pure and noble conscience. And now here I sit in a sauna at the Russian mission, sweat dribbling down my torso into my pants, bargaining with Lemtov like some unscrupulous D.A. cutting a backroom deal with the local gang boss. Sweet Jesus. What price my conscience now?

"Tomorrow morning at nine," I say, slicing my hand through the air, bringing the bargaining to a close. "That's it."

Lemtov gazes at the stones. His choices are clear: Sit tight or run. If he sits tight, remains in New York, he will be gambling that Russia's influence in the General Assembly will be enough to protect him from any charges emanating from the Secretariat. And if the Special Committee fraud turns out to be the sum total of his crimes, he might even ride out the storm, his career stymied for a time but not destroyed. But if he has been involved, as I strongly believe now, in something worse—money laundering? Toshio's murder?—my wager is he will run. Maybe back to Moscow, where his network of high political contacts will shield him, or maybe to some sun-drenched isle where he can play golf with people who will accept him unquestioningly as one of their own, another brilliant guy who proved how smart he was by getting his hands on the loot.

Lifting his head, Lemtov asks me to reconfirm that the report will not go to the SG within forty-eight hours.

"You have my word."

"But what is the guarantee?" he asks. "If the Headquarters Committee releases the girl at nine tomorrow, what is the guarantee your report will not pass immediately to the Secretary-General?"

"I've just given you my word."

"Your word," he says, smiling crookedly.

And that does it. That look, the cynicism that defines the whole man, it is finally too much for me to take. Rising, I run the towel over my chest and shoulders, then drop it on the bench. I point at Lemtov over the water barrel, through the steam. And in a voice that is unmistakably threatening, I say, "Don't wait. Get yourself on a plane. Get yourself out of the country. And before you go, make sure you speak to your friend the Tunku. I want my daughter released. By nine."

———

Outside, the September air is cool, the afternoon turning to evening, office workers spilling onto the sidewalk and heading for home. Mike crosses over from the 16th Precinct and falls in beside me. Handing him my jacket, I turn up my collar and start knotting my tie.

"Early bath?" he inquires.

"Lemtov's in denial."

"About everything?"

"We didn't discuss everything."

"Rachel?"

I finish doing my tie, then turn down my collar. Taking my jacket, I explain that there will be a Headquarters Committee meeting to-morrow at nine A.M. to discuss Rachel. I do not say a word, of course, about the deal I have struck, the threat I have made. I know that Mike would not approve. But then, Rachel is not Mike's daughter.

He stops and turns me around to face the 16th Precinct. "See up there," he says. "Third-floor window?"

"So?"

"Good view of the Russian mission."

Nodding, I pull on my jacket. Two cops emerge onto the precinct steps; Mike turns and draws me after him.

"Well, here's the scoop," he says. "Last month the Bureau was up there for a week." The Bureau, the FBI. "Listening gear, cameras, the whole nine yards. Interesting, no?"

I am not hugely surprised, and I say so. Spying always has been, always will be, a permanent if unsavory fixture of the diplomatic game.

"The Bureau," Mike repeats emphatically. "Not the goddamn CIA. Not the State Department. These guys were investigating a crime. And I'm telling you, NYPD and the Bureau, they don't get along. Like a

Bloods-versus-Crips thing. Territorial. No precinct captain's gonna let those guys bring a setup like that on his turf just to check out parking infringements. It'd have to be a major crime. Serious shit."

I turn that over. "You're thinking money laundering."

"That's what I'm thinking."

"Can we find out?"

"I got some ideas." As he flags down a cab, he explains that he's due at some hotel a few blocks downtown, a UN event where he has to straighten out the security. He wants me to go with him and brief him on my talk with Lemtov; he also wants to discuss how we're going to approach the FBI. As the cab pulls up, a squad car goes racing past, siren blaring. I glance back over my shoulder at the precinct and the Russian mission. Surveillance, I think. People watching people. A thought, some connection, hovers just out of reach. Then Mike bundles me into the cab.

"Frigging cocktails," he mutters, referring to our destination. "You believe it?"

Up ahead the squad car swings left, downtown, and disappears like a wailing specter into the darkening city.

32

"CAKE!" SOMEONE SHOUTS. "TABLE'S READY, BRING IT OUT!"
The place is hung with flags. The French tricolor in honor of the hosts, a number of UN banners, and a scattering of national pennants that appear to be purely for decorative effect. Silver trays of canapés are ranked on white tablecloths. A small army of cocktail waiters is busy laying magnums of Krug on beds of ice. Abundance; riches abounding, the stunning cornucopia of the Western world. When two waiters hurry over to open the doors for the entrance of the cake, I am suddenly twenty-six years old and driving home with Sarah from the one and only UN cocktail party she ever accompanied me to.

We had a fourteen-year-old girl on the ward today, she told me. A druggie.

At the time, Sarah was an intern in an obstetrics ward up in Washington Heights.

She lost her baby, Sarah said. We did the blood tests. They came back with the lowest iron readings on record.

Anemia? I inquired, the diagnostic reflex of the medical intern's spouse.

Sam, the girl was malnourished.

Naive, I know, but I was shocked. Malnourished in America, not some famine-blighted basket case in Africa but right here in New York. Ironic, considering the fate of our own daughter. She was barely four years old at the time, a healthy kid. Sarah never mentioned it again, but thereafter I attended all UN gala events alone.

And now when the chef wheels in a cart creaking beneath the weight of an enormous cake crowned with a marzipan model of

UNHQ, I decide that it is time to follow Sarah's example and absent myself from what promises to be a spectacularly extravagant and tasteless affair. Rising, I signal across the room to Mike that I am leaving. He has been darting in and out with the harassed hotel manager for the past half hour, catching a few words with me each time he passes by. Now he waves and calls to me that he will be right on it tomorrow morning. What he'll be right on is the half-assed plan of action on which we have agreed. Mike will make an unofficial approach to an ex-colleague from City Hall, the liaison officer for the plethora of state and federal law enforcement agencies at work in the city. Mike is confident a meeting can be set up between us and the FBI, maybe as early as next week. Given my recent chat with Lemtov, next week might as well be next year for all the good it is going to do anyone now. But I nod anyway, and Mike dives through a rear door in pursuit of the hotel manager.

I am already halfway across the ballroom, when the Brits, led by Lady Nicola, come rolling in. Lady Nicola peels off from the entourage and comes over. Her cream dress, spangled with white sequins, reaches to the floor. Her hair is piled high, held in place by two bright silver hairpins.

"Unfashionably early," she remarks, smiling as she casts a glance around the empty space. "My driver's always hopelessly punctual. What's your excuse?"

I nod toward the door. I tell her that I am just leaving.

"Not still smarting from Ms. Dale's comments in the side chamber, are you?"

"No," I lie.

"I understood you were friends." She gives me a look. I decide not to rise.

"We're acquainted."

"Tempers wear rather thin. Especially on a day like today. I'm sure you can understand that, Samuel."

Samuel. Not Windrush, just Samuel. As if she hadn't presided over the verbal mugging inflicted on me by Jennifer. As if Lady Nicola still holds the same personal regard for me that she had before this whole thing started. And it is a bleak testament to the lessons of the past few days that my first thought is, what does she want?

When I move to step by her, she lays a hand on my arm.

"Might I ask why you found it necessary to visit the Kwoks?"

I stop dead. Her face is unreadable. The Kwok brothers. Jade Moon Enterprises. Finally, guardedly, I manage to speak. "It was part of the investigation into Toshio's death."

"Oh?"

"Can I ask one?"

"Please do."

"Who told you I was there?"

"The Kwoks," she says after a moment's reflection, and seeing my surprise, she adds, "Not directly. They went through our mission."

Her look turns cryptic. By now, of course, I begin to get the idea. Wang Po Lin, scourge of the British imperialists, brought low. But God almighty, I am so tired of diplomats' games. Leaning toward her, I lower my voice.

"The rumor was that your people were responsible for Po Lin's recall."

"My people?"

"The Brits. True or false?"

"Po Lin was responsible for his own recall."

"All those speeches he made about the damn Opium Wars. Hong Kong. Don't tell me you weren't glad when he was recalled."

"That hardly makes us responsible."

"What do you want, Lady Nicola?"

She drops her gaze and turns aside. I chop my hand sharply in the air.

"I'm very tired. I'm very pissed off. And if one more person misleads me, tells me one more goddamn lie, I might just do something stupid. Now. You wanted to let me know you've got a line into the Kwoks. That they're working for you or something. Maybe helped you entrap Po Lin. Great. So now you've told me. So now you can tell me how Po Lin ties in with Hatanaka's murder. Uncoded. Plain English."

"Entrapped?"

I make a face.

"The Po Lin incident is closed, Samuel. We don't wish it reopened. And we'd rather you not bother the Kwoks."

I cast a glance around the ballroom. A string quartet is tuning up near the open doorway to the balcony. The British contingent, Lady Nicola's entourage, is watching us curiously, so I take Lady Nicola by the elbow and guide her firmly out onto the balcony. Though surprised, she makes no attempt to pull away. Outside, I turn her, but she steps back against the stone balustrade. She draws her cashmere shawl up around her shoulders.

"You tell me exactly what went on with you, the Kwoks, and Po Lin," I say. "If you don't, I'll have the NYPD go in and turn the Kwoks upside down. And if I do that, how long do you think the

Kwoks are going to keep quiet about the assistance they've given you?"

"This isn't a Secretariat affair."

"It's my affair. And this is your one chance, I'm not asking again."

She stares past me, silhouetted against the New York night. Car taillights disappear behind her, then come snaking over her shoulder and move on up the avenue. Just when I think I have lost her, she faces me again.

"The Kwok brothers gave us some useful information on Po Lin. I'm not denying that. But that information had nothing to do with Hatanaka's death."

"How can you be sure?"

"I'm sure."

"Not good enough."

We study each other.

"Very well," she concedes. "Correct me if I'm wrong, but you've been investigating Po Lin because he was on the UNDCP Special Committee. The committee Hatanaka was investigating in relation to the fraud."

I nod.

"Po Lin wasn't recalled because of any fraud, Samuel. He was recalled by his government for the crime of moral turpitude. And the suspicion that a foreign government had used that to turn him."

Translation: The rumor is correct. The Brits set Po Lin up for a catastrophic fall.

"His predilection for gay porn?" I venture. "Or something worse?"

She looks at me levelly but says nothing.

"What about all the companies Po Lin bought into? Those investments he made."

"Investments?"

I have worked with Lady Nicola frequently enough to have seen her full repertoire of misdirection. And this is not part of it. Head half turned, brow creased, she is puzzled, and her puzzlement I know at once is real. I hang my head a moment. Po Lin's investments still do not fit. Not anywhere. The underhand intrigue sketched by Lady Nicola, the blackening of Po Lin's name courtesy of the Kwoks that ended in Po Lin's recall, all that squares with what we know. But Po Lin's investments? They remain a totally disconnected and unaccountable fact.

Inside, the quartet starts to play, the first champagne cork pops loudly.

"I trust I can rely on you, then," says Lady Nicola, sliding seamlessly into professional affability. "No more visits to the Kwoks?"

I lift my eyes tiredly. How different is she—are any of them, in the final analysis—from Yuri Lemtov?

"I wouldn't want to embarrass you."

Her eyes grow somber. She straightens her shawl. "When I accepted the ambassadorship, an old and very wise head in our Foreign Office gave me two very good pieces of advice. Perhaps you've heard them. Nothing's personal. And always remember that it's only a game."

"Po Lin might disagree."

Lady Nicola smiles at that. And I know then that the British spooks in Beijing have missed the news. So I lay a hand on her shoulder and look hard into her eyes.

"Po Lin's been executed."

Her pupils dilate when she sees that I am in earnest. Her wrinkled neck beneath the line of her makeup flushes pink. She is appalled. As someone who has inadvertently taken a human life should be. But she is a professional diplomat; tomorrow morning she will be back in her Security Council chair, debating some weighty resolution, putting the world to rights, shuffling the diplomatic pieces and playing the game. She might even have some harsh words to say about the tawdry Chinese record on human rights. But right now she knows and I know. And to make sure of that, I lift my hand and tap her twice on the shoulder.

"You're responsible," I say.

And before she can speak I bow my head politely, turn my back on her, and go inside.

———

Out in the lobby, the French delegation has just arrived. Ambassador Froissart and the senior French delegates have brought their wives, the women all dressed like models from a Chanel fashion shoot. The talk is loud, coats passing from hand to hand toward the cloakroom as I edge by. Then, over the heads, I notice Marie Lefebre, dressed in jeans and a white shirt and sweater. She is speaking with the concierge. Catching her eye, I direct a glance toward the main door. She takes the hint.

"You have my story?" she asks as she joins me on the sidewalk outside.

"The Japanese went down in a screaming heap. You heard it here first."

"Huh," she says.

"I haven't got anything for you, Marie. I want something from you."

"Maybe you don't know what you have." Her glance wanders inside. Froissart is mustering his forces now, preparing for an advance on the ballroom.

"Do you have anything on Po Lin you're holding back?" I ask. "The dates on those investments? Anything?"

Pulling at her sweater, she says, "I must change," and her gaze wanders back to the lobby. I am not blind. I get the idea. Marie does not want to miss her chance by standing here talking to me. She wants to scoot off and change so that she can get back in time to mingle with the big guns like Lady Nicola and Froissart. Maybe the SG might even put in an appearance later. Journalistic nirvana.

"Marie." I open my hands, a despairing gesture.

She considers me a second, then takes my arm. "Come." She turns me around and leads me to the curb. She checks both ways down the street, then hauls me out through a break in the traffic. "You can talk and complain," she says, casting an envious glance at another delegate's wife stepping from the rear of a limo. "I can look at my wardrobe and cry."

———

Marie's apartment building is by an old Huguenot church, an elegant redbrick building that seems stranded from another time. A strong aroma of coffee seeps out of the apartments into the stairwell as we climb; many of the nameplates on the doors are French. And Marie keeps up the same inconsequential patter she launched into when we left the hotel. I am beginning to wonder if she intends to tell me anything useful at all. Then a guy sticks his head out from the apartment below and calls, "Monsieur!"

A fat guy in a Chicago Bulls sweatshirt. He gives me what can be described only as a leer; then he shouts, a short burst of French.

"*Le plus beau moment de l'amour*"—something I don't catch, then—"*l'escalier!*" Stairs?

He withdraws his head, slamming the door, and I look to Marie for the translation, some explanation. She continues to climb. "The super," she tells me. "He is a pig."

Taking out her keys, she leads me to a door just off the next landing. Her apartment is tiny. The front door opens onto two square yards of hall, an open door to the left leads into the bedroom. From the hall I can see the high bed in there and the dark drapes over the window. To the right of me is the living room, shelves piled with books, and a sofa against one wall, and immediately in front of me is the kitchenette. Marie flicks a switch in the kitchenette, then disappears into her bedroom.

"*Alors,*" she calls back. "Now, what is my story?"

"Which one do you want?"

"The one that makes me famous." Her face reappears in the open doorway. She smiles. "The one that gets me the job at *Time.*"

I tell her, only half jokingly, that I have not reached the conclusion to that one just yet. Her face disappears. I hear her opening and closing a closet, a drawer sliding.

Go in, she calls. Sit down.

So I wander into the living room, run my eyes over the framed floral prints on the wall, then slump onto the white sofa. A woman's room. I put my hands behind my head. If I closed my eyes now, I would sleep.

"Did it help you," Marie calls, "what you stole from our files?"

My eyebrows rise. I decide after a moment that I have not misheard her. "What I stole?"

Laughter from the bedroom. "I saw when we returned from the vote. The filing system is not so bad like it looks." She recites the date of the article on Lemtov that I purloined.

I am embarrassed, of course, but I have a feeling that an apology is not expected here. Marie's somewhat blasé acceptance of my breach of faith seems to signal that we are to handle this after the Gallic fashion, purely pragmatically.

The article was, I admit now, helpful.

Marie makes no response. I give it a moment, then raise my voice. "I said it was helpful."

"Good."

My head swings around. Marie is standing in the doorway dressed in a red cotton robe; my eyes make an instinctive sweep down her body.

"I need to do this," she says, holding up a compact and lipstick. "I cannot hear you out here. Come in."

When she withdraws, I ponder the situation a few seconds. Then I rise and go in. She is standing in the bathroom, the door open behind her, leaning over the basin. She inspects herself in the mirror, then she applies her makeup, a well-practiced routine, while she talks.

"Does Lemtov become the new Russian ambassador?" she asks me.

"I wouldn't waste my time writing that one up just yet."

She wrinkles her nose at the mirror. "You mean no."

"Who gave you all that detail on Po Lin? His connection with Jade Moon. Those investments."

"A friend."

"Your friend's name?"

She continues with her makeup. Eyeliner now.

"When was the last time you interviewed Lady Nicola?" I ask her.

Marie shrugs.

"Weeks?" I prompt.

"Months." She pushes her hair back from her face. "And it was not one-to-one with her. I am not so privileged. Always she has a press aide. Someone to hold her purse."

"Not your favorite ambassador."

"A bitch," Marie declares, straight to the point.

From which I think I can safely conclude that Lady Nicola is not Marie's source on Po Lin. But then, Lady Nicola would not be the only one in the British delegation to be aware of Po Lin's connection with the Kwoks. I take a quick mental check of the senior British delegates. It strikes me that at least two of them might be susceptible to the charms of a woman like Marie. I mention one of them by name, but Marie ignores me.

"Are you ready for tomorrow?" she says.

I prop my shoulder against the door frame. She puckers her lips at the mirror, applying a bright shade of red.

"Today everyone is crazy on the vote," she explains. "Interviews. Features. Why the Japanese lost. Tomorrow everyone who flew in, they will fly out." A considerable number: More than a thousand journalists have been given temporary UN accreditation this past week. She dabs a perfumed finger on her throat. "Once they are gone," she says, "people like me will ask different questions. For example, I am not the only one curious why Ambassador Asahaki left like that Tuesday night."

"He came back."

"Yes. Too late to save the vote. And everyone knows his relationship with Hatanaka was not good." She studies me in the mirror; she is fishing again. Which was meant to be my role here.

I say another name: John Bradley, a British delegate, my next best guess as to Marie's source on Po Lin. Marie pulls a face, then turns.

"Is it true your daughter has been detained for Hatanaka's murder?"

The question catches me like a slap. I actually flinch. She sets down her perfume.

"It is true," she says, amazed.

I guess it really was too much to hope this would not get out. And if Marie knows, others can't be far behind. My imagination momentarily runs riot. I see the banner headlines. Father and daughter in UN murder pact. Full story inside.

"It's true she's been detained," I admit. "The rest is crap."

We look at each other. She does not know what to say to me. Finally I go into her bedroom and slump into a chair.

"Stay," she orders, then, going out to the kitchenette, she tosses back a few candid remarks on my appearance. "Terrible" is about the mildest. Returning with a glass, she presses it into my hand.

"What is it?"

"Drink it," she says.

Absinthe. It burns my throat, tears film my eyes.

More, she says, and I take another shot. She stands by the chair, surveying the battle-fatigued figure that is me. A day that started with an explosive rearrangement of my internal organs has not much improved; I am not, I imagine, an attractive sight. When I glance up, Marie is checking her watch.

Putting the glass down, I try to get to my feet, but Marie presses a hand on my shoulder, nodding to the glass.

"Finish it."

Then, moving around the bed, she picks up a black dress that shimmers in the light. She signals for me to turn and face the window. Which I do. As if this situation is as unremarkable to me as it seems to be to her; as if my heart is not suddenly racing or my mouth, despite the absinthe, strangely dry.

I hear her cotton robe swish down softly, the muffled sound of her feet on the carpet, a quiet groan as she struggles into the dress. "Where are you going to now?" she asks me.

"Secretariat."

"Everyone will be at the cocktails."

"Not everyone."

Reaching from the chair, I part the heavy red drapes. There is no view, just a long row of office windows across the street.

"Your daughter?" she says.

I make no reply.

"I do not understand it," she tells me. "What is happening there?"

Letting the drapes fall, I sip the absinthe, then study the moon of light in the glass.

"You can turn now," she says.

So I do. The black velvet clings tightly to her curves, her shoulders are bare and pale. She takes up her bedside clock and sets it.

"Use the shower if you want."

I say with no real enthusiasm that I really should be leaving.

"Two hours, I have set the alarm." She places the clock on the bedside table. "Call your daughter. She will understand you need some rest." Diving into the bathroom, Marie takes a last look in the mirror as she gives me some final instructions. Towels in the dresser. Food and drink in the refrigerator. Then, stepping past me, she grabs her purse from the bed and hurries to the door.

"You will be gone when I get back," she tells me. "Make sure the door is locked. Pull it hard."

Opening the door, she pauses. It is like a whirlwind suddenly dying. "Like this," she says, poised to demonstrate.

"Marie—"

But the door has already banged shut. And Marie Lefebre has already gone.

33

QUIET. FOR THE FIRST TIME TODAY, SOLITUDE. MY first thought, of course, is that I should just hit the lights and leave, but instead of that I find myself sinking back into the chair. Traffic passes down on the street, sirens wail in the distance, everything moving and urgent while I sit here totally exhausted, momentarily becalmed. My eyes run tiredly over the unfamiliar feminine touches around me: a vase of asters, a framed black-and-white poster of a barge on the Seine, the patchwork quilt on the bed.

By this time tomorrow the worst should be over. By this time tomorrow Rachel should be free, but somehow even that thought fails to buoy me right now. Because right now, looking back over the events of the past few days, pondering everything that has occurred, I feel that I have been involved in a highway pileup and that I have staggered from the wreckage, torn and dazed, and in a brief second of lucidity before total collapse turned to survey the scene. And the scene is bloody.

Toshio is dead and we still do not know who killed him. Patrick O'Conner and the entire perm five are scapegoating me for Japan's failure to obtain a permanent Security Council seat. Rachel is a hostage, and I have brazenly bartered for her freedom any prospect of bringing Lemtov to justice for the fraud that I am convinced now he was involved in. Closing my eyes, I smell lavender. And the downward spiral of my thoughts touches Jennifer.

I do not understand her. There was a time when I believed I did, at least the major lines of her character. Her thoughtfulness. The fearless drive and resolution. Her fierce intelligence and her honesty, qualities that made her such a daunting figure at Columbia but that have been a steady shining light to me these past few months, a growing promise of personal hope and renewal. Now? After the pasting she dished out to me in the side chamber earlier, I find myself grasping at a shadow, the insubstantial figment of my own imaginings: the woman I thought I knew.

And then my own behavior, the fuck-you scene in the corridor. How exactly does that square with the glowing self-portrait I carry around in my head? Was that the behavior of a civilized man, or something I might have expected from Patrick O'Conner?

Leaning my head back, I breathe deeply. And my thoughts come to rest at last on Rachel. I put down my glass. I pick up Marie's phone and dial my cell phone.

"Rache? It's me."

"Hey, Dad." Quiet, but in control.

"I'm uptown. I can get over to see you in an hour or two. I just wanted to check if you're okay, if you wanted anything."

A pause. "No," she says at last. "And you don't have to come and see me, Dad, I'm fine. Weyland's here."

In fact, she does sound okay. Tired, of course, but not wallowing as I feared in some dark pit of despair. She tells me that she's up on the North Lawn with Weyland, getting some air. We take a few more stabs at conversation, but these go nowhere and our voices trail into silence.

"Rache?"

"Don't say something corny, Dad."

I smile at that. A small one. "I'll be over there soon."

"Go home. Nothing's happening here."

"We'll see."

Another pause. I can hear the traffic down on the FDR Drive, and I picture Rachel and Weyland on the walkway, looking out over the East River.

"I love you too, Dad," she says, and hangs up before I can speak.

I put down the phone. Then I get up and wander into the bathroom, hang my head over the basin, and splash my face. I glance at the dripping shower head, then behind me to the bed. Two hours. Marie has set the alarm to go off in two hours.

———

When I wake, the first thing I see is the black velvet dress. It is draped over the chair beneath the window. A phosphorescent orange glow slants in from the night outside, lighting the dress and the chair and my right arm, which hangs over the side of the bed. The traffic noise seems distant now, subdued. Still drowsy, I reach for the clock: eleven fifty-five. Five minutes to midnight. Softly I groan.

"I did not want to wake you."

The words, not a whisper but spoken quietly, come from a place just inches behind me. For a long while I lie very still. I can hear her breathing now, and I can feel the warmth of her breath on my neck. At last she speaks again.

"Sam?"

The skin on my neck tingles. What is the etiquette, I wonder, for a man stripped to his boxers, waking from slumber in a strange woman's bed, to find that that woman has joined him?

"I missed the alarm," I say, unmoving, my voice thick.

"*Oui,*" comes the response from behind.

I wait. She waits. Then, raising myself on one arm, I begin to push back the covers. Her hand shoots across, her fingers close on my hip. I stop. "My daughter's waiting for me."

"She will be asleep."

That's right, I think. Rachel will be sleeping now, peacefully; why wake her? I glance at the clock: eleven fifty-six.

"You also sleep," says Marie.

But for a second I remain just as I am, raised on one arm, gazing at the light slanting through the window, struck still by the strangeness of things, the awful power of the unpredictable in life. Sarah flies to Pakistan to help women give birth and within three weeks lies dead on a snowswept Afghan hillside. Rachel puts on her UN jacket and wanders into Turtle Bay one morning, only to find herself detained as a suspect in a murder. I start the day believing that I know the woman with whom I will probably share the rest of my life, that woman proceeds to dump a truckload on me, and I end the day in another woman's bed. And God doesn't play dice with the world?

"If you want," adds Marie.

Her hand all this while has not left my hip. Now I feel one long-nailed finger trace a slow line along the bare skin toward my navel, and an involuntary sound whispers deep in my throat. Then the hand is gone and my penis, swelling, brushes lightly against my thigh.

I could turn now, she must be expecting it, but I don't. I lie quite still, intensely aware of every sound and every movement: the stir of the curtain, muted voices on the stairwell, the clock. When I was sixteen and sleeping with the high school beauty queen, I was introduced to a game she called Wait for It. It was what it sounded like, the moment of congress delayed in order to heighten the pleasure, winding ever upward to an exhilarating pitch of anticipation and final release. That, at least, was Leanne Brady's theory. At sixteen I did not really see the point, and when Leanne turned a barely acceptable delay of minutes into hours, then days, as our regular daily meetings in her father's woods slipped to once a week, I dumped her. Thereafter I expended my sexual energies on more straightforward fare, primarily Gracie Morton, a plain-faced girl of sweet disposition and tremendous breasts whose own sexual inclinations could best be described as Keen for It.

But right at this moment it is Leanne Brady whose spirit, undeniably, unexpectedly, hovers over me. Wait for It. Behind me, Marie lies absolutely still. The air seems to thicken in the room, the back of my neck and my spine prickle with the intense awareness of her presence just inches away. I can feel my own heart beating. And holding my breath, I listen; finally I hear it, her breath, no longer on my neck but faint, irregular and trembling.

I turn my eyes to the clock: twelve-oh-one.

"Marie?" Quietly.

No answer. So I roll slowly onto my back, pause, then turn my head on the pillow to face her.

She is lying on her back. Her eyes are closed, her lips fractionally parted, and as I watch her hand where it rests on the covers on her chest, the shallow rise and fall as she breathes, my first thought is that she has fallen asleep. But then I feel the touch of her hidden hand beneath the covers. Just one finger that slides up my left side over my ribs to the nipple, where it circles. My heart seems to pound in my throat. Then her hand flattens gently against my chest and feathers lightly down over my stomach and comes to rest on the straining bulge in my shorts. She strokes me through the cotton, a rhythmic movement that brings me up onto my elbow, suppressing a moan.

Then my hand moves down her soft belly into the thick mat of dark hair. My knee presses between her thighs, her legs part, and my fingers slide into her.

Her head lolls back on the pillow. She closes her eyes and bites her lip.

She says, "Ah."

But when a minute later I go slamming into her, her head twists sharply and she emits a cry of real pain.

I hesitate, begin to withdraw. But she clutches her hand to the small of my back, she says no. Her hand grabs my shorts, dragging me back into her.

Her head is pressed hard into the pillow, her body still rigid with the shock of pain. She looks at me directly, still clutching my shorts, and lifts her free hand to her mouth. Very deliberately, slowly, she crooks her index finger, slides the knuckle between her teeth, and she bites. Bites hard. So hard that her eyes instantly brim with tears.

And suddenly, weirdly, I am lit. Her other hand jerks at my shorts and a spasm ripples over my back and I slam into her again. The muffled cry in her throat now is like a siren call, pure and sweet. Her eyes are fixed on mine, her tears running now. I hesitate again. Again, almost angrily this time, she jerks at my shorts. When I plunge into her, she goes rigid, her head thrown back, but she has my shorts gathered like rope in her hand now and she pulls hard, the material squeezing my scrotum. I drive into her again. And again. Marie's head jolts on the pillow beneath me with each fierce stroke, the knuckle of her finger clenched so hard between her teeth, she must be drawing blood.

It does not, of course, last long. Within a minute I come, a shuddering explosive release that is like a great wave crashing, my body taut and rigid, then falling, finally smashing into the shore. Sensation splinters, whispering through every cell of my body.

When I slump down on her, exhausted, wrecked, Marie lets the knuckle slide from her mouth. She turns her face into the pillow and wipes her eyes. Her chest, like mine, is heaving.

After a while neither of us has spoken, and I raise myself. Her head is turned from me, her eyes closed. And when—due to belated gallantry? a sense of obligation owed?—I press my hand down between her legs, intending to bring her to climax, she rolls away from me, swings her legs to the floor, and disappears into the bathroom.

So I lie here alone, my hand on the warm sheet that still bears the impress of her body, and I drift, my mind like my muscles loosened and relaxed. I am completely spent, a piece of drifting flotsam. The last thing I hear before I close my eyes, before I sleep, is the shower.

———

Somewhere a phone is ringing. I sit up, shaking my head as I reach for where the phone should be. Then I remember. This is not my bed or even my apartment. And that is not my phone.

"*Merde,*" says Marie, rolling, then reaching from beneath the covers beside me. "*Merde, merde, merde.*" Locating the phone in the semidarkness, she puts it to her ear. "Yes?" Irritably.

I glance at the clock: six thirty-five.

Christ, I mutter, pushing back the covers, easing my feet to the floor.

Beside me Marie says, surprised, "Yes, he is here."

I rear up. Who? I mouth silently, pointing to the phone.

Marie frowns, flicks up a hand, and listens. Finally she holds out the phone to me. "About your daughter," she says.

I clamp the phone to my ear. "Windrush."

"Hello."

My stomach sinks, suddenly weighted with lead. It is Jennifer. The weight spreads to my limbs. The silence that follows is filled with an awful significance, but when I drop my head and try to straighten out my thoughts, I cannot find the words. Any words.

At last Jennifer speaks again, her voice pressed hard beneath the strain of control. "I've been requested to supervise the handover of your daughter."

Chilled, I stare at the floor between my feet.

"Did you get that?" she says.

"What handover?"

"The Headquarters Committee wants to pass her to the New York police. You'd better get down to my office."

The Headquarters Committee. The Tunku. Oh, Jesus, I think, the skin prickling up my spine. Oh, Lord. I have left one base uncovered. And Lemtov has found it.

"The NYPD?"

"Homicide," says Jennifer. "The Headquarters Committee's asking for Rachel to be charged with Hatanaka's murder. They're requesting a prosecution by the New York D.A. A trial under New York statute."

New York statute. My head rises, I sit up straight.

"What is it?" whispers Marie behind me.

I shake my head. I ask Jennifer where she is. At the Waldorf, she tells me, but she's just about to leave for her office now.

When I hang up the phone, the room sways; I have to pause for a second and breathe. Like a river in spate, Marie's questions come streaming, but she could be miles away, her voice barely audible above the blood that is singing, roaring in my ears. A trial under New York statute. New York, the state with the D.A.'s office where the name Samuel Windrush ranks with Benedict Arnold as one of the world's great traitors. The city with the prosecuting attorney's office where Randal White presides. Randal White, who would cheerfully walk through fire, over glass, and—I have no doubt— over the dead body of an eighteen-year-old girl to demonstrate his fitness for high office, his no-nonsense approach to crime. New York, the state that did away with the death penalty, then changed its mind.

I pray then. Silently and urgently. Dear God, save my daughter. Help me. Dear God. Dear God.

FRIDAY

34

B ULLSHIT," I SAY, "TOTAL BULLSHIT."
     But I continue flipping through the file of witness statements
Jennifer has handed me, the ones she says she received from the
Tunku earlier this morning. Her cab arrived moments after mine;
now we're standing out by the side entrance to USUN. Neither one
of us has mentioned the phone call that found me in Marie Lefebre's
bed, and now, while Jennifer searches for her keycard in her purse, I
keep my head down, desperately scanning the catalogue of truth,
half-truth, and lies, searching for some way out.

"Bullshit maybe," says Jennifer, finally swiping her card down the
slot, shouldering open the door. "But extremely damaging."

"Oh, come on. You believe this?" I slap the file with the back of
my hand as we go inside. The file appears to contain five statements.
One from a UN guide, an Uzbeki, one from a lowly Afghan bureaucrat in Political Affairs, two from junior members of the
Turkmenistan mission to the UN, and the final one from a Russian
working in the Dag Hammarskjöld Library. Each of them recounts
in improbable detail conversations they claim to have had with
Rachel, incidents they claim to have seen. Walking down the corridor with Jennifer, I read one notably risible line out loud. " 'Then
Rachel Windrush said to me, "I will have my revenge for my
mother." ' " I look up. "Does that sound like Rachel, for chrissake? I
will have my revenge for my mother? That's not Rachel. That's some
stupid political hack from Kabul, that's not an eighteen-year-old kid
from Brooklyn."

"She's not a kid."

"You know what I mean."

"They're signed statements. If this gets to a court and the witnesses stand by their statements, a jury will have to take them seriously."

We stop by the elevator, Jennifer presses the button. Beneath the surface of her controlled exterior I have the sense of a burning heat.

"She's innocent," I say.

Jennifer throws up a hand.

"Really." I hold up the statements. "This is trash."

Stepping back, Jennifer points through a window to the UNHQ grounds across First Avenue. "See that? That's a place I visit. Somewhere I wander across to for meetings or conferences. Even the occasional vote. But it's not where I work." She points to the floor. "Here's where I work. And you know the difference? Here I know what's happening. The NSC and State Department disagree on policy? I know. Our media people spin a story in the press? I know. Bruckner wakes up with a goddamn headache and I know that too, because I work here, Sam." She points again to the UN grounds. "That's foreign territory. Over there I get to know only what the locals feel like telling me."

"We were discussing Rachel."

"Three days ago Hatanaka was murdered over there. Since then we've been flying blind on this side of the street. Suddenly yesterday I hear a rumor that your security people have detained someone. This morning I find out who that someone is. We are discussing Rachel. Now, what in God's name's been happening over there?"

This is not the moment, I realize, to try to cover myself with the fig leaf of Article 100. The elevator arrives; as we get in, I give her the truth.

"Rachel got dragged into the investigation somehow. She was at the NGO reception, she went down to the basement briefly to grab her coat. Dragging her in as a suspect was someone's idea of a way to muzzle me. But this stuff"—I slap the statements—"this stuff is crap."

She looks from the statements to me. "In a couple of hours I'm due a visit from NYPD Homicide," she says. "We're all going to troop across to the UN guardhouse, where I'll notify the guards that the NYPD stands ready to take Rachel Windrush into custody. The Tunku will have a piece of paper for me to sign. I'll sign it. And once I've done that, Rachel will be surrendered into the custody of the New York police. She'll get her Miranda rights read to her, then she'll be carted down to the station and charged with murder. Once that happens, the only way you'll be able to help is by getting her a decent lawyer. And that stuff"—she nods to the statements in my hand—"that stuff is not going to look like crap to a prosecuting attorney. That stuff is going to look like manna from heaven."

"It's lies."

She looks at me a long while. Then she taps a finger on her cheek. "Lipstick," she says.

The elevator stops. She gets out and heads for her office while I trail after her, rubbing a hand across my cheek and feeling small. "You've got to stop the handover," she says when I catch up to her.

My head swings around to her, but she walks straight on, eyes fixed firmly to the front. "While she's on UN territory she can't be charged," she says. "I'll try to straighten this out. In the meantime, you have to make sure she stays there."

"How?"

"Your problem."

She unlocks her office door and goes in explaining how she might be able to give me some time. When the Homicide people arrive, she will ask to see some paperwork, signed papers from the D.A., warrants sanctioning the handover. Anything she can think of. "They'll be bending over backward to make sure they don't screw this up. I'll give them the legal runaround, send them to the D.A.'s office or somewhere for more documentation. That'll give us both some time." Slinging her coat on a chair, Jennifer sits behind her desk, then forages in a drawer.

She is offering to delay the cops. Obstruction of justice. Jennifer Dale.

As so often these past few days, I have a sense here that the truth is sliding by me, that I am missing the real meaning of actions, that the motivations I search for are being carefully veiled, that those I have found I have misunderstood.

"Why?" I say.

Jennifer keeps her eyes on the drawer and does not answer me. I step nearer her desk. "Why didn't you just do what you'd been asked? You didn't have to call me. You don't have to delay the cops, that's not part of the USUN legal counsel's brief."

She asks me, ironically, if I am trying to say thank you.

I do not buy that. Not for one moment. Jennifer's principles are too firm, her faith in the legal proprieties too securely anchored for her to be compromising herself on a personal whim. I am not fool enough to believe that she is offering to delay Rachel's arrest for the sake of any feelings she might still retain for me. I look down at the witness statements in my hand, and I chew it over. What I know about Lemtov. What I know about Jennifer.

"Do you know these are bullshit?" I ask her finally.

She lifts her head from the drawer.

"Is that it?" I say as she averts her eyes. "Is that why you want to help, why you called me?"

"I'm helping you. Just accept it." She cannot look at me. And she cannot look at me, I realize, because I have hit the target. I toss the statements on her desk.

"You know these are bullshit. You know Rachel's being framed."

"I never said that."

I move around her desk so fast that Jennifer rears back in surprise. Bracing one hand on the open drawer, the other on the arm of her chair, I lean over her.

"This isn't a legal debate. There's no professor here to give you an A plus when you show him how fucking smart you are. This is my daughter's life. And you know she's innocent. And if I can't work something out, you're just going to let it happen? You're just going to stand there and watch her get handed over to the Homicide cops? How do you justify that?"

"Sam—"

"What do you take, the Nuremberg plea?"

"For chrissake—"

"Just following orders?"

Her hand is so quick, I don't see it. There is just a loud clap, my head jolts sideways, and my left cheek is suddenly burning.

We stare at each other, both furious, both ablaze with our own different fires. Rachel in a UNHQ basement room. Me in Marie Lefebre's bed. God, I think as the sting in my cheek dies away. God, where are we? How in the world did we ever get to this place?

Jennifer finally shoves my hand off her chair. She swivels back to her desk and hefts a thick wedge of pages from the drawer onto the desktop. "I presume you noticed the connection between all those statements," she says tightly.

I have, of course. Each statement has been given by a national whose country's fate is tied in some way to Russia; in the case of the librarian, a Russian national himself. When I say that, Jennifer looks up at me.

"You're not surprised?"

"I've got no evidence against anybody," I tell her.

She lays a hand on the wedge of pages she has just produced from her drawer. And she studies me, appearing to weigh something up. "You haven't seen this," she decides.

I crane my neck to read the title, but it's hidden by her hand.

"It's the FBI report," she tells me, "on Yuri Lemtov."

My mouth opens. An FBI report on Yuri Lemtov? That Jennifer had until this moment assumed I had seen?

"Jesus," Jennifer murmurs. She takes a second with herself, then she rises and goes to the door. "I've called the agent in, he's meeting me downstairs. Maybe you can take a look at that"—she tosses her head toward the report on her desk—"before he comes up."

She exits. Crossing to the door, I stick my head out and call her name, but Jennifer walks straight on, hurrying, and turns out of sight at the end of the hall. I take a step after her, then change my mind and return to the desk. An FBI report. On Yuri goddamn Lemtov. And the words are right there at the head of the first page: Money Laundering. When I flip to the introduction, I find that the report is a summary of an FBI investigation that has been running for nearly a year. An investigation into the financial activities of the deputy Russian ambassador to the UN, Yuri Lemtov. I lift a hand to my head. My stomach knots painfully. How long has Jennifer had this damn thing?

In the table of contents I notice a chapter dedicated to various accounts at the Portland Trust Bank, so I quickly locate that chapter and scan my way through. I cannot quite believe it at first, the sheer size of the numbers I am looking at, the staggering quantities of money involved. Not just millions of dollars. Tens of millions. As if some enormous sluice gate has opened and sent money pouring like a river through Lemtov's accounts, a wide and deep-flowing Mississippi of cash. The BB7 account into which the defrauded UN money disappeared, that is listed here. But it is only one of many accounts, and the few hundred thousand dollars of defrauded UN money is simply inconsequential, a bubble on the stream, completely dwarfed by the scale of the money-laundering operation the FBI seems to have uncovered.

Dipping into other chapters, I find more of the same, a bewildering array of bank accounts and a volume of cash that beggars belief. Finally flipping to the back, I read the report summary. It is damning, the evidence irrefutable: Lemtov is as guilty as hell. But then comes an addendum from the senior FBI lawyer on the case. Diplomatic Immunity, says the title.

Rising, I wander up and down by the crossed U.S. flags, the State Department eagle, as I read. The whole addendum sounds like some weird legal master class, a case study from a law student's worst nightmare. I end up by the window, one hand braced on the frame. Diplomatic Privilege. International Protocols for Foreign Missions. The Convention on the Protection of Persons of Diplomatic Standing.

The phrases are all here, and they add up to a frustrated lament, a keening wail from FBI Legal. Lemtov's position on the Russian delegation, his diplomatic accreditation, has totally screwed the FBI. The addendum is signed and dated. Then I notice another date, the date when this report was delivered to the USUN legal counsel. Lifting my eyes, I see the guards at the UNHQ guardhouse across the street. They have finished stacking the crowd barriers; now they stand on the steps, sipping coffee, watching two other guards haul flags up the poles. All totally normal. Sometime later this morning those guards will be handing my daughter over to NYPD Homicide.

I bow my head over the report and read the date again: July. She knew, I think. All this time.

When Jennifer reenters the office, my throat is so constricted with anger that my words can barely escape. "You knew this from the start. From the goddamn start. Why in hell didn't you say?"

Jennifer glances back to the open door. When the guy enters behind her, I cannot believe it. Asian. Mid-thirties, with a ponytail.

"Agent Nagoya," says Jennifer, crossing to her desk. "This is Samuel Windrush." The guy comes and offers me his hand somewhat unsurely. He ventures a half-assed smile. Agent Nagoya. An Asian-American from the FBI.

"You," I say. His look is contrite, but I swipe his hand aside. "You broke into my apartment, I'm not shaking your goddamn hand."

"Sam," says Jennifer.

"You want me to pretend like we're pals? Listen, this guy—" I turn from Jennifer to Nagoya. "That was you in the car yesterday, right? Up in Harlem?"

He nods.

"No explanation?" I say. "No 'sorry you crashed your car for no damn reason'?"

"Sam," Jennifer intervenes, "do you want to hear this or not?"

I drop the report onto a chair and clasp the back of the chair with both hands. Jaw tight, I glare at Nagoya. He asks me if I have read the report.

"Enough. What were you doing bugging my apartment?"

"That was an error of judgment."

An error of judgment. Civil rights in the U.S. of A.

"We had Hatanaka's apartment under observation. You were seen entering it. You tampered with our bugs."

"Your bugs," I say.

"We were attempting to establish the nature of Hatanaka's connection with Lemtov," he tells me. "From our surveillance of Lemtov, we knew he was seeing Hatanaka. Hatanaka was the UN's man on Afghanistan." He points to the report. "We suspected it was drug money. That Hatanaka might be involved."

Toshio Hatanaka, international drug baron. I swear softly and turn aside. I am almost too angry to stand here and listen. How much more wrong could these guys be? "Toshio was investigating the man, for chrissake. That's why he was seeing Lemtov."

"The Bureau didn't know that," Jennifer cuts in.

"Look," Nagoya says. "We haven't had this easy. Lemtov came to our attention early this year. Since then it's been in and out with our lawyers the whole time debating the dos and don'ts. By July we thought we had a pretty decent case against the guy. You saw the numbers?"

I nod curtly.

"Well, we wanted him shut out, closed down. Only our lawyers couldn't figure a way to bring the hammer down on the guy."

"You're too modest, Mr. Nagoya," says Jennifer, and for the first time I sense her coolness toward him. She does not like this guy. "Mr. Nagoya and his team," she tells me, "didn't pay quite the attention they should have to their legal advice. The evidence they gathered against Lemtov is tainted."

I look at her. She nods to the report. "It's unusable."

"It's evidence," says Nagoya.

"Not in court. Not a snowball's chance in hell," says Jennifer. "A phone tap at the Russian mission. At least three breaking and enterings. Mail tampering."

"A guy like that," Nagoya asserts, "it wasn't easy."

Jennifer addresses me. "At the end of July the FBI took what they knew to State." The U.S. Department of State. "Washington dumped it on us."

I turn that over. At the end of July Pascal was still scratching around the Special Committee paperwork, trying to figure out if it was Asahaki, Po Lin, or Lemtov who had misappropriated the UN money.

"And you just sat on it?"

"I went through the report half a dozen times," she says. "If there'd been just one piece of evidence that wasn't tainted—"

Nagoya snorts and turns his head.

"Three weeks ago I decided it was hopeless," Jennifer says. "I recommended to the ambassador that the report should be passed to UN Legal Affairs. Bruckner gave it to O'Conner."

Silence for a moment as I take this in. "Three weeks ago Patrick had this?"

"Count them. Twenty-one days."

"I never saw it."

"Obviously."

We look at each other.

"Yesterday in the side chamber," she says, "who did you think I was talking about?"

Understanding dawns, and I groan out loud. Not who I thought: not Patrick O'Conner. It was Lemtov she was accusing me of protecting.

"You weren't exactly clear."

"What was I meant to do, point at Lemtov and say 'Arrest that man'?"

I put up a hand. The recriminations can wait, we still have Rachel's handover to deal with. I grab the FBI report and beckon Jennifer as I turn to leave her office. "Not you," I tell Nagoya when he attempts to join us. Jennifer instructs Nagoya to stay put, then follows me out.

"What feedback have you been getting from Patrick?" I ask, steering her to the elevators.

"Zero. Just like I told you Wednesday."

Wednesday. When she summoned me to her office, when she was so pissed off with me and made that threat I never really understood. Last warning. Now, too late, I get it.

"You've been pushing Patrick all this time?"

"Like pushing string," she says despairingly. "We gave him the Bureau report to use as a lever. Something to help him get Lemtov's UN accreditation withdrawn. He kept telling us he was working on it. Then the Security Council vote was closing in. I guess we let the Lemtov thing slide. The next thing we know, Hatanaka's dead, Asahaki's back in Tokyo, and everyone's speculating on some connection." We get into the waiting elevator, I push the ground-floor button. "God," she says, "Bruckner hit the roof. Then you let it slip that Hatanaka's been investigating this fraud in the UNDCP Special Committee."

"Of which Lemtov and Asahaki were both members," I say.

"We knew one of them was a big-time crook. You knew it too, at least Patrick did. But instead of concentrating on Lemtov, you seemed to have it in for Asahaki. And that time you were wasting in Chinatown, what was that about?"

"So you guessed from the start that Lemtov was behind Toshio's murder."

"Not from the start. But when you mentioned the fraud, Hatanaka investigating that UNDCP Committee, well, come on. But it was only a guess, it still is. And we couldn't do a damn thing about it anyway, our hands were tied."

I make a sound. She knows what I'm thinking, how much her silence has cost.

"The moment I saw those statements this morning," she says, "as soon as I was told what they wanted to do with Rachel, I called you."

I lift my eyes to the elevator ceiling and clap a hand on my neck. Jesus, diplomacy. Everyone with his own little secret; everyone putting one over on the next guy, frightened the next guy's putting one over on him. All so busy with the big game that they fail to notice a man like Lemtov among them. Their hands were tied. By which Jennifer means that they could not risk upsetting the Russians because the Russians with their permanent seat on the Security Council could have vetoed the ascension of the Japanese. International affairs, I think, shaking my head. Global politics, how goddamn grand.

"I couldn't discuss it with you," says Jennifer. "I gave Bruckner my word."

I had, of course, assumed as much by now. And as a lawyer I guess I can even understand it. The USUN legal counsel could not be involved in this. However guilty Lemtov might be, if the Russians discovered that Jennifer had been acting hand in glove with the Secretariat, preparing a case against him, it could poison U.S.-Russian relations at the UN for a generation. If the Russians ever asked her straight out if she'd ever discussed it with anyone in the Secretariat, she had to be able to look them in the eye and tell them no. The moral high ground. High ground that Jennifer surrendered the moment she called me this morning.

We alight from the elevator and move toward the front door. "How long can you delay the Homicide people?" I ask her.

"An hour. Maybe two. They're due here any minute."

While Jennifer keys in the code to unlock the front door, I look through the glass to UNHQ across the avenue. The guards are raising the last flags, the pale dawn light colors everything gray. Down in the basement, Rachel will be waking. Maybe Mike and Weyland are already telling her what the Headquarters Committee—what Lemtov—has done.

"I can have Bruckner phone Patrick," Jennifer offers.

"No."

"Won't that help?"

"It won't help me break Lemtov's hold over the Headquarters

Committee," I tell her as she opens the door for me. Clutching the FBI report to my chest, I hurry out past her. "Delay Homicide as long as you can."

"What are you going to do?" she calls after me.

I hit the sidewalk, then jog across First Avenue without looking back. The guards at the guardhouse greet me, say good morning. I lift my hand and jog on by. What am I going to do? Not so much a plan as the only option left open to me, a last desperate hope. I am going to try to free my daughter. I am going to try to use what I now know to dislodge Lemtov. My last hope is to make Lemtov run.

35

RACHEL HAS HEARD, I SEE THAT AT ONCE. She is wearing no makeup, her face is pale, and her red-rimmed eyes are bloodshot. She has on a baggy gray sweater, my old baseball cap, blue jeans, and sneakers, and she is holding a crumpled tissue in one hand. Weyland looks at me sympathetically as I cross to Rachel's bunk and sit down beside her. For her sake, I try to smile reassuringly; my arm goes around her shoulders and I mumble the platitudes. I'm here. You're okay.

"Eckhardt and the Tunku been down," Weyland tells me. "They told Rachel the situation, gave her those statements." He points to Rachel's pillow, where a few loose, crumpled pages lie scattered. "I called Mike. He's coming on down."

"I didn't tell them anything, Dad." Easing away from me, Rachel wipes her eyes.

"You've read them?" I ask, nodding at the statements.

"It's lies. All of it." Tears gather.

"It doesn't matter, Rache. Hey," I say softly, "it'll be okay."

"No it won't."

I lay a hand on her knee, speechless.

"I've been telling Rachel," Weyland says to me, "maybe it's better like this, you know. U.S. justice. She'll be better off outta here, could be."

But Weyland is an ex–NYPD cop. He has seen too much of U.S. justice to be able to put any real conviction in his voice; his remarks leave an unintentionally somber air.

"Why are they saying this stuff?" Picking up one of the statements, Rachel tosses it aside, then sweeps all the statements off her bunk onto the floor. She hauls her legs onto the bunk, grips her ankles in her hands, and presses her heels against her butt. Her head lolls back against the wall. "This fucking place," she says bitterly.

She is not referring to this room. She is referring to this whole place, the United Nations and all its members and functionaries. We are marshaled together beneath my daughter's scorn.

"Did Jennifer get you?" she says. Then, seeing my surprise, she slides a hand beneath her pillow and brings out my cell phone. "She couldn't get you at home. When she got through to me I gave her the number you called me from last night." She hands me the phone. "Here," she says.

I take the thing and pocket it, lips clamped tight. Then Mike arrives and takes in the scene: Rachel on the bunk with me, and Weyland, elbows resting on his knees, leaning toward us like a third member of the family.

"You've seen these?" Mike says to me, holding up what I guess must be another copied set of statements.

I squeeze Rachel's shoulder. Hang in there, I tell her, then I lead Mike back out into the hall.

———

"So what did you say to the guy?" Mike turns on me the moment we're alone. He is more than just unhappy, I see now; he is very pissed off. "Yesterday at the Russian mission. I told you, go careful. Tread easy. Jesus, didn't you get the idea down at Brighton fucking Beach? Lemtov's not a guy you go messing with." He waves the statements at me; he obviously has no doubt who is behind them.

"Maybe I pushed him too hard."

"That's not what you told me yesterday." Mike screws up his face. "You threatened him, right? Like I told you not to." My look is all the answer he needs. "Get ahold of your girlfriend," he advises. "Fast."

I thrust the FBI report into Mike's hands. "Lemtov's been laundering money on a grand scale. The Bureau has known about it for months, and I got this courtesy of Jennifer."

Mike looks from me down to the report, swearing softly. As he turns to the introduction, I guide him away from Rachel's holding room.

"Remember that surveillance from the Sixteenth Precinct?"

Mike nods, thumbing the pages of the report, trying to wrap his mind around this, trying to see how it fits. I can see it's a struggle.

"Here's another one," I tell him. "The guy who put that report together is the same guy who broke into my apartment." Mike's head rises quickly. "Agent Nagoya," I say. "The FBI. And he was the one over at Pascal's when I crashed my car."

Mike thinks a moment. "The phone tap at Hatanaka's?"

"Agent Nagoya."

"Fuck."

"It gets worse." I point to the report in his hands. "That stuff is useless." When I explain that the FBI has broken every rule in the book in order to obtain their evidence, Mike groans in dismay. "Here's the kicker," I tell him. "Patrick had it three weeks ago."

Mike stares at me.

"I never saw it, Mike. I swear. Jennifer never told me. And neither did Patrick. It went from the Bureau to USUN. Bruckner gave it to Patrick three weeks ago, the first I heard was this morning."

"Jesus fucking Christ."

"USUN figured Patrick would get Lemtov's diplomatic accreditation withdrawn."

"And Patrick just sat on it?"

"Apparently."

"That money-laundering conference in Basel," he says, looking down at the report. "Lemtov and goddamn Patrick."

We stop by the giant double doors of plate glass. On the far side, tourists wander from the souvenir shop laden with UN T-shirts and coffee mugs, then cross to the bookshop. A gang of schoolkids swarms past, clutching postcards and heading for the UN post office booth, a tiny and somewhat preposterous emblem of UNHQ's territorial independence. Immediately to the front of us through the doors, a UN guard seems to be explaining to a couple of senior citizens that the cafeteria behind him is temporarily closed.

"Remember Patrick's reaction Tuesday morning?"

Mike nods. "No forensics team. Suicide."

"Later on I thought maybe he was covering for Asahaki. But look at it this way. Patrick knew Toshio and Pascal were going through some accounts down at the Portland Trust Bank. And this report— which Patrick had mid-August—this makes it plain that nearly twenty million bucks went into Lemtov's account there. BB7. The same account the defrauded UN money disappeared into."

"You said that account was Asahaki's."

"Maybe Lemtov and Asahaki both had access, that's not important. The point is, what if Patrick really was involved with Lemtov."

"He would have told Lemtov about the report."

"And he would have told him what Toshio was doing. Lemtov knew the kind of guy Toshio was. He would have been more worried about Toshio than he was about the FBI. If Toshio could prove the defrauded UN money went into BB7, Toshio could eventually subpoena the account details. Legitimate access. Once that happened, Lemtov wouldn't just have his UN accreditation withdrawn, the Bureau would have legally solid evidence they could use against him too. Lemtov wouldn't have let that happen, he would have dealt with it. Not necessarily how Patrick intended."

"So Lemtov had Toshio murdered, then just hung around here?" Mike is not so sure that I've got this right.

"Listen." Taking Mike's arm, I turn him back down the hall. "In less than two hours Rachel's going to be charged with murder. We can't afford to wait till we've crossed all the t's. We've got what we've got. Now we just have to use it."

He gives me a sideways look. We, he says.

"I need your help, Mike. You and Weyland both."

"We can't release her."

"I don't want you to."

He grunts in surprise.

"If you release her now, she either stays in the UN grounds and gets picked up by Eckhardt and handed over to the NYPD, or she leaves the UN grounds and becomes a fugitive. Releasing her now won't help. I want her moved, Mike. Get Weyland to take her across to the Secretariat building, the conference rooms, anywhere around the grounds, but move her."

"That's doable," he concedes, "but what's the point?"

"If Lemtov hears Rachel's been released, that some real evidence has turned up on the real people behind Hatanaka's murder—"

"He's not gonna buy that from you."

"He's not going to hear it from me."

We stop outside Rachel's room, B29. I take the FBI report from Mike. "I'm going to dump this on Patrick. Along with the news that you've released Rachel. If Patrick comes down here with Lemtov to check, she can't be here."

Mike turns that over. "Patrick tells Lemtov, plus word's out on the Bureau report—that's gonna rattle Lemtov's cage, make him disappear?"

When I nod, Mike squints. He does not like it.

I point west, in the direction of USUN. "The Homicide cops are probably in Jennifer's office. So unless you've got a better idea right now, this is it."

Mike considers it a second. Then, shaking his head, he shoulders open Rachel's door, and while he goes and instructs Weyland to retune the walkie-talkie and get ready to move, I squat down by Rachel. I rest a hand on her knee.

"We're going to try to flush out the guy behind those," I tell her, indicating the crumpled statements on the floor. "It won't be easy, but we're going to try."

"You know who it is?"

"We're not sure. Maybe. What matters is, you stick with Weyland. Do what he tells you. Go where he says."

"They're letting me go?"

"Not yet." I glance over my shoulder. Mike has finished with Weyland; he signals to me with a jerk of his head toward the door.

Squeezing Rachel's knee, I stand. And when she looks up at me, I see that her red-rimmed eyes have taken on a quickened light of hope. But a hope that has not displaced her fear.

"I have to go, Rache." She nods apprehensively. Before I can say more, Mike takes my elbow and guides me out the door.

In the elevator I hit the button for thirty-five, Patrick's floor. Mike reaches past me and hits the button for his own floor.

"You're a schmuck," he tells me.

I face him.

"You've forgotten Brighton Beach?" he says. "You don't speak to these guys without some backup."

"This isn't Brighton Beach."

"Go tell that to Hatanaka."

"I haven't got time to round up a damn posse, Mike."

"I am the damn posse," he says. "And when this thing's over, we're gonna be needing some kind of evidence. You ain't going anywhere till we got you wired."

36

"D ON'T ASK," SAYS PATRICK O'CONNER, "BECAUSE I CAN tell you already the answer is no."

I have found him up in UN Central, the Operations Room. He flicks off the PC, some e-mail he has been reading, and moves along the table.

"Your daughter, right?" Bending, he reads a fax as it comes off the machine. A report from our observer team in West Papua. "Maybe I didn't make myself clear yesterday, Sam. So listen up. Last time. It's out of my hands."

"The Headquarters Committee wants to hand her over."

"They're going to hand her over," he corrects me, his voice surprisingly subdued. "And there's nothing I can do about that." He shoots a glance up at me. "Nothing you can do either."

Dwight Arnold, the Operations chief, comes over then, and I step back while he and Patrick study the long fax from West Papua as it continues to run off the machine. They fall into a discussion of the implications. The Indonesians and the New Guineans are apparently accusing each other of incursions across their mutual border. Overnight, Indonesian soldiers have been murdered in a West Papuan town. A crisis brewing.

As I listen to Patrick muse on a possible escalation of the conflict, it occurs to me that with the vote behind us, real UN life, the daily lurch from one international crisis to another, has resumed. Toshio's death, Rachel's fate, these are questions that Patrick would now like to see pushed off the Legal Affairs agenda. My presence here is a stark reminder to him that that is not going to happen. Patrick tears off the fax, telling Dwight that he will take it straight up to the SG.

When I follow Patrick into the hall, his expression becomes pained. "Look, you want some time off, get some lawyers lined up for your daughter? Take it. Whatever you need."

"I don't want her to leave the UN grounds."

He lifts a hand, calling for the elevator to wait. We get in with half a dozen others; I have to hold my tongue till we emerge on thirty-five.

"The Tunku went down and saw Rachel this morning," I tell him.

Patrick peruses the fax as we walk. I try again. "He left her in tears."

"Man's a dickhead." Patrick turns in to his office. He drapes the fax over his desk, then searches his in box. He starts talking about West Papua, the problems our observers are having; and when he crosses to the mini fridge, reaches in for an OJ, he has his back turned to me. I reach into my shirt pocket and depress the button on the recorder Mike has given me. Not a wire, but the best Mike could manage at such short notice. The recorder vibrates lightly against my chest.

"You got Rachel into this, Patrick. I'm not asking for remorse. But don't you think you've some kind of obligation to use whatever clout you've got, wherever you've got it, to help me get her out?"

He downs the OJ in one gulp, then contemplates the empty plastic bottle a moment. "Remorse," he says, tossing the bottle in the trash as he returns to his desk. "Waste of fucking time." He bends over the fax, but after a few seconds I still haven't spoken and he lifts his head. "Listen. If I detained Rachel for no good reason, why's the Headquarters Committee handing her over to the cops? Why's there a bunch of statements here"—he stabs a finger onto a file on his desk—"that put Rachel right in the frame? Are you blaming me for that too? Okay, so she's your daughter, it can't be easy. But, hey, get your head outta your ass. Open your eyes."

"You honestly thought she was guilty. You really believe you just did your job."

"I did my job," he says. He squares the blotter in front of him, reaches for a sheet of paper, and takes a pen from the mahogany holder. He commences to write. "Now, how about you bugger off and do yours."

Even from the opposite side of the desk I can see the name that Patrick had scrawled at the top of the page: Gary Sumner. The Australian ambassador to the UN. Patrick, it seems, has decided to implement his exit strategy, to pull the cord on his parachute. After the debacle of yesterday's vote, Patrick O'Conner knows that his glory days here at Turtle Bay are behind him. So he is doing what you would expect a man like Patrick to do—he is using his current position to help ease his passage into his next job. The West Papua situation is an ongoing foreign policy nightmare for the Australians, their gratitude for firsthand information from the field would be immense. This might have been going on for months. Probably has been, I think as I watch Patrick's pen glide.

"So you won't help me?"

Patrick mutters something inaudible. I slide the FBI report from beneath my arm and place it down by the blotter. Then I open the report so that the title page is visible. Patrick's glance wanders across; after a moment he reaches and casually flips through the report with his left hand.

"What's this?"

Nemesis, I think. The undoing of Patrick O'Conner.

But what I say is "Don't screw me around."

He continues to flip through the report, his look becoming thoughtful. Finally he lifts his eyes. "The Dale woman," he decides aloud.

"Where I got it isn't the issue here. You had this three weeks ago. Three fucking weeks."

"What can I tell you? You think you should have seen it earlier?" He closes the report. "You're probably right." And then, unbelievably, he returns to his memo on West Papua. He consults some legal pamphlet. He writes.

"Patrick, you've been covering up for Lemtov. Protecting his ass, for chrissake, are you going to deny that?"

He makes a face. "You want to go upstairs, speak to the SG, ask him how I've been protecting Lemtov's ass?" Patrick points his pen to the ceiling. "Go on. Be my guest."

"You're full of it."

He rises from behind his desk and crosses to the bookshelves. His hand trails over the leather spines. "Go and ask him. Ask him why the guy you think's been protecting Lemtov's ass has trooped up to the thirty-eighth floor with daily updates on Toshio's investigation of that FBI report." Removing a heavy volume, he brings it back to the desk. "Ask him that."

Toshio's investigation of the FBI report? I say the only thing I can think of. Bullshit.

"What do you think Toshio was doing in Basel?" he asks me. A question I intended to ask him. Patrick lays a finger on the FBI report. "He was looking into this as I told him to. And maybe if you'd done as I told you to, you wouldn't have made such a bloody pig's ear of this. Maybe your daughter wouldn't be in the shit she's in. You wanna blame someone, try looking a little closer to home." Patrick picks up his pen and returns to his memo, referring to the thick volume now as he writes.

I feel unsteady on my feet. Patrick's explanation. His attitude. At last, way too late, I seem to be getting something that resembles the truth.

"Why didn't you tell me that?"

Patrick sticks his tongue into his cheek. Then he recaps his pen and kicks back in his chair. He swivels left and right. "Hatanaka was investigating the Special Committee. A month ago he's telling me he's cracked it, that he had the guy. Asahaki." Patrick swears. He still cannot quite believe it. "Asahaki. Christ, how likely was that?"

"You thought Toshio was lying to you?"

"Let's say I wasn't too sure about his motives. This was a month before the vote on the Japanese seat. It seemed a little too convenient, you know. The self-appointed opponent in chief of the Japanese seat. Him up there, pointing the finger at the Japanese ambassador, crying fraud. If that got out, he knew bloody well what that'd do to Japan's chances."

I turn that one over. "And you did too."

"Sure, I knew it too. I told Toshio to hold off, show me more evidence, anything, wait till the vote was over. After that he could have Asahaki arrested in the street for all I cared." He glances down at the report. "We were still butting heads over it when that thing arrived."

Quite a moment, if he is telling me the truth. An independent source, the FBI, suddenly fingering Lemtov as a big-time crook.

"Once he read the report," says Patrick, "even Toshio had to admit that maybe the Special Committee fraud wasn't all down to Asahaki. Toshio knew he had to do some more work on it. At least take another look at Lemtov."

"You showed the Bureau report to Toshio immediately?"

My surprise surprises Patrick. "Of course I showed it to him immediately. I wanted him off Asahaki's back."

He gives me a curious look. And my belief in a Lemtov-O'Conner association begins to waver. Would a money-laundering associate of Lemtov's, even a man with Patrick's brazen front, be reacting like this? I remark that Pascal never mentioned the Bureau report to me.

"Nyeri wasn't told. Just me, Hatanaka, and upstairs." The SG.

"Dieter?" I ask.

Patrick shakes his head. But it seems incredible that Dieter

Rasmussen, the head of Internal Oversight, wasn't informed, and I
say so. Patrick rises, walks around his desk, and seats himself on the
sofa arm.

"Listen," he says, "we weren't going to announce it to the world
just like that. This is the U.S. accusing the deputy Russian ambassador. I mean, think about it. How did we know this was a genuine
FBI report and not something dreamed up by the U.S. State
Department to stir up trouble for the Russians? Using us here in the
Secretariat to do their dirty work." He points. "Which, incidentally,
is why you weren't told."

I draw back. This is one angle that I missed totally: the possibility
that this report is just a pack of lies. It simply had not occurred to
me that my countrymen would do that. And though I do not believe
they have, I can see now the impossible position in which Patrick
found himself. My connection with Jennifer automatically excluded
me from the loop. Patrick really did no more than his job in having
Toshio check the report out alone.

The recorder in my pocket whirs quietly. What it has recorded is
no good to me at all.

"So why Basel?" I say. "Why did Toshio need to go there?"

"We needed to confirm some transactions from the FBI report,
authenticate the thing." Patrick shrugs. "We decided the U.S.
Federal Reserve wasn't necessarily going to be a reliable source, they
might have been gotten to by State. I know some people at the Bank
for International Settlements in Basel." His glance drifts away.
"Toshio saw them. Confirmed a few major transactions from the
FBI report. After that we knew the report was kosher. Lemtov was
definitely laundering money."

"For whom?" I say. "From what?"

"You want my guess, it's tied in with all the IMF loans that disappeared into the Kremlin. Toshio guessed drugs. But, hey, take your
pick, the way that country's run, it could be any bloody thing. That
wasn't our problem. Our problem was Lemtov, how he was abusing
his diplomatic accreditation."

It all sounds so plausible. Except for one thing. "Did you ever
mention to Toshio that you and Lemtov had been in Basel together
three years ago?" Patrick's eyes return to mine slowly. "That conference on money laundering," I say.

Patrick studies me awhile, thoughtful. Then he points at me. "You
think I'm tied up with Lemtov."

I don't answer. I look at him and wait. At last he puts his hands
over his face. "Christ almighty," he says. "You've got a damn genius, you know that? A genius for getting things wrong." His hands

drop, he goes back to his desk. "Is that what you're doing here? You figure I'm in something with Lemtov, I can get him to take the pressure off the Headquarters Committee, get his friends to retract those statements, set Rachel free?"

"You attended that conference with him in Basel."

"I didn't attend it with him. He attended it. I was there to give a seminar." Patrick signs his memo to the Australian ambassador, then folds it. When he lifts his eyes, he sees by my look that I am not satisfied. "That's what happened. What do you want, an affidavit?"

I ask him if he would like me to take what I now know to Dieter Rasmussen.

Patrick touches his forehead and swears. Because he knows that if I take what I have to Dieter, Dieter will have Internal Oversight tear him apart. Not telling them about the FBI report, screwing around with my investigation of Toshio's murder, failing to adequately explain his connection with Lemtov. After yesterday the SG will not be stepping in to protect him, and the Australians will not want to take Patrick on in any capacity whatever if he comes to them trailing a cloud of UN scandal.

Patrick chews it over. And finally decides that he cannot afford to let me tear a hole in his parachute. "All right, I gave a seminar at the damn conference. It was just for a handpicked few. Senior officials from countries we were all worried about. Central America. The ex-Soviet countries. Places where drugs and crime had bought their way into politics. Money laundering was the big worry. Money laundering under the protection of the state, what that could do to the financial system. My job was to give these guys an idea of the legal loopholes, what they should be watching out for. Things they could stamp out themselves or report directly to the BIS."

"And Lemtov was there."

Patrick nods. "The focus of the seminar was a hypothetical case I put together. We spent the whole day on it." When he looks up, his cheeks have flushed a light shade of pink. "The hypothetical case was of a high-ranking diplomat. One who laundered money under cover of diplomatic immunity."

"Jesus Christ."

"There's no reason for you to mouth that around," he says, pointing with the memo.

I look down at the FBI report, then back up. "You taught him how to do it. You showed Lemtov how it was done, and he went out and did it."

"Lemtov wasn't a bloody diplomat back then, and I wasn't vetting these guys anyway." And as soon as Patrick saw the FBI report, he tells me, he acted on it. "Frankly, what you've got into your head about me covering up for Lemtov, it's a bunch of crap." He slips the memo about West Papua into his breast pocket. "So now that you know, how about you get off my back." He moves past me toward the door.

But my astonishment at the bizarre nature of Patrick's complicity in Lemtov's crime is fast turning into something else. Taking the FBI report from his desk, I pivot.

"So with all this in front of you, and what you knew you'd taught Lemtov, you went right ahead and detained Rachel?"

Patrick faces me. And he repeats his increasingly improbable line: that he believes Rachel still has a case to answer, that there remains absolutely no proof that Toshio's murder was connected with the investigation of the Special Committee or Yuri Lemtov.

"There's no proof," I remind him heatedly, "because you wouldn't let a proper forensics team into the grounds. And the reason you detained Rachel was because you didn't want me rocking the boat before the big vote. And not just that. You didn't want me getting to the bottom of this." I hold up the report in my hand. "Because this, your role in it, it was just too damn embarrassing for you. You were worried it might make you look like a goddamn clown."

Patrick sets his jaw, he smooths down his tie. He tells me that we can discuss it later, that right now he has an appointment with the Australian ambassador.

I just cannot help myself then. I hurl the report across the room. Patrick flinches aside as the report smashes into his giant framed photograph of Sydney Harbour. A shower of splintered glass rains down. Patrick turns his gaze slowly from the broken picture to the glass, then to me.

"She has a case to answer," he says.

One step, one move in his direction, and I would not be able to stop myself. I would break every bone in his body.

And then my cell phone rings. My hand is still trembling with rage as I answer it. "Yes."

"Sam?" Jennifer, her voice strained. "The Homicide detectives brought an attorney with them. They won't wait. We're coming over now."

37

M OVE RACHEL!"
    Startled by my sudden entry, Mike leaps up from behind his desk. He makes a gesture with both hands: Keep it down.

"So how'd he take it?" he says.

I try to keep my voice low, inaudible to the guards next door. "Homicide's on its way over. Rachel's got to be moved, Mike."

"Oh, fuck."

"Right now."

He grabs his walkie-talkie and we go down the hall a way, out of earshot of the guards. Mike speaks into his walkie-talkie, instructing Weyland to get Rachel moving.

"Don't run," Mike warns Weyland. "Take it steady, like you're both just stretching your legs, taking a walk."

We are on the west side of the Secretariat building, there is a clear view to USUN across First Avenue. While Mike relays his instructions to Weyland, I watch the USUN front entrance. I know it is about to happen, I am expecting it, but when Jennifer suddenly appears on the USUN steps with three men, I feel my legs start to buckle. My hand reaches to the wall for support.

Mike looks at me.

"Jennifer," I say, directing his attention out to where Jennifer and the men are now descending the USUN steps. In a couple of minutes they will be at the UN guardhouse, formally requesting that Rachel Windrush be passed into their custody. Arresting her for the murder of Toshio Hatanaka.

"I thought she told you a couple of hours," Mike complains.

Down the hall a guard sticks his head out from the Surveillance

Room and informs Mike that Weyland appears to be taking Rachel for a walk. Annoyed, he adds that Weyland's two-way seems to be switched off, they can't raise him.

"Musta got tired listening to you guys bitch," Mike says.

The guard laughs, then withdraws. His butt is covered. He has informed his boss.

Mike turns to me. "So, has Patrick gone to do his stuff with Lemtov?"

I press my lips together. I shake my head and explain that we got the nature of Patrick's connection to Lemtov totally wrong. Mike is skeptical, but I am pretty sure Patrick has told me the truth this time. Now he is just going to keep his head down, wait for Rachel to be taken into custody by the NYPD, and see how it pans out. What he is not going to do is act precipitously. And he is not going to do what we'd hoped. He is not going to make Lemtov run.

"Well, Weyland and Rachel won't be able to give everyone the runaround for too long," Mike warns me. "You wanna make Lemtov bolt, you got twenty or thirty minutes max."

He leads me back to the open doorway of the Surveillance Room where we stand a moment, watching the bank of black-and-white screens. What in the name of God are we going to do now? I wonder.

On the top left monitor, Weyland and Rachel are ambling through the basement corridor. They look like Mike told them to look, as if they are just stretching their legs.

On the large central monitor the Security Council sits in session, Lady Nicola presiding. Lemtov, arms folded, not a care in the world, is seated behind his ambassador. Froissart, the French ambassador, is reading a statement, presumably something about the incident in West Papua. Then I notice that poisonous little man the Tunku hovering with his delegation in the "interested parties" seats, waiting to give the world the benefit of his opinion on the big question of the day. At the sight of him the muscles across my shoulders bunch tight.

The next screen down, the General Assembly Hall, is filled with a picture of NGO representatives.

How? I think desperately.

Beside me Mike cracks his knuckles. Then with no conscious effort I find my eyes focusing on the General Assembly screen. On the NGO representatives. And then on the representative in the back row with the white suit, the sunken face, and the goatee.

Juan.

Then I say it, a low whisper of desperate hope. "Juan."

———

"Hi," he says when he emerges from the General Assembly Hall. Though smiling, Juan is clearly puzzled to find that I am the guy who sent the guard in to fetch him. He cocks his head. "So what's happening with Rachel?"

Taking him firmly by the elbow, I lead him away from the guards.

"Hey," he says, jerking his arm free. "What's going on?"

My instinct is to grab his lapel and haul him after me. Instead, I lower my voice and explain the situation as succinctly and as urgently as I can. "I want you to come with me to the Security Council chamber, Juan. I'll explain why on the way. But if you don't come with me right now, Rachel's going to be charged with Hatanaka's murder."

He pulls a face. Say what?

"And the way things stand, she has every chance of being convicted. Now, are you coming with me?"

Mouth open, he hesitates, and then nods. Turning together, we jog to the escalators.

"You've got an in with the Tunku?"

"I wouldn't call it an in," Juan says.

"Whatever. He thinks you're one of his big buddies this session."

Juan rolls his eyes at the thought of it.

"So he won't think it's strange," I say, mounting the escalator, talking over my shoulder, "when you go running to him with some rumor you just picked up. Something you're wondering if he can confirm."

"That's what I'm doing?"

That's what you're doing, I tell him.

Juan considers a second, then nods again. He doesn't have a problem with that. "So what's the rumor?"

"Rachel's been released," I say. "And the UN guards are about to arrest the guy who really murdered Toshio."

Juan's head goes back. "Jesus," he says. "The Tunku?"

I am silenced momentarily by the misunderstanding. Then, stepping off the escalator, I tell him no. Not the Tunku. "But he'll pass the rumor on."

"Ah," Juan says. I can see he doesn't really get it. Then, as we approach the Security Council Chamber, he asks, "Why don't I go straight to this guy, the one you wanna tell?"

"Because you can't reach him. The Tunku can."

He turns it over. He still doesn't get it.

I stop him outside the Security Council Chamber door. "Your story is you've picked up the rumor from a pal. Some guy in one of the NGOs."

"Amnesty?" Juan suggests. Amnesty International, keeper of the flame of human rights.

"Perfect," I tell him. "You knew the Tunku had an interest in the whole business through the Headquarters Committee. Now you're just asking him if he can confirm the rumor."

"This rumor. It's not true, right?"

If only. When I shake my head, Juan hesitates.

And for a moment I have an awful vision. A vision of myself at Juan's age being approached by Harry Bright, the deputy prosecuting attorney in the D.A.'s office, a decent man of some twenty-five years' experience who requested that I discreetly bury a file. He would not tell me why. And I—stiff-necked, youthfully self-righteous, and a complete innocent in the hardball political game being played in the office—I would not do it. Reciting my principles, I refused Harry Bright's request. Two weeks later the contents of the file, a case Harry had handled poorly decades earlier, became the ammunition used to destroy his career.

And now suddenly I am Harry Bright. Only it is not a file I want buried, it is a lie I want told. And it is not my career on the line but my daughter's life.

"This helps Rachel?"

This helps Rachel, I tell Juan evenly.

He thinks some more. Finally shrugs. "Sounds cool."

Relief buffets me like a swirling gust of wind. I squeeze Juan's shoulder. He nods and turns to the door, and I wait just long enough to watch him enter the Security Council before I back away and turn. And then I run.

———

"What's happened?" I whisper, blowing hard as I careen to a halt by Mike, who still stands in the doorway of the Surveillance Room. He is watching the screens over the heads of the seated guards.

In the Security Council, Chou En is speaking; the others at the horseshoe table have their earphones on for the translation. At the bottom of the screen I can make out Juan's white suit; he is in the middle of the Malaysian delegation. A few heads are leaning toward him, apparently listening to what he has to say.

"Where's Rachel?"

Screen five, says Mike.

I locate the screen. Weyland and Rachel, well clear of the basement room in which she was being held, are sitting near the stairs. While I watch, Rachel gets up and speaks to Weyland. Weyland rises, and the two of them disappear together into a side room.

Up here in Surveillance a phone rings. The guard who answers it swivels in his chair and holds the handpiece out. "The guardhouse," he tells Mike. "Again."

The guardhouse. Where Jennifer and the Homicide people are waiting for Rachel.

Mike takes the phone. "Yeah?" He looks at me while he talks, his expression grim. "Yeah, yeah. We're doing it. Just give us a little time. Okay—I don't care what they're telling you. This is me, Jardine, I'm telling you. Wait. Yeah. Ten minutes." He hangs up.

"Ten minutes?" I whisper.

"If we're lucky," he mutters beneath his breath.

Then one of the guards at the console points to the Council screen. He wonders aloud what the problem is. Peering closer, I see one of the Malaysian delegates go bounding up the stairs, exiting the Council Chamber. Not the Tunku but one of his young offsiders.

"Keep an eye on him," Mike tells the guard. There is no hint that this is anything more than a routine request. Then Mike backs into the hall, drawing me after him. "The guardhouse has called three times now," he whispers. "They'll give it ten minutes. After that they'll go over my head, call Eckhardt."

I make a face. Mike's boss will turn out all of UN Security, if necessary, to carry out his orders. And his orders will be those from the UNHQ Committee: Deliver Rachel up to NYPD Homicide. If this gets to Eckhardt, we are screwed.

Mike goes back to stand in the open doorway, arms folded. He chews the fat with the guards at the monitors like nothing out of the ordinary is going on, but the guards are obviously growing uneasy. They tell Mike that Weyland and Rachel have not reemerged from the basement side room into which they disappeared, out of sight of the security cameras. And a minute later, when the young Malaysian exits the elevator into the basement corridor, they speculate with real concern on what he is doing down there.

Mike repeats his relaxed instruction to just keep an eye on the guy.

"He's heading for that room," one guard says. Basement Room B29, he means, where Rachel was being held. The room Weyland and Rachel vacated just minutes ago. I ease myself into the doorway beside Mike and watch the screens.

The Malaysian halts outside Basement Room B29. He knocks on the door and waits.

"They went for a walk," one of the guards up here mutters.

On the screen, the Malaysian opens the door and puts his head in. Then he goes right into the room, disappearing from the screen.

The tall guard twists in his chair, addressing Mike. "What's his game, sticking his nose in there? You want I get someone down there?"

"Wait," Mike tells him.

The guard darts a glance at me, then turns back to the screen.

Within seconds the Malaysian reappears. He is not jogging this time; he sprints down the corridor to the elevators, arms and legs pumping. Mike makes a sound.

I close my eyes, almost sick with relief.

"You got nothing yet," Mike warns me quietly.

The surveillance guards are talking now, speculating about the Malaysian, what he was looking for, whether there is any connection with Weyland and Rachel's timely stroll. They know that something is not right. One of them suggests sending a guard to fetch Weyland and Rachel. Mike overrules the suggestion, telling them to wait.

Two minutes later the Malaysian messenger boy arrives back in the Security Council Chamber. He hurries down the steps and rejoins his delegation. The heads all lean toward him. Juan, I notice, is still there.

Beneath his breath Mike says, "Yada, yada, yada, the girl's been released. Now over to Lemtov."

But it does not happen that quickly. The Malaysians appear to discuss the news for a while among themselves; the Tunku keeps turning to Juan, whose replies are punctuated by emphatic nods and a flurry of hand-waving.

My nerves, already stretched taut, begin to sing. Get up, I think, willing it through the screen as I focus on the Tunku. Get up, for chrissake. Walk over to the Security Council table. Tell Lemtov. Get up. Tell him Rachel's been released. Tell him his own head's on the line. But the Malaysians continue their discussions as though they have all the time in the world.

I cheat a glance at the screen where I last saw Rachel and Weyland. Nothing. They have stayed sitting tight in the basement side room.

At last the Tunku rises. He shuffles past the other members of his delegation and crosses the open expanse of floor to the Security Council table. He crouches behind Lemtov. And Lemtov very casually leans back and listens as the Tunku whispers in his ear.

Now run, I think. Make your excuses and go.

For a moment that's what seems to be happening. His news passed, the Tunku retreats to his own delegation while Lemtov leans forward and has a quiet word with the Russian ambassador. Then Lemtov stands and steps away from the horseshoe table, but instead of heading for the exit, he goes to where the British are seated behind Lady Nicola.

"The fuck?" murmurs Mike.

I, too, am adrift. Lemtov crouches to speak with one of the Brits. After hearing Lemtov out, the Brit goes forward to have a quiet word with Lady Nicola. Almost immediately she turns and addresses the whole Council, cutting Chou En off mid-flow. When the perm five ambassadors all rise as one, I finally understand it: Lemtov has requested a private session in the Security Council side chamber.

"Oh, shit," I say. "No."

Mike shoots me a severe look.

Now Lemtov and the other deputies follow their ambassadors out of the main chamber. Mike points to another screen. Another camera picks up Lemtov and the rest of them filing through the door into the side chamber, then the door swings closed at their backs. Guards take up position to either side.

Mike grunts and looks at me from the corner of his eye.

Appalled, I stare up at the screen, at the closed side-chamber door. Maybe Lemtov is just stalling, I think. Maybe he is trying to figure it out. Maybe in fifteen minutes he will emerge from the side chamber and head straight for the exit. But in fifteen minutes Rachel will be in the hands of NYPD Homicide. If Lemtov runs in fifteen minutes, it will already be too late.

Here in the Surveillance Room the phone rings. The senior guard answers it again, and this time he sits up straight. "Sir," he says, then hands the phone to Mike. While Mike hangs his head and listens, the senior guard galvanizes his colleagues at the monitors. He wants to know which guards they have free in the Assembly building. He tells them that the order from Eckhardt is to get the girl over to the guardhouse at once.

My throat feels clotted. Mike hangs up the phone, then draws me out into the hallway. "Eckhardt," he says, frowning. "So wild he's just about busting a gut."

"Just five more minutes, Mike."

Mike jerks his thumb back toward the Surveillance Room. "Eckhardt's given these guys a direct order. You can't stop it. I can't stop it. She's gonna be handed over."

"No."

Mike lowers his head; he can't bear to look at me. "Jesus," he says.

Fear has dried my throat, I have to swallow before I speak. "Give me your two-way."

Mike lifts his head. "What?"

Reaching, I yank the two-way off his belt. "Go get yourself another one," I tell him with quiet urgency. I point to the Surveillance Room. "You stay here. Tell me what's happening. Just keep me and Rachel away from the guards."

"You and Rachel?" Mike screws up his face when it registers what I'm asking him to do. "Christ. You think they won't catch you?"

"Look, tell Eckhardt about the FBI report. Try to hold him off. Lemtov's just buying time. When he figures it out, he'll run."

"Says you."

We look at each other. Urgent voices rise in the Surveillance Room, everyone calling in the spare guards around the building.

"Fucking mental," says Mike, shaking his head. Then he points to the two-way in my hand. "Reset it to three one one," he instructs me, backing away. "And you don't speak to me on it. You just listen. Go on." Turning in to his office to find himself another two-way, he shouts back over his shoulder, "Go!"

38

"DID IT WORK?" RACHEL ASKS THE MOMENT SHE sees me. She and Weyland have been sitting on the floor, their backs to the wall. They both scramble to their feet as I tell Rachel no, that it has not worked as we planned. She lets out a moan.

"But it still might," I add quickly. "We just need some more time." I point to Weyland. "Some guards are coming down to get Rachel in about two minutes. She can't be here when they arrive."

He doesn't say a word, just thinks a moment, then nods. When I explain what I want him to do, he considers that a moment too. He can see it makes sense, the only way he can help us and not lose his job, and he nods again.

I beckon Rachel over to me by the door and take her hand; our palms are filmed with sweat. Then Weyland comes and touches Rachel's arm and smiles his encouragement. He tells her she is going to be okay, but when she tries to smile back, her eyes are wide with fear. Weyland gestures to the door; he is ready.

"You set?" I ask Rachel.

She stares at the door blankly. When I squeeze her hand, she nods, so I step up and pull back the door.

Weyland takes three long strides, then launches himself out into the hall, arms spread out in a dramatic sprawl that looks just as it's meant to look, as if I've caught him by surprise and delivered a mighty hit. But he has miscalculated the dive. He actually strikes the wall with his shoulder and cries out, an instinctive shout of real pain. Crumpling to the floor, he lies there, groaning.

As we emerge into the corridor, Rachel hesitates, then bends over Weyland. I have to drag her up the stairs.

Suddenly Mike's panicked voice blurts out from the two-way, "If they keep going up those stairs, we've got them!"

I pull Rachel to a jarring halt beside me. And we listen. There is no sound from above, from below us only Weyland's soft groaning. We stand like two cornered animals, frozen.

"Yeah." Mike over the two-way. Watching us in the monitor as he talks to the Surveillance Room guards. "If they'd taken the elevator, they'd be clear."

"The elevator," I say, dragging Rachel back down the stairs.

Weyland, still stretched on the floor, holding his shoulder, looks up at us as we shoot past. He moans and rolls aside. Down the hall, we skid to a stop by the elevator. Rachel presses the button.

"Which floor?"

"Up," I answer stupidly.

Rachel giggles, the giggle rising in pitch, and I take her firmly by both shoulders. "Keep it together, Rache."

She looks back toward Weyland, her eyes brimming with tears.

"Keep it together," I say again, shaking her. Bowing her head, she wipes a hand across her eyes.

The elevator arrives, the doors open. Mike speaks over the two-way. "They stop on one, they're history."

Suddenly guards come racing from the stairwell and into the passage behind us; they pause when they see Weyland sprawled on the floor. Pushing Rachel into the elevator, I hit the button for three. Out in the basement hall the guards shout and come running. I keep my thumb jammed on the button, cursing the doors. "Come on. Come on."

At last, finally, they close. The shouts die as the elevator rises. Slumping against the wall beside me, Rachel tilts back her head and closes her eyes.

"You okay?" I ask.

She nods, but she looks pale and terribly drawn.

"At three," I tell her, "we go straight out. We'll try to get across to the Secretariat building. Not so many guards over there. And whatever you do, stay near. Stick with me." Her eyes remain closed. "Rache?"

When she opens her eyes, I see that she is fighting back tears. I squeeze her arm, then the elevator stops, the doors slide open, and I take her hand and set off running across the polished cream linoleum straight down the passage toward the Secretariat building, south.

"You got no one in front of them," Mike tells the guards as if he is wildly pissed off.

No one in front of us. We charge straight on, not looking left or right, the side corridors flashing by, our shoes slapping on the linoleum.

"Where are the guards?" says Rachel, breathless, as we push through the corridor doors. In front of us the long, wide passage to the Secretariat building is empty. Probably over at the General Assembly Hall, I think. Or the Council Chamber. I urge her desperately on. "Keep going," I say. "Run."

Seconds later we burst through the open doorway into the Secretariat building, I grab Rachel's arm and stop her dead. People. Secretariat bureaucrats, guys with briefcases, women carrying folders, half a dozen or more strolling toward us, heading over to minister to the needs of the delegates in the Hall. Sliding a hand beneath Rachel's arm, I walk her left toward the stairs. The Secretariat staffers pass by us without a second glance.

"You got anyone on the stairs?" Mike asks the surveillance guards. Then he swears. "Floor fucking ten maybe? What good's that?"

Rachel and I exchange a look. Moving as one, we take to the stairs. Five floors up I am sucking air, blowing like a winded horse. Behind me Rachel has her hands on her hips, canting forward, still climbing. And then a long way above us, several flights up, we hear a door open. Two guards enter the stairwell, arguing over whether they're meant to be heading up or down.

Edging along the wall, we get ourselves onto the next landing, then quickly and quietly step out of the stairwell.

"Okay," says Mike, "they're on eight."

The eighth floor is just like most floors of the Secretariat, a long central corridor and countless ranks of veneered doors to either side. Plenty of places to be cornered but nowhere to hide. I touch the two-way on my belt. I want to ask Mike what's happening with Lemtov, but I can't do that without alerting the surveillance guards as to how Mike is helping us. I turn right, take a step, then swing to the left. With Rachel panting beside me, waiting for me to call our next move, it comes to me with a stark and numbing clarity. In a few minutes we will be caught. This is not going to work.

"Dad?" says Rachel, sensing my sudden loss of direction. Her face is pale, her eyes shine. Her shoulders rise and fall with each breath. I am her only hope of getting out of this; she is relying on me absolutely to tell her what to do next.

But all I can do is lift a hand helplessly. And then like the voice of an angel Mike barks over the two-way, "Twenty-nine through thirty-two? I don't fucking believe it. You shut down three floors' worth of security cams for maintenance, you tell me that only now?"

My heart beats hard into my ribs. Hope. Mike goes on chewing out the surveillance guards, making sure that I've got the message. And I have. Between twenty-nine and thirty-two the guards are blind. Grabbing Rachel's hand, I run, a wild dash for the elevator, praying that our luck holds, that we can get all the way up to twenty-nine.

Hitting the elevator button with the heel of my hand, I step back and watch the numbers climb. Five. Six. Seven. Finally eight lights up; there is a ping as the doors begin to open, and I shove Rachel in ahead of me. And then I see the guard. A young guy, he stands in the elevator, his finger poised over the buttons. My gut clenches.

He glances from Rachel to me. And then he smiles pleasantly. "Floor?" he says.

Rachel shoots me a look. I glance down at the guard's belt. He isn't carrying a two-way, he has not heard.

"Twelve," I say, stepping in.

He hits the button, the doors close, and we ascend in silence. The kid tries to make eye contact with Rachel, but she keeps her gaze firmly on the numbers over the door. Long seconds pass. When the doors finally open at twelve, Rachel hurries out. The kid looks faintly disappointed.

As the doors close behind us, Rachel hunches over and makes a strangled noise in her throat.

"Stairs," I say, turning her in that direction, explaining the plan as we go. The elevators run in three banks, floors one through thirteen, thirteen through twenty-six, and twenty-six through thirty-nine. By getting off on the twelfth floor, we might misdirect the surveillance guards into thinking we're not trying to get much higher. By taking another elevator at fifteen, they might not immediately assume that we're heading straight for twenty-six, and they won't necessarily place guards there ready for our arrival.

Rachel says "Ah-ha," but she hasn't listened to a word.

We race up the stairs past thirteen waiting for some warning from Mike over the two-way. No warning comes. Then, emerging onto the fifteenth floor, we pause. The silence from the two-way now is eerie. Rachel crosses to the elevator and hits the button.

"Wherever we go, they'll find us, Dad."

"We're buying time. That's all we can do."

She makes a face. Despair.

The elevator arrives, the door opens, and two middle-aged men in suits are standing there. Faces I vaguely recognize, deadwood from Protocol.

"If they don't get in the goddamn elevator—" Mike says, and my hand snatches at the volume control, turning it down. The guys in the elevator look at the two-way, then up at me curiously.

I think, What? If we don't get in the goddamn elevator, what? We're caught? We're not caught? What?

"Going up?" says one of the Protocol guys.

Steeling myself, I bow my head and usher Rachel into the elevator in front of me. We watch the doors slowly close. Then a cry comes from somewhere on the floor.

"Hold it! Hold the elevator!" The urgency is unmistakable; it has to be a guard.

But when one of the Protocol guys reaches for the buttons, I brush his hand aside and hold my thumb firmly down on Close Door. Twenty-six is already lit; these guys are going to the same place.

"Charlie," I say, tossing my head toward the cries out on the floor. "Thirty pounds overweight. He can take the stairs."

The doors close, we start to rise, and the two men exchange a glance. Neither one is smiling.

Rachel has her back to the wall, her arms folded, and her chin sunk on her chest. Perspiration beads on her forehead and trickles down her cheeks to her neck. She is breathing hard, like me. When the guy nearest Rachel bends to look at her more closely, she raises a hand to her face. His glance slides across to me, and I lift my eyes to the numbers over the door: twenty-one, twenty-two, twenty-three. At last he turns back to Rachel.

"Something wrong?" he asks her.

She turns her head, eyes fixed on the floor. She could not look more frightened, more in need of help, if she tried.

Twenty-four, twenty-five.

The two guys exchange another glance, clearly thinking about that shout down on fifteen.

"You in a hurry somewhere?" the same guy asks Rachel.

"A meeting," I interject. "Last-minute rush."

They consider me doubtfully.

Twenty-six. The bell pings.

"Who with?" the guy says.

As the doors slide open, I cast around for a name. "Jim," I say finally.

"Yeah?" He cocks his head. "Which one?"

Rachel steps out past me. I nod stiffly to the two men, then get out and steer Rachel away quickly. Leaning toward her, I whisper, "Soon as we're through this door, run. Straight up to twenty-nine. Don't look back."

Behind us now we can hear the two Protocol guys debating what to do as they step out of the elevator. We're almost at the stairs when they call out that we're heading the wrong way for the offices. We keep right on walking.

"Miss!" one of them calls after Rachel.

I shoulder open the stairwell door and tell her, "Run."

I take the stairs two at a time; at first Rachel tries to keep up, but she simply cannot do it. After two flights she stops, slumping against the banister. On the flight above I stop and urge her on. Then she lifts her head, I see her face, and my heart leaps into my throat. She has gone white. Her eyes seem sunken and the skin is stretched tight over her cheekbones. Physical exertion and fear have sapped her strength totally. She drops her head and sobs.

Leaping down the steps, I wrap an arm around her waist. She rises and puts her arm over my shoulder, then leans in to me. She keeps saying sorry.

"A couple of more floors, Rache. We'll get there."

She nods, then looks up. Easing her away from the banister, bearing much of the weight of her slight frame now, I start to climb. She lifts her legs, struggling, climbing beside me. Another flight, then the door back down on twenty-six opens. A few ineffectual cries of "Hey!" and "What are you doing?" drift up the stairwell. The Protocol deadwood; thank God they make no effort to follow. They yell something about reporting me to the guards and then they withdraw.

Rachel and I are both perspiring freely now, both breathless. My heart palpitates strangely as we stagger onto the twenty-ninth-floor landing. Rachel disengages herself, leans back against the wall, hands on hips, and tries to catch her breath. Clinging to the banister for support, I follow her gaze up to the security camera fixed high on the wall above us. Then I turn up the volume on the two-way.

"Dad—"

"Shh."

A few seconds more, then Mike speaks. "They're up there. We've lost them."

When I look at Rachel she presses her lips together, her mouth trembles.

"Okay," I say, finally pushing away from the banister, hauling myself upright, moving toward the door.

Be strong, I think. She needs you to be strong.

And I almost manage to keep my voice steady as I tell her, "Now let's get you hidden."

39

OUT ON TWENTY-NINE THE MACHINERY OF LEGAL Affairs ticks over. Most people are locked away in their offices, dealing with paperwork; others roam the corridors, files in hand, looking concerned. When Rachel and I walk briskly down the central hall to my office, the only one who even notices us is the cleaning lady, Celine, a tiny old Jamaican lady who has worked here since before the Flood. "Ouda the way," Celine demands, pushing a trolleyload of rags and buckets between us, her skinny arms extended, her head down. A strong antiseptic odor wafts over us as we hurry on by.

A minute later and we are in my office. Rachel closes the door. "I can't stay here," she says. "God. This is the first place they'll look."

"You're not staying." My hand dives into the desk drawer.

"How do we find out if Lemtov's gone?"

"Mike'll let us know."

"He hasn't said anything."

Keeping my head down, I go on searching for the key to Toshio's locked office.

"Dad, this isn't working."

"Hang in there."

"You said it was all—"

"Rache!" I lift my head. "I'm not a goddamn marine, okay. But I'm doing my best here." We look at each other. She wraps her arms around herself, turning away. "You're doing great," I tell her, lowering my head, searching in the drawer again. "Just hang in there. A few more minutes."

My hand finally alights on the key. Crossing to the door, I open it and check both ways along the hall. Celine is gone; the hall is empty.

But as I am about to step out, I glimpse movement, a door opening along the hall, and I pull my head back sharply. Then, holding my door open just a crack, I peer out. It is Toshio's door that has opened. And now someone comes out of his office, a file beneath his arm.

"Dad?"

Turning to her, I press a finger to my lips. Rachel screws up her face.

I look out again and I can see who it is now. Pascal Nyeri. He must have come up to check on some paperwork on the Special Committee investigation. He relocks Toshio's door, then walks away down the hall toward the elevators. A cold bead of perspiration trickles down my spine. A minute earlier and we would have walked right into him. When Pascal disappears from sight, I beckon Rachel to join me by the door. The hall is empty now.

"Last move," I whisper, then I lead her out and across the hall to Toshio's office. A formal notice is pinned to the door beneath Toshio's nameplate. LOCKED BY ORDER. NO ENTRY WITHOUT UN SECU-RITY AUTHORIZATION. The notice is signed by Eckhardt.

As I unlock the door there is a ping from the elevator down the hall, then the voices of guards as they emerge onto twenty-nine. Dragging Rachel into Toshio's office, I quickly close and relock the door. I put a finger to my lips again, and we stand facing each other, waiting. My heart rate is off the scale, I can hear the blood beating in my ears. It must be only a minute, but it seems like an age before we hear the guards coming along the hallway, opening and closing doors.

We stand absolutely still. Rachel has gone a sickly shade of white.

The guards seem not to have been told exactly who it is that they're chasing. As they get closer we can hear them asking everyone they meet if a man and a young woman have come running this way. Nobody has.

Outside Toshio's door, our refuge, they stop. "Hatanaka," one says, evidently reading the nameplate.

"The dead guy?"

"I guess."

One of them tries the door handle. Rachel flinches. Then there's a loud bump, one of them putting his shoulder to the door, and she closes her eyes.

"Leave it," says one of them, moving away. "If we can't get in, they can't get in."

Released, the door handle flips up. The voices fade as the guards carry on their search along the hall.

"Give me your sweater," I whisper.

Rachel opens her eyes. Shedding my jacket, I hold out a hand. "Take off your sweater, come on."

Frowning, she takes off the baseball cap and pulls off her sweater. "They'll come back," she says.

"Not for a while they won't. They've got three floors to search."

Pulling on her baggy gray sweater, I tug the two-way off my belt and go and sit behind Toshio's desk. Mike, I know, is not going to appreciate this. But I do it anyway. I press the transmit button on the two-way and speak. One word.

"Mike?"

Down in the Surveillance Room, Mike will instinctively want to curse me. I hope he'll be able to make his way to somewhere private, where he is free to talk. I set the two-way on the desk and turn down the volume.

"I want to find out what's happening with Lemtov," I explain to Rachel quietly. "After that, I'm going to run decoy."

I ask for the cap. She hands it over. Then she looks at the cap and the sweater. "You don't even look like me," she says hopelessly.

Adjusting the band, I pull the cap down firmly on my head. "Be thankful," I say.

She grimaces. Then, folding her arms, she goes and sits in a corner chair and draws her legs up beneath her.

Something about that simple movement, how she looks, makes me think quite distinctly, This will destroy her. If I can't get her out of this somehow, if I can't stop the handover, Dr. Covey's worst-case clinical assessment, my own worst fears, will be realized. Emotionally she just isn't equipped to withstand any more of this. And to be charged with murder? To face month after bruising month of a trial? They will not need the death penalty. I have an awful vision of prosecuting attorney Randal White appearing at Rachel's bedside in the Special Needs ward at Bellevue, asking persistent lawyerly questions as Rachel relentlessly starves herself into the grave.

"You can't say it, can you?" Rachel tells me now.

When she faces me, I lift a shoulder: Can't say what?

"Aren't you even gonna ask me, Dad? Even now?"

Her eyes are clouded, her arms folded tight. I know, of course, what she means. But instead of asking the question I have carefully avoided the past two days, I bow my head over Toshio's desk and with a flick of a hand I wave the whole thing aside. I stare at the two-way, waiting for Mike's reply.

"It's the library, isn't it," she says. "All that stuff I requested down in the library."

"This isn't the time, Rache."

"You know why I requested it? All that stuff on Mom's camp, where she was murdered?"

I raise a hand. I tell her very firmly that I don't want to hear this.

"I requested it because you did."

My hand slowly falls. "I never told you I'd been through that."

"I was looking up something else," Rachel says. "I got talking to the librarian and she just mentioned you'd been down there a lot a few years ago. I guess she mentioned the camp." Rachel lifts a shoulder, makes a face. "I was curious."

I make a sound. Understanding of what has happened gathers slowly. "You requested to see everything I'd requested?"

She nods. "I never even read it. There was like volumes of it. What do they think, I sat there for two weeks or something? Do they think I'm crazy?"

"You never read it?"

"I just glanced at it." She shrugs.

Rachel never read it. She has no idea any questions were ever raised within the Secretariat about Toshio's conduct of the hostage rescue mission.

"When you went downstairs Tuesday night," I say.

She looks straight at me. "To get my coat."

To get her coat. She went downstairs to get her coat. And at the Dag Hammarskjöld Library she simply requested the old files I'd requested. Because she was curious. Is there anything, anything at all in this whole affair, that I have gotten even partly right?

"I didn't do anything wrong," she says. "And you know what? That just doesn't matter." She draws up her legs and presses her face into her knees.

Now I hit the two-way, whispering urgently, "Mike?"

Still no answer. Rising, I move around the desk toward Rachel, intending to do the only thing I can: hold and reassure her, promise her that while a single breath remains in my body she will not have to face a trial alone. But then I stop suddenly. And I look down at the pink folder in Toshio's in box. A pink file. In bold black letters an inch high the word *confidential* is stamped right across its cover. I stand very still a moment, then I take out the file and open it.

The first page is a memo from Patrick, a masterly piece of bureaucratese that gives Toshio full responsibility for the investigation of the UNDCP Special Committee while retaining full rights of intervention for Patrick. Next come a few pages of notes on Asahaki, Po Lin, and Lemtov—background profiles—and then three separate sections that appear to be information Toshio turned up on each individual during his investigation. The largest by far is the section on Po Lin. When I flick to the conclusion of the section on Lemtov, there is no mention of his money-laundering activities and not even a passing reference to the FBI report.

Closing the file, I look at the in box. And I picture the scene. On the morning of Toshio's death, when I came up here with Mike, I placed the entire contents of the in box in my lap and went through it page by page. I am absolutely sure of that. I have not misremembered. And I am absolutely certain that this pink file, at that time, was not here. Not in the in box. Nowhere in the vicinity of Toshio's desk. And since that morning the door to this office has been locked.

"Sam!"

I snatch up the two-way. "What's happening with Lemtov?"

"Zero. They've called the Tunku into the side chamber. Froissart's gone to the can. That's it. Zip."

I glance across at Rachel. She rocks back and forth, her eyes fixed on the two-way. "Who shut down the security cameras up here?" I ask Mike.

There is a pause. "How the fuck do I know? You haven't noticed, I been busy down here."

"Can you find out?"

"Listen, forget that shit. You want, you got about two minutes to get yourselves outta there. The south stairs are still open, but the elevators, everything else, we got covered. You wanna move, move now."

"Find out who shut them down," I tell him, then I grab the walkie-talkie and the pink file. I go to Rachel and crouch beside her, shoving the file beneath my shirt as I speak.

"Don't open the door for anybody except me. Not Mike. Not Weyland. Anyone says they're going to smash the door in, let them. More likely they'll go find a key. It'll buy us some time. You just sit tight right there."

"I knew it wouldn't work."

"It's not over, Rache."

She continues rocking, hugging her knees, and I embrace her, hold her close while she buries her face in her knees. Bending, I kiss her head as I used to kiss her when she was a child. She doesn't respond. And when I cross to the door, she doesn't say a word either.

Stepping warily into the hall, I take a final glimpse at her before I close and lock the door. Rachel is rolling onto her side on the chair, curling into the fetal position. Curling up tight like a ball.

40

THE SOUTH STAIRS ARE CLEAR AND I DESCEND with speed, one hand skating down the banister for balance, the other clutching the file against my stomach. My legs jar with each leaping stride. Passing beneath the first security camera, I hear Mike tell the surveillance guards, "They're coming down. What's covered?"

I keep on going, racing now, getting as far from Rachel as fast as I can. The farther I can lead the guards astray, the more time I have to figure this out, the more time Lemtov has to run.

"She's alone," says Mike, meaning me. He sounds uncertain, he knows something's not right. And then, "Okay, you've got someone where? The stairs on twenty? Right. And those other two on twenty-nine, they're coming back to the stairs? Yeah, fine. Kid stays in the stairwell, she's trapped."

Diving out of the stairwell at twenty-two, I sprint to the elevators; one has just arrived. When the two maintenance guys get out, I jump in and clap the button for fourteen, praying that the guards on the stairs at twenty don't have time to get to the elevator. The doors close. I hold my thumb on the button; the elevator seems to descend so slowly that it might be moving through molasses. As I pass twenty-one I find that I'm instinctively holding my breath. Number twenty lights up over the door. Move, I think, move. But the light seems to stay on and on, then suddenly winks out. Nineteen lights up and I am still descending, and I think, Oh, Jesus, no more.

"How many guys you got waiting on fifteen by the elevators? Five guys?"

Nineteen. Eighteen. Paralyzed, momentarily hypnotized by the numbers, I watch as they wink on and off above the door.

Seventeen.

Then I slam the heel of my hand into the button for sixteen. The elevator stutters. Then it slows, stops on sixteen, and the instant the doors open I am running again, straight down the hall. It won't take the guards a minute to get up here from fifteen, and once they're up here, guided by the Surveillance Room, it won't take them a minute to collar me. There are security cameras at both ends of the hall. Running is useless. If I keep running now, it is over.

In a moment of desperation I improvise. Just before I reach the corridor that cuts at right angles across the hall I'm running down, I turn left into a conference room. It is empty. Out of sight of the security cameras now, I pull off the baseball cap and Rachel's sweater, dumping them in the trash as I cross to the door that leads into the adjoining corridor. Then I pull the pink file from beneath my shirt, tuck my shirt back in my pants, and smooth down my tousled hair. Taking a breath, I step out into the corridor, file open, head down. I turn right. Now I am just another office gofer in shirtsleeves, examining the paperwork. Just another UN bureaucrat with a file.

I examine the paperwork, praying that the sudden switch has thrown them. I study the paperwork in the file and keep walking.

Then I turn right again, heading back toward the elevator, retracing the path I've just run. A woman steps into the corridor in front of me; she hardly seems to see me as she hurries by. I am almost at the elevators when I hear the guards come bursting from the stairwell around the corner.

"You've got her," Mike says flatly. "She's still in the room."

I quickly switch off the two-way. The next moment four guards appear; I step aside and they charge past me without a glance. Keeping my head buried in the file, I cross the last few yards to the elevators, waiting every moment for a cry at my back. But no cry comes. And the last thing I see of the sixteenth floor is a view of a long, empty hallway between the closing elevator doors. Then I bend over Toshio's pink file again. And now I am not just pretending. Now I am actually reading what is recorded here in these pages.

————

"Mike!"

He is standing in the doorway of the Surveillance Room; his head jerks back at my call. When he sees me, he comes jogging.

"They found the sweater and cap," he tells me, drawing me into his office. "They figure she's still between twenty-nine and thirty-two. All the guards are back up there, searching."

"Who shut down the security cameras?"

"Some guy, Matate they're telling me." Mike goes and taps at his PC keyboard. "Name mean anything to you?"

Shaking my head, I move to where I can see the screen. Mike is calling up this Matate's personnel file.

"Rings bells with me," says Mike, biting his lip as if something about the memory has him worried. And then Matate's file appears, a large mug shot of the man in the top left-hand corner of the screen. Mike groans. "This is one of the guys I interviewed. Part of the team that shut down the cameras for maintenance when Hatanaka died." Mike flicks the screen with his finger. "You wanna tell me what the fuck's going on here?"

"You said the maintenance crew had alibis."

"For the murder, sure. This Matate was working with two other technicians. Three of them in the same room the whole six-hour shift. They bring their own sandwiches. There's a can right off the maintenance room. These guys were in each other's pockets the whole six hours. This Matate"—Mike lays his finger on the screen— "this guy never had a chance to kill Hatanaka. No way."

I study the face on the screen. Matate. His hair is like thick black fleece, tight curls, but not wet and dripping as it was when I last saw it. There's no question in my mind that this is him. The broad, flat cheeks, the wide smile, and the quarter-inch gap between his two front teeth. Not the kind of face that is easy to forget. Mike has not forgotten him. And neither have I. Matate. Whom I last saw wearing nothing but a towel, dripping his way through an overcrowded apartment up in Harlem.

"Where is he now?"

"Christ knows." Mike considers a moment. "If he's working on the security cams, he's probably still down in Maintenance."

I tell Mike that we need to find Matate. Find him fast.

"He couldn't have done it, Sam."

"Yeah, well, Rachel didn't do it either."

Mike looks at me.

"Upstairs now," I say. "I didn't ask her, she just told me. And I believe her."

Mike throws up a hand. He mutters something about Eckhardt setting heads rolling, then leads me back to the Surveillance Room.

The monitoring guards turn to update Mike as he enters. Then they see me. The senior guard rises, pointing at me over Mike's shoulder, telling Mike in a tone of angry amazement that the son of a bitch is right here.

"You found the girl?" says Mike gruffly.

They haven't. The senior guard starts in again about me.

"Save it," Mike tells him sharply, nodding at the bank of screens. "Show me Maintenance. I'm looking for that guy Matate."

"Ain't we all," says another guard farther along the console. He tells Mike that they're still trying to raise someone in Maintenance to get the cameras up on twenty-nine through thirty-two switched back on. No one in Maintenance is answering.

"Here," he says, pointing to a screen. Nothing. A picture of a closed door marked Maintenance and an empty section of passage.

"If nobody's answering," Mike remarks, "could be nobody's there."

The guard shakes his head. He tells Mike he saw someone go in there two minutes ago. From along the desk another guard with a phone to his ear calls across that he's still getting no answer from Maintenance.

My glance slides over to the Security Council screen, where there is a sudden stir of movement. First Lady Nicola, then the other senior diplomats come filing back in from the side chamber and retake their places at the horseshoe table. Chou En. Froissart. Bruckner. For a second my heart leaps wildly. Lemtov is not there. It has worked, I think. He has run. Light-headed, I point to the screen to show Mike. But Mike is already shaking his head, and then I see him too: Lemtov. He takes his place behind the Russian ambassador and leans across to share a joke with one of the Chinese.

The surveillance team here is receiving reports from the guards searching for Rachel over in the Secretariat. The guards report that they have swept thirty-two and thirty-one; now they're moving down to thirty. Twenty-nine after that.

Mike looks at me. He is finished; there is no more he can do.

Drawing him out into the hall, I turn my back on the Surveillance Room. "This is Toshio's file." I slap it with the back of my hand. "The one that went missing? The one we couldn't find? I just found it up in Toshio's office. On his desk."

"You're shitting me."

"Listen. Matate turns off the cameras on twenty-nine, the missing file reappears. He shuts the cameras off in the basement, Toshio ends up dead. Spot the connection. And one more thing. Matate's got a roommate. Name of Pascal Nyeri."

Mike's eyes narrow.

"And guess who I just saw leaving Toshio's office?" I ask, holding up the pink file.

It takes a moment for the pieces to come together. When they do, Mike swears.

"Sir?" says a guard from the room behind us. We turn to find him pointing up at the Maintenance Room screen. The Maintenance Room door has opened; we watch two men come out, one dressed in the white coverall of a technician, the other wearing a suit. Africans.

"Matate," says Mike.

But it is not Matate I am looking at. Going over to the screen, I reach up and place a finger on the suit. "Pascal Nyeri." Even as I speak, they part. Matate goes left, Pascal right. Pascal walks briskly and after a second Matate breaks into a run.

"Oh, shit," says Mike. "Shit. We got every spare guard upstairs chasing Rachel, for chrissake." He points to the screen, giving the surveillance guards their orders. "Keep them two runners on-screen. Warn the gates. I want 'em both collared. No fuckups."

I stand here staring. I cannot believe it. We have come this far and now for no good reason we've blown it. In five minutes Pascal and Matate could be gone, over a fence into New York, where we have no jurisdiction, then into a cab and straight out to the airport. Lemtov is sitting calmly in the Council Chamber. And Rachel is still going to be handed over, charged with a murder in which she had no part.

I give Mike the pink file. "Which exit's Nyeri headed for?"

"Sam."

"Which exit?" I shout, backing out of the Surveillance Room, switching on my two-way.

Mike glances at the screens. "North."

North, I repeat, and I am already running.

———

The three-dimensional game of chase recommences, this time with me the pursuer, not the pursued.

"Nyeri's in the basement, still going north."

Several floors above Pascal, I race north down the hall.

"He's coming up to the public area. The cafeteria and post office, all that."

Cutting past the Delegates' Lounge, I head for the elevators.

"Okay, he's in the public area." A pause, then Mike says, "What the hell?"

I snatch up my two-way. "What's he doing, Mike?"

"He's gone in the goddamn bookshop, we've lost him. Hang on, we're trying to bring up the screen."

"What?"

"Hang on." Another pause, then he says, "No, it's okay, he's coming out, wrong turn or something. He's headed for the stairs now, going up."

Leaping into the elevator, I press the ground-floor button. When Pascal gets to the top of those stairs, he will be fifty yards from First Avenue, where neither Mike nor I can touch him.

"Where are you?" Mike barks. "He's up on the ground floor."

The elevator finally stops, and I shoulder my way out of the opening doors. Tourists wander like sheep around the North Concourse, some lining up for the security check, others flocking over for the guided tours. I charge through a line of schoolkids near the Meditation Room; their teacher shouts after me.

"Nyeri's out," calls Mike.

I can see that for myself through the plate-glass wall. Pascal has just gone out the concourse exit and turned left toward First Avenue. He hasn't seen me, but he is walking fast now, striding out. Sprinting through the concourse, I leap over the rope barrier, carve my way through the tourists, then swing left out the exit, hard on Pascal's heels.

"We'll stop him at the guardhouse," Mike says confidently.

But with Rachel cowering in Toshio's office, NYPD Homicide still waiting to collect her, there is no way I am leaving this to the UN guards.

Pascal doesn't hear or see till I am right up beside him. As his head turns, I slide my hand beneath his arm and take a firm hold. I bring him to a stop. He makes a sound and pulls away, but I hold on tight.

"You want to talk to me, Pascal?" Then I point up ahead to the guardhouse. "Or them?"

Pascal jerks his arm again, but I hang on grimly. At last he tries to act as an innocent man might. "What?" he says, his mouth struggling to smile in feigned surprise.

The UN guards appear from the guardhouse with Jennifer; I shake my head and wave them off. While they confer on their two-ways with someone upstairs, I tug roughly on Pascal's arm, hustling him around the giant knotted gun-barrel statue, down the steps, and across the North Lawn. When Jennifer tries to follow, I shake my head again and wave her back.

Pascal starts asking me what's happening, what this is all about, but I don't answer him immediately. I lead him to a stone bench on the promenade over the FDR Drive, then push him down onto the bench and stand over him. He tries to rise. I push him down again. He looks up at me defiantly.

"What is this for?" he says.

Fury wells up in my chest. Toshio Hatanaka is dead. Rachel has been deprived of her liberty, dragged back to the edge of a personal abyss, and at this moment lies quivering with fear, waiting to be arrested and charged with murder. Put on trial for her life. What is this for? I think, my heart silently raging. It's for two innocent lives. It's for Toshio's life already lost, and Rachel's, now hanging by a thread.

My tongue is thick, my throat dry. I breathe deeply a few times to calm myself. Something in my look gets to Pascal; his eyes dart down to the slab beneath the bench.

It's while he's like that, head down, wondering how much I know, what lies he can get away with, just how much he is going to tell me, that I muster enough sense to reach into my shirt pocket and press the button on the tape recorder that Mike gave me to use on Patrick. There is a faint vibration against my chest as the tape turns. Then I sit myself down on the bench. When Pascal attempts to rise, I pull him back down.

The rumble of traffic passing below us along the FDR Drive is a useful background hum; even I can't hear the recorder. I fix my gaze on the old Pepsi-Cola sign across the East River, its color faded; the clouds above scud low and gray. I gather myself a moment. This is it, I think, my last chance. When I face Pascal, he is not looking at me but out over the river. I lean toward him and I ask my question.

"So just how long have you been working for Yuri Lemtov?"

41

FOR A LONG WHILE PASCAL IS SILENT. NO angry denial, no exclamation of surprise, nothing. He just sits there, staring at me, as if my question has tipped him into a sudden catatonia, as if he is too shocked to reply or move.

"What was it," I ask, "the money?"

More silence. Then at last he looks at me, his brow furrowed with a single deep line. "Lemtov?" he says.

"Okay, try this." I jerk my thumb over my shoulder toward the Secretariat building. "Fifteen minutes ago your roommate Matate shut down the security cameras up on twenty-nine. Ten minutes ago you arrived there with Toshio's missing file. The one on the Special Committee investigation. And you deposited it in Toshio's in box. Would you care to tell me why?"

"I did not."

"You were up there."

Looking me straight in the eye, Pascal denies being anywhere near Toshio's office today.

"What have you got, an identical twin? Listen, I saw you, Pascal. I saw you come out of Toshio's office. When I went and checked in there, the damn file was on his desk. In his in box, for Pete's sake. And it wasn't there when the office was locked by Security. I know that because I was there Tuesday morning. And that file was not there."

Caught in the lie, Pascal drops his gaze. He rests his forearms on his knees and studies the concrete slab beneath his feet.

"You're in serious trouble here, Pascal. You know that."

He doesn't say anything. Then a movement catches my eye to the left; when I turn I see two guards closing in. I flick my hand, warning them off. One consults his walkie-talkie, and they retreat to the cover of the trees. Pascal, head down, sees none of this.

"When this gets out," I tell him, "Lemtov's going to deny it. He'll deny he ever asked you to put that file there. You know that too, don't you? He's not going to stick by you, he's got no reason to. All he has to do is deny it. And that's what he'll do. If you point the finger at him, say he was behind it, he'll deny it flat out. And who's going to believe you? Dieter?"

Pascal lifts his eyes and stares at nothing.

"Dieter's going to be after your head," I say. "You'll be on your own. You'll take the fall. And Lemtov, he'll just walk away from you."

No response. Impossible for me to even guess what he is thinking.

"Now do you want to tell me what happened?"

"Nothing happened," he says quietly. A young man a long way from home, and though he hides it well, afraid.

"I can't make you talk to me, Pascal. But if I get up from here and walk, you're on your own. There won't be a single person in the Secretariat wanting to hear your side of it. Not one who's going to listen when you finally decide that talking might not be such a bad idea. So if you want to put in your side of the story, this is it, your last opportunity. I can't make you. But if you think Lemtov's going to protect you now, you're a fool."

Elbows on his knees, he leans forward but remains silent.

"How about Matate?" I ask, changing tack. "Was that how Lemtov approached you?"

Pascal gives a brief shake of his head.

"But Matate turned off the security cameras for you, right?"

No reply. I glance back to the Secretariat building; it looms up behind the Assembly Hall away to our right. Up there on twenty-nine they will have found Rachel by now.

"Pascal, you just came down from Toshio's office, you went straight to the Maintenance Room, you spent five minutes with Matate, then you both ran. You can't tell me Matate wasn't involved in this."

Pascal shoots me a look from the corner of his eye; he is obviously startled by how closely his movements have been monitored. And in the next moment the realization of what this means seems to reach him. Matate has probably been caught just as he has. Someone from Security is probably questioning Matate right now. Pascal's eyes close fractionally, his shoulders droop.

"Matate turned off the cameras so that you could get into Toshio's office unnoticed. Yes or no?"

"He was not involved."

"Matate turned off the cameras."

"He didn't know the reason."

"A favor?"

Pascal nods.

"And some kind of payment?"

"No."

That simply isn't plausible, and I say so. Crap. A lie. I remind Pascal that if he is not straight with me, I will get up and walk, and he will have to face the music alone.

"Five hundred dollars," he admits finally.

"Did he know what you were doing?"

"No."

I don't know if I buy that or not. But I sense that this is one part of his story he won't be changing, and as it's not really what matters anyway, I don't push it.

"The money came from Lemtov?" I ask, turning a little on the bench, the recorder whirring quietly. I pray for Pascal to answer my question with something more than a nod.

The prayer goes unanswered. He simply inclines his head.

"Yes?" I prompt.

"Yes," Pascal says and adds, to my considerable satisfaction, "The money came from Lemtov."

"And how much did he pay you?"

Pascal seems to weigh where this is taking him. "Two thousand," he says.

"Dollars?"

Dollars, he agrees, darting a glance past me. I have the distinct impression that he is gauging some distance, setting himself to run. So I place a finger firmly on his knee.

"We haven't finished."

His eyes come back to mine and then down. His hands are braced on the bench now, on either side of his thighs.

"What exactly did Lemtov get for his money?"

"He gave me the file. I put it in Hatanaka's office."

"That's all?"

Another nod.

"Why do you think he wanted you to do that?"

Pascal shrugs. But by now there is a light sheen of perspiration on his face, and I can see the carotid artery pulsing in his neck. I need to be careful here. If I push him too hard, too fast, I'll get nothing. Too soft, too slow, the same.

"You told me back on the day this all started that the evidence you had on the fraud pointed just one way. To Bunzo Asahaki."

"It did," says Pascal.

"Then maybe you can tell me why Toshio's file on the investigation, the file that you just put there in his office, maybe you can tell me why it has a whole stack of paperwork that implicates Po Lin in the fraud. Had all that just slipped your mind?"

Pascal reminds me of Toshio's final visit to the Portland Trust Bank. Toshio, he says, did not show him everything.

"Maybe not. But that paperwork on Po Lin, it's basically numbers. Accountancy. And you're expecting me to believe that Toshio put that together by himself? He didn't even consult you? You, the accountant who was working with him on this?"

Pascal shifts his weight uncomfortably on the bench.

"I don't believe that it just slipped your mind, Pascal. That stuff wasn't there. It's been put there sometime between when the file disappeared and now. And it's been put there by someone who understands numbers. Someone who knows his way around this investigation. And there's only one person who fits that bill."

Pascal's eyes stay down and I cheat a glance over my shoulder. Half a dozen guards have emerged onto the terrace; a few more are loitering on the North Lawn behind us.

"Lemtov didn't just get you to put the file back. He got you to tamper with it first. He got you to point a lot of fake evidence at Po Lin."

No response.

"Who actually paid you the money?" I ask.

"Lemtov."

I lift my head in surprise. "Himself?"

Pascal nods.

"Where?"

"The Russian mission," he says.

I consider that. "There's no way he did that just to get you to put the file back. If it was just that, he would have used an intermediary. He wouldn't have gotten involved himself. Not from the mission. He must have had some other reason for wanting to deal with you directly."

Pascal tilts his head back and gazes at the sky. "How can you help me?"

"You doctored the file."

A moment's hesitation, then Pascal crosses the Rubicon. "Yes," he says.

"For the money?"

"Yes."

"That's all?"

He lowers his head, nodding. Though clearly frightened, he is not about to break, to get down on his knees and confess all. He is a much tougher man than that. As a man who has dragged himself up so far from his birth must be.

"I don't believe you, Pascal."

His tongue passes over his lower lip.

"I don't believe you did it for two thousand bucks."

But Pascal hardly seems to be listening to me now. His hands ball into fists on his knees and he stares out to the faded Pepsi-Cola sign across the river. He has said all that he is going to say.

On the tape in my pocket I have Pascal's confession, his testimony that Lemtov has screwed around with the fraud investigation, but I have nothing that implicates anyone directly in Toshio's murder. And I don't know if what I have is going to be enough to stop Rachel's handover to the New York authorities.

Which is why, finally, I do what I never intended to do. One last shake of the tree to see what falls. I bend forward, hands joined, elbows resting on my knees. My gaze follows Pascal's across the river.

"I see this young guy," I say evenly. "He's come a long way from where he started, but now he's turned thirty and he's looking around and he's not quite satisfied with what he finds. He's hit a ceiling in his career. Until his boss and a dozen more senior guys retire or die, he's going nowhere. He's making maybe thirty-five grand a year. Not great, but back home his family thinks that's a lot of money, millionaire class, and they've probably made a lot of sacrifices to help get him to where he is, so he's got obligations. And he pays them. Remits what he can to his family, but he's living in New York, he's got his own problems, rent to pay, taxes, other expenses his family can't even imagine. In the richest country in the world, thirty-five grand a year, and this guy is poor." Pascal darts me a glance. I continue. "He just doesn't see any way out of that. He can't quit his UN job because he hasn't got a green card; he'd have to leave the country. And he can't go home because the shame would kill him. Besides, his family needs the money coming in. And they simply wouldn't understand it either, why anyone would give up the good life in America to return to some dirt-poor village in the Cameroon."

Pascal makes a sound.

"It's not the life he dreamed of," I say. "It's not nights at the opera, discussing Voltaire, none of that. It's waking up in a crummy tenement in Harlem, standing in line for the shower, trudging into work, getting shouted at by Dieter Rasmussen, then going home to decide whether he should dry-clean his suit or send the twenty bucks back home, where his family needs it for food. That's the picture. A young guy trapped by his situation, no fault of his own, looking for some way out. You recognize it, Pascal?"

Hands on the bench to either side of his thighs, he bows his head. Against my chest the recorder hisses faintly.

Over my shoulder I glimpse Jennifer standing with the guards and the Homicide guys at the guardhouse, watching us. "And then," I say, "Lemtov appears. Somehow he's found out that the Special Committee is under investigation. He knows that sooner or later the paper trail is going to be traced back to him. He can't let that happen. But he can't stop the investigation either, so he does the next best thing."

Pascal rises. I grab his arm and drag him back down to the bench.

"Lemtov turned the investigation. And he used you to turn it, Pascal."

"No." Vehemently.

"You didn't just replace that file for Lemtov. You've been working for him longer than that, haven't you?"

"No."

"You tampered with the evidence. Toshio didn't know how to read the paper trail, all the numbers, but you did. And he relied on you, didn't he? Down at the Portland Bank it would have been just the same as with me. You sifting through the paperwork first, picking out anything that might be construed as pointing to Asahaki, passing that up the table. Anything that pointed to Lemtov, you buried. Those papers you showed me that nailed Asahaki, they were copies, remember?"

Pausing now, I recall what Patrick told me this morning. Toshio wanted it to be Asahaki. If Asahaki was implicated, Toshio guessed that Japan's run at a Council seat would fail. And Toshio wanted that. If Pascal kept pushing "evidence" against Asahaki at Toshio, was Toshio likely to question it? Wouldn't he have done what Patrick said he did, used the evidence to try to bring Asahaki down? In truth it probably wasn't so difficult for Pascal to turn the investigation. Toshio, initially at least, would have been an unwitting but willing accomplice.

"Are you going to deny that?" I ask Pascal.

His mouth hangs slightly open; his gaze is fixed on his feet.

"You didn't do that for a lousy two thousand dollars, Pascal. Two thousand dollars isn't going to change your life. And that kind of fooling around, what you were doing for Lemtov, that was a big risk. If someone figured it, you'd be out of a job, on the next flight home to the Cameroon, no second chances. Lemtov must have offered you plenty. Enough to make a real difference in your life."

"You don't know that," he says suddenly. His neck muscles are bunched like thick cords of wire. "You don't know me, my life. Nothing."

"I know what you did."

His eyes meet mine, then immediately slide away. By now Rachel must have been caught, I think. By now the guards will be bringing her down.

"A couple of weeks ago something went wrong, didn't it? Suddenly Toshio wasn't so eager to swallow everything you gave him on Asahaki. Suddenly he was asking you some difficult questions about Lemtov. Yes?"

Pascal's face hardens. He seems determined now not to speak.

My guess now is Toshio never breathed a word to Pascal about the FBI report on Lemtov. But the moment Patrick showed the report to Toshio, Toshio's suspicions must have been aroused. So Toshio shut Pascal out, went and did some investigating on his own. The unaccompanied trip to Basel. The private visit to the Portland Trust Bank. He wasn't just doing what Patrick assumed, checking out the FBI report. He was also discovering how badly Pascal had misled him.

"Toshio figured it out, didn't he? That you'd rigged some numbers, pointed him at Asahaki and away from Lemtov. But this is Toshio. He didn't just run upstairs and report you. Not his style. Not Toshio. He knew how the game was played, he'd been dealing with guys like Lemtov most of his career. You were just a pawn. He knew that. So what did Toshio do? I mean, you'd been working with him on the Special Committee thing for a while, he knew you, maybe he even thought of you as a friend. Maybe he'd even been to your apartment, saw how you were living. He knew if he reported you, you were gone. Everything you had, your career, prospects, everything destroyed. Was Toshio the kind of guy to do that to you?"

This touches a nerve. Pascal blinks a few times, then presses a thumb and forefinger on his closed eyelids.

"He confronted you, didn't he? He told you he knew what you'd done."

From Pascal, silence. Down on the FDR Drive the cars rumble on while the recorder in my pocket whirs quietly. I need Pascal to speak. Looking back to the guardhouse, I see Jennifer spread her hands to me, a questioning gesture: Where's Rachel? What the hell's going on? Behind Pascal's back I gesture to her: Wait.

"Maybe Toshio even asked you to turn again, help him nail Lemtov," I suggest. "Whatever. That's how things stood Monday night. That's why Toshio was over at the Japan Society, that's why he copied out that poem for Asahaki. Some kind of reconciliation, Japanese style. He knew by then that Asahaki wasn't guilty of the fraud."

Pascal stands, I jump up and grab his arm.

"And by then you were afraid. Afraid of what Toshio knew, what it could do to you. And more than that, you were afraid of Lemtov."

Pascal jerks his arm free; we stand facing each other. The recorder in my pocket seems to be searing my chest. Speak, I think. For chrissake, Pascal, speak. But Pascal Nyeri maintains his stubborn silence. So I do the only thing I can. I raise my hand and point. My final shot.

"Lemtov gave you the heroin, that syringe. Matate shut down the security camera for you. And you, Pascal, you killed Toshio."

Pascal stares straight through me. Not stunned, not even thoughtful, more like he is somewhere else, reliving some scene in his mind. Then slowly his expression changes. His shoulders bow and his eyes cloud with tears. And at that moment I see Pascal just as he feels, alone now in all the world. Then he speaks, not to me but to himself. *"Le plus beau moment de l'amour c'est quand on monte l'escalier."*

And then from behind me there comes a wail of real terror.

"Mama!"

My heart seizes. Rachel. Crying as she cried as a child, screaming for her mother.

I swing around. She is up on the terrace, a guard at either side of her holding her arms, leading her toward the guardhouse, where Jennifer and the Homicide guys are waiting.

"Rachel!" I shout.

Up there, they all turn. And Pascal seizes his moment; he runs. Caught flatfooted, I lift a hand helplessly after him and he goes left, sees the guards stepping from behind the trees, then breaks right along the walkway toward the conference rooms. But now guards seem to be coming from everywhere. Three of them go sprinting past me after him and three more appear on the walkway up ahead of Pascal. He is surrounded; he will not escape.

As I move toward the terrace, Mike comes running from the building. He shouts at the guards holding Rachel. Bemused, they release her and she comes stumbling down the steps and across the lawn where I gather her in my arms. She clings to me, pressing her face into my chest while I stroke her hair and kiss her head. I keep telling her that it's over. Up on the terrace, Jennifer confers with Mike.

Then a guard behind us on the walkway shouts, "Move in now. Grab him!"

Still holding Rachel, I turn.

Pascal has been corralled. A semicircle of guards has trapped him against the low wall of the walkway. He can't escape but he is clambering onto the low wall. Below him, a clear fifty-foot drop, is the FDR Drive. Beyond that, way too far to jump, the East River. Crouching, he holds on with both hands, and there is nothing distant about his look now. He is simply terrified, a guilty man at the mercy of fear. And what he fears is not the drop but capture. One guard, caught up in the moment, has drawn a gun.

On the terrace Mike shouts, "Back off! Don't shoot, for chrissake. Back off!"

But the guards, totally focused on Pascal, don't seem to hear.

Clamping a hand to the back of Rachel's head, I keep her face pressed against my chest. But I can't take my own eyes off the scene. It is the awful inevitability, the dreadful certainty of what is about to happen that is so sickeningly mesmerizing. As if the moves are somehow preordained.

The guard with the drawn gun takes one step forward. And Pascal rears back. Rears back and overbalances. His hands are suddenly clutching air, his arms flailing skyward. The other guards seem to freeze. Pascal's head swivels. Wild-eyed, he looks down, sees the FDR Drive, instinctively straightens one leg and reaches back for the wall, and then he is suspended a moment, poised against gravity, against time. Suddenly he twists in the air, his body jackknifing, falling, his arms reaching skyward again as he disappears soundlessly behind the wall.

The silence seems to go on forever.

And then down on the FDR Drive there is the scream of braking tires, the sudden blare of a horn, and the bang and the long, slow crunch of crumpling metal.

42

PANDEMONIUM. A WOMAN, SOME TOURIST UP ON THE terrace, begins to scream. The guards rush to the walkway wall and look over, shouting at one another, shouting down to the Drive, where a whole chorus of horns is suddenly blaring. Then Mike goes running past me to the walkway, calling back over his shoulder to Jennifer, telling her to get an ambulance down there fast.

Rachel lifts her face from my chest and looks around, startled as a deer.

More tourists emerge onto the terrace, drawn by the screaming woman. One guy tries to calm her; another is pointing to the walkway, shouting in Spanish as a crowd gathers.

Rachel looks up at me, says "Dad?" and I quickly wrap an arm around her shoulders and steer her across the North Lawn, away from the commotion, the raised voices, and the gathering rush of people. I keep telling her that it's all right, that everything's okay, but my legs seem to be moving of their own volition. The picture of Pascal momentarily suspended in the air is seared like a lightning flash onto my mind's eye. When we reach the tree-screened privacy of the Eleanor Roosevelt Memorial, I ease Rachel onto the bench. Then I sit down beside her. My legs are trembling. The voices over on the walkway are distant now, Mike's bawling voice the only one I can really make out. Close the area, he cries. He shouts for the guards to get the tourists out.

"What happened?" says Rachel.

I draw her to me. She hunkers down close. I stroke her hair, and after a moment she lies down on the bench and rests her head on my thigh. A squirrel forages through the ground ivy, rustling the fallen leaves near my feet. And though I watch the squirrel, it is Pascal I still see. His final words that I hear.

What happened? I think.

And the alarming truth is that I am suddenly not sure I know.

———

Pascal Nyeri has been killed. By the fall, by the first or second car that went careering over his body. It hardly matters. Fifteen minutes after the event you can still hear the sirens down there on the Drive, police and ambulance men sorting out the wreckage. The North Lawn and the whole terrace area have been cleared of tourists; there is a line of UN guards ushering the last sightseers from the concourse straight out to First Avenue. The tourists crane their necks to where some guards and gawking delegates lean against the low wall, looking down ghoulishly to the mayhem on the Drive. Two TV news choppers are buzzing like dragonflies out over the East River, filming the chaos, something dramatic to lead tonight's broadcast. Just near the bench Mike and Jennifer are standing together with the attorney from the D.A.'s office, three heads bowed over the tape recorder I have given them, listening to the final scene of Pascal's short life. The sound quality is surprisingly good; I can hear my own voice quite clearly.

Matate, so Mike has told me, was caught over at the East Forty-third Street exit. Apparently he could not wait to relate his side of the story. And everything Matate has confessed squares with what Pascal told me, right down to the payment of five hundred dollars. Matate denies any part in Toshio's murder. He says he told Pascal about the scheduled security camera shutdown in the basement Monday night. Pascal talked to him about it several times that weekend, confirmed that it was definitely happening, but beyond that Matate claims to know nothing.

Matate's admission, coupled with the tape and with Pascal's reaction when I accused him outright, should be enough. Rachel, God willing, should walk away free. And yet my relief in the aftermath is not exultant. The last minute of Pascal's life, my accusation, his attempted escape, the silent fall—all of it keeps playing over in my mind. Shock has printed it there indelibly. Could I have handled it differently? Better? Did he really have to die?

"Sam," Mike says now, and I touch Rachel's shoulder as I rise from the bench. Mike and Jennifer have finished listening to the tape. When I join them, Mike is speaking into his two-way.

"I'll have to take a copy later," Jennifer tells me, tapping the recorder. "Keep Rachel on the grounds here while we straighten it out with the D.A.'s office."

"No arrest?"

She turns to the attorney, the Homicide cops' legal escort. He looks down at Rachel on the bench and shakes his head. No arrest, he says. Once the D.A. is informed, the guy says he is sure that Rachel will be free. The guy bobs his head at me and Jennifer, then walks back toward the guardhouse.

I look at Jennifer. I cannot quite believe that the ordeal is over. She places the recorder in my hand, then squeezes my arm.

"I'm glad for you," she says, glancing at Rachel. "For both of you." She seems about to say more, but the attorney calls to her and she goes to join him. They head toward the guardhouse together.

"Eckhardt's bringing Patrick down," Mike tells me, sliding the two-way onto his belt.

"Lemtov?"

"Still in the Council Chamber."

"He hasn't run?"

Mike drops his voice. "Lemtov's a thirty-eighth-floor problem now. Leave it alone. You got Rachel outa this. Be happy."

Weyland comes ambling down the path, and when he reaches the bench, Rachel gets up and embraces him. She clasps his shoulder and he turns aside gingerly. It seems he has really done some damage there.

I turn the tape recorder over in my hands. Then I give it to Mike. "Make some copies once you've played it for Patrick and Eckhardt."

"You're not staying?"

"Can you call your people in Surveillance, let them know I'm coming up there to review the tapes?"

He nods, looking straight at me. He repeats his warning for me to leave it alone.

I go have a quick word with Rachel, warning her not to leave the UN grounds till I say so. I thank Weyland and shake his hand. And as I move away across the lawn, Mike calls after me, "You wanna tell me what you gotta review?"

I keep right on walking.

After all the grief I have caused them today, the surveillance guards are understandably not pleased to find that they are now expected to assist me. But Mike has given them their orders, so I am allocated a screen at the far end of the room while they track down the sections of the security tapes that I want to see. Video cartridges come sliding along the floor to me every few minutes. As I review each tape, I jot down the times from the bottom right-hand corner. I note the places where the events are occurring, carefully putting everything in sequence.

It is an hour before I am done. Then I play it through tape by tape before kicking back and staring at the blank screen in front of me. I am silent. Numbed. The senior guard calls over to me from his console, asking what I want to see now.

I shake my head. Nothing, I say.

He gives some button a savage punch and a picture appears on the blank screen I am staring at. The Security Council Chamber. A live transmission.

There they all are, the big guns of international diplomacy, the enforcers of the new world order, the self-selected elite. Only Bruckner, reading from a prepared statement, shows any sign of animation. Lemtov, Froissart, and Chou En, each wearing headphones, look bored, half asleep. Lady Nicola glances at her watch, then puts her hands to the small of her back and stretches. They will have heard by now that Pascal Nyeri is dead. Maybe they have already taken a second brief adjournment to the side chamber, which seems likely, but from their faces you would never know that anything untoward has occurred to disturb the morning's deliberations.

The presiding body of international affairs doing what it does best. Looking banal. Inviting the curious viewer to switch channels, to turn that curiosity someplace else.

Then I hear Mike passing along the hall outside. He is talking to a guard, debating what to do with Matate. But for a while longer I sit thinking, staring at the screen. Finally I rise and go down to Mike's office, where I find him alone, one phone to his ear, another ringing on his desk. He sees me and throws up a hand in despair as he carries on his conversation. With the local NYPD precinct captain, it seems, a man on the warpath about the disaster he is blaming Mike for causing down on the FDR Drive. I signal to Mike. He rolls his eyes and covers the mouthpiece with his hand.

"If he wants," I say, pointing to the phone, "I'll go down and identify Nyeri's body."

Mike nods, grateful right now for any help he can get. He scribbles an address on his memo pad, at the same time confirming with the precinct captain that he has the right morgue, that the place has not moved.

"Yeah, yeah," Mike tells the precinct captain. "I'm sending some-one down there now."

Mike rolls his eyes again and cradles the phone beneath his chin as he tears the page from his memo pad. He gives me the address and carries on his conversation as I reverse out the door.

43

MARIE LEFEBRE FLIPS ASIDE THE PEEPHOLE COVER AND peers out, then the bolts go back, the chain jingles.

"You did not buzz," she rebukes me lightheartedly as she opens the door.

In answer, I hold up the tape recorder. "I've got your big story."

Her glance flickers from the recorder back to me. "A joke?"

"No joke."

She pushes a hand up into her hair and tilts her head to one side. Then slowly she smiles. Conspiratorial. She and I, two adults in the know. Stepping back into her kitchenette, she ushers me into her apartment where a strong smell of coffee fills the air; there is an espresso maker on the stove behind her, hissing steam. When Marie reaches for the recorder, I shield it with my body as I shuffle by her into the living room.

Pour two cups, I say. I tell her that we can listen to the tape together.

Marie looks at me with playful ferocity, but when I simply smile, she disappears into the kitchenette. "Pig," she calls, laughing.

Then I hear a cupboard open, the sound of crockery clattering. Placing the recorder upright at the center of the glass coffee table, I take a slow turn around the room. The collection in her CD rack is standard fare, classical and jazz, but her small bookcase contains a surprising mixture of French classics and contemporary romance. Judging by the wear on the spines, they have all, at some time, been read.

"Will I get my job at *Time*?" she calls from the kitchenette.

"You want to know if the story's big enough?"

"*Oui.*"

"It's big enough."

She laughs again, delighted. Farewell Radio France. "What was it, that call this morning about your daughter?"

"She's okay."

Marie appears with two tiny cups and saucers on a tray, which she places on the coffee table by the recorder. "How you left, so quickly—"

"She's okay," I repeat, firmly cutting off any further inquiry in the direction of Rachel.

Marie's eyes shoot up. She has gotten the message. "So are you going to tell me this big story?" she asks.

Leaning against the wall, I point to the tape recorder, suggesting that she might want to take some notes.

She fetches a memo pad and a pen, then settles onto the sofa, her legs tucked beneath her. The pad rests on a thigh. When she glances across, her look is not exactly lascivious, but it holds out a certain promise. She reaches over and presses the play button, turns up the volume, then eases back onto the sofa. Her eyes are fixed on the recorder now.

Silence, then the background hum of traffic down on the FDR Drive suddenly cuts in.

"This is me and a guy from Internal Oversight," I tell Marie. "This morning. We're out by the walkway on the North Lawn."

Marie nods. And then, on the recorder, I speak.

"So just how long have you been working for Yuri Lemtov?"

Four times already this afternoon I have listened to it, heard myself say the words, yet now I cannot help the same bleak thought rising anew. Stupid, I think dismally. Sometimes I really am so goddamn stupid.

At the mention of Lemtov, Marie's eyebrows have risen. But when she looks up at me, I redirect her attention to the recorder, where the conversation continues. A very one-sided conversation. In fact, listening to it becomes progressively more painful for me, my own voice droning on, figuring, probing, and Pascal Nyeri hardly responding at all. Marie makes a sound of surprise from time to time, scribbling furiously. On the tray the two cups of coffee sit untouched.

Finally I shove off the wall; I really do not want to hear any more of this. Telling Marie that I'm going to the bathroom, I pass by the kitchenette and enter her bedroom. The strong aroma of coffee is in here too, but beneath that, Marie's sweet scent, an uncomfortable memory. At the sink I splash my hands and my face, then I flush the toilet before returning to the bedroom. The clock is right there on the bedside table. Checking the alarm setting and the time, I turn the clock over. The alarm has been switched off.

When I reappear in the living room, Marie has stopped scribbling in her pad; she just stares at the recorder and listens. I do too, enduring another minute of it before my voice on the tape rises in pitch to deliver the final damning judgment.

"Lemtov gave you the heroin, that syringe. Matate shut down the security camera for you. And you, Pascal, you killed Toshio."

I hit the stop button. For a few moments neither one of us speaks. I look at Marie, but her eyes remain on the recorder. At last she tosses her pen and pad onto the table, drops back onto the sofa, and exhales.

"This Pascal, he is from Internal Oversight?"

"He was."

Marie tilts her head to one side.

"A few moments after that"—I point to the recorder—"he died."

Slowly she eases forward, swinging her feet out from beneath her, setting them on the floor. Her eyes have not left mine.

"Trying to escape the guards," I say. "He dropped onto the FDR Drive."

"He jumped?"

"An accident."

Her look lingers, then her eyes return to the recorder. "So everything—the fraud, Hatanaka's murder—it was all Lemtov."

Concealed in my hand till now, I place the clock from her bedroom down by the coffee cups on the tray. No reaction from Marie.

"Hard to believe, isn't it," I say.

She gestures to the recorder. "This was this morning?"

"Just a few hours ago. None of your colleagues called you?"

"No."

I tell her to tune in to the evening news. They'll have some great pictures.

"Who else has heard this?" she asks, nodding to the recorder.

"No other journalists. Just you."

At last she is unable to keep her eyes from wandering to the clock.

"That was our deal, wasn't it?" I say. "You kept what you knew about the fraud under your hat, I'd give you the big exclusive?" Tossing my head toward the phone, I ask her if she wants to call the people at *Time*. "You never know how long they'll keep that job open. With what you've got now, maybe they'll recognize how good you really are. Send you straight to the top. Editor in chief, *Time* magazine. Sound like something you could go for?"

By now, of course, she is getting the idea that I have not come to pick up where we left off this morning. Not even to fulfill my side of the deal we made Wednesday. Pulling a slip from my breast pocket, I place it down by the clock. Time *magazine,* it says. *Editor, International Desk,* and then a New York number.

Marie considers it a moment, then turns her head as if she is baffled. By the number. By me.

"You told me there was a job waiting for you at *Time,* Marie. You told me you just needed a big story to land it."

"*Oui?*"

"I called them." Bending, I touch the slip. "There's no job. And they've never heard of you."

"Why did you call them?"

"Is that really the point here?"

"Why?" she demands, rising suddenly. This abrupt flare of anger I recognize for what it is, a practiced attitude, a screen behind which she can compose herself. I don't intend to give her that opportunity.

"Here's another one. Between when Pascal left Toshio's office and me starting that conversation with him on the North Lawn, there were about ten minutes. And when I saw him leaving Toshio's office, he wasn't panicked or scared. But by the time I caught him, he was running. Even before I started asking questions, he was a frightened man. How do you explain that?"

"You are asking me?"

"Matate and Pascal both ran. But Matate took the regular way out, he headed straight for East Forty-third. Pascal didn't. He went for the public exit."

She lifts a shoulder. Looks perplexed.

"No comment?"

"Only perhaps you are wrong," she says, stooping to pick up the slip, the *Time* number, from the tray. "Like with this." She folds the slip into a tight square and drops it onto the table.

"I've checked the surveillance tapes. I watched Pascal run through the building, what he did from when he got in the elevator on twenty-nine after leaving Toshio's office."

Marie picks up her notepad and pen and takes them over to her desk by the bookcase. She keeps her back turned to me.

"Just before he got to the Maintenance Room he received a message on his pager. That's when he ran. He dived into that Maintenance Room like he'd just been hit with a thousand volts. But when he came out he didn't make for the nearest exit with Matate. No, Pascal headed for the public exit. Because on his way to the public exit there was a place Pascal needed to go, wasn't there, Marie? Something he needed to get."

"Speculation I cannot use in my story."

"The UN bookshop," I say. "Pascal was in and out of there in fifteen seconds. He wasn't there for the books."

Marie comes back over and picks up her espresso. She takes a sip, then wrinkles her nose. Cold, she says, replacing her cup on the tray.

"Pascal went straight to one particular shelf," I tell her, determined to see this through. "He stuck his hand down behind the books and brought out an envelope. Once he had it, he headed for the nearest exit. It's all on the security tapes."

"Should I make a note?"

"You put that envelope there."

Marie bends to collect the tray and cups, an act of unconcerned domesticity.

"That's on the security tapes too," I say. "Just minutes before Pascal arrived in the bookshop. You were there. The same shelf. And you planted that envelope." Taking the clock from the tray, I hold it up. "See that? Set for eight-thirty." I turn the clock over. "And see this?"

She lifts a brow.

"It's off. I didn't sleep through the goddamn alarm. You never set it. Or if you did, you switched it off when you came back."

She starts to turn from me. I chop a hand down hard on the tray and it crashes to the floor. Cups go flying, something breaks. Marie fixes her eyes on the coffee stain that has suddenly appeared on her ivory-white sofa.

"Leave," she says.

I remain planted to the spot.

"Now," she says, lifting her eyes.

"I went and identified Pascal's body. They let me take a look at his personal effects. His passport. Things like that."

Marie pivots, heading for her bedroom. Taking two strides, I grab a handful of her sweater and she screams and lashes at me with her heel. Then she jerks to one side, breaks my hold, and dashes into the bedroom. But when she tries to close the door behind her, I drop my shoulder and shove hard and she falls backward. I grab her shoulders, fling her down on the bed, and plant one knee on her stomach. She thrashes around, her nails rake my right hand, then I manage to clutch another handful of sweater and pin her down.

Her head goes back, her body arches, and she screams. Screams loud. In one sharp movement I cock my arm and bring it down hard, backhanding her across the mouth. Her head jerks sideways, her scream dies.

My body is poised over hers now, our chests are heaving. Then she looks at me. Looks at me hard. And in the next moment, I can hardly believe I am feeling it, she lifts her hips and grinds her pubic bone against my shin. Her eyes remain fixed on mine. My hand goes back and then stops. She tilts up her chin, waiting for the blow. Inviting the strike. I waver. And then, swearing, I shove away from her and step back from the bed.

"You know why you didn't have to let me in from the street? Because I didn't buzz you. I buzzed your super. He let me in."

She stares at the ceiling. The skin around her mouth is turning red.

"You know, he's got a serious thing about you."

"*Cochon,*" she says.

"Keeps an eye on you. Like when I was here last night, that kind of stuff he notices. Turns out he's a big-time racist. I guess you knew that too." I take the UN personnel photo of Pascal from my pocket and hold it up. She glances at it, then away. "Your super, the pig, he recognized it. Almost went crazy when I showed him." I flick the photo onto the bed beside her. "Pascal Nyeri. He's been a regular nighttime guest of yours for the past three months."

"You are jealous already?"

"He's dead," I say, barely able to speak, my voice squeezed tight by the constriction of my throat. "The guy you've been screwing for the past three months is dead. He's dead, and you knew that before I got here, and what do I find you doing? You're brewing coffee, for chrissake."

She sits up and straightens her hair. Then she reaches across to her bedside table, picks up a pack of cigarettes and taps it until a cigarette drops into her hand. She looks around for her lighter. But her calm is too studied to be natural. She is trying to recall, I guess, all the coaching she must have had in order to deal with this situation. Cover blown. The endgame.

"Pascal killed Toshio. But he didn't do it for Lemtov. He did it for you, Marie. For you. For the French passport you offered him. His ticket to a new life. The life he'd been dreaming of since he was a kid. Paris. Culture." In my mind's eye I see the books by Pascal's bedside in Harlem. Voltaire. Montaigne. "French civilization," I say hoarsely. "He did it for you and your fucking country."

Marie rolls and searches for her lighter in the other bedside drawer.

"You people never changed your policy, did you? When France finally gave in and agreed to let the Japanese seat go to a vote, Bruckner high-fiving it with everyone thinking he'd made the big breakthrough, that was all horseshit. Bruckner hadn't changed your minds. You just let him believe he had. But you people never for one moment wanted Japan to get that seat. Your country doesn't want a new world order. The old world order suits France just fine."

"This is your fantasy."

"You're an agent of your country. You report to Froissart. And you used Pascal to murder Toshio."

She turns and looks straight at me. She does not deny it. She does not say anything; she simply points to the door and waits for me to leave. She knows, of course, that there is not a snowflake's chance in hell that I am going to let her back into UNHQ. I have already entered her name on the security blacklist, and as soon as I can I will be making sure that her press accreditation is permanently withdrawn. But I am pretty sure that now that she knows what I know, she will be removing herself from New York anyway. Two men are dead, and if I have figured it out, someone else might do the same. Her speedy departure is the best I can hope for too, hence my visit here. To let her know what I know. To get her gone. What evidence I have against her would not stand up in a court of law, but it is not only that. The fact is that my brief carnal sojourn with her last night, as Marie no doubt intended, has given her a weapon. If I make an accusation against the French, she will attribute any personal motive she pleases to my words. Froissart might even manage to drag Rachel back into the fray. And the thought of Rachel being flayed on the altar of my stupid indiscretion, the idea that my thoughtless action might have rendered her vulnerable again, is simply too painful to face.

So now I have done what I came to do. Marie Lefebre knows what I know. The moment I walk out the door she will be packing her bags to leave. But seeing her sitting now, so composed on the bed, I cannot help thinking of the scene down at the morgue and Pascal's broken body; and the scene Tuesday morning in the basement, Toshio's glassy eyes staring at nothing.

This should be worse for her, I think.

Reaching down, I grab her arm and haul her out to the living room. She swears in French and tries to pull away.

"Pascal sent you a message." I lean over to the recorder.

She looks from the recorder to me, thrown now and uncertain, while I hold her arm tight. With my free hand I crank up the volume, then I hit rewind a moment, and then play.

"—and you, Pascal, you killed Toshio."

Traffic noise on the tape, distant, from down on the Drive. In my mind's eye I can see Pascal's face. He is looking right through me. Thinking, I know now, of Marie. Here in the living room I watch her beside me. At last, on the tape, Pascal speaks.

"Le plus beau moment de l'amour c'est quand on monte l'escalier."

Marie makes a sound, her lips part. *Le plus beau moment de l'amour c'est quand on monte l'escalier.* The same words Marie's super shouted after me. The same words he must have been shouting at Pascal for the past three months as Pascal followed Marie up to her apartment. The best part of passion is the walk up the stairs.

How right he was, I say.

She continues to stare down at the recorder. Finally I release her arm and turn away. When I get to the door, I look back, but she has not moved. The tape plays on.

Rachel's crying for her mother, sobbing into my chest; Mike up on the terrace shouting at the guards on the walkway, ordering them to back off; a few moments' silence and then that sound of crumpling metal, a six-car pileup over Pascal's broken body.

Marie's eyes remain dry.

I let myself out. As I move across the landing I hear a cry rise behind me and I pause, but it is not her. Not Marie, but the tourist who witnessed Pascal's fall, the woman up on the UN terrace caught forever in the fatal moment, screaming. My hand on the banister, I hang my head and descend the well-worn stairs.

SATURDAY

44

A FTER THE MORNING'S BIG POWWOW UP ON THIRTY-EIGHT I spend a couple of hours in my office, playing catch-up with the paperwork on my desk. Problems arising from the General Assembly session and the more usual troubles from out in the field. Added to these is a flood of queries relating to Afghanistan; it seems that someone has suggested my office as an alternate destination for anything addressed to Toshio Hatanaka. I will probably be receiving this stuff for weeks before the mix-up is straightened out. In the meantime I pile it all into a box. Then, when my own work is done, my desktop visible again, I take the box down the hall to Toshio's locked office. The box is perched on my thigh, my knee pressed against Toshio's door, and I am digging in my pocket for Toshio's key, when Mike comes strolling toward me down the corridor.

"Heavy?" he inquires.

I hand him the box, then open the door. He follows me in.

"Misdirected mail," I explain as he deposits the box on the desk. I tell him about the mix-up and my admittedly crude solution: The problem is now someone else's. Mei Tan, Toshio's secretary, will have the task of guiding Toshio's yet-to-be-named replacement through all the paperwork in here.

Mike turns to the open door and starts peeling off the security notice, the No Entry sign.

"You pleased how things went this morning?" he asks me. The big meeting upstairs, he means. Mike and Eckhardt were both there, along with me, Patrick, and the Secretary-General.

"I'm pleased it's over," I say.

He leans back, tearing the notice off in one sweeping motion. Then he crushes it into a large ball.

"How's Rachel?"

"She spent the night back home."

"Permanent?"

"Nope."

Almost the first thing Rachel said to me over breakfast was that she wasn't staying, and the next thing she said was that she'd made an appointment for herself with Dr. Covey. After the emotional roller coaster she has been on the past few days, I had, naturally, feared the worst, that she might revisit the dark territory of withdrawal, the place into which she retreated after Sarah's death, the first stop on the way back to anorexia and the intensive care ward. Instead, she seems to have come through it, battered but determined to go on. Determined not to be one of life's victims. Though I cannot take any credit for how well she seems to have coped with what has happened, I am more pleased and more relieved than I ever believed possible to find that my daughter has discovered in herself that kind of quiet courage. I take it as a sign, I suppose, that in the years since Sarah's death, I have not failed totally as a father.

"Look at the pluses," says Mike. "For one, you don't have to see the goofballs she brings home for supper."

I give him a look.

She's a good kid, he says. She'll be fine.

Though being a good kid is no shield from harm, certainly not in this city; that is not what Mike really means. He is simply telling me that I cannot lay a protective hand over my daughter's head forever. From Mike I appreciate the platitude, the reassurance and hope that he wants to convey.

We stand by the desk a moment, looking around Toshio's office just as we did Tuesday morning. The knowledge of what has happened since, everything our investigation uncovered, seems to have given the place a darker, more somber aspect. And when my gaze falls on the place where Rachel lay curled up and quivering yesterday, a cold hand seems to touch me. Whoever the next occupant of this office might be, this is one place that in the future I will be going out of my way to avoid.

As we head back to my office I ask Mike what he's doing up here anyway. "What happened to the grand Security review?"

"We just finished phase one," he tells me. "Eckhardt kicked my butt for an hour, I went and kicked ass downstairs."

In the aftermath of Toshio's murder, the discovery of how it was done, the inevitable reassessment of security procedures has been set in motion. Upstairs this morning the SG made it clear that he was not a happy man. He spent much of the time pacing the floor, yelling, while the rest of us hung our heads, jotting unnecessary notes in our files. He has demanded a full review of UN Security, to be followed, naturally, by a full and lengthy report. There will be no glory in the task, so Eckhardt has palmed the whole thing off on Mike. Which Mike ruefully accepts as a justified penance for everything that has gone wrong in his department.

"I was thinking maybe you had something to tell me," Mike remarks now, lobbing the balled-paper wad into the trash can as he strolls into my office.

"About Rache?"

"No."

When I glance over, the look Mike gives me is unexpectedly direct and probing. Sitting down, I rearrange the pens on my desk.

"Actually," Mike says, "I was thinking you had something to tell everyone. Upstairs this morning."

I shrug and shake my head.

"You sure?"

"What's this, a quiz?"

When I smile, Mike very pointedly does not. "I went down the morgue, Sam. Spoke to the guys you saw when you identified Nyeri's body. I saw the stuff from his pockets."

I take a moment with that.

"Also," he says, "I talked with our guys in Surveillance. Thought I'd better smooth things out there, put them straight about you. Let them know you're not the jerkoff they think you are."

"Did it work?"

He just looks at me. "They tell me you went back there, got them to help you with the editing. That you spliced together some of yesterday's tapes."

"Guilty."

"So have you got something to tell me now?" he asks, and by this time, of course, it is clear to me that this is no offhand inquiry.

I had asked myself, naturally, how it would be if someone wasn't satisfied with the Lemtov-Nyeri tie-up, everything that seemed proven by my taped conversation with Pascal out on the North Lawn. Lemtov, unsurprisingly, denies the whole thing categorically, denies any relationship whatsoever with Pascal. But last night the SG invited the Russian ambassador up to the thirty-eighth floor to peruse the FBI report. That, along with Pascal Nyeri's death and my tape of the final conversation, has convinced the Russians that Lemtov is finished. The carefully constructed edifice of his career is

in ruins; his ambassador is in no mood to listen to his pleas of inno-
cence. And for her part, Jennifer has accepted the chain of events at
face value too; and so, apparently, has Patrick. But the possibility
that Mike Jardine might not be satisfied, that he might independ-
ently uncover at least part of the truth, that one I missed. On reflection, I really shouldn't have.

"You saw the passport?"

"Ah-ha," Mike says. "French. And I saw the date of issue.
Yesterday."

"You noticed that."

Mike waits. He has me on the hook, he has no intention of letting
me slip free. So at last I reach into my desk drawer and take out the
videotape. I turn it over in my hands.

"Lemtov should never have been here."

"Says who?"

"He should never have been here, Mike. And I don't mean just
what he put Rachel through. This is a guy whose only interest in the
UN was the cover it gave him. Now he's out, and if I had any part in
that, I'm not sorry."

"Okay, so you're not sorry." He points. "What's on the tape?"

"Do you want Lemtov back here?"

"Sure. Great guy." Mike squints. "What are you saying, do I want
Lemtov back here? Guy's a crook. I want him back here like I wanna
dose of the clap. Now, what's on the goddamn tape?"

No way around it. On my way to the VCR in the corner I close
my office door; then, as I slide the tape into the machine,
Mike comes and stands by me. The tape clicks, begins to play, and
Mike leans forward.

"When's this?" he asks.

On the screen the members of the Security Council are trooping
into the side chamber. There is a date and a time in the top left-hand
corner.

"Lemtov's just gotten the word from the Tunku that Rachel's
gone," I tell Mike. "This is when Lemtov asked for a recess in the
side chamber."

Mike grunts and watches the screen.

"Outside the side chamber now," I say, locating the visual as the
scene changes to a guard by a door and an empty corridor. I point to
the time on the screen: a few minutes after the previous footage in
the Security Council. "You're still in Surveillance," I tell him. "I've
gone to help Rachel run."

On the screen the side-chamber door opens and Ambassador

Froissart comes out. Mike nods, remembering. "He went to the can."

We watch as Froissart passes beneath three different cameras. Then another figure appears, a woman holding out a microphone.

"Journalists," Mike comments quietly. "Man can't even take a leak in peace."

Froissart appears to give the journalist the brush-off, then he disappears into the men's rest room. And to Mike's surprise my edited tape stays with the journalist. Marie Lefebre. Mike turns to me, puzzled.

"Watch," I say, touching the screen.

He does, silent for the next two minutes. We see Marie send a message from her pager; then she hurries along the corridors, down the escalators to the public concourse. Then down another floor to the basement. At last she enters the UN bookshop, where she crouches unnoticed and takes the envelope from her purse. When she places the envelope behind a row of books, Mike's head goes back. His glance shoots from me back to the screen. After a moment Marie goes hurrying out of the bookshop. The tape jumps, fastforwards, and when it slows again we see Pascal arrive. He goes straight to where Marie deposited the envelope, reaches behind the row of books, collects the envelope, then leaves.

"Fuck." Mike frowns. And then recalls the contents of the bloodencrusted envelope down at the morgue. "The French passport?"

I hold a finger up: Wait.

We watch the final scenes play out. Pascal hurries up the stairs, tries not to alert the guards by running. He gets himself to the exit as fast as he can. And then he is out. Striding fast. And suddenly, right behind him, I appear. When I grab Pascal's arm, the video freezeframes.

"You saw what happened after that," I tell Mike.

"That woman," he says, facing me. "The journalist."

"Marie Lefebre."

"She was like, what, the go-between or something? Between Nyeri and the French fucking ambassador?"

I incline my head. Gesturing to the VCR, I ask Mike if he would like to view it all again. He declines the offer, then takes a quiet moment with himself, refiguring the whole sequence of events. He asks me, finally, where Lemtov fits in.

"He doesn't." Ejecting the videotape, I return to my desk and lock it away in the bottom drawer. Then I clasp my hands together on the blotter. "Lemtov had nothing to do with Toshio's murder. And it

wasn't Lemtov who was using Pascal to fool around with the paperwork. It was the French."

"So why'd Lemtov frame Rachel?"

"Because he thought I was framing him. I mean, see it from his
side. He'd defrauded UN funds, he was laundering money big-time,
but what were we chasing? We were looking for Toshio's murderer.
Lemtov was guilty of plenty. That's why he wanted me off his back,
that's why he used Rachel. But he didn't know a damn thing about
Toshio's murder."

"Plus, you threatened him. Like I told you not to."

I open one hand, acknowledging the error. Mike looks at me
askance.

"And this all came to you in a dream or something? You had a vision the French ambassador did it, so you went and checked the
tapes?"

I remind him about the French passport. After finding that on
Pascal's body, it was really just a matter of working backward.

"Seem to recall you volunteered to go identify the body only after
you already looked at the surveillance tapes," he says.

"Remember the missing pink file? The one Pascal returned to
Toshio's office? Soon as I saw it I knew it was wrong."

"You guessed straight off Nyeri spiked it?"

"It was all those figures on Po Lin's investments again. Company
names. Details we'd seen before. Even Jade Moon got another mention. The Kwok brothers."

Mike lifts his head. "Whoa back. Nyeri spiked Hatanaka's report
with information we already had?"

"And do you recall where we got that information?"

Mike pauses, remembering what I told him. My source was a
journalist. Then he glances back at the VCR.

"Not her," he says. "Please."

"Marie Lefebre. The very same."

"That trip down to Chinatown?"

"We were wasting our time. Just like she meant us to."

Mike rests his forehead in his hand a moment. The realization of
just how wide of the mark our investigation remained throughout
has hit him hard in his professional pride.

"All those investments of Po Lin's?"

"Total crap." Rising from my chair, I come around and prop my
butt against the desk. I fold my arms. "The French must have picked
up on Po Lin's connection with Jade Moon from the Brits. Probably
the Lefebre woman again. The French made up some numbers, then
pointed us at Po Lin and the Kwoks. They knew that'd stir up trou-

ble, at least keep us busy. They wanted to direct us away from Asahaki and Lemtov because both those trails touched Pascal."

Mike considers that. "You figure that's why Lady Nicola told you what she'd been up to with the Kwoks."

"Right. It was like she said, she considered the Po Lin business closed. She figured I wouldn't lay off till I knew, so she told me."

"So the Brits were just innocent bystanders."

I make a sound. The confirmation of Po Lin's execution came through this morning. "Innocent bystanders" hardly seems an appropriate judgment on the Brits.

Mike thinks some more, not quite sure where this leaves us. He returns to the fact he has a handle on. "Nyeri did it, yeah? He was the one whacked Hatanaka."

"What I said to Pascal out on the North Lawn yesterday, what you heard on the tape. Everything about him wanting something more, a better life, well, that was right. But it wasn't Lemtov who offered him a better life, I got that wrong. It was her. Marie Lefebre."

"Come on. You're guessing."

"I've spoken to the super in her apartment building. Pascal was a regular nighttime visitor at Marie's for the last three months."

Mike's hand drops. He looks at me.

"That's the key," I tell him, unfolding my arms, bracing them on the desk. "Our man from Internal Oversight was conducting an affair with Marie Lefebre, a French journalist. Only she wasn't just a journalist. She was also an agent of the French Foreign Ministry."

"She was screwing Nyeri?"

I bow my head. She was screwing Pascal Nyeri, I agree.

"And somehow," I say, "she got to know what Pascal was working on, his investigation with Hatanaka. Or maybe that's why she moved in on him in the first place. Anyway, somewhere along the way she makes her big suggestion to Pascal. Point the evidence of the Special Committee fraud at Asahaki."

"Why?" says Mike. But in the next moment he gets it. "The Council seat?"

"Right. The Council seat. Blacken Asahaki's name, screw Japan's chances at the vote, and no change on the Council. What France always wanted, despite public statements to the contrary."

Mike shakes his head in disgust at the intrigue. "Jesus."

"My guess is that's all they planned. A dirty trick, Asahaki's reputation destroyed, roughhouse politics, but everyone still walking at the end of it. Only something happened they hadn't figured on. The FBI report. Toshio suddenly had a whole pile of dirt on Lemtov. And Patrick was pushing him to confirm it, at least take another look at

Lemtov. Toshio must have wondered, naturally, why Pascal hadn't found anything like that earlier. So Toshio went back and checked Pascal's work, everything that Pascal had been feeding him. And he would have found that Pascal had been feeding him some lies."

"He confronted Nyeri?"

"He must have. Only Toshio would have thought the same as I did, that Pascal was covering for Lemtov. He wouldn't have seen that Lemtov's crime, the fraud, was being used by a third party to frame Asahaki. And Pascal would have told Marie that Toshio was onto him. After that, what choice did the French have? They couldn't afford to have it come out, what dirty game they'd been playing. So they dug themselves in deeper. The French government supplied the heroin, that's why it was so pure. It wasn't from the street. And having Pascal murder Toshio didn't just get Toshio out of the picture. It gave them another crime to pin on Asahaki."

Mike looks at me sideways.

"That's where we came in," I say. "Pascal called Legal Affairs within hours of our finding the body. He wasn't just being helpful. He wanted to make sure we had Asahaki right there at the top of our list of suspects. As long as we kept the pressure on Asahaki, we were doing what the French wanted. Keeping him out of Turtle Bay while they undermined the pro-Japanese vote."

"You've really nutted this out, haven't you?"

The evidence was all there, I tell him. I tell him it wasn't so hard to figure out once Marie Lefebre's role became clear.

"So it's pretty much how you called it yesterday," Mike says. "Only with Nyeri working for the French, not Lemtov."

Pretty much, I agree sadly. But the reason for Toshio's murder, Pascal's motive, I was way out there too. Not even close. When I say so, Mike brushes the remark aside.

"Nyeri did it for what he could get out of it. Money. Passport. Comes to the same thing, don't it? A new life? Like you said."

But Mike's world-weary assessment, I am sure, is way off beam here. He did not know Pascal as I knew him; or Marie Lefebre, if it comes to that.

"I don't think Pascal committed a murder just for a French passport."

"For the woman?"

"Not for the woman either." Moving away from my desk, I wander over to the bookshelves, the wall of documents, and trail a finger idly across the spines. *Law of the Sea. The Protection of Intellectual Copyright. Security Council Resolutions.* Nothing, frankly, that a truly civilized man would want to waste his time reading. Nothing, for example, by Voltaire. "I think they must have threatened him."

Mike scoffs.

"Not at first," I say. "The woman, the promise of a passport, that was probably enough to get Pascal to fool around with the numbers. But once he'd done that, the French had him. One call to Patrick— hey, look what this Nyeri's been up to—Pascal would have been out. Fired. A one-way ticket back to the Cameroon, maybe even prosecuted and into the slammer. Not so much a new life, more like a disastrous end to the one he already had."

"You're justifying the guy? He killed Hatanaka, for chrissake, we're meant to feel sorry for him?"

I turn and focus on the USUN building across the street. Justifying, is that what I'm doing? Pascal, whatever his motives, murdered Toshio Hatanaka. But does that fact stand alone? To what degree do a man's circumstances mitigate his crime? Isn't that one of the oldest and deepest questions of jurisprudence? To discover what moral difference lies between the man who steals to feed his family and the man who simply steals. Never forgive, or always. Isn't it between these two extremes that the fraternity of lawyers does daily courtroom battle? Now I ask myself if I would really wish to plant my feet beneath the defendant's table on this case, to rise and claim extenuation for my client. Pascal Nyeri was tricked. He was threatened, Judge. Consider his life. He really had no choice.

Mike does not believe that. And in my heart of hearts, I guess, neither do I.

Though I cannot defend what Pascal did, I can still feel for him. I can understand the ardor of his desire, not just for Marie but for his own dreams, and I can see the web in which he was trapped, in the end fatally. I can see all that, empathize deeply, because I, too, passed through Marie Lefebre's bed. I, too, committed a crime, one for which no court will ever condemn me. An inexpungible crime of the heart.

In truth, maybe that is what I am trying to justify here. The unjustifiable. Not Pascal Nyeri's actions but my own.

"Not to feel sorry for him." I face Mike again, raising a hand vaguely. My voice trails off. "Understanding?"

"Like all the great understanding he gave Hatanaka? Come on. He got what he deserved. Eye for an eye. Right there in the good book."

But in the good book there are other lessons too, like forgiveness and mercy. Now, however, does not seem the appropriate moment for me to be quoting Scripture, so I let it pass. I glance at my watch. I tell Mike that I'm due downstairs in five minutes. Rachel has come in to return her UN uniform; her brief career as a guide at Turtle Bay is over. But Mike isn't done yet.

"Lemtov wasn't involved in the murder, but you're letting him take the fall for it?"

"That's right," I admit.

"All that 'he should never have been here' crap. That's what you meant, yeah? Lemtov should never have been here, so you're helping him leave." He thinks a moment. "You were worried that Bureau report wasn't gonna be enough. Worried the SG might just tick Lemtov off, tell him to change his ways, let him stay. But this way, implicated in Toshio's murder, he's out for sure."

"Lemtov's not even going to be charged, Mike. But with his diplomatic cover removed, the Bureau can take a real shot at him. He'll be dodging extradition orders for the rest of his life. For the Special Committee fraud he gets nothing. He won't be jailed. He's just out."

"For a crime he didn't commit."

"You're justifying the man?"

Mike doesn't smile. He says, "That's not you, Sam. Me? Sure. I don't care too much how a guy like Lemtov gets nailed so long as it happens. But you?" He pauses, then alights more quickly than I would have hoped on the answer. "Payback, right? For what he put Rachel through."

I bow my head, then raise my eyes. I ask Mike if he has any other questions.

"The Lefebre woman. Where can I find her?"

"She's gone."

"Address?"

"Gone gone. Back to Paris."

Consulting my calendar, I find the number, the same one I tried earlier this morning, then I dial Marie's apartment. I put her answering machine message on the speaker for Mike. Marie's voice is calm and businesslike. She says that she has been temporarily reassigned to the Agence France-Presse head office in Paris, that she can be contacted there. She gives a number and then the same message is repeated in French. After that there is a long beep. When I hang up, Mike stares at the phone a long while.

"It wouldn't have made any difference if she'd stayed, Mike. With Pascal dead, there's no way we could have proven anything. The most we could have done was withdraw her press accreditation. Now we don't even have to bother." Opening my arms, I attempt a smile. "At last," I say, "someone ran."

But Mike's face does not move. Letting Lemtov take the fall for a crime of which he is innocent, that Mike can live with. But this evasion of retribution by Marie Lefebre strikes at Mike's deep sense of justice. He was assigned to bring Toshio's murderer to book, and he has failed.

"Cunt," he says at last.

I pocket my pen. I take my jacket from the back of the chair. And while he is still trying to digest what he has learned, trying to reconcile himself to the highly unsatisfactory outcome, I make a few consolatory suggestions. The French Foreign Ministry, I say, has lost a key intelligence asset here at UNHQ, there is absolutely no chance Marie Lefebre will risk coming back. And though Ambassador Froissart cannot be touched with what we have—that apparently innocent meeting with Marie by the side chamber—I tell Mike that over the coming weeks the two of us can figure some way to let Froissart know what we know. Maybe we can make him jumpy enough to follow Marie Lefebre's example and beat a voluntary withdrawal back to Paris.

In response to these somewhat hopeful remarks, Mike simply pulls a face. He doesn't swallow one word of it.

"At least we can try."

"So when was I gonna hear about this?" He gestures to the VCR, then the phone on my desk. "Sometime soon?" He raises a brow. "Sometime never?"

"I didn't think it would help. I wasn't sure you would have wanted to know."

"Wrong. Both counts."

Unable to hold his gaze, I pull on my jacket and I ask him what he intends to do now.

"You mean about Lemtov?"

About all of it, I say.

He takes a few seconds with himself, then faces me squarely. "You've told me everything, right? No more rabbits outa goddamn hats. No more French passports in dead guys' pockets."

I shake my head.

"If that's everything," he says reluctantly, "I don't see that we have a choice. We just let it play out. Lemtov takes the fall, the woman stays gone." Then his look becomes penetrating, unwavering, as if some deep instinct for suspicion has been stirred. "That *is* everything?" he says levelly.

If there was ever a moment to confess all, to wipe the slate clean, this is it. But what price a clean slate, an unsullied conscience? If I told Mike, as a friend, what really happened between Marie Lefebre and me, how could Mike Jardine, deputy head of Security, ignore that information? Me, a senior figure from UN Legal, wrapped in the amorous embrace of a French spy, my one-night stand with her sandwiched between the deaths of Toshio Hatanaka and Pascal Nyeri. Maybe I could convince him that I was the innocent dupe, but even if I could, where would that leave Mike? How exactly would my confession assist the cause of truth? Mike would be left wrestling with his own conscience, wondering whether he should do his duty and report me to Eckhardt and Patrick. And all the while, of course, cursing me for putting him in such an impossible position, for not keeping my mouth shut. But here in my office, his eyes narrowing, he sees none of that.

So whose slate stays clean? Do I shrug the burden onto his shoulders, or do I lie and carry the burden alone?

Sensing my hesitation, he tilts back his head. Finally I nod.

"That's everything."

He looks at me a moment longer. "No," he decides with a sad kind of ruefulness. "That's just everything you're gonna tell me. But, hey, you owe me nothing, right?"

We look at each other, my lie hanging between us like poisonous vapor. Later I might find the strength to tell him the truth, but not now. For now it is all I can do to hold myself steady, to meet his unflinching gaze without wilting.

"I expected better," he says at last. He does not wait for a response. He leans toward me, chucks my shoulder a little too hard, then he goes.

45

WHEN I FIND RACHEL, SHE IS SITTING WITH three other guides in the room behind the UN Public Information Office in the basement, drinking Coke. Unlike her uniformed friends, Rachel is dressed in jeans and a sweater; she has her own UN guide's uniform draped over the chair beside her. The talk dies when I put my head in, so I keep it brief. Is she ready to go? Not yet, she's waiting for her boss, she says. There are some more forms she has to sign. How long? She shrugs and tells me maybe fifteen minutes. Then I hesitate in the doorway.

"Did you see Jennifer?" Rachel asks me, and a gentle heat immediately moves up from my neck, suffusing my cheeks. I shake my head. Two of Rachel's friends exchange a look; one of them rolls her eyes. "She was down here," Rachel goes on. "She just came in and asked me like, if I was okay. She said she might see you. I think she went back to her office."

I tap my hand against the door frame, casting around for some dignified way to make my exit. At last it is Rachel who speaks. She says that if she finishes up here soon, she'll come looking for me across the street, then she smiles and sips her Coke through a straw.

When the marine guard overhears the USUN receptionist tell me that Ms. Dale is not in the building, he steps forward to inform me that Jennifer has just gone around the corner to see her son. So a minute later I find myself standing on the sidewalk outside the kindergarten where Jennifer's son, Ben, spends five mornings a week. On the far side of the glass wall there are balloons and a low table bearing a large cake decorated with white icing and four stubby red candles. The teacher appears to have opened this place on a Saturday morning so that some four-year-old kid whose parents are busy saving the world across the street at the UN can celebrate his birthday. But with so few kids in attendance, the place looks empty, and despite the cake and the balloons, not festive but sad. Jennifer, somewhat incongruously, is wearing a green paper party hat and a sober gray business suit. Crouching by Ben near the cake, she glances up now and sees me looking in from the street.

"Hi," she says, coming out to join me on the sidewalk a few moments later. Then she gestures past me. "I saw Rachel. She's quitting?"

"Only her job."

Jennifer considers my remark. Then, hearing music start up behind her, she glances back over her shoulder. She stays like that, apparently unwilling to face me directly.

"Jennifer."

"Mmm?"

When I touch her arm, she faces me again.

"You wanted to see me," I tell her. At this, Jennifer looks momentarily puzzled. "You told Rachel?"

"Oh, that." When her hand wafts up in airy dismissal, a heavy weight settles in my gut. Her words to Rachel were no more than a parting aside. Jennifer was not, as I thought, hoping to see me. In fact, judging by her demeanor, her apparent unwillingness even to look me in the eye, it seems that my unexpected arrival is far from welcome. For a moment I actually consider leaving this for another time, but that thought quickly passes. Time is not going to make this any easier.

I nod down the street. I ask if she minds if we walk.

Dead leaves, the first of fall, go scudding past our ankles, driven by a sudden gust of wind. Overhead the sky is a brilliant cloudless blue. Walking beside me, Jennifer reaches up to sweep the green paper hat off her head.

"So Lemtov's out," she says, pushing the hat into her jacket.

UN tom-toms, I think. Patrick has passed the word to Bruckner, and Bruckner has told Jennifer. Probably a few more of the U.S. delegation. By Monday morning the entire General Assembly will have the news. But Jennifer's tone is surprisingly downbeat.

"Isn't that what you wanted?"

"Hatanaka and Nyeri are dead, Sam. And the Japanese lost the vote. If the Secretariat had acted on the Bureau's report when we gave it to you—"

I raise a hand, cutting off the retrospective apportionment of blame. She draws her jacket tight around her waist.

"We've all made mistakes on this," I tell her meaningfully. "All of us."

She contemplates her feet as she walks. Then, scuffing her shoes over the fallen leaves, she offers a few remarks about Bruckner's reaction to the whole sorry episode. Apparently he has decided that the Secretariat had some hidden agenda all along, that we were working to block the Japanese ascension to the Council from the start. I absorb these remarks in silence. I do not, of course, tell Jennifer that the hidden agenda belonged to one of the U.S.A.'s fellow perm five members, France; that dirty political battle has been waged, won, and lost, and a public revelation of the truth now would simply introduce an element into the Security Council, into the whole UN system, as corrosive as acid. It is not lost on me either how easily my own role in the affair could be magnified and distorted by the French into villainous caricature. So I just walk, keeping my gaze straight ahead now and nodding from time to time.

Then I hear her say, "So how's O'Conner seeing it?"

I stop. A few more steps, then she stops and faces me.

"How's O'Conner seeing it?" I repeat.

Surprised by my reaction, she cocks her head. But after a few seconds it registers, and she raises a slender finger and points. "I asked you that before."

"Right."

"Tuesday morning. The opening."

"And do you remember what I told you then?"

She ruminates a moment, gives a wry smile. I told her, as she now remembers, nothing at all.

"Jennifer—" My throat is suddenly dry. "Jennifer, I didn't come over here to discuss O'Conner's political opinions on the state of the world. It wasn't the USUN legal counsel that I wanted to see. It was you."

"Same thing."

"You know it's not."

We study each other awhile.

"Look, if you can put your hand on your heart, tell me you don't care if you never see me again, I won't make this worse."

She doesn't reply.

"Can you tell me that?" I ask her. "Honestly?"

"It isn't that easy."

"Hand on heart?"

"Don't push me, Sam," she says quietly, walking on.

After a while, tentatively, I lay a hand on her arm. She makes no move to pull away.

"I'm sorry, Jennifer. Is that what you want to hear from me? I made a mistake. A big one, and I'm so goddamn sorry, I just can't tell you—"

Her eyes, when she lifts them, are clouded. "I can't do it, Sam. I can't go through it all, not a second time."

"Jennifer—"

"Please." Her face goes tight. She turns suddenly and heads back toward the kindergarten. I go after her, then fall in step beside her. She presses the heels of her hands into her eyes, then shakes her head. "I guess if this is apology time, I really wasn't too understanding either."

"You?"

She pulls a face. "About Rachel, I mean. What you were going through."

I wave a hand, dismissing her apology.

"No, really," she says.

But in truth my own behavior and language were nothing to be proud of, and I tell her that now. It is her turn. She waves my apology aside.

"So we're agreed. We're both total lowlifes, scum of the earth." A corner of her mouth rises. We stop by the sandbox outside the kindergarten. She looks in through the window to where the birthday candles on the cake have been lit. Ben is staring at the candles wide-eyed, he has not seen her yet. In a few moments she will be going in to join him.

And what is left now for Jennifer and me to say to each other? So long? It's been a fine few months, pity how it ended, but good luck with the rest of your life?

"I slept with her once, Jennifer."

Her gaze stays fixed on her son.

"I'm not excusing myself here, but that's the truth. It wasn't some ongoing thing. She was chasing a story. You were breaking my balls. I slept with her. If it's any consolation, she's gone back to Paris."

"It isn't."

"Okay." I take a breath. "I just wanted you to know that."

"Can you imagine how I feel right now, Sam?"

When I don't answer her, she turns. "I feel," she says, looking straight at me, "like I really could murder you."

She does not look like she could murder me. The look in her eyes is not fierce or wild, but wretched. Totally spent.

"Only that's not what I'm thinking," she says. "What I'm thinking is that you made a mistake, like you said, and that you're sorry. And I think you are. In my head, Sam, I believe you, I really think you are. But in the end, you know, that just doesn't help. Because what I feel, how I feel, that wins every time. You're standing there saying sorry, and I'm so mad at you I'm having visions of meat cleavers and knives." She smiles crookedly. "A pretty shaky foundation for a relationship, don't you think?"

"We could work it out."

"No."

"You don't want to try?"

"Trying has nothing to do with it." Her expression and her voice are now strained. "That's what I'm saying. I have tried. And what I've found is that I can't do it. This thing." She lifts a hand; she cannot even bring herself to say the words. Betrayal? Adultery? Finally she gives up, facing the kindergarten window again. "I really am so goddamn angry with you," she says, folding her arms, hugging them close.

For a moment my heart beats erratically, painfully. When I open my mouth to speak, she cuts me off.

"Don't," she says.

"Can't we just give it some time?"

She shakes her head, a short, sharp movement. She is hating every second of this, but she has steeled herself against persuasion. And this is Jennifer. She is unlikely to weaken.

And me? By now I am dying inside.

"I have to go," Jennifer says.

When I lift my eyes I see that she has offered me her hand. And after a moment I take it. But when she attempts to withdraw, to retreat to the refuge of the kindergarten, the solace of Ben's loving embrace, I hold her hand firm. I fix my eyes on hers as I speak.

"If I thought you had something better lined up, someone better than me, I wouldn't stand in your way. I wouldn't make it this hard. You know that. If you had a better life to go to, if I honestly thought you had, I'd stand aside. I'd even wish you luck. But that's just not the way I see it, where you go from here."

She pulls her hand free.

"The way I see it, if I just step aside now, you'll retreat into your career. And maybe a year or two from now you'll figure having a great career isn't the same as having a great life. And you'll look around then, Jennifer. Maybe you'll find someone. But that guy, Mr. X, he won't be perfect. Because that's not the way we are. None of us. And so what are you going to do when Mr. X screws up? Or the next guy?"

She drops her head but says nothing.

"We can have a future together. A good life. And I don't pretend to know what you want, but I know what I want." Reaching, I touch her arm. At last I speak the words that I know she has been waiting to hear from me for months now; I hope is still waiting to hear. The only words that will prove to her that I am ready to take another shot. At love. At some kind of life that is deeper and more complete and true than the life I have. "I want you, Jennifer. I want you."

For a long while she is still. Then she moves close to me, rises on tiptoe, and clasps my arm as she presses her cheek hard against mine.

It's too late, she whispers.

Then she turns and bows her head and walks away. My heart, for a moment, ceases beating. I look up at the sky. And I know then, beyond hope, that it is over.

EPILOGUE

TOSHIO HATANAKA'S BODY IS BEING RETURNED TO JAPAN. When Moriko called with the details of the arrangements, I went up to Patrick's office for the first time in days and told him I was going out to the airport. I thought someone from the Secretariat should at least make that effort.

"You asking for my permission?" he asked me.

"No," I said.

He waved a hand to the door and I silently withdrew. Since announcing his resignation Monday, he has spoken to me just once apart from this morning, when he called to inform me that the rumors were true, that he'd been appointed the Australian High Commissioner in London. His resignation will take effect within weeks; by the end of the month we will have a new Undersecretary-General for Legal Affairs. I could not pretend either surprise or sorrow. And yesterday I heard from a source on the thirty-eighth floor that in Patrick's letter of resignation the customary parting courtesy of the Undersecretary-General to his deputy was omitted: The name Windrush did not appear on his list of recommended candidates to succeed him. Though as a U.S. citizen I never would have expected to be a serious candidate for the post, I really would have appreciated the gesture. But Patrick, true to form, has remained graceless to the end.

After leaving Patrick's office I went downstairs to get Mike, but he was too busy with his own reestablished routine to spare the time for a trip out to JFK. I get the impression Mike would like to forget about Toshio and the whole affair as soon as he can; he does not regard the investigation or the outcome as anything like his finest hour. But he suggested I phone Jennifer, that USUN might want to send someone to fly the flag. I wound up my courage and finally called her. Jennifer relaxed a little when she understood that the call wasn't personal.

"I can't make it," she told me.

I suggested Bruckner. Jennifer laughed at that; then with a few carefully chosen words she let me understand that a commemorative farewell to Toshio Hatanaka was not high on the list of USUN's priorities.

"You heard Patrick's leaving," I said, knowing of course that she had.

"Ah-ha. Stay tuned for the bulletin from over here."

I took a moment with that. "Bruckner's leaving?"

"Stay tuned," she repeated before hanging up.

So we are talking again. And I am not really surprised by the news about Bruckner. There is no political mileage in trying to rebuild the pro-Japanese consensus; it will be years before Security Council reform gathers enough momentum to make it back to an Assembly vote. Like Patrick, Bruckner wants to put this failure behind him; his career path will have to undergo a sharp change in direction. Maybe a Senate seat, but wherever he goes I doubt Bruckner will be staying in New York to endure the daily reminders of this week's fiasco at Turtle Bay. And wherever he goes I guess Jennifer will be going with him. On reflection, maybe that "stay tuned" was a subtle way of breaking it to me that she is leaving. One to mull over in the quiet of my apartment tonight.

Now that Rachel has returned to Juan's place in Alphabet City I have plenty of downtime in the evenings to think things through. Something I've thought through already is that there is no going back to the half-life I was leading. If nothing else, my time with Jennifer has shown me that. On the personal front I am ready—no, more than that—I really do want to take another shot at life. But for now the hint of an impending departure from Jennifer causes a powerful ache somewhere in my heart. It hurts like hell. It will not be fatal.

Out at the airport it is raining, a fine drizzle, not really much more than a heavy mist. The guy from the airline holds an umbrella over me as we cross the wet tarmac to the hangar where the giant doors are wide open. He gestures me in, then retreats back to the warmth of his office.

It is the flags I notice first, UN and Japanese, one of each draped across the brass-handled coffin. The coffin lies on a baggage trolley, ready to be towed out to the plane. Moriko is standing there. She raises a hand when she sees me, and my head dips in sad acknowledgment. Then, as I begin the trek across the oil-stained concrete, I recognize the man at her side. Bunzo Asahaki. I walk on, then come to a halt by Moriko.

"He would have been glad you came," she says, touching my arm.

I apologize for those who could not make it, people she might have expected to see. Patrick. The SG. She nods and bows slightly. She tells me that she understands. Then I reach across her, offering Bunzo Asahaki my hand, but he does not deign to notice the gesture. Finally I let my hand slide into my pocket, then I turn and face the coffin.

It looks too small. And in some strange way that seems appropriate. The coffin looks too small for the body just as the body always seemed too small for the life it contained. He meant so much to so many people. That fact has been brought home to everyone these past few days as the letters and tributes have poured in from innumerable NGOs and governments, UN staffers all over the globe. The same sentiments keep recurring. Toshio listened. He tried to understand. He made every effort to solve problems instead of dropping them into the black hole of UN bureaucracy. He did not hide behind the UN Charter. And there are frequent addenda to these notes asking to whom in the future the writer should apply for assistance at UNHQ.

Though none of these tributes will ever make the headlines or the history books, they are a genuine and fitting testament to a life well lived. Toshio is gone and his absence really matters to those he left behind. I have brought a few of these notes along to show Moriko later, but for now I just watch in silence as a guy in white coveralls couples the trolley to his cart.

I have decided not to take the job with Goldman at Columbia. If Patrick had stayed, if things had worked out differently with Jennifer, I guess then maybe I would have gone. Someday I might regret not making the move, but at this moment in my life it seems the right decision. When I was young I was going to change the world. Now in my maturity I face the harder labor, to change myself, to work to become a better man. Maybe Toshio's life can be something for me to live up to. Not the headlines or the history books, but just this, people to whom my absence truly matters when my turn comes to leave the world behind.

The man in white coveralls throws a tarpaulin across the flags on the coffin, then climbs aboard the cart. When Asahaki gives the signal, the cart and the trolley move off: Toshio Hatanaka's body is going home. In solemn cortege we three bow our heads and follow the coffin out into the softly falling rain.

ACKNOWLEDGMENTS

Nita Taublib, Deputy Publisher
Beth de Guzman, Executive Editor
Betsy Hulsebosch, Creative Marketing Director
Yook Louie, Art Director
Susan Corcoran, Associate Director of Publicity
Kelly Chian, Glen Edelstein, Maggie Hart, Madeline Hopkins,
and Production

7-01